HARD KNOCKS

FORGE BOOKS BY HOWIE CARR

Hitman
Hard Knocks

HARD KNOCKS

HOWIE CARR

A TOM DOHERTY ASSOCIATES BOOK

NEW YORK

This is a work of fiction. All of the characters, organizations, and events portrayed in this novel are either products of the author's imagination or are used fictitiously.

HARD KNOCKS

Copyright © 2011 by Frandel LLC

A Forge Book
Published by Tom Doherty Associates, LLC
175 Fifth Avenue
New York, NY 10010

www.tor-forge.com

Forge® is a registered trademark of Tom Doherty Associates, LLC.

Library of Congress Cataloging-in-Publication Data

Carr, Howie.
  Hard knocks / Howie Carr. — 1st ed.
      p. cm.
  "A Tom Doherty Associates book."
  ISBN 978-0-7653-2640-9
  1. Private investigators—Massachusetts—Boston—Fiction. 2. Murder—
Investigation—Fiction. 3. Corruption investigation—Fiction. 4. Boston
(Mass.)—Fiction. I. Title.
  PS3603.A77423H37 2012
  813'.6—dc23
                                                              2011024947

First Edition: January 2012

Printed in the United States of America

0 9 8 7 6 5 4 3 2 1

To the three C's—
Carolyn, Charlotte, and Christina

HARD
KNOCKS

Chapter One

MY JAILBIRD BROTHER got me into this whole jam. It wasn't the first time Martin T. Reilly had dragged me into something, but the difference this time was, he wasn't even around. He was doing another bit, this one in the federal prison up in Ayer at the old Fort Devens Army base.

The feds got a "tip" from a so-called Top Echelon Criminal Informant, and a combined FBI-ATF-MSP task force bagged him down on the Connecticut line, on I-84, driving a truckload of cigarettes that did not belong to him. Marty stood up, not that he had a lot of choice in the matter. Fuckups like Marty either keep their mouths shut or they get whacked. People think everyone in the quote-unquote mob who gets arrested nowadays immediately flips and goes into the Witness Protection Program, but it's only for guys a lot higher up in the hood hierarchy than Marty.

So my little brother was up at Devens doing federal time, which now means 85 percent of the sentence, and when he and all the rest of the wiseguys (there's a misnomer) aren't either working out in the weight room or trying to concoct bogus technicalities for an appeal in the law library, they're yapping away, swapping lies, dropping names. And poor Marty, what did it say about his utter lack of stature either inside or outside the joint that the biggest name he had to drop was an ex-cop's, namely mine?

The day I got the call that started the whole thing, I was sitting in my house, which is actually the first-floor apartment of a three-story row house in the South End. That's where I've lived my entire life, except for three years in the Army and a few more in the suburbs when I was trying to do the family thing, which did not work out.

Business was slow, a not-uncommon occurrence in my current line of work, which is officially private investigations, although I'm not so much a peephole gumshoe as a—well, let's just say the services I presently offer include almost nothing you'd want to see embossed on a business card, if you get my drift. On top of that, or maybe because of that, I was pretty much tapped out. I was sorting my unpaid bills into two piles. One stack was the bills I couldn't afford to pay until the direct deposit of my monthly city disability-pension check, my kiss in the mail, into my checking account. The second pile included all the bills I couldn't afford to pay, period, until business picked up, assuming it ever did. That was when the phone rang.

"Reilly Associates," I said with as much enthusiasm as I could muster.

"Is this Jack Reilly?"

"Speaking."

"This is Bucky Bennett." It didn't ring a bell. "I know your brother." The bell was ringing now. It was an alarm. "I knew him down in Otisville." Another federal pen, in upstate New York, inhabited by a lot of Northeast organized-crime types, among them, at one point, my brother.

Marty's friend spoke softly, but he might have been trying to lull me. "He told me to give you a call sometime." That was mighty white of good old Martin T. Reilly. "I got a big, big problem, Jack." Ex-cons often do. "Hello? Are you there?"

"Yes," I said with a sigh. "I'm here."

"Jack, you don't know me, but I heard a lot about you. I heard you used to handle a lot of work for the mayor, the old one, and I know you were a cop, and now you're on your own."

That certainly was the CliffsNotes version of the life of Jack Reilly, a man teetering on that fine line between has-been and never-was. I sensed a pitch was imminent.

"I gotta talk to you. They're looking for me. I gotta screw before they find me."

"Who's they?"

A hollow chuckle. "Can I meet you somewhere?"

Some people claim they can smell money. Me, I can smell no money, and I can smell it a mile away. "Pro bono" is just Latin for "deadbeat." I decided to try to lose the guy.

I asked him, "Have you thought about calling the police?"

Another nervous laugh. "Marty told me you were a funny guy."

"Look," I said, staring at the two piles of unpaid bills in front of me. "I'm kinda busy right now."

"Please, man, I'm desperate. I know what I must sound like, but I got some stuff, I gotta make sure it gets into the hands of the right people or I'm dead. You're on Shawmut Ave., right? How far are you from Foley's?"

Oh great. Not only was I not going to get paid, now I was going to have to buy him a drink, in my own place on top of everything else. James Michael Curley used to say that it's nice to be important, but it's more important to be nice. That's excellent advice, I suppose, if you're running for office, but who exactly was I trying to impress? Still, Bucky wasn't going to take no for an answer.

"I like old J. J.'s," he said. So do I, especially if someone else is buying. This, however, was not shaping up as one of those magic moments.

"Lotta cops there," he continued, talking more to himself than to me. "Almost Southie, but not quite. No-man's-land, nobody's home turf, so nobody hassles anybody else. It sure ain't the Ace of Hearts."

The Ace of Hearts? That was a gin mill on the other side of the bridge, in South Boston, where a lot of the local bad actors hung out. The guys my brother was "associated" with, as the prosecutors sometimes put it at his sentencings. Maybe I'd underestimated Bucky, or perhaps he was still engaging in that eternal jailbird pastime—name-dropping.

"Okay," I said, "I'll meet you at Foley's in a half hour."

"I'll need about an hour," he said. "Marty told me you look like him, only shorter and not as good-looking."

BUCKY BENNETT looked just about how I'd figured he would. Somewhere in his late forties, early fifties, thinning dark hair, maybe five-eight but fairly well built. They're all in great shape when they get out of the can. At least the organized crime guys. If you split your days between the Nautilus machines and the prison's law library, you tend to come out physically fit and well read.

Bucky had a little paunch on him, though, which by my calculation meant he'd been out at least a couple of years. I knew my brother hadn't been in Otisville for at least two years himself. His latest home-away-from-home, Devens, was supposed to be a hospital of sorts, although I was pretty sure Marty didn't have anything wrong with him, unless terminal stupidity has been declared a disease, in which case Marty will be eligible for SSDI the moment he hits the street.

Bucky had that furtive, darting-eye look of a guy from a tough neighborhood who's always been on the fringes, just close enough to the action to get seriously burned on a fairly regular basis. He was wearing sweatpants—thanks for putting on your Sunday best for the occasion, Bucky. I was decked out the way I used to dress when I worked at City Hall—Oxford shirt, no tie, V-neck sweater, and a blue blazer.

The mayor always told me, and probably everybody else on his payroll, "Dress British, think Yiddish." Five years off the city payroll, this was as close to dressing British as I could manage, but then, it was no skin off my ass if Bucky noticed the frayed collar on my shirt, or the missing button on my sport-coat sleeve. Bucky was just another con between cons looking for something on the arm.

He glanced around Foley's bar, where everyone was standing. Let the record show that I bought the first round.

"Got enough cops in here?" Bucky Bennett said. "This is like an after-hours club."

"That's two doors down," I said. "We call it For God and Country."

At Foley's, the cop presence keeps the local hard guys out, and the bums from the Pine Street Inn a half block away know better than to come in and panhandle. The *Herald* is a block north, and when you threw in the reporters and the salespeople with the cops, Foley's was just a shade too downscale for most of the hipsters, either gay or artsy-fartsy or both, who live in the renovated lofts farther south on Harrison Avenue.

This afternoon, with the shift just changing at Area D-4, Foley's was a cop bar, and they were packed in shoulder to shoulder at the bar, pounding them down, everyone on their feet of course, because there are no barstools at Foley's.

Bucky Bennett stood next to me at the bar and watched an older sergeant chase a shot of blended Canadian rye with a Pickwick Ale draft.

"You see that cop over there?" he said.

"Yeah." I told Bucky his name.

"He busted me once when I was a kid," Bucky Bennett said. "One night, after the bars in Quincy Market closed, I was down Mondo's with a bunch of guys, legless, and after we ate, we waited until the counterman turned his back, and then we all booked it out the door."

"The old chew 'n' screw," I said, staring straight ahead at my reflection in the back bar mirror.

Why me? Why do they always attach themselves to me? Do I look like a probation officer? Bucky must have noticed my exasperation with his aimless chatter, because he looked both ways to make sure no one was listening. Then he whispered to me, "Is there somewhere we can go that's a little more private?"

I nodded, picked up my beer without saying a word, and walked to the jukebox. Bucky followed as I turned left and kept walking until I reached the stacked-up empty beer cases at the back of what we call the Berkeley Room, on account of it's on East Berkeley Street. When I reached the last table, I put my drink down on it, and Bucky did the same. We both pulled up wobbly chairs and then I asked him, as noncommittally as I could, why he had sought me out.

"I'm from Charlestown," he began, and I resisted the urge to offer my condolences. "I got a problem," he said once again, and I nodded, politely, as if he were a paying customer, which he never would be, not in this lifetime.

"Like I told you on the phone," he said, "I was in Otisville there with your brother. Lotta other Boston guys there too, as you probably know." So far, no surprises. "Anyway, you know how it is inside. Guys say, when you get out, give me a call, maybe we can do some business, blah-blah-blah."

"What were you in for?" I asked, just to keep up my end of the conversation.

"Armored car down in Holbrook, Jazzbo Mangan's gang."

I remembered Jazzbo's little crew. They had a nice run there, but their last time out the FBI had been waiting for them at the bank, just like they'd been laying for my brother down on the Connecticut line. The general suspicion was that Jazzbo or maybe some of the other guys with him were getting a little too big for their britches over in Southie and that the guys who hung out at the Ace of Hearts had arranged for all of them to take a nice long vacation.

I said, "I thought you guys all got thirty years on and after for that machine gun."

"Hey, you got a good memory there," he said. "Come to find out, that machine gun they give us wasn't even a working piece. It took me a while, but I finally realized, the two guys sent it over to fuck us."

Is there no honor among thieves? Say it ain't so, Bucky.

"But that's what saved our asses in the end. They were too cute by half. It's just like them two guys, they give you a gun that don't work and they hope you pull it on the feds. You do that and the best thing that can happen to you is you get thirty years on and after, and the worst thing that can happen is you get your head blown off trying to fire a piece that don't work, which this one didn't. No firing pin, wasn't that thoughtful of our friends from South Boston? But the way I look at it now is, if it'd been a real gun, I'd still be in there, like your brother, no offense."

"None taken."

"So we go up on appeal," said Bucky, "and the judge says he can't hand anybody, not even a so-called career criminal like me, thirty years on and after for pointing a toy gun at a fed. Not yet anyway."

He took a long sip of his beer as he pondered the troubling implications of the continuing erosion of the Bill of Rights.

"So I get out," he said, "and I've got a phone number that turns out to ring in the Ace of Hearts. I go over there, just checking in, you might say. Paying my respects to the two guys there. Maybe pass on a message or two, like from your brother."

"The two guys have anything for you?"

He smiled. "That's not their style, you know that. Their style is, have you got anything for them?"

I was getting antsy. Enough with the teases, Bucky.

"One thing I should tell you," he said, "even though I was along for the ride on that last thing with Jazzbo down there in Holbrook, I wasn't in on all their other jobs." He again looked both ways and then leaned across the table, lowering his voice. "What I am basically is a burglar. I'm real good with locks."

I began silently counting and recounting the empty Bud Light beer cases stacked up against the walls. I sighed deeply.

"I know, you got other places to be," Bucky said. "I'm getting to it. Long story short, you ever hear of Cooperative Trust?"

"Bank in Medford. Got burgled on a holiday weekend. They grabbed millions out of the safety-deposit boxes. Turned out a lot of them had been rented under phony names."

"You do have a good memory. It was Memorial Day, two years ago."

"The two guys at the Ace of Hearts did that?"

"Oh God, no. Like I told you, the only thing them two do is provide 'protection,' if you know what I mean. That, and maybe kill you, if you don't buy what they're selling, which is protection for anything you want to do in their territory, which by their definition is anywhere they can get to before the ginzos."

I nodded. I was beginning to get the picture.

"So you pulled off this big bank burglary," I said, "right after you'd been in to see the two guys."

"Not right after. Six months maybe, which I guess was close enough so that they could claim I was holding out on them, by not cutting them in."

"They come looking for you?"

"Did they ever. And when they come lookin' for you, they generally find you. The way they figure it, if they know you, they own you. So as far as they're concerned, they had first dibs on me and my friends from the Cooperative Trust job."

When the two guys figure they got dibs on you, and you disagree, that's usually when you get a rocket in your pocket.

"Once they figured out who was in with me on the job," Bucky continued, "they went out and picked off the weakest link. He was a Townie like me, a junkie, been on dust ever since he was a kid— then Ecstasy, Oxys, whatever. He meant no harm, basically, just another project rat looking for his next fix. They snatch him right off'n the street, take him down to some basement somewhere, in Southie or Quincy'd be my guess. Then they strap him into a dentist's chair and they pull out his teeth one by one with a rusty pair of pliers until he tells 'em where we got everything stashed, which they then go pick up."

He paused. "Long story short," he said, repeating that annoying phrase, "I don't get a dime off my own job."

"Even if he was in on the job," I said, "why would you ever tell a junkie where you stashed your loot?"

"Good question," he said. "But it didn't seem like such a big deal at the time. It's a little nothing bank, we thought we'd maybe grabbed two hundred large, tops. You think we'd have even done the job if we knew every goombah in the city had a box there?"

Yeah, Cooperative Trust was very popular with In Town, which is what the indigenous wiseguys call the local Mafia. I was still thinking about the two guys' dental work. It sounded like an urban myth.

"How do you know all this?" I asked. "About the teeth and the pliers, I mean. This guy that got snatched, I'm assuming he won't be down for breakfast."

"That's a good assumption all right. But I know. You hear things."

"Wasn't there some story going around at the time," I said, "about how the two guys sold In Town on letting them take you guys off the board as some kind of public service to all wiseguys everywhere."

"More'n likely that's exactly what happened," he said. "'Cause we had all kinds of jewels and stolen bonds and negotiable securities and shit that the wops had stolen off'n other wops. We had it stashed in a garage in Everett. The two guys got it all—every damn thing there was. Stole a truck and backed it up to the garage and took everything. Some of the loot I guess they gave back to In Town, but knowing them guys, I'd bet they kept most of it."

I asked Bucky, "How come they didn't grab you too?"

"No need to, once they had everything. I took it like a man, you know. What could I do?"

"You could try to shake them down. You didn't get any bright ideas like that, did you, Bucky?"

"I ain't that crazy. But there was a lotta other stuff in those boxes, papers and shit, that we just threw into the canvas bags along with everything else. Figured we'd sort through it all later. Remember, we had all weekend—a three-day weekend—to go through them boxes. And the two guys didn't come looking for us for maybe a month—they had to have all these sit-downs with the guineas so nobody loses any face. Mafia protocol and all that horseshit. So I had plenty of time to go through a lot of the papers we took out of the bank, looking for bonds and shit. Most of it was just routine legal stuff, deeds and wills and shit like that. But some of it—it was hot. Some of that shit I made copies of, kept the originals and put the copies back. Don't ask me why."

"I'm getting the drift," I said. "Some of this stuff was so hot it was burning a hole in your pocket."

"Couldn't have been that warm if I've been sitting on it for close to two years," he said. "But yeah, it had started smoldering, you might say. I mean, I set up the whole score—"

"All by yourself, Bucky? You set the whole thing up, is that what you're telling me?"

He grimaced. "Okay, maybe I had a little inside help, but the thing is, it was my job, biggest one around here in years. And I got nothing to show for it. I'm still humping every morning outta the day-labor pool over to Local 25. At my age, still worrying about shaping up every morning at six. But what am I gonna do, I got alimony and child support and tuition and—"

"Welcome to the club," I said.

He again leaned across the table, looked first to his left and then to his right, a bit theatrically considering we were alone in the room. He paused, then whispered:

"So I wrote a letter to a certain party and I told him what I had on him and I told him I needed some money, a lot of money, and I needed it fast."

"Blackmail," I said. "And that is when you heard from the two guys whose names we're not supposed to mention." I got up, walked over to the bar, and returned with two more beers. It was now two rounds for me, none for Bucky. I sat back down, pushed his beer across the table, and shook my head.

I didn't even want to know who Bucky was trying to shake down. I also didn't want to know what dirt he had on whoever it was he wanted to blackmail. All I needed to know was that the two guys believed they had a proprietary right to whatever Bucky had. If I knew what Bucky knew, then I would be joining him on what my father used to call the Lucky Strike Hit Parade.

"Bucky," I said, "you got the kind of problems you need the cops for. I'm thinking Witness Protection Program."

He smiled weakly and shook his head. "Being a cop, I figured you'd know about the FBI. Guys like me call the FBI about those two guys, they end up getting grabbed off the street, by the two guys, like my friend there in the dentist's chair. I could give you names. The feds set up a meeting somewhere, and it ends up it's one of the two guys that shows up. You line up a score and forget to cut them in and either they come looking for you themselves, like they did with us, or the feds are waiting for you on the next job. Like Jazzbo, for instance. Why do you think your brother got lugged down on I-84? Guy he was driving for forgot to cut the two guys in. Them guys got a direct line into the feds, and they use it. They rat you out, and then, just before you're getting sentenced, they buy you a drink and they say, Tough luck Bucky, or Marty, or whoever, come see us when ya get out. Don't you ever talk to your brother about any of this shit?"

I hesitated, not wanting to give him a confirmation which he might take as encouragement that we were both in this together. We most certainly were not. Bucky looked at his watch. I looked at his teeth.

"You know what they say about your brother over there at the Ace of Hearts, don't you?"

I shook my head. We were approaching the too-much-information threshold.

"They say Marty does good time."

"He should," I said. "He's done enough of it."

We sat in uncomfortable silence for a few moments.

"I messed up big time with this play," Bucky finally said. "They're after me, so I'm outta here."

"So I guess you won't be needing me, then?"

"You guessed wrong. You're in it."

"I don't think so."

"I think so." He smiled and showed me some Bureau of Prisons dental work. "I'm going to get you the shit that I was going to use to shake down this other guy. If you don't hear from me, you'll hear from someone else how to get the stuff. If they get me, I want you to get them, all of them. You're going to be my insurance policy."

"Insurance policy?" I shook my head. "If I try to go after these guys, I'll be in the same boat as you. That's not an insurance policy, my friend, it's a suicide pact. You're not thinking straight. Why not go to the Staties? They're clean. I still know some of 'em, I'll make the call for you."

I reached into my coat pocket for my cell phone.

"Too late," he said, shaking his head. "I'm dealing myself out. The stuff is already out of my hands. You should have it in the next couple days, and then you can figure out what you want to do with it. Me, I think you're on to something with that Staties angle there. Maybe you should hand it off to them."

"Don't be an asshole, Bucky. Look, maybe my brother didn't quite explain to you what I do. I'm not like some private detective on TV, you follow me? I'm not a muscle guy, I work for politicians and I, I—"

"I know what you do," he said. "Your brother didn't pull no punches. He told me pols hire you to dig up shit on guys who are running against them and then blow them up with it. He says at least half the crooked hacks that get taken out by the papers, you did it, at least the ones from City Hall and the State House."

I shrugged. Half seemed a bit high, though. Maybe a third.

"What you need right now is muscle," I said. "You got staying-alive problems. What that means is, you need somebody other than me. You need a staying-alive guy, not a digging-up-shit guy."

He smiled, ever so slightly.

"I'll be the judge of that," he said.

I shook my head. "I don't accept the job," I said. "You send me something, I'm throwing it away."

"It's not going straight to you," he said. "You think I'd send something directly through the mail? They got guys down the Postal Annex, just like they got guys in Walpole and at the State House and City Hall and every other damn place."

"Whatever you got," I said, "it's not worth me getting killed over. If the two guys ask me for it, I'm giving it to them."

"I don't think so." He smiled. "You talk a good game, but this is too good, this shit you're getting. I remember Marty telling me that sometimes when you were at City Hall you were known to take guys off the board just for shits 'n' giggles. That right?"

"Not lately," I said. "Everything I do now I get paid for, if you see what I'm getting at."

He saw what I was getting at all right. But as I suspected, he wasn't biting, because he couldn't. Bucky was broke, or he never would have dug this deep a hole for himself.

"Once you see this stuff," he finally said, "I'm pretty sure you'll do the right thing."

"By settling an old score for you?" I said. "How is that the right thing for me?"

"Sorry, man," he said, standing up, "but I need someone to back me up, and you drew the short straw."

He reached into his pocket, came up with a crumpled twenty-dollar bill, tossed it underhand onto the table. I shook my head.

"Beer's on me, Bucky. This is my place."

"It ain't for the beer," he said, looking down at me. "It's a retainer. You want to get paid, I'm paying you. Consider yourself hired."

"For a double sawbuck? You're a little light."

"It's the thought that counts," he said. "See you around the campus, Jack."

Then he turned on his heel and walked out the door. The last light of the early-March afternoon was fading, and he was leaving a roomful of armed cops and heading out into the darkness, less than a half mile from the Ace of Hearts.

SO THERE I was sitting by myself in Foley's, nursing the dregs of my second beer. My back was turned to the main bar so I didn't see him come in, but when I suddenly heard Bing Crosby crooning "Far Away Places" on the jukebox, I knew that City Councilor-at-large Delbert Raymond "Slip" Crowley was in the house. It was his theme song, at least in Foley's.

He figured that every time he punched it up, as soon as they heard Bing Crosby, everyone in the barroom would think of him. Cheaper than thirty-second spots on the radio, he always said. I didn't even bother to turn around because I knew what was coming next. A cold longneck landed in front of me on the table, and Slip pulled up the chair Bucky had just vacated.

"Who was that maggot you were sitting with?" he said. "He reeked of the lockup."

Slip took a sip of his mixed drink—he had to be the last guy in America who drank 7&7s. "Haven't seen you around much lately," he said. "How's business?"

"How's business?" I said. "You saw who I was just talking to. How do you think business is?"

"That bad?" he said, and let the subject drop.

Slip pulled out a pack of Kools and lit up. In the twelve-to-one vote in the City Council to ban smoking in all public buildings in Boston, Slip was the one. After a good long puff, he extracted his glasses from his breast pocket. Then he removed a sheet of paper from the same pocket, unfolded it slowly, and perused it with great deliberation. It was the list of wakes he would be attending this evening.

"Slow night on the circuit," he finally said, looking up over his bifocals. "Gotta go to Southie for a pair of my old-timers, and then over to Langone's for a paisan."

"Nothing in the southern tier?"

"Nothing that ain't Haitian," he said. Sixty-seven years old, and still going strong. He could have stood to drop about fifty pounds, but the extra weight wasn't as noticeable since he'd traded in his belt for a pair of suspenders. He looked like a caricature of an old-time Boston pol—red nose, busted capillaries everywhere on his face, and a full head of white hair combed straight back.

His yard signs still described him as a "veteran," and he had to be the only pol left in Massachusetts outside Bristol County who still routinely carried a gun—a .38 caliber Police Special.

Both newspapers had permanent contracts out on him—when endorsing his opponents every other year, even the *Herald* would routinely dismiss him as "pistol-packing," as if that was a jab that cost him votes he'd have otherwise gotten in the chi-chi wards. The *Globe* once described him in an editorial as a "reprobate," and after Slip looked it up in the dictionary, it had become one of his favorite words. The definition of reprobate, Slip always said, was "asshole."

Behind Bing Crosby, thirty wakes a week, the police and fire unions, and a sixty-five-year-old girlfriend from West Roxbury named Helen, Slip was still good for forty thousand votes every two years—half as many as he used to get, but that didn't much matter, because only a third as many people voted now in city elections as twenty years ago, when he was first elected to the Council. Slip's base was white, native, nongay Catholic Boston—nowadays fewer than 90 of the 251 precincts in the city, and shrinking every year. It wouldn't be enough much longer, but then Slip only cared about the next election—the one coming up in November.

"Don't suppose you'd be interested in hitting the trail tonight?" he said, and I shook my head.

"I get it," he said. "You've got some gash lined up."

"Gash?" I said. "That's a little retro even for you, isn't it, Slip?"

"I was not aware," he said, "that I was addressing a meeting of the Beacon Hill Civic Association."

We batted the breeze for another couple of minutes or so, mainly to ascertain if we still agreed on certain major issues of the day. We did. Property taxes were too high. Harvard buying up Allston sucked. Harvard losing twenty billion dollars from its endowment definitely did not suck. Rich people moving into the neighborhoods sucked. Illegal aliens moving into the old neighborhoods sucked worse. The projects ruined Roslindale, but thank God the Greeks had moved in. Then I remembered that I had a problem by the name of Bucky Bennett.

"Are you up on the FBI?" I asked.

"Wouldn't trust 'em as far as I could throw them," he said. "You know that reprobate from South Boston, Finnerty—the one with the red hair. Ask the cops about him. They call him Agent Orange."

"He's the one pinched my brother on that last hijacking beef."

"Exactly. On orders from a certain bucket of blood in South Boston would be my bet, for reasons I am not privy to, and I'd like to keep it that way, thank you very much. Lemme tell you a little story about Agent Orange. I'm down in West Palm two weekends ago, you know my Helen's just retired from Boston

Gas, or whatever they call it now, and she bought a condo down there and—"

Suddenly we heard a loud commotion outside. They always say gunshots sound like a car backfiring, but when was the last time you heard a car "backfire"? This outburst sounded like the police firing range at Deer Island. *Bang-bang-bang.*

Slip instantaneously went for his shoulder holster and came up with his .38. He'd be telling a greatly embellished version of this story on the floor of the Council for months to come—a cautionary tale on the eternal need to uphold and venerate the Second Amendment. But neither Slip nor any of the armed cops who had just finished the day shift had the opportunity to make like Dirty Harry, because almost as soon as the gunfire ended, we could see blue lights all over the place.

All the cops at the bar ran outside, badges in one hand and service revolvers in the other. The civilians inside the bar settled for crowding around the front door. It was dusk, and the street-light was out, so the only illumination, inadequate as it was, came from the ancient flickering beer sign in Foley's front window.

Schaefer . . . Schaefer . . . Schaefer . . .

I ended up just outside the front door, on the tiles between the East Berkeley Street sidewalk and the front door that opened into Foley's. I had a pretty good hunch who had just bought the farm, but as close as Foley's is to the MS-13 gangbangers in the Cathedral projects and beyond that Roxbury, there was a faint chance this was a Third World hit. But I doubted it.

Now the cops had surrounded a body lying in the gutter, shining their flashlights on it, talking into their shoulder radios, calling for EMTs who would have only one duty here—to remove a corpse to what they used to call the Southern Mortuary down on Albany Street.

Slip was standing directly above the body, so I sidled up behind him and looked down.

It was Bucky Bennett, all right, and he was lying faceup, mouth wide open with blood trickling out. I counted two exit wounds—he'd obviously been shot in the back of the head, from the backseat no doubt. One bullet had exited through his mouth, shattering most of his front teeth. The other gaping exit wound was in his forehead, the coup de grâce. It was an old-fashioned mob hit. Two in the hat.

Slip turned around and I instantly knew what he was about to do, but there was no way to stop him. Without even thinking about it, Slip was going to deal me in.

"Hey Jack," he said, "ain't this the shitbird you was just sitting with?"

Now all cop eyes turned toward me, and I knew the free-associating that was going on in their minds. Cops are like anybody else—they believe everything they read in the newspapers. Most of the cops knew who I was, or thought they did. I was not going to get any benefit of the doubt from this crew.

One of the uniforms stepped between me and Bucky's body.

"You're Jack Reilly, aren't you?"

I nodded but said nothing. I was keeping my own counsel. I was dummying up.

"Do you know who this guy is?" the cop asked.

"I believe he said his name was Bennett."

"Then you were talking to him." This guy was good. He was bucking for detective.

"I'll ask you again," he said. "Were you talking to him?"

"I was." Deposition mode is what I was in. Several cops had already gone back to shining their flashlights around the street. Rousting me would be a chore for the plainclothesmen. The uniforms' job was to wait for the TV crews to arrive so they could gather behind the yellow crime-scene tape for some heavy-duty milling around.

"What was he doing at Foley's?" the uniform asked me.

"I believe he was having a Bud Light."

The cop smiled and nodded. "Okay, I get it. Wise guy. I heard plenty about you at the academy. You're the one the feds got on a wire down at Doyle's. Then you went out on a disability pension. Yeah, I know you. You're Jack Reilly."

SLIP CROWLEY vouched for me, so the cops let me go back inside Foley's until the detectives arrived. I abandoned my table for the bar, switched to club soda, and tried to organize a rousing game of liars' poker, but everyone seemed to be shunning me as they awaited the arrival of the meat wagon. Tough crowd, Foley's.

Conveniently for local TV, Bucky had expired just in time to provide a live shot for the top of the early newscasts. As the news crews arrived, and were filled in on the sketchy details by the cops, they quickly began poking their heads inside the front door and eyeballing me, the Last Person to Talk to the Victim.

I retreated from the front of the bar toward the back, far enough away so that the TV people couldn't videotape me through the front window. But the way they were staring at me, I realized they were committing my matinee-idol profile to memory just in case I decided to duck out the back door, which is exactly what I would have done if the cops hadn't ordered me to stay put.

Slowly, the cops were piecing together what had happened, and inside, we were getting it secondhand, hearsay as it were. When Bucky had walked out of Foley's, he took a left and started toward the Back Bay. He was hardly beyond Washington Street, less than half a block from Foley's, when a nondescript car pulled up beside him and a white guy with a gun, wearing a Red Sox cap and a Bruins jacket, jumped out of the passenger side and made him get in. That information was still a little sketchy; so far every eyewitness to the snatch that the cops had turned up had been either a Mandarin or Cantonese speaker. Chinatown is seeping not so slowly southward.

With Bucky now inside their car, the hoods had apparently doubled back around on Tremont, and then turned right again on Herald Street. The plan was probably to get him over to the Lower End somewhere for a root canal. At the corner of Herald Street and Harrison Avenue, Bucky must have noticed a Transit Police cruiser in the rearview mirror, because he made a lunge for the door. He got it open, but the hoods dragged him back in, at which point the T cops behind them astounded everyone by observing a crime in progress that they themselves weren't committing.

They turned on the blue lights.

With the T cops on their tail, the thugs sped up as they turned right onto Harrison and they made the obvious call. They capped Bucky right then and there, in the car, after which they cut right onto East Berkeley. Personally, I would have continued south on Harrison into Roxbury, where there's less traffic and not that many working streetlights. You can drive faster and it's very dark, in more ways than one.

But fewer and fewer white people know the 'Bury, which meant the killers were probably young, relatively speaking anyway. These days a "young" mobster is anyone under fifty.

After they clipped poor Bucky, his killers pushed the body out of the car in front of Foley's. The two guys at the Ace of Hearts would not be pleased—they like clean hits, preferably the mysterious disappearance that inevitably "baffles" the police. But it's hard to get good help. After Bucky's body was pushed out the door, the T Police cruiser slowed down just long enough to give the hoods a chance to vanish. The murder car, no doubt recently reported stolen in some nearby blue-collar suburb like Malden or Revere, would soon turn up in some housing project parking lot, wiped clean of fingerprints.

Now that I had the bare-bones story, I treated myself to another club soda with a twist and returned to solitary confinement in the Berkeley Room. About five minutes later, the detectives arrived. I could see that the one walking toward me was a guy I knew as "Plain View"—Detective Mike Evans, a classmate of mine at the academy way back when. Back then he'd had brown hair. Now it was mostly gray, what little of it that was left, and he combed the few wisps back.

Plain View probably had it figured down to the hour how long he had to go until he could retire and start collecting his 80 percent pension. He'd been known to bend rules now and again— hence the nickname. But all in all, he wasn't a bad shit. For a shit.

Plain View was wearing a blazer and a tie, something you didn't see too much of anymore in the police department, or anywhere else.

He nodded at me, pulled up a chair, and sat down heavily across the table from me. Apparently due to the circumstances of my departure from the job, I didn't rate a handshake. A heavyset crew-cut female officer with a steno pad planted herself in a chair to his right. I had already made up my mind how I was going to handle this initial inquiry. Mum's the word. Loose lips sink ships.

"This is going to be your official statement, Jack," he said. "We'll do it here because I know how much you like to speak on the record in bars."

Another needle about that small embarrassment of mine from long ago.

"Now that we've dispensed with the small talk," he said, "let's get down to business. What were you discussing with the late Mr. Bucky Bennett?"

"The National Register of Historic Places. He thought Foley's was long overdue for inclusion."

He paused to let that sink in, then shook his head.

"Same old fucking Jack," he finally said. "All these years off the job, and you still think your shit don't stink." He quickly looked over at the stenographer. "That's off the record." He turned back to me. "Let's start over. I repeat, what were you and the late Mr. Bennett talking about?"

"He told me he and Jazzbo Mangan were framed on that armored car heist down in Holbrook. He wanted to find the guys who were really robbing those armored cars. He suspected they might be Colombian drug dealers and he was wondering if I had OJ's prison address in Carson City."

Plain View sighed heavily. "I don't get it. I try to give you a break. I'm letting bygones be bygones here and you're busting my balls." He looked over at the female stenographer, made a chopping motion with his hand, and she nodded, put down the pad, and primly folded her hands.

Plain View said, "You ain't got the juice now, pal. You ain't the mayor's Mr. Fixit no more—notice I ain't calling you a bagman, I'm being as polite as I can. But the fact is that you got no clout, either at City Hall or anywhere else. All you are, Jack, is a broken-down crooked ex-cop pretending to be a private fucking eye, and this is a murder investigation, and you've got a license issued by the state—"

"Are we at the point now where you tell me we can do this the easy way or we can do this the hard way?"

"No, we're at the point where I tell you to fuckin' wise up, because we got a pretty good idea who whacked this fine upstanding citizen, and so do you I bet, and there ain't nothing to be gained by playing footsy with these guys, as you should know as well as anyone except maybe your brother." He leaned back in his chair and yelled over his shoulder toward the bar. "Am I right, Councilor Crowley?"

"I never inject myself into disputes between two of my loyal constituents," Slip said, his back still turned to us as he stood at the bar. "You lose two votes that way."

I hadn't noticed that Slip had drifted back inside, but it couldn't hurt to have someone standing within earshot who was at least somewhat on my side, whatever my side was at this moment.

Plain View turned back toward me and tried to look benevolent. "Did he do time with your brother?"

I pondered that one for a moment. "You know, I believe he did mention Otisville."

He waited for me to continue, but I'd said my piece. I sat there and prepared for him to start yelling at me again. It didn't take long.

"You got the same piss-poor attitude you always had," he said. "Even when you was in that photo finish with the grand jury—"

"A photo finish that I won, by the way." I caught the stenographer's eye and said to her, "And that is on the record."

"Your problem," Plain View said, "is that you've always been a freelancer, on the job or off. Which is fine, especially now that you ain't on the job no more, and don't have to abide by the, the—" He winced as he struggled to come up with the right phrase.

"The code?" I suggested. "The code of ethics, so-called."

"How 'bout we just call 'em the rules and leave it at that? Now that you're not on the job, you don't have to abide by our rules, and once they took away your badge I could not care less what you are or are not doing, believe me."

So why was he pointing a finger at me and yelling if he didn't care?

"But what I don't appreciate is that right now you might be able to assist us in a murder investigation, and yet you still got this hard-on after all these years. I got every right to be asking you these questions, and you damn well know I do, but even now you wouldn't tell me if my coat was on fire. You got a big chip on your shoulder, I understand that, but it's a free country and you got every right to have a chip on your shoulder. What you don't have is the right to withhold evidence."

He was wrong about the bitterness. I've moved on, as they say. My monthly check provides me with all the "closure" I'll ever need. Plain View may get 80 percent when he goes out, but I get mine right now, 72 percent, tax-free, and it goes up with every new union contract.

"The only possible conclusion I can draw here," Plain View said, "considering your somewhat checkered past—and checkered is a charitable way of putting it—is that you, Jack Reilly, must figure there's a score in here somewhere for you, and I'm just telling you, if that's your play, then you're fucking with the wrong guys, and I don't mean the BPD."

"Thank you for your concern, Detective," I said.

"You're fighting above your weight class here," he said.

"Ten-four, good buddy."

"Okay," he said, standing up. "I got other things to worry about tonight, but I'm gonna come looking for you in the morning, and you sure as hell better have a better line of bullshit ready than what you've been handing me tonight."

FOR ONCE in my life, I wanted to escape Foley's. But I also didn't want the cops to think I was spooked. It would be bad for business, assuming I ever got any. So I figured I had to hang in for at least another half hour or so. I was about to treat myself to some more of what made Milwaukee famous when Slip came over with a fresh longneck for me and another mixed drink for himself. He sat down across from me.

"May I offer a helpful suggestion?" he said.

"Do I have a choice?"

"No," he said. "You know, you could have handled that a little more smoothly. A little blarney might have gone a long way there."

"Yeah, but what's the point?"

"The point," he said, "is that sometimes you gotta duck. I shouldn't have to be telling you this stuff. You should have learned it long ago, at City Hall."

I took a long sip of beer and considered reminding Slip whose big mouth had brought me to Plain View's attention in the first place. But if it hadn't been him, somebody else would have ratted me out. It's one of the downsides to drinking in a cop bar. I stared at Slip's 7&7 and mulled switching over to the high octane myself. I like rye and that's no lie.

Slip shook his head slowly. "Now you're pissed at me. I knew I should have kept my mouth shut. No good deed goes unpunished."

I smiled and said, "Can I quote you on that?"

Gerry Foley came over with two more drinks that we hadn't ordered, and from the dismal look on his face I knew again that sorrows always arrive in battalions, or something like that.

"The press requests the pleasure of your company, Jack," he said, gesturing with his head to the bored collection of cameramen and reporters at the front of the bar. "I gotta let 'em in. They drink here too. But if you want me to, I'll hold 'em off while you screw out the back."

I looked over at Slip. He sparred with these people every day. I asked him if I should take it on the lam. Slip shook his head.

"Might as well do a gang bang," he said. "Otherwise they'll just be chasing you all over town tonight, and my guess is you got other people you need to be worrying about chasing you all over town tonight."

No doubt about that. I asked Gerry if he wanted me to deal with them outside, but he said they could do it inside as long as they confined themselves to the Berkeley Room and didn't shoot tape of any of the other patrons whose wives might be under the impression that they were at the Arch Street Shrine making the stations of the cross. I told Gerry to send them right down. I stood up and watched as they approached. Four cameras and a half-dozen or so reporters, which meant one from each TV station, plus the two papers, and the all-news radio station.

"No NPR?" I whispered to Slip.

"They only come over from Cambridge for the hate crimes," Slip said out of the side of his mouth.

They all got their mikes in front of me, and then a tall, dark, and vacant 42-long TV airhead asked: "Why do you think Bucky Bennett was murdered?"

"I haven't the slightest idea," I said. And that was about as good as it got—stupid questions from them, even lamer answers from me. It occurred to me that all I was doing was providing up-to-date video that would make it a lot easier for certain parties to recognize me on the street. I was just about to wrap it up when, off to the left side of the pack, I heard a female voice:

"Did Bucky ever do time with your brother?"

A decent question, finally. I looked over at the reporter, and dimly saw that she was in her early thirties, nice round face, light brown hair, wearing a suit coat over a short skirt, and the high black boots of the type favored by first-team female anchors on the Fox News Channel. My gaze naturally drifted to her left hand—no ring.

"Who are you?" I said.

"Katy Bemis, *Herald,*" she replied. "Did your brother do time with the deceased, and is your brother still incarcerated?"

The other reporters were glancing over at her. She would be asking most of the questions from now on.

I said, "My brother, Martin, yes, he is still in custody of the BOP, and I believe Mr. Bennett did serve part of his sentence with Martin."

I glanced over at Slip. He frowned and shook his head.

"Are you aware that Mr. Bennett was a suspect in an unsolved bank burglary in Medford a few years back, and that at least one and perhaps two members of his gang have since vanished?"

"I just met Mr. Bennett this afternoon," I said. "We didn't discuss his life story."

"Are you aware of the rumors that there was an underworld contract out on Mr. Bennett's life?"

Slip stepped in front of me. "Thank you very much, Mr. Reilly," he said. "That will be all the questions he takes here tonight."

"Why don't you let him answer his own questions, Slip?" Katy Bemis said. "Are you his PR man? I thought you were a full-time city councilor."

"Don't push me, sister," Slip snapped at her, before turning to me and saying out of the side of his mouth, but loud enough for everyone to hear, which was the whole point, "I know this broad from City Hall. She's no damn good."

I turned back to catch Katy Bemis's reaction, and saw a bemused expression cross her face. Slip had made her day.

"Can't he answer for himself, Councilor?" she said. "You handled tougher questions than this in front of the grand jury, didn't you, Mr. Reilly?"

"Call me Jack," I said. "But really, uh—what was the question again?"

"There was a contract out on him. Did he mention that to you?"

"No," I said. Well, he didn't, not in those exact words anyway. Besides, I wasn't under oath. Since when was it against the law to lie to a reporter?

With his head, Slip motioned toward the back door, and I said thank you very much. He put his arm around me and turned me around toward the back door. He got me outside and then lit up a Kool as we started walking toward his car, the cameras recording our flight.

"Goddamn broad," he said. "I know her type in my bones. Thinks her ass is ice cream and you've got to lick it."

I'd heard this rap from Slip before. Many times, in fact. The perfidy of the Yankee—a hardy perennial of a topic in Slip's social circles, and in my late father's too, for that matter. The cheap bastards, the statewide Know-Nothing landslide of 1844, the burning of the Ursuline Convent, and don't forget the Licensing Board and the Boston Finance Commission. . . .

"You know something," I said to Slip. "I'll bet she goes—"

"To a wooden church. Fucking right she does. Eats cucumber sandwiches with the crusts cut off. And she'd rather put out for a big—"

"How do you know who I put out for?" Katy Bemis yelled, leaning out the back door of Foley's, a smirk on her face.

"Fuck you," he yelled back, "and the polo pony you rode in on."

———

IT WAS a business decision to clam up. Don't get me wrong, it's not like I live by some ancient Sam Spade private-eye code or anything like it. But ratting out a client, even one of the twenty-dollar variety, would be bad for all private eyes, as Mr. S. Spade once observed. Especially for one PI in particular—me.

Ratting out anybody, even a dead ex-con, was the kind of thing that would always be used against you. In a couple of days, everyone in the world would have forgotten Bucky Bennett. Everyone, that is, except the people who had an ax to grind against me. People like that never forget, and they make sure everyone else always remembers it. Reilly? they would say, whenever I got a shot at some decent money. Yeah, you could use Reilly, but remember how he spilled everything to the cops when Bucky Bennett got hit?

Eventually what little I did know would come out in the wash—it always does. That's why Plain View hadn't really pushed me at Foley's, because he figured that in a few hours, if there was anything to spill, somebody would spill it.

Besides, as my old man always used to say, Never sell yourself short. Why throw in a hand before you've even taken a peek at the cards? What if it turned out there was something in those papers or whatever it was that Bucky was sending my way?

Something salable.

I was glad to get away from the reporters, but home held no particular appeal. So we got in Slip's car and rounded the block a couple of times until the reporters dispersed, then we parked the Slipmobile on Washington Street, hoofed it back down East Berkeley, and re-entered Foley's through the side door. Just in case any scribes were still loitering at the bar, I ducked into the Berkeley Room after handing Slip Bucky's double sawbuck and telling him it was my turn to play whip-out.

He returned a minute or so later, laid down Bucky's twenty-dollar bill and set the beer on top of it. I protested mildly but he wouldn't hear of it. I stared straight ahead and considered my next move. Slip lit another cigarette and started talking.

"So as I was saying, before I was so rudely interrupted," Slip began, as if nothing had happened, "I'm down in West Palm two weeks ago, and it's Monday morning and I'm flying back—"

I wasn't in the mood to pay much attention to what Slip was saying, but Slip's the kind of guy who doesn't really care. He figures as long as he can hear the sound of his own voice somebody else must be listening too, which means he's banking votes for the next election.

"—and I'm flying coach, of course, because otherwise people would talk, and as I'm boarding, guess who I see is already hoisting a glass of bubbly up in first class with a bimbo whose hair is even redder than his own. None other than FBI Special Agent John Finnerty. Also known as Agent Orange."

"No shit?" I said, and now I was paying attention.

"My question is," Slip said, "where the fuck does Special Agent Finnerty get the money to fly first class? Inheritance? I don't think so. And why exactly is he still in the Boston FBI office after all these years? I always thought the standard operating procedure in the FBI was never to rotate anybody through their hometowns. It leads to trouble, it has led to trouble."

A few years back at the State House, a crooked state rep had been tipped that the "lobbyist" he was taking bribes from was actually an undercover G-man who turned out to be from Dorchester. The rep instantly returned the cash (with different serial numbers), and ended up beating the attempted-extortion rap, after which he was subsequently elevated to the state Senate by his grateful constituency. The last I'd heard, he was chairman of the Ethics Committee.

So yeah, now that Slip mentioned it, there was something rather fishy about Finnerty's permanent posting in his hometown. Too bad I hadn't been listening more attentively to Bucky. I asked Slip if Finnerty had recognized him on the flight.

"He most certainly did," Slip said. "Not only does he recognize me, he offers to get me upgraded to first class."

"Maybe he wanted someone to talk to."

Slip shook his head. "No way. He only had eyes for the bimbo. They looked like twins, I shit you not. I get back to the hall, I'm curious, I make a couple of calls, come to find out his secretary's got red hair too. Also, he's out of the house, slipped the surly bonds of matrimony, you might say. He's living with this selfsame flame-haired spitfire from the steno pool. Stop me if you've heard this one before."

"Costs money, doesn't it?"

"My point exactly. Where's it coming from? My guess is, if you hang at, say, the Ace of Hearts, it would be nice sometimes to have information before the competition does."

I took a long gulp of my beer. "Competition whose last names end in vowels."

"In Town or anyone else," Slip said. "But it gets worse. You heard how the mayor's about to appoint the new police commissioner—guess who's getting a big-time push for the job? Hint: he has red hair."

"You're shitting me," I said.

"The heat's coming down big-time from the State House," he said. "They say the Speaker wants this one, bad. He's got the full-court press on."

I took an even longer guzzle. "How come you never told me this?"

"How come?" Slip said. "You never write, you never call. Until tonight, I haven't seen you since Christmas maybe. Sometimes I think you're giving me the swerve."

"I heard you were running for president of the Council," I said.

He snorted. "President of the City Council? That's like being admiral of the Swiss Navy."

Chapter Two

I OWN MY house on Shawmut Avenue in the South End, but I didn't just inherit it. I've paid for it, twice. First, after my parents died, I bought out my brother Marty's half. That money went to pay the retainer for his lawyers on the rap before this one, which involved some stolen artwork he was trying to fence out in Illinois on behalf of the traditional parties both known and unknown to the grand jury, as the indictment put it.

Then a few years later I bought out my ex-wife as part of the divorce settlement. So I own it, lock, stock, and two mortgages. It's easy to spot—it's the only house for blocks that still has a coat of paint on the front door.

I'm the third male in the Reilly family to own it, just like I was the third Reilly to serve on the Boston Police Department. The only memento from my grandfather's brief service—he was one of the 1,500 cops fired by Governor Calvin Coolidge in the Boston Police strike of 1919—is an old-style bobby hat that I found in the basement a few years back. After Silent Cal broke the strike, the BPD never went back to bobby hats. Too many bad memories, I suppose. My grandfather's hat now rests in the nearest thing to a place of honor that I could find for it, on the mantel above the nonworking fireplace in my living room.

Even though my house is only two blocks from Foley's I figured it'd be safer to accept a ride home from Slip, especially since he was armed, and I wasn't. Once I let myself inside I went straight to my bedroom closet and got down my old Army steamer trunk and assessed the Reilly Bros.' dusty collection of firearms—registered and otherwise. My brother always likes to keep a few extra pieces on hand, and so do I. It's one of the few interests we share. I settled on one of my brother's unregistered pieces, a Taurus, a cheap Brazilian knockoff of a Smith & Wesson .38. I loaded it and returned to the kitchen.

I put the phone on automatic answer, poured myself another beer, and did a little more bookkeeping with the bills in the Have-to-Pay pile. It was the second of the month, which meant it was time for The Check. Not mine, from the city, but hers, my ex-wife's, from me. John Barrymore once said you never know how short a month is until you pay alimony. It's one of those sayings the brilliance of which you never quite grasp until it's too late.

Then the phone rang, and the caller ID said UNAVAILABLE, which is another way of saying Martin T. Reilly. I picked up on the third ring and heard an asexual computer-generated voice telling me that I had a collect call from a facility run by the Bureau of Prisons, and would I be willing to accept the charges?

Of course I would. On her deathbed, I promised me sainted ma that I'd forever be watching over her ne'er-do-well son, or should I say her other ne'er-do-well son, even as she was watching over me from heaven. She always bought into that Catholic mumbo jumbo hook, line, and sinker.

The disembodied voice said press one if you accept charges. I pressed one and immediately heard a familiar voice.

"Was Bucky in Foley's for the reason I'm assuming he was in Foley's for?"

So much for the traditional salutations. It was my brother Marty. If they ever name a street after him, it'll have to be one way.

"Listen," he said. "You understand I can't say much, right?"

The feds tape all conversations, and so does the state, although I'm more familiar with the BOP than with the Department of Correction, because my brother mostly does federal time.

He said, "They think you have something of theirs."

He didn't have to say who "they" were.

"They say they don't want any trouble."

"They always say that," I said.

"Look, I'm just the messenger here, and the message is, you've really hit the jackpot this time."

"What does that mean, exactly?"

"It means they'll do whatever they have to do to get whatever it is you have that they want, and of all the things they don't like, cute is right at the top of the list. Do I make myself clear?"

Crystal clear. No cops.

"They liked how you played it just now, down the street. That's the way they want the whole thing to go down. Dummy up and they'll make it a win-win."

Wonderful. They might have some work for me. Wet work, no doubt. How Marty already knew what had transpired in Foley's less than two hours ago, I didn't want to know, even if he'd been able to tell me.

"Suppose I was to tell you," I said, "that I not only don't have what they want, but I don't even know what it is that they think I have. What would they say to that?"

"They would say that is not a satisfactory answer."

I was afraid of that.

"Let me ask you something else," I said. "You know those toys of yours that you used to stash in my trunk?"

It wasn't the smoothest code ever devised, and it took Marty a few seconds to figure out what I was talking about.

"I've been thinking of traveling with your Brazilian friend," I said.

"Mr. Taurus, I presume?" he said, catching on.

"Exactly. Would you recommend I take Mr. Taurus on a tour of the city?"

"That would be a very prudent thing for you to do."

That was all the wisdom Marty had to impart this evening. I hung up the phone and let the answering machine pick up the rest of the calls, most of which were hang-ups or TV news producers wanting me to do a live shot at eleven. Yeah, right.

About nine thirty, though, my cell phone rang. I figured it must be somebody I knew, so I picked it up.

"Back in the news you are," a male voice said, not identifying himself.

"Who is this?"

"A paying customer," he said. "Cash 'n' carry. Reasonable doubt at a reasonable price. Forgotten but not gone. Invincible in peace, invisible in war. Need I continue with the amusing catchphrases of yore?"

No, he needn't. It was Representative Daniel Patrick Mahoney (D-Dorchester), majority leader of the Massachusetts House of Representatives, better known to one and all as Jiggs, a nickname lifted from the henpecked Irish husband of the long-forgotten Hearst comic strip, *Bringing Up Father.*

I said, "Are you calling to commiserate in my time of troubles?"

"I wasn't aware that you were in trouble," he said. "I took you at your word when you told the TV reporters you didn't know the deceased gentleman."

"Did I hear something about cash?"

He chuckled. "Same old Jack Reilly. Yes, you did."

I knew better than to ask him any questions over the phone. I also knew that if I told him that my present circumstances precluded me from doing anything for him immediately, then he would find somebody else, immediately. I couldn't afford to miss a payday, especially one that would surely involve cash. Jiggs gave me the name and address of a bar in Central Square in Cambridge. He asked me if I could meet him there at eleven tomorrow morning. *Dominus vobiscum,* I said. *Et cum spiritu tuo,* he replied. It was a date.

I WAS considering whether to have another beer when my cell phone rang again. I picked it up and said hello.

"This Reilly?" It was an older, male Boston voice.

"Speaking." Maybe I should have asked who I was speaking to, but in my line of work, curiosity sometimes does kill the cat, or at least the job. The same rules that applied to Jiggs went for this guy too.

"I'm a friend of Bucky's," he said. "He asked me to give you something."

"Yeah?" I said. "So what is it?"

"Don't you know?"

"He didn't tell me anything."

The voice had no response to that, but somehow I discerned that he was as skeptical of my story as Plain View.

"Well, I gotta get rid of this shit Bucky gave me," the voice said. "I seen what happened on the news and I don't need that kind of trouble."

"Why don't you mail it to me?"

"Mail it?" he said. "I thought you didn't know what it was."

"You can't mail it?" I said. "What is it, a Brinks truck?"

He chuckled. "How 'bout we meet somewhere, smart guy? Tonight."

I didn't care much for that idea, but I had a feeling he was going to be adamant, whoever he was.

"Okay," I said. "How about Foley's?"

"That's where you ran into Bucky, right?"

"Right."

"Then I don't know about that."

"What are you afraid of, ghosts?"

"How 'bout we meet somewheres downtown?" he said.

"How 'bout we meet tomorrow?" I said. "In the daylight."

"I'll be long gone by then, mister. It ain't safe around here right now, being a friend of Bucky's."

"Look, pal, I think I'm going to call it a night."

"I wouldn't, I was you. Them guys that killed Bucky, they'll be looking for you soon enough, if they aren't already, and they want what I've got, and I'm not planning on sticking around long enough to meet up with them."

I considered that for a moment. What if he did have . . . whatever? He'd suggested downtown, so maybe he'd go for a busy place, down near Quincy Market.

"How 'bout the Purple Shamrock?" I said.

"How 'bout Longo's?" he said, referring to a joint on Broad Street.

"What's wrong with the Purple Shamrock?"

"What's wrong with Longo's?"

"How many people there, this time of night?"

"What are you afraid of, ghosts?"

I told him I'd meet him there in a half hour. I figured, with any luck, I could get whatever it was, put this all behind me, and get back to some paying jobs. Besides, how much of a trap could I be walking into? Just by going there, wasn't I proving that I didn't have whatever it was that Bucky had that the two guys were looking for?

Still, better safe than sorry. I wore an overcoat, with the Taurus tucked in the right waist pocket. I couldn't even remember the last time I had carried a gun, and although I could have sworn I still had a shoulder holster, I couldn't find it. Maybe I should have taken someone along with me. But my problem was the same one that had plagued the late Bucky Bennett. I was fresh out of backup.

It didn't take long to drive to Broad Street, but I wanted extra time because I didn't like the parking situation. Garages were out until further notice, especially at night. Ditto alleys and side streets, which is all there is down in the Financial District. I finally decided to park on Broad Street in front of the joint and take my chances, or actually, my lumps, considering how thick the meter maids are on the ground there, even after business hours.

I strolled into Longo's as casually as I could manage, and counted only four hands on deck, all male, including the bartender. It was a lunch place, mostly, and the dining room, the kitchen, and a couple of private function rooms were all cordoned off and dark at this time of night. Evenings Longo's was nothing more than a gin mill, with a circular bar in the middle of the room and booths all around. I planted myself on the other side of the bar so I could keep an eye on the front door.

I ordered a beer and waited for something to happen.

After about five minutes, a short, older guy who'd been sitting across the bar from me wandered over with his beer and sat down beside me. He looked about sixty, in good shape for his age with no gut, and he was wearing a Red Sox cap.

"Hey," he said, "don't I know you from someplace?"

I gave him a quick once-over. "I don't think so."

"Yeah, I'm sure I do," he said. "You're Jack Reilly, ain't you? Used to drive the mayor around, am I right?"

I looked at him again. "Listen, pal, I'm sorry, but I'm waiting for somebody."

Suddenly he was off the stool and in my face. "You're waiting for me, motherfucker. I'm Knocko Nugent."

Knocko—one of the two guys whose name you were never supposed to mention, unless you used the proper measure of respect, which was by referring to him as The Man.

I respected The Man enough to not even think about going for my gun. I also respected him enough to instantly bolt for the door, but despite the fifteen-year age difference, he was faster, and stronger. He grabbed my right hand by the wrist with his left hand, and in the same motion leaned over and came up with a knife out of his boot. Instantly the shiv was up against my neck, and I could see that it was a serious-business knife, with not one, but two blades. In the service, we called them Arkansas toothpicks. On the Military Channel, you'd see them on specials about the British SAS. They're not for cutting, they're for stabbing—a statement knife, as it were.

"Now walk slowly, into the back room," Knocko said, "and don't bother to yell, because the nearest civilians are the meter maids outside, and they're too busy writing a ticket on that shitbox of yours to hear you scream."

Two of the other guys sitting at the bar slid off their stools and followed us inside the function room. The bartender stared straight ahead. Once the four of us were inside the back room, one of Knocko's henchmen slammed the door shut behind us. Knocko pushed me roughly toward a table and then ordered me to sit down in a rickety chair, after which he did the same, directly across from me. The other two sidled up behind me and assumed standing at-ease positions, awaiting orders.

Knocko pointed a finger at me. "Don't fuck with me!" he said. "You fuck with me, you're a fuckin' dead man. You got that, you fuckster, you?"

Now he stood up, knocking over his chair as he rose. He was really yelling now.

"You know how I handle a fuckster like you across the bridge? I get a garbage bag and I put it on the floor and I make you step in it. Then I point a .45 at the top of your head, and I pull the trigger. You know what happens?"

More than likely, I die.

"I'll tell you what happens, fuckster," he said. "All the blood and brains and shit just drains right into the bag. No mess, no fuss. You understand what I'm telling you, fuckster?"

Fuckster—I'd never even heard the word before, and now I'd been called one maybe five times in the last thirty seconds.

"I oughta give you a good fucking beating, right here and now, just on general principles for being a lying fucking crooked cop, but you got something I want. So I'm gonna give you something else to think about, you fuck, you."

He looked over at one of the thugs, the thinner, younger one.

"Frisk him, Kevin, then cuff him."

Then he turned to the fatter one, who had to go at least four hundred pounds. He had his pants pulled up way high, as if that would cover his sixty-inch waist.

"You got the cuffs there, Kevin?"

So both of them were named Kevin. But it was Thin Kevin I had to worry about first, because he quickly located the Taurus. He opened his palm to show it to his boss. He said, "Look, Jimmy"— Knocko's real name—and then brought it over to him. Knocko took the gun from his underling and studied it with disdain. As

Knocko watched, Thin Kevin pulled me up out of the chair, after which he drew my hands behind my back and cuffed me. After I was handcuffed, Knocko strode up to me and shoved the Taurus into my stomach.

"Were you thinking of trying to kill me?" he said, and I had no good answer.

"I asked you, fuckster, were you thinking about trying to kill me?"

"I was thinking," I finally said, "about defending myself."

"Here's something you should know about me. I never killed anybody who wasn't trying to kill me."

In Knocko's vocabulary, I'm sure the word "kill" had as many meanings as Eskimos have words for snow. "Defending oneself," was defined as trying to kill him, no doubt. Another synonym was "beating Mr. Nugent to a parking space," or so it was said about an unsolved Christmastime murder of a father of three shot to death in his minivan at the South Shore Plaza a few years back.

Knocko prodded me in the stomach with the gun and pushed me backward toward a little service bar in the corner that I hadn't noticed before. Fat Kevin followed him, and when we reached the sink, from somewhere Fat Kevin pulled out a white terrycloth sash, the kind you see on bathrobes. Knocko crossed his arms and watched, smiling, as Fat Kevin wrapped the sash around my neck. He took one end and Thin Kevin took the other, which he held over the sink.

Knocko showed me his expensively capped teeth. "You know what this is about, fuckster?"

No, this fuckster didn't. So Knocko walked over to the sink, and turned on the garbage disposal. It made the customary grinding sound.

"Gimme the sash," Knocko said to Thin Kevin, and then he dangled it over the garbage disposal. Until now, I'd figured I was in line for at most a beating, because the fact that I'd come here at all proved that I didn't have whatever it was Knocko wanted. But now I began to wonder if Knocko would kill me anyway, simply because he couldn't help himself.

"Know what happens if I feed the sash into the disposal there while Kevin's still holding on to the other end?"

"I can figure it out."

"Tell me, then."

"The blade rotates, it grabs the sash, and it pulls me down, and unless Kevin lets go of the other end, my neck breaks."

"Very good, fuckster." He smiled. Then he dropped the sash, and told Fat Kevin to do the same, after which he told Thin Kevin to unlock the handcuffs. The tempest seemed to have passed, for the moment. He told them to bring me back to the table and sit me down, which they did, after a few hard shoves to show Knocko that they were tough too. Knocko stood over me and reached into his pocket again and I cringed, which he noticed, and that made him laugh. When he laughed, the two guys behind him laughed. Then he pulled his hand from his pocket and instead of a weapon, he was holding a crumpled piece of paper, which he tossed at me.

I looked down at it, but I didn't want to make any sudden moves with my hands.

"Go ahead, pick it up," Knocko ordered, and I did. He gave me a few seconds to study the scrawled notes, which were mainly numbers and a few addresses.

"Anything there look familiar to you?" he said. "That first one there's your ex-wife's home address in Canton, and under it's the license plate on your daughter's car—it's an O-six Sable, gray, another real piece of shit, and she works three nights a week at the Beef 'n' Brew right off ninety-five there, and right below that one is your son's license plate, the address of his dorm room at UMass, and his cell phone number."

Knocko allowed himself a sadistic little grin. "You know, we could grab your slutty ex-wife some morning when she's driving to the courthouse, but I know you cheap-ass cop types. You'd love to see her gone, wouldn't you, to save on the alimony."

Cripes, could he read my mind on top of everything else?

"Here's the deal, maggot. When we get our stuff back, I throw away this little list here. We don't get our stuff back, well, you don't even want to think about that. You understand?"

I nodded.

"Maybe you're wondering how come I recognize you tonight. You want to know how I made you?"

Did I have a choice?

"You used to work for the mayor, right? At night sometimes you used to drive him over to the Boston Athletic Club for his candy-ass workouts, you remember that? I'll bet you never knew this, but one time, I had both you cocksuckers in my sights. We were up on the roof of the packy across the parking lot there. We had automatic rifles, M-16s, we were going to take both of you out, him first, then you."

I didn't say anything. The silence lingered.

"Look at him," Knocko said, flashing an affectionate smile at the younger, thinner Kevin. "He's wondering why did I want to kill him? But he doesn't dare ask, because he's afraid I'm going to kill him now." He chuckled and bared his teeth at the same time. "You're fucking terrified, aren't you, fuckface?"

I still said nothing, which may have been pushing it at this point. I was wondering to myself, was fuckface a promotion or demotion from fuckster?

"Stand up!" he finally screamed, and I knew another thunderstorm had shown up on the Doppler. "Get up on your feet, you motherfucker."

I stood up, and he was quickly right back in front of my

face—my chin, actually, because I had four or five inches on him. He couldn't have been much over five six.

"Go ahead," he said. "You can ask me. Say, 'Why were you going to kill me and the mayor, Mr. Nugent?'"

"Why were you going to kill me and the mayor, Mr. Nugent?"

"Why?" he repeated now, looking over at Fat Kevin. "He wants to know why Mr. Nugent was going to kill him and the mayor." Then he turned back to me, bent over, and pulled the knife out of his boot again. He shoved the tip of the blade under my chin, pressing it hard enough against my skin that I had to move my entire head up and back to avoid being cut.

"Why was I thinking about clipping the mayor?" Knocko said. "It was because at the time we owned the City Council president. We whack your boss, our guy's the new mayor. We win."

He flicked the knife just enough to break my skin. I squirmed, involuntarily, more in surprise than pain, and that must have turned Knocko on, because then he twisted the blade. It wasn't in deep enough to really do any damage, but when he jerked the blade he must have hit a vein because blood—my blood—started dripping onto the floor.

Then he suddenly lost interest in shanking me. He deftly slid the Arkansas toothpick back in his boot.

"Where's my shit?" he said to me. "You got my stuff and I want it back."

"Look, Mr. Nugent," I said, "if I had the stuff, as you describe it—"

His eyebrows arched, and he again fixed me with the kind of demented grin you usually see only on television when Charles Manson is pitching the California parole board for an early release.

"Did you hear him, boys?" he said, then looked back at me.

"He says, 'as you describe it.' Why, you must be one of those high-class fucking college boys. Are you a fucking college boy, college boy?"

"UMass Boston," I said quickly. "Look, if I had the stuff, would I have come down here when you told me you had the stuff?"

"Very good, college boy," Knocko said. "You finally put two and two together."

He stood up again and walked back over to where I was still standing, flanked by the Kevins. A small puddle of blood was forming at my feet. My blood.

"This was a test," he said. "You passed it when you walked through the door. The rest of it . . ." He shrugged. "Let's just say, I had to deliver a message to you, and I don't much like telephones."

I said nothing. With guys like this, you're never really out of the woods. Sometimes all it takes is one look—it doesn't matter what you mean by it, it's how they read it. They're insane, all of them, more or less, and Knocko more so than anyone else around here, ever.

"Don't you want to know what the message to you is?" he asked.

I had a pretty good idea, but he obviously wanted to make sure I got it.

"The message," he said, "is that if you get out of line—" He made a slashing motion with his hand across his throat. That was the message I'd be taking away, assuming I got away. Another large drop of the message had just dripped onto my right shoe.

"When you get that thing of mine," he said, "I want it back. It ain't yours, it's mine. You got that?"

"I got it," I said.

He turned on me, walked back over to the table, grabbed the slip of paper with the numbers written on it, stuffed it in his breast pocket, and then told the Kevins it was time to leave. He stuck my gun in his belt and walked to the door. I was still standing there, bleeding. Then he turned back around and smiled at me.

"Don't you want to know why I didn't whack you and the mayor that night at the Boston Athletic Club?"

Actually, the thought had crossed my mind.

"I'll tell you why," he said. "It occurred to me, while I was lying on my stomach on that roof across the street waiting for you two lyin' lowlifes to come out, I realized it would be cheaper to just keep paying off your boss."

He turned again and walked out the door, slamming it behind him.

I waited a minute or so, then gingerly walked over to the door and cracked it. I glanced across the room at the bartender, but it was a new guy. He was the only one in the house. I opened the door and walked into the main room, to the bar. I leaned over and grabbed a clean hand towel from behind the bar, and used it as a bandage for my wound. The bartender didn't even bother to turn around. I think he was cutting up fruit, and I had no desire to strike up a conversation with anyone holding a knife in his hand. Besides, there was no point in asking the bartender if he'd seen anything because I already knew the answer to that question. I walked quickly out to my car and saw an orange seventy-five-dollar ticket fluttering under the windshield wiper.

DRIVING HOME, glancing up at the rearview mirror every few seconds to make sure no one was tailing me, I kept dabbing at the cut with the bar towel. The bleeding eventually slowed to a trickle. I briefly considered heading down to the emergency room at the Boston Medical Center to get a stitch or two. But I was in enough pain already without putting in God-knows-how-many hours just watching the parade of illegal aliens in that Tower of Babel.

Instead I just drove straight home, all the while trying to figure out just how many people Knocko had to have on the pad to come up with that much information on me that quickly. He knew my kids' names—that meant someone close to my family (Marty again, perhaps?) or someone in Town Hall in Canton, where their mother, my ex-wife, lived. He had their license plates—that meant somebody either in the Registry or a cop, and running tags isn't as nearly as easy as it used to be, now that every computer inquiry leaves a trail. He knew my son's dorm room at UMass—so he had somebody in the university system. He knew my ex-wife had a job at the courthouse—which meant he had sources in either the judiciary or the legislature, or both. Probably both.

And he'd put the whole package together in a couple of hours, while he was simultaneously setting me up.

Plain View was right—I was fighting above my weight class here. What was even more depressing was how effortlessly he'd been able to handle me. He'd dangled the bait, and I'd bitten. And the worst thing was, he knew he could get away with it. I had no "protection." He could threaten me and my family with impunity and I had no way to push back.

I'd lost my chops. In the old days, I'd have come looking for him, with a badge and the mayor behind me. He would have considered me a threat. Once I'd had clout, even if it was secondhand clout, clout-by-association. But now? Now I was nothing but a fuckster.

Chapter Three

I DIDN'T CALL my kids, because what could I really do other than scare them out of their wits? As for my ex-wife, anything I told her would eventually end up in an affidavit in support of a motion for either a restraining order or, more likely, an increase in alimony or child support or whatever other euphemism her PC judge in the quote-unquote family court is using to describe the monthly check this year.

Back home I made sure every door and window was locked and bolted, after which I tried to get some sleep. All night I tossed and turned, until around seven A.M., when I trudged to the bathroom, turned on the light, and lifted my chin to examine the cut. The scab hadn't quite formed yet, and the cut was still oozing blood. I wet a washcloth with warm water and dabbed at it. I looked like death warmed over.

Then I went online to read the morning papers.

GANG WAR was the front-page headline in the *Herald*, which was technically accurate, I suppose, if you considered Bucky's little burglary crew a gang. As for the part about a "war," if that's what it had been, it was surely over now, although Katy Bemis was doing her best to paint a bull's-eye onto at least one more target's back:

> *Just before being forced into the death car, Bennett was seen at J. J. Foley's, a South End bar. Witnesses said he was talking with Jack Reilly, a rogue ex–Boston cop turned private eye who retired on a full city disability pension days after surviving a federal grand jury probe of an alleged City Hall police promotions racket.*
>
> *Reilly, who was not indicted, confirmed to the* Herald *last night that he had spoken to Bennett, but declined to reveal what they had discussed. He described Bennett as a jailhouse pal of his brother, Martin, a minor figure in local organized-crime circles who is now serving a 10-year federal prison sentence for truck hijacking. . . .*

Rogue ex-cop? They always call me that in the papers. It's their code for "crooked," which they don't dare call me directly because I was never convicted. They never accurately describe my brother Marty either. What he is is a degenerate gambler. They call him a "career criminal," which he is, but the root cause of everything is the gambling. My brother is a guy who has got the fever so bad that he'd bet on the WWF if he couldn't find any other action. When Marty gets out, he's going to go crazy when he discovers ESPN Classic on cable. He'll grab for as much action as you want to give him on a tape of the 2008 Super Bowl, and he'll pick the Pats over the Giants every time.

Around 8:30, the landline rang. I picked it up.

"Look outside, handsome." It was Plain View. "You've got a police escort this morning."

"I'm not going anywhere."

"That's what you think. Come on downstairs."

"You forgot the magic word."

"You mean Knocko?"

I sighed, logged off the Internet, and trudged downstairs. Plain View was in the front seat of an unmarked vehicle. His driver was a black guy—Plain View introduced him as Willie.

After I climbed in the backseat, Willie pulled the car over and parked it next to a fire hydrant.

"I thought we were going for a ride," I said to Plain View.

"You'll be going for a ride soon enough, if you don't start playing ball."

Then he noticed the cut under my chin.

"Jesus," he said. "What happened to you?"

"I cut myself," I said. "Shaving."

"When did you start shaving with an ice pick?"

I tried to ignore that by changing the subject.

"Right now," I said, "I'm paying attention to the rearview mirror, and what I see is Myrna the meter maid waddling this way, and she is one nasty bitch, as I can tell you from personal experience."

Plain View craned around in the seat to get a look at her. She was about five two, 180, Dominican would be my guess. Standard modern-issue meter maid, in other words. Plain View told Willie to go have a chat with her. Willie didn't seem terribly pleased to be playing Birmingham Brown to Plain View's Charlie Chan, but he knew enough to follow orders.

"I don't get it," I said to Plain View. "Your license plate's gotta be untraceable, so what does it matter if she writes you a ticket or not? Nobody has to pay, and no one will ever know you parked next to a fire hydrant."

"It's the principle of the thing," Plain View said. "You can't let a meter maid push you around."

He watched Willie gesturing as he tried to convince her not to write a ticket. Willie flashed his badge. She kept writing. He showed her the badge again. She tore the ticket off her book and handed it to him, a triumphant expression on her face. One ticket closer to her quota for the day, the quota that City Hall always claims doesn't exist.

"Do you think there's really a ticket quota?" I asked Plain View.

"Are you going fucking soft?" he said.

We watched Willie accept the ticket and then climb back into the front seat, muttering to himself, motherbleeper PR this and motherbleepin' spic that. Once more I feared for the future of the Democratic coalition. Willie was not celebrating diversity. Finally, Plain View told Willie to calm down and then turned back to me.

"Did you get yourself a good night's sleep?" he said.

"As a matter of fact, I did. Thanks for asking."

"I was wondering if maybe you had any nightmares," he said. "I mean, about being snatched off the street and taken somewhere and strapped into some dentist's chair in some basement or warehouse."

"Funny, you're the second guy to mention dental work to me lately."

"Really?" he said. "This other guy who liked to talk dentistry, would they be waking him today at O'Connor's, visiting hours two to four and seven to nine?"

I stared out the window at Myrna and said nothing.

"Enough with the small talk," Plain View said. "You better start talking, or maybe there's another shaving accident in your future, would be my guess."

I asked him if we could agree I spent twenty minutes tops my whole life with Bucky before he got whacked. He said yes, he would be willing to stipulate that. Then I asked him if he really thought I had anything to do with Bucky getting clipped. He said no.

"So what can I possibly tell you?" I said. "Do you think I know why he got hit?"

"I think you know more than I do, at the very least, and if you'd help us out, it might give us something to work with."

Translation: no one had spilled. If something didn't break very shortly, the Bucky Bennett hit would be going into the books as unsolved. So they were going to lower the boom on me.

"Why are you rousting me?" I said. "You know who did this, and you know what happens when you go up against those guys. There's no percentage taking them on. You can't win. Nobody can. If you're a civilian, you disappear. If you're a state cop, you're shipped out to the boonies. If you're a Boston cop—"

"Early retirement," Plain View said.

"Which I can personally tell you ain't all it's cracked up to be," I said.

"I don't know," he said. "You can't be doing all that bad, living in this fancy tail-gunner neighborhood and all."

I let that one slide too.

"Seriously," I said, "why are you here?"

"Seriously?" he said, and now Willie glanced up into the rear-view mirror at his boss. Obviously he had been asking himself the same question. "Seriously? If you go missing in the next forty-eight hours or so, I want to have it on the record that I warned you, personally."

"So that explains Willie," I said. "He's your corroborating witness."

Plain View shrugged. "I could have hauled you down to head-quarters, gotten some more witnesses for when the time comes, if the time comes, and I sincerely hope it doesn't. But instead of

dragging you in for an official warning, Willie and I are just trying to accommodate a taxpayer as he begins what I'm sure will be
another very trying day in the Dreaded Private Sector."

"You're not kidding, are you?"

"I'm not a big kidder, Jack, in case you've forgotten." He
handed me his business card. "Think about it. You can always get
me at that cell phone number there."

He opened his door, got out and walked around to the other
side of the Crown Vic, and opened my door. All he said to me was,
"Now, screw."

I THOUGHT about driving to Central Square for my meeting
with Jiggs, but my late father's '87 Oldsmobile looked serene there
in a legal neighborhood-only, Myrna-proof parking space. So I
decided it was time for a walk.

It was relatively pleasant for early March. The sun was shining, the snow was mostly gone, even from the shadows next to the
buildings, and it was only a mile to Park Street, where I could
catch the Red Line to Cambridge.

The only problem with walking was that someone from
South Boston might decide to give me a lift. But it was daylight,
and like a Boy Scout, I would be prepared. Despite the warm sun,
I selected my heaviest topcoat from the closet, removed a couple
of almost-fossilized mothballs from its pockets, as well as an ancient football card that said it was "For Amusement Purposes
Only." How old was the card? It was so old there were plays on
two NFL teams from L.A. I tossed the card into the wastebasket
and tried the jacket on for size.

The label said it was from Kennedy's, which has been out of
business for maybe twenty years, and I don't remember ever
shopping there, so it had to have belonged to my late father. I

noticed a few moths had braved the barrage of mothballs to chow down on the sleeves, but that was okay too.

After all, I wasn't out to impress the carriage trade. Jiggs was hiring me for my expertise, not my wardrobe. I went back to the steamer trunk, and this time I selected the Rossi, a fine piece. I silently congratulated myself on my prescience in not taking it to Longo's last evening. It fit snugly inside the coat's right-side waist pocket, which was where I planned to keep my right hand all the way to Cambridge. I figured that would serve as enough of a warning to Knocko's steadier hit men, however many of those he still had. Cocaine had changed everything, and not for the better.

It turned out to be an uneventful trip on the Vomit Comet across the river. I stood, as I always do when forced to travel on the "rapid transit." Just give me a strap and I'm satisfied. In the front of the car, a grimy Gabby Hayes lookalike had removed his boots and was cutting his toenails, which were ricocheting around the car at the speed of sound. All the seats were taken except one, where a suspicious-looking yellow fluid was sloshing around. A couple of aspiring rap artists were tossing f-bombs about the car, and everyone else was staring straight ahead, trying to avoid making eye contact with anyone else. If somebody shot the "rappers" today when they got off the train, the papers tomorrow would say they'd been turning their lives around, working on their GEDs, making every single meeting with their probation officers. Their tearful "fiancées" would be interviewed. . . .

Next time, I'm driving. I don't care how good a parking space I have to give up.

At Central Square, I fled the train and took the stairs two at a time until I reached the daylight on Mass. Ave., where I just managed to dodge a steaming pile of fresh dog shit.

I walked two blocks and then cut down Brookline Street to a little shabeen. Jiggs had to have somebody there, somebody who owed him something. That was how Jiggs operated. He did favors, and expected the same in return. One hand washed the other, and Jiggs scratched your back, maybe, if you'd scratched his first.

My right hand still plunged deep into my father's topcoat, I walked past the barroom the first time, detecting no hostiles inside. I kept walking until I reached the old diner next door, which was packed with an early-lunch crowd of beefy locals. I did an about-face on the sidewalk in front of the diner, sauntered back past the gin mill, and this time stopped to peer in. In the back I could see Jiggs, sitting by himself in a booth, reading the *Herald*.

At the bar behind the tap, I spotted a solitary barman doing his morning chores. The layout looked legit, but so had Longo's last night. I kept my right hand firmly on the Rossi as I walked right in and strode up to Jiggs, who smiled but didn't rise or offer his hand.

"Long time no see, Jack," he said, none too originally, but glib was never Jiggs's middle name. If it came down to a choice between stealth and menace, he'd take menace every time. He was big, borderline fat, with slicked-down gray hair and a permanently ruddy complexion. He'd been a cop for a few years before getting himself elected to the legislature, and he still carried himself like a deputy superintendent. Someday Jiggs would keel over with a massive stroke or heart attack and the newspapers would call it the "end of an era." Some era.

He was the majority leader, the number-two guy in the House. He'd always reminded me of what my cop father called a bull—an old-style cop who hit you first and asked questions later, while you were spitting your teeth out onto the sidewalk. He was wearing an expensive red tie, but the knot was stained by the perspiration from his three chins.

After leaving the job when he was elected state rep, Jiggs had gone to night law school at what was then called Portia. In the early days his practice had been mostly drunk drivers and common nightwalkers, i.e., whores. Jiggs didn't mind knocking heads at the courthouse or the State House, any more than he had out on the street. That was what made him such an effective floor leader. Everybody was scared shitless of him.

"That's a nice piece about you in the rag today," Jiggs said, gesturing at the open *Herald* on the table. "You got a knack for steppin' in it, is all I can say."

I could have mentioned a few bad mornings he'd endured himself out there on the front page. Let's put it this way, Jiggs has never been named Solon of the Year by the League of Women Vultures. But I said nothing. The customer is always right.

"I hate to do this to you, Jacko," he said, "but do you mind standing for a frisk?"

"For chrissake," I said, "you called me."

He shrugged, stood up, and grabbed his coat off the chair. It was no bluff. Either I took a frisk or the jig, you might say, was up. Jiggs was ready to walk. He didn't trust me, any more than I trusted him. We were, after all, both cops.

I sighed and put my hands up.

"I'm carrying," I said, and he went right for my pockets. The piece he didn't care about. Jiggs was looking for a wire. He preferred to do business in swimming pools, and if he'd known anybody at the Cambridge Y on Mass. Ave., we'd have been meeting in the shallow end of the pool. He patted me down, pits to tits and back again, after which he nodded and then sat back down, which was my cue to do the same.

"I got some things I need taken care of," he said, "and you're the only one who can handle them."

Translation: Nobody else would get within ten feet of whatever he had in mind for me. He dropped his voice an octave.

"You know The Man?"

I nodded. Who didn't? To my brother and the late Bucky Bennett, Knocko was The Man, but for Jiggs, The Man could only be one person—Representative Harold Lynch of Oak Square, Brighton. Most people called Lynch Mr. Speaker, pronounced "Mistah Speakah." He was Jiggs's boss, and at the State House, as in most places, the boss was always looking over his shoulder.

I hadn't thought about the Speaker in months, and now his name had come up twice in less than twenty-four hours. I considered asking Jiggs if he was really pushing Agent Orange for police commissioner, but you never tip your hand to a guy like Jiggs. He wanted to talk about Lynch.

Jiggs said, "He's gonna whack me."

This wasn't the Mob, not exactly anyway. When reps talked about getting whacked, what they meant was that they were about to lose their nice offices and their extra pay and their gold-embossed stationery and their reserved parking spots under the dome next to the lieutenant governor's. What the Speaker said went, and if he said Jiggs was going, Jiggs was gone.

It seemed an appropriate moment to ask why.

"Because he thinks I'm gonna whack him. He's changed, Jackie. Something's wrong. He's drinking like a fish. He started smoking again. You know where his office is, right? Outside the window it's knee-deep in butts—ask anybody. I'm surprised it hasn't made the papers yet."

That meant he'd tried to plant a story, but hadn't succeeded—yet.

"Newport Lights. He smokes 'em down to the filter and then tosses 'em out the window, one after another. Drinking stingers and smoking Newport Lights. He switched from Marlboros."

"So you're gonna clip him because he smokes menthols?"

"Please, Jackie." He sagged, trying to appear hurt. "You know me. I'm a go-along-to-get-along guy."

He was applying the Vaseline rather heavily. Apparently he'd forgotten that he was the guy who'd tutored me on the rules of life at the State House:

1. Nothing on the level.
2. Everything a deal.
3. No deal too small.

Now he was telling me he was on the level.

"Look," he said, "I got twenty-four years in up there. I'm twenty-fifty."

That means twenty-plus years in, fifty-plus years old. Two very important numbers in the public-pension game.

"I'm vested up the ass," he said. "All I need now is a couple of years on top. Then I'm set."

"Set for what?" The old rhetorical question. "All I ever remember you wanting was a few jobs for the boyos at the T or the Edison."

"The Edison? You're living in the dim fucking past, Jacko. The Edison ain't even its name anymore, in case you haven't noticed on your bill. It's NStar, or was. Maybe it's National Grid now, I can't even remember. The phone company's Verizon—it ain't even NYNEX no more, forget New England Telephone. Jordan's is Macy's. Filene's is Macy's. Harvard Trust got bought by BayBank which got bought by BankBoston which used to be First National Bank of Boston, which got bought by Fleet, which got bought by BankAmerica, which ain't really BankAmerica either, I forgot what that used to be, but the point is, everything's changed. You been down to my district lately? I'm telling you, Gallivan Boulevard don't look like Dublin no more. Just give me four years, I'm riding off into the sunset, saya-fuckin'-nara. I get my two terms in as speaker, and after that, if you want to talk to Jiggs, you'll have to call Jupiter."

That would be Jupiter, Florida, the original sunny place for shady people, at least if they're Boston pols. My theory is they all love the Intracoastal Waterway because it gives them the opportunity to run over manatees and other endangered sea mammals in their powerboats with the clever names on them like *On City Time* and *Payroll Charlie*.

Jiggs was filibustering now: "The old days are over. Selling T jobs, taking cash for racing dates—sooner or later you get a target letter from the feds. Everybody's a snitch now."

Which was why it was so important to be a lawyer if you wanted to survive in politics and didn't start out with beaucoup bucks. You needed a way to launder the payoffs. Chairman of Banks and Banking was a particularly large mammary—that explained Jiggs's familiarity with the genealogy of New England financial institutions, and if I recalled correctly Jiggs had finally been able to buy that summer cottage in Harwich Port shortly after taking over as "Mistah Chairman."

Later on Jiggs became chairman of the Rules Committee. In case you were wondering, there's only one rule. Whatever the speaker wants, he gets, because he rules. Actually, there's a second rule. If you don't vote with them, as a rule they kill you.

The only other guy in the place, the bartender, stared at the TV set mounted above him and ignored us. Even if he could hear Jiggs's monologue, he apparently didn't find it nearly as fascinating as the commercial from a local ambulance chaser who also served on the Governor's Council—"a name you can trust," the announcer said, against all evidence. The counselor was soliciting new fake-injury cases. Someone in his office could even *habla español*. The toll-free number was 1-800-I-GOT-HURT, or maybe it was 1-800-I-FAKED-IT.

"Are you listening to me, Jack?" Jiggs said. "I said, all I want is two terms."

Unlike most of these guys, it wasn't about the pension for Jiggs. Oh sure, he'd happily take it—about ninety thousand a year would be my guess, with the Option C for his future widow, whose name escaped me, and quite possibly Jiggs himself by this time.

What I did know about Jiggs was that he would have the same plan going in as speaker as all the guys before him. Once he took the gavel, he'd "resign" from his little law office in a cubby-hole on Tremont Street—sitting legislators never got hired by the white-shoe firms downtown. But all his old Dorchester and South Shore cronies would suddenly become lobbyists. You don't have to pass any tests to become a lobbyist. There is no board of registration, only a form you fill out with the secretary of state, after which they take your mug shot—good practice for what can, and quite often does, happen when a lobbyist gets careless.

What the reputed reformers outside the building never seemed to figure out was that the real money wasn't in passing legislation, it was in killing it. The big paydays come when you can shake down whatever industry is petrified at being disemboweled by some bill that they know the leadership can deep-six if the right palms are greased. The next session, the same legislation can be refiled, and the game begins anew. It's like an annuity, the yearly shakedown. And the lobbyists make sure that their marks, er . . . clients, all buy a table at the Speaker's annual "time," which is usually held on his birthday and always at Anthony's Pier 4.

It's all strictly legit, at least as long as you're legally permitted to call a bribe a campaign contribution, and who's going to change that law? Certainly not the hacks pocketing the bribes.

I asked Jiggs, "How do you know for sure that the Speaker's coming after you?"

"How do I know? He's always moving around with this kid from Northampton, Norton, he's the new whip. Kid moves his lips when he reads, I shit you not. He went to North Adams State—which by the way has also changed its name, don't ask me why. But this Norton kid, he has season's tickets to the Bruins, he's a fucking Elk, what more can I tell you? Dumber than two rocks. Just the guy I'd pick as my own majority leader—too fucking stupid to figure out how to set you up."

"I thought the days of setting people up were over."

"Aw, c'mon, you know what I mean. The Man's paranoid, is all. He thinks I'm lining him up for a head shot."

Which of course he was, right here in Central Square, negotiating with an assassin, namely me. Good old Jiggs, the legislature's Cassius with the lean and hungry look, hold the lean.

A hulking construction worker outside cracked the door open but without even removing the cigarette from his lips the bartender yelled out at him, "Closed 'til noon."

Jiggs leaned back in his chair and crossed his arms. "You can't call him Hal no more, did you know that? It's gotta be Mr. Speaker. Not for himself, he says, but for the dignity of the office. The dignity of the office? Are you shittin' me?"

I suspected Jiggs was telling the truth, or at least a partial version of it, his version.

"So," I asked, "what exactly do you want me to do about Mistah Speakah?"

ONE THING about the legislative leadership is that no one much trusts each other. They speak elliptically, always figuring they're being set up and perpetually fretting that someone might be taping them, which is why they seldom mention anyone by anything other than a nickname. If you aren't The Man they call you Green Teeth or Hi Test or Shit for Brains or some other such endearing moniker. If you're fat they call you Slim and if you're slim they call you Tubbo.

The reps in leadership also feel justified in clipping absolutely anyone who might become a threat two, four, or even six years down the line. The only ones who are safe are the Republicans, because there aren't enough of them to mount a challenge to anyone with a D beside their names. As for Jiggs, he tried to keep his head down. He believed in the old adage, never write when you can speak, never speak when you can whisper, never whisper when you can nod, never nod when you can wink. . . .

He glanced around again at the bar, reached over to the other side of the table to get his overcoat. He grabbed a folded *Herald* from beneath the coat and I saw a thick manila envelope wedged between the folds of the tabloid. He put the *Herald* on the table and pushed it across to me.

"I've pulled every public document for you," he said. "It's all in there."

Well, yes and no. It would be the usual crap, most of it as worthless as tits on a bull. Speaker Lynch's campaign expenditures report, his driving record from the Registry (as if a speaker drives himself a lot), even his annual SFI—Statement of Financial Interest—from the State Ethics Commission.

"So tell me," I said, "what am I being retained to turn up that you couldn't find on your own, master schemer that you are?"

"I want you to get the answers to certain questions I cannot afford to be asking personally," he said. "First thing, he's selling off his real estate. Looks to me like somebody's squeezing him."

"And you know this how?"

"He just put a third mortgage on his house in Brighton."

"No shit?" Now that was an interesting tidbit. I'd never known anyone who'd had a third mortgage on his house.

"When did he do this?" I asked.

"Couple of weeks ago," Jiggs said. "It's public record. It's on file down at the Registry of Deeds."

"So why don't you just leak it to the newspapers?"

He grimaced, and then sighed deeply.

"I have to move carefully here, you understand? Why do you think I'm talking to you?"

"Who might try to put the arm on such a distinguished statesman?"

"That's what I'm paying you to find out."

"Anything else?" I asked.

"He's got a girl."

"Oh my God, stop the presses."

"Not that kind of girl. Well, he does have that kind of girl, but she works in Transportation for Hey Good Looking, and Hey Good Looking's girl is on my payroll—"

"Whose payroll is your girl on?"

"I don't have a girl," he lied. Same old Jiggs—wouldn't say shit if he had a mouthful.

"Listen to me, will you?" he said. "This girl, she's a woman, she's in her late forties. Not his girlfriend, you follow me? Gets hired about a year and a half ago, which happens to be about the time The Man started falling apart. She makes a lot of trips—island trips, and not the kinda islands you get to by catching the ferry at Woods Hole, you know what I mean? She's going to the Cayman Islands. You know, where all the offshore banks are."

"Sounds to me like all you need to do is just drop a dime to the newspapers."

"Let me finish, okay? She's not making the runs for him, or at least I don't think she is. The punch line is, her last name is M-A-S-S-I-M-I-N-O." He nodded. "She's a Massimino. One of *those* Massiminos. You see my problem now?"

I did indeed. His problem would be Massimino, as in Anthony Massimino—Tony Miami, Knocko Nugent's partner, the other guy whose name you're not supposed to mention. I know Tony Miami a little bit, but not that well, or I wouldn't have gotten caught flat-footed last night.

I asked, "What have the two guys got on him?"

"That's what I'm hiring you to find out. But no fingerprints."

He still hadn't mentioned the Speaker's candidate for police commissioner. If Slip knew, Jiggs knew. He was playing some kind of game here, but I'd known that going in. That's what these guys do—play games.

"Do you want the job or not?" he said.

"I charge five hundred bucks a day—"

With his right hand, Jiggs waved me off, and with his left, he reached into his left breast pocket and came up with an envelope that he slid in a single motion into the folded *Herald*.

"There's thirty-five hundred cash in there, and if it takes you longer than a week, you ain't gonna get what I need. One more thing—you know about the Convention Center Authority, right?"

The Speaker's "legacy." All these windbag crooks always want to leave behind some monument to their careers in alleged public service, although in the end most of their grandiose schemes amount to nothing more than a few newspaper exposés of waste and fraud, followed by indictments and, most significantly, several new taxes—revenue streams, they prefer to call them—none of which ever go away. It is immortality of a sort, I suppose, to go along with the immorality. The Speaker had personally shepherded the enabling legislation through to create this new authority, which was now fitfully constructing an absolutely unneeded convention center down on the waterfront.

"The Convention Center Authority?" I said. "Didn't they get the city to sell them the Under-Common garage?"

Jiggs nodded. "The Speaker put a gun to the mayor's head— the authority had to have it as the revenue stream to pay off the bonds it was selling to build the new center. So the deal was, if the authority didn't get the garage, then the city would get no increase in local aid, ever. You might say the Speaker made the mayor an offer he couldn't refuse."

I was thinking about how, when I worked for the mayor, I used to put neighborhood guys down at the garage. That was when the city still owned it. I always used the garage for the guys who needed "jobs," as opposed to work, to keep their probation and parole officers at bay. The garage was where you sent the ele-ment. They robbed the place blind. It was expected of them.

"The garage is worse now than it ever was when the city had it," Jiggs said. "The cashiers they got now make the Pike toll col-lectors look like Mother Theresa. First he hires Tony Miami's sister, and then he turns the whole authority into just one big Mob hiring hall."

"Define Mob," I said.

"Hard harps from the Valley, Mafia guys from Providence, Hell's Angels from Lynn, all kinds of teamsters and longshoremen and every last one of them a no-show; you also got tow truck driv-ers from the North End, I'm just talking about the ones I person-ally know of. Not to mention at least one cocaine dealer I know runs a bar in Hyde Park—shall I continue?"

It was another perfect opportunity for Jiggs to mention Agent Orange, but that was apparently going to be his little secret. He leaned forward again, as if he were in danger of being overheard.

"You remember Sal DiGrazia, right?"

Now it was my turn to smile. "That's my rep, Jiggs. The pride of Ward Three. When he was a kid he was one of my precinct captains."

"Sal's had what you might call a meteoric rise," Jiggs said. "He's the assistant whip now. Number four. He files all the bills the Speaker wants everybody to know are his, okay? Shit that The Man can't personally come out for because it smells so bad, but everybody knows they can't vote no because DiGrazia's his guy and his name's on it. You get it, right?"

"I get it," I said.

To me this was inside baseball, and is there anything more mind-numbing if you're not in the game yourself? Jiggs must have noticed my flagging attention, because he reached into his breast pocket and extracted a small sheet of paper with printing on both sides of it. It was a bill, a legislative document, H. 4103. He placed it on the table between us.

"It's a land conveyance," Jiggs said. "A ninety-nine-year lease of two prime acres of state land on Route 1, next to the Golden Melon."

"The strip joint?"

"The Mob strip joint. DiGrazia filed it for The Man. He's giving away state land, to the Mob, for the traditional buck a year."

"How come this isn't in the papers?" I said.

"Who would you suggest I call? I'm just an old hack from Dorchester, remember? The *Globe* ain't interested. They own the Speaker now. Remember, he kept the gay marriage referendum question off the ballot last year. That's all they care about now, gay marriage. Whenever they mention Hal now they say he's 'grown.' That means he does what they tell him to do. As long as it doesn't cost him any money."

I looked down at the number of the bill—H. 4103—and committed it to my increasingly leaky memory. Jiggs saw me studying the bill and grabbed it and stuffed it back into his pocket. Then he gave me a list of his phone numbers. Should someone else answer, I was to identify myself as "Mr. Black." If anyone else picked up my phone—not likely—he would of course also be "Mr. Black." If there's only one name, it's easy to remember. In my experience, the only place people give each other multiple fake names is in the movies.

"If I do find out anything," I said, "what are you going to do with it?"

Jiggs smiled. "There you go, Mr. Black, asking questions you don't need to know the answers to. As Ted Kennedy said to Mary Jo Kopechne when she told him she was pregnant, We'll cross that bridge when we come to it."

"His father was a cop, wasn't he?"

"Ted Kennedy's?" Jiggs said.

"The Speaker's," I said. "I think he was an inspector."

"You'd know better than me," he said. "All I know is, when he mentions the old man, it sounds like he's talking about the Pope."

"Funny," I said, "that's not my recollection of him."

"I don't know too many cops up for sainthood myself," Jiggs said. "Present company included."

I suddenly remembered something.

"Haven't you guys got some big vote coming up in the next couple of days?"

"Don't tell me you still read the newspapers?"

"It's all coming back to me now," I said. "The Speaker's got a rules-change vote coming up, and it'll abolish the eight-year term limit on being speaker."

"Very good. It took you long enough, but you've finally put two and two together."

"So that's what this is really about," I said. "The Man isn't looking to hit you, at least not directly, but if they keep term limits in place, his eight years are up. He's gone next January after the elections, and you take over. But you're not going to get the gavel now because once that term limits rule is gone, he's speaker for life. . . ."

"Maybe not life, but I'm no spring chicken myself. I'm ten years older than he is. And now I gotta worry about that god-damn Elk from the west with Bruins season tickets."

"But if you let him ram it through, and then a few days later somebody drops a dime, then maybe somebody else could end up speaker for life. . . ."

Jiggs smiled as he stood up and reached for his topcoat. I remained seated. He didn't need to tell me that it wouldn't look good for us to be seen leaving an obscure barroom together. Even if it was in a foreign land, occupied territory—Cambridge.

"Always remember," Jiggs said before he turned and walked out. "I didn't see you, and you didn't see me."

Chapter Four

EVEN BEFORE I got on the Red Line to head back to Park Street, I found a branch of my bank and deposited Jiggs's thirty-five hundred in cash. On the deposit slip I wrote "Jiggs." It's nice to work under the table, but in my line of work, dealing with politicians, it's not healthy.

If a guy gives you cash, and you don't report it, someday he might find himself in a jam and decide to trade you up, or at least try to. You don't ever want to have to worry about winding up as a chip in somebody else's plea bargain.

I guess this is as good a time as any to describe my line of work, such as it is. On my business cards, it says I'm a private investigator, but that's not really true. There aren't any real "private eyes" left anymore, if there ever were any to begin with. No-fault divorce killed the peephole business. Guys still come to me occasionally and ask me to dig up dirt on their cheating wives. I always buy the first round and then I tell 'em, I could probably do it, but it'd cost you an arm and a leg, and ultimately the judge doesn't care; as a matter of fact he (or increasingly she) can't care under state law.

You want to know what no-fault divorce is? Nowadays, if a broad catches her husband with a gal pal, he owes her a million bucks. If a guy catches his wife with a boy toy, he owes her a million bucks. It's as simple as that. Worst deal in the world ever for white guys, worse than affirmative action, even. Another "reform" that hits the working man right between the eyes. The other main piece of PI business back in the old days was employee pilferage— "shrinkage," the chain stores call it. Now everybody's got surveillance cameras, plus I'm not exactly fluent in the language of most entry-level shoplifting-prone illegal aliens—excuse me, "undocumented workers."

But I've adjusted. Actually, from the moment I went out on my disability, what I have been is a shit broker. I dig up shit, and then I spread it around. See, I used to work at City Hall and, later, the State House, so I know plenty of politicians. And they're always in the market for somebody with my very specialized skills, which I honed in my previous life, working for the mayor.

For instance, let's say you're an incumbent and you've got some ambitious kid who's planning to run against you. You need this punk taken off the board, and to do that, you need a little Oppo—Opposition Research.

Or, as I call it, shit.

You tell me the kind of excrement you're looking for and if it's there I'll find it. I run down criminal records, property liens, lawsuits, pissed-off tenants, pissed-off landlords, outstanding parking tickets, unpaid child support, overdue library books, plagiarism, defaulted student loans, prescription drug abuse—whatever this bastard was or is mixed up in, if you give me a lead or two I'll track it down for you.

That was one of my many chores at City Hall for the mayor. Oh sure, I was a precinct captain and then a "ward coordinator" for a while. I was his driver too, off and on, as well as a collection agent (a phrase I much prefer to bagman). Later on I was also the mayor's Mr. Fixit at the State House with my own little office tucked away up on the fifth floor. But what I was really good at, where I excelled if I do say so myself, was in extracting shit from records, public and otherwise, to throw at any poor bastard who crossed us. It helped in my investigations that I had a badge, of course, but I can still accomplish just as much now as when I was on the job. Maybe more, with the Internet. Digging up shit is a lot like riding a bicycle. You never really forget how to do it.

For example, I can get you somebody's credit card bills, although that'll cost you a little more, but not quite as much as I charge for obtaining medical records from any major HMO. Since HIPPA, the medical privacy act, coming up with hospital documentation has become a much trickier, more expensive proposition. But as I tell my clients, when it comes to forcing some ungrateful piece-of-shit selectman out of a primary fight, there's nothing quite like an incontrovertible record of an HIV test, even if it came back negative, or a doctor's notations of a penicillin shot for an STD. You present any fresh-faced young family man with records of treatment for a deviated septum, as in cocaine abuse, and I guarantee you he will lose his enthusiasm for a campaign against a fading but treacherous and well-heeled incumbent, which is what almost all of my clients are.

Reilly's the name, shit's my game.

I'm not exactly getting rich, but I don't need to make that much to make ends meet, considering that I've got two tenants in my building, plus my disability pension, or should I say "disability" pension? In a couple of years, the monthly child-support payments, or should I say "child-support" payments, will cease, at which point I'm home free, and I won't have to be sorting my bills into two piles at the beginning of each month.

I got back to the South End from Cambridge around one thirty. The mail was in the slot, and there was nothing there from Bucky Bennett. Maybe he'd been bullshitting me all along.

I wanted to get right to work on Jiggs's case, so I called my first captain on the police force, who is also my godfather. His name is Brendan Mulcahy—Uncle Brendan, I always called him, except on the job. I asked him if I could come by his house in West Roxbury later in the afternoon to discuss a personal matter.

"Who's getting lit up now?" he said.

"That's a cold thing to say to your godson."

"I repeat, who's about to step on a land mine?"

"Ever hear of Speaker Hal Lynch?"

Just the slightest pause. "Let me guess—you're interested in the old man."

"Bingo." He said he had a few errands to run but that he could see me at three. No sooner had I hung up the phone than it was ringing again.

Against my better judgment I picked it up, and when I did I heard the jailhouse recording again. I pressed number one to accept the charges.

"Now what?" I asked.

"They want a sit-down."

"They had a sit-down with me last night."

"So I heard," he said.

"No more sit-downs."

"They're sorry about what happened."

"Not as sorry as I am."

"I'm not reaching out for the guy you sat down with last night. I'm reaching out for the other guy." That would be Tony Miami.

Funny, how these names were starting to recur. Funny peculiar, as opposed to funny ha-ha.

I said, "You're talking about the guy I know?"

"Affirmative. He says old acquaintance should not be forgot. Says he hasn't seen you since you were driving for the mayor."

"Yeah, those were the days all right."

"Look, I'm just the messenger here," he said. "He's very concerned about this matter."

"He can't tell me this himself?"

"He wants to. He wants to square things with you."

I said nothing. What was the point?

"He knows you're pissed," Marty said. "He says he'll meet you at the usual place."

"My usual place, or his?" No way was I going down to Roxbury. Guys—and women too, occasionally—have gone into his place, the Marconi Club, and never come out, or if they have, it was feet first, after dark, wrapped in a surplus Army blanket.

"He says your place. The place on Dover Street."

Which was the old name of East Berkeley Street. That's where Foley's is, and no blow-in drifter FBI agent from Des Moines would ever know that, except maybe Agent Orange himself, who was from Gate of Heaven parish. But I doubted Agent Orange was working a fresh wiretap this afternoon. We had one other swerve we used to keep any G-men who might be listening in away from Foley's. Sometimes we called it "the Chinese place." You know, Fo-Lee's.

Marty said, "He says he wants to talk to you, and you should trust him."

"Should I?"

"Fuck no."

"So why would I want to do something like that, if it's not too healthy?"

"Because it might be even more unhealthy if you don't do it, plus, it might also be unhealthy for some other people you know."

Meaning himself. In the prisons, Knocko and Tony Miami had screws, they had snitches, and they had enforcers. Sometimes they were all one and the same.

"Marty," I said, "have I thanked you yet for dropping my name to the guy who made this all possible?"

"What do you want me to say? I screwed up again. That's why Ma asked you to watch out for me."

He always had to bring that up. After all the years I'd been taking care of him, and his lawyers, and his bookies, and his shy-locks, he would always fuck up again.

"You still there?" Marty asked. "Hello?"

"Why should I go down there?"

"Because he's reaching out to you. It's your joint, and there's a lot of cops, so that's how he's letting you know he's on the level."

"Is he on the level?"

"Oh, God no." He paused a moment. "But whatever it is he thinks you got from our late friend, he must want it back real bad."

"I know how bad they want it," I said. "I found out last night."

"What can I tell you?" he said. "Are you going or not?"

"What time?"

"As soon as you can get there. Me, I wouldn't set foot inside unless you see there's at least three or four cops in there. And I mean ones you go way back with, not some guys who you don't know who might be playing for the other team. And if it's only Stan the Polack bartendin' in there, just keep walking, 'cause they'll just take him out too if they really want you."

That was their modus operandi. There was no such thing as an innocent bystander. They were very Colombian in that regard.

"Hey Marty," I said.

"Yeah?"

"You gonna drop my name with any more of your jailbird pals?"

"What makes you think I haven't already?" He laughed. I didn't.

I PUT on my overcoat, picked up the Rossi, made sure it was loaded and the trigger lock was off, and then placed it in a small paper bag. My plan was to walk into Foley's with the gun pointed at Tony Miami. My only bow to subtlety was the paper bag covering the gun. It would fool no one, but after last night, I didn't much care. I set off on foot for Foley's, and when I got there, I pulled open the front door and stood outside on the tile threshold to check out the lay of the land.

No problem: Two uniform cops stood at the bar talking to Stan the Polack, and three plainclothesmen from District 4 were drinking lunch at a front table. I knew at least two of them; not the brightest bulbs on the Christmas tree, but they weren't particularly dirty either. They were just drunks.

I strode past them and considered checking out the two bathrooms, but finally decided that five cops were protection enough. I turned the corner into the Berkeley Room, keeping my right hand in the bag, my finger on the trigger. Then I saw him, sitting at a table by himself, no drink in front of him.

"Jack," Tony Miami said. "How's your hammer hanging?"

Tony Miami had to be close to sixty now. A few years younger than Knocko. The word always was, Tony could have gone In Town—Mafia—but never considered it because he couldn't abide the idea, even in the abstract, of ever having to share anything of his with anyone else, especially money or women. Even more, it was anathema to him to have to take orders, or show "respect" to those goombahs. He and Knocko were equals, they were birds of a feather. They just plain didn't give a shit about anything or anybody else.

Tony Miami had black hair, hazel eyes, and a deep tan—hence the nickname. He was only about five seven, and unlike Knocko, he was not a gym rat. But you wouldn't want to run into him in a dark alley, because you probably wouldn't even see him until he was on top of you, slitting your throat.

He had both hands folded in front of him on the table. I decided to remain standing, with my hand in the bag.

"How's your brother, Jack?" he said, gazing placidly up at me.

"Funny you should ask. I just spoke to him."

"Oh yeah? What a coincidence. He's a good shit, Marty. A stand-up guy."

As in, stand-up guys do hard time, for other guys. He looked up at the bag over my hand.

"You know, Jack," he said, "if I didn't know you better, I might get the idea you don't trust me."

"I had a problem last night."

"I heard," he said. I waited for him to say something else, but that was it. He'd heard.

"I got something for you," he said, staring at my right hand in the paper bag. "It's on the floor, next to my chair, but I don't want to be making any sudden moves until you're more at ease."

"Push it out with your foot to where I can see it," I said, and he did. He had brought a paper bag of his own.

"You forgot something when you left last night," he said. "A guy I know said he picked it up for you."

I leaned over and looked down into the bag. Inside was my Taurus, along with the bullets.

"You'll notice," Tony Miami said, "it's unloaded." He extended his hands, palms up. "We don't want any trouble."

I kept watching him as he used his booted foot to push the bag closer to me.

"Why don't you have a seat, Jack? Take a load off."

I sat down warily, and cocked my ear to make sure I could still hear the cops boozing it up at the bar.

"What's with the attitude?" Tony Miami said. "We go way back, you and me."

I nodded. Look, I admit I worked for the mayor, but I wasn't married to him. Whatever business he had with the two guys, I wasn't privy to. I didn't want to know, then or now. I was just the guy with the badge and the license to carry who drove the mayor around, at least on those occasions when he had to sit down with someone like Tony Miami.

"First of all," he said, "I apologize for last night." He leaned forward. "I wasn't in town, you understand? If I was here, I would have called you myself, no bullshit, and we woulda had a sit-down, just like we're having right now, and we woulda got this thing re- solved with none-a that gangster bullshit. He had no business working you over."

You've heard of good cop/bad cop. This was Tony Miami, good gangster.

"I heard some things were said about your family, what you might call threats," he said, shaking his head and closing his eyes in mock sadness. "Not about Marty, I mean, but about your kids."

I stared at him, trying to play a dead hand. No emotion. These guys are like dogs; you can't let them see fear, ever.

"I just want you to know, Jack, I told the other guy, I told him he was way out of line there," Tony Miami said. "You gotta un- derstand, sometimes The Man just loses control and nobody can do nothing."

"So I've heard," I said.

"All I'm telling you is, don't worry about all that bluster of his last night about license plates and dorm rooms and shit. Nobody's gonna hurt nobody's kids, okay?" He paused. "The problem is, something of ours is gone, and we have to get it back."

"If I told you that not only do I not have whatever it is you want, but I don't even know what it is, how would you respond to that?"

He smiled. "I'd respond, Jack, that you can't shit a shitter."

"Can you tell me what it is exactly that I'm supposed to have that belongs to you?"

He shook his head slowly and then scratched his chin.

"Let me start over," he said. "I know you got a pension from the city, but I'm guessing that after alimony and child support and all that shit you basically ain't got a pot to piss in. We know lots of people. We could throw plenty of work your way."

Just as I had suspected. Maybe I could get the contract to hit the next Bucky Bennett, after which I would get hit.

"We're always looking for help, you know, and we both been watching you for a long time."

Here's how it works when you're "partners" with these guys. If the business does great, they assume you're skimming off the top, because that's what they'd do. If everything goes south, they assume it's because you're stealing, busting the place out, because that's what they'd do. They don't want to know how business is. They don't care. That's your problem, how business is. They just want to know how much they're getting this week.

Eventually, something happens and you go missing. A couple of days later your picture's in the *Herald*, a one-column mug shot, and the caption underneath says "Missing from Usual Haunts" or "Foul Play Suspected."

"We've been following you ever since City Hall," Tony Miami said. "We notice how you keep your mouth shut, and you can straighten a thing out, and we can always use another guy that can straighten a thing out."

A limitless future, in other words, until they decide to straighten you out.

Tony Miami asked, "You were in the service, right?"

I nodded. "Army."

"Remember what your DI told you in basic? Or mine did anyway. He said don't worry about the bullet with your name on it. Worry about the one that says, 'To whom it may concern.' You know what I'm saying?"

He was saying it wasn't my fight. He was right about that. I nodded again.

"Good," said Tony Miami. "Then you will hear from us, okay?" He stood up and gripped my left forearm just above my wrist. He squeezed hard. "Go along to get along. When you get right down to it, we ain't that different from City Hall or the State House. We gotta get this thing resolved, and we don't need any concerned citizens getting mixed up in something that don't really concern them. You know what I'm saying. You been around the block a few times."

I took it all in silently. Sometimes it's best to keep your mouth shut, lest something you say be taken as a commitment. I didn't want Tony Miami thinking he had my "word" on anything.

"Your mother was Italian, wasn't she, Jack?" he said, looking down at me, and I nodded yet again.

"So when I say to you, don't be *stunatu*, you know what I'm saying, right?"

Stunatu—I guess the nearest English word to it would be "stupid," or maybe "dopey." For instance, asking Tony Miami about his sister working for the Speaker, that would be *stunatu*. Very *stunatu*.

"Your brother, Marty, he can be *stunatu*. No knock on him, but it's true, am I right?"

This time it was my turn to shrug.

"Don't you be *stunatu*, not on this thing." He looked down at the bag. "And don't leave your little piece behind this time."

He saluted me, then turned and walked out of the Berkeley Room, into the main area and over to the table of detectives, shaking hands all around while motioning Stan the Polack to send over a round. I suppose he was trying to show me that I had nothing to fear, because if he were planning to whack me, would he really be buying a round, yapping with some witnesses, especially cops? Of course, if I were going to get clipped, someone else would handle the chore, and Tony Miami would be far, far away when the hit went down, with the JetBlue boarding passes and credit card receipts to prove it. Tony continued casually chewing the fat with the cops, which I took as my cue to leave. I got up, grabbed my two bags, and headed for the side door.

"See ya, Tony," I yelled over my shoulder as I quickened my pace.

"Be good," he said. "Don't be a stranger."

That's exactly what I was afraid I wouldn't be.

BACK ON Shawmut Avenue, I checked my phone messages.

Katy Bemis, the *Herald* reporter, had left a message asking me to call her about some information from her "sources" that I might find interesting. She was looking to corner me for a no-comment so she could thump me again. I'd endured enough TKOs for a while, so I hit the Delete button, locked up my house, and walked back outside. Despite Tony Miami's reassurances, I took both guns with me.

I climbed into my Oldsmobile and drove away from the best parking space I'd had in weeks. I spotted Myrna lurking in a doorway and waved at her. She glared back at me.

I was headed for West Roxbury, to visit my godfather, and by that I mean in the Catholic, as opposed to the Mafia, sense of the word. He'd been my father's best friend, ever since they'd met at the police academy right after World War II, when Curley was still mayor, doing his final stretch during his final term, for mail fraud, down in Danbury. Uncle Brendan had been my first boss when I went on the job.

Now he was eighty-six, and his wife—my godmother—was dead, and his kids had all moved away. He liked company, not that I ever provided any, except at times like this, when I needed something.

I parked in front of his house, which I noticed could have used a fresh coat of paint. He met me at the door with a cane, and he looked even frailer and more stooped over than he had the last time I'd visited, almost a year earlier. His cardigan sweater enveloped him like a shroud. Only a few wisps of his white hair remained, plastered onto his liver-spotted scalp.

Once inside, as we slowly walked down the musty front hallway, he silently pointed to the same framed picture he always showed me—a black-and-white photograph of him and my father, in the old-style double-breasted police uniforms. They were standing under the now-demolished Orange Line elevated train tracks in Roxbury.

Next to that picture hung a framed, yellowing front page of the old *Boston Record-American,* with Brendan escorting a beefy thug, wearing a fedora and a wide-lapelled suit, into the old courthouse in Pemberton Square. The headline was PUNCHY WON'T SQUEAL.

After completing our traditional homage to the photos, I followed him as he hobbled back to the front of the house. As we looked out the picture window in the living room, he gave me an update on the neighborhood he'd lived in since 1949, the year Curley finally lost to John B. Hynes.

"You remember the Costellos?" he asked, pointing across the quiet suburban street, and I said yes, even though I didn't. "They moved to Fort Myers. Sold to the Chins."

Like everywhere else, Ward 20 was changing. His hand trembled ever so slightly as he pointed at the house next door. The O'Malleys had moved to the Cape after selling out to two women from New York.

"Lesbians," he said. "Nice people." Pause. "I guess." Another pause. "The younger one, the fat one—she's pregnant. These people have babies now, you probably knew that. Gay-bies, they call them."

The prolonged standing by the picture window was taking its toll, and I saw him starting to sway. I grabbed him by the arm and guided him away from the window. He flopped down heavily in a stuffed chair covered with antimacassars. He had to take several deep breaths before the color began returning slowly to his cheeks. His house would be the next one in the neighborhood to turn over. His children would visit one of those Medicaid lawyers who advertise on the radio, and for five thousand dollars, the lawyer would generate documents for Uncle Brendan to sign that would transfer his assets into a trust, and after the legally prescribed waiting period, he would be packed off to a nursing home. It was all legal, moral, and ethical, as the ads say. Congress said so.

And six months later, the old man would be dead.

"How're the kids?" I asked.

"Great, I guess," he said. "They tell me, get a computer, get on-line, we can video-chat, whatever that is." He waved a bony hand dismissively. "I'm too old."

"Hey, you're doing fine, Uncle Bren," I said, and immediately regretted it. Even at his age, he was not someone to be patronized. The last thing to go on Brendan Mulcahy would be his bullshit detector. He fixed me with his piercing blue eyes.

"How about you, Jack," he said. "Are you doing fine?"

I mumbled something inane, so he followed up with a question about my ex-wife. Her name is Cheryl.

"She's still at the courthouse," I said.

"That was part of the deal, wasn't it?" he said. "When you went out."

"It was part of the deal," I said. "Saves on the alimony is what it does."

"Do you ever see the kids?"

I studied him, to see if he was giving me the needle. But I saw no malice in his eyes. I never had, which was why I had always wondered, even as a kid, how he'd survived as long as he did on the job. About my kids, he was just making a polite inquiry, the way he would if he ran into someone at the Christmas tree sale at Holy Name. For a second I considered telling him, I see my kids about as often as you see yours, but what had he done to deserve a dig like that?

He was an old man, and I wasn't, not yet. He wasn't my father, and I wasn't his son, but somehow I had disappointed him. He'd gotten old and I'd gotten bent. I saw him only when I needed some shit and I needed it fast.

He said, "How about your boy? Is he in college yet?"

"UMass Amherst," I said. "He's a sophomore."

"Does he ever talk about . . . the job?"

I shook my head. "He's old enough to remember what happened to me, you know. And they got the city-residency requirement now."

"He couldn't use Shawmut Ave. as his address? He wouldn't be the first to have a mattress address, would he?"

"No, he wouldn't," I said. "But there's another problem. The pigmentation problem."

Uncle Brendan sighed. He was almost old enough to remember the signs: "Help Wanted—No Irish Need Apply." Now the ancient policy had been reinstated, this time in the name of Political Correctness.

He said, "Didn't I read that the mayor's son just got on?"

"That's the only kind of whites who get hired now," I said. "Same with the fire department. You gotta be connected, period. It doesn't matter if you get a 100 on the exam, it doesn't even help if you're in the National Guard, you gotta be a veteran. Only other way a white kid gets on now is through the cadets, and the only way to get on the cadets is to have some serious clout at City Hall, which is something I'm fresh out of."

That was it. I'd spoken my piece, and he had nothing to add. The silence lingered, awkwardly, and I was afraid he was going to ask me about the cut on my face. But he decided to move the conversation in another direction.

"When you called," he said, "you mentioned something about Inspector Lynch."

I immediately relaxed. Now we were on more comfortable ground. No need to be judgmental or defensive about one another—I was just the wet-behind-the-ears kid again, relying on his institutional memory.

"I'm doing a little research on the Speaker," I said, and he looked away. He had his suspicions, which he didn't want to confirm, about the nature of my research. "So I figured you'd be the guy to talk to, about his old man."

"Would you mind putting on a kettle?" he said. "There's some green tea in the pantry."

"Green tea?" I said. "What happened to Constant Comment?"

"The Chins," he said. "I told you they were good neighbors. You oughta read the literature on green tea, Jack. Great for the prostate."

"Or," I said, "as the new mayor calls it, the prostrate."

We both laughed and I headed out into the kitchen. As I

prepared his tea, we continued talking. Out of each other's sight, our voices slightly raised, we could somehow chat more amicably. By the time I finally brought him his cup, with a saucer of course, we were pals again, or at least not enemies. He was talking easily.

"You know one way you can tell when you're getting old, Jack? When there's a powerful guy out there, and you realize you knew his father a lot better than you know the son."

"If you're talking about the Speaker, then I must be getting old too, because I knew his father a little bit too," I said. "The Inspector. He was just getting through when I came on the job."

"A more miserable human being you've never seen," Brendan said, with unusual venom. Usually the worst he'd ever say about anybody was that "he's not my favorite."

"The Inspector was one of those cops who thought every hooker found him irresistible," Brendan said. "I shouldn't be repeating this, but you know what your father used to say about him?"

I shook my head.

"Your father said he'd fuck the hair on the barber's floor."

I smiled. My father said that about anybody who cheated— any guy who had, as he also put it, touched everything but the third rail.

"He had another line, your father," Uncle Brendan said.

"Let me guess," I said. "Did he say the Inspector would fuck the crack of dawn?"

He put his head back and roared. Then he took another deep breath.

"There used to be this joint in Kerry Village—Bay Village they call it now. The Mid-Town. One or two nights a week, it was all dykes, lesbians. If you caught them dancing, it was a crime— lewd and lascivious. A lot of 'em were society dames—it was walking distance from Beacon Hill, the Back Bay. So our friend would haul 'em out to his prowl car and he'd give 'em a choice—"

Arrest, and a write-up in the *Record* that would ruin them, or . . .

"Ever hear of the Restroom Regiment?" he continued without missing a beat, and I shook my head.

"They used to have public toilets at every MTA station, and I suppose you can figure out what was going on in the men's rooms—"

"Was the Inspector a switch hitter?"

"I doubt it," said Uncle Brendan with a frown. "The Restroom Regiment gave him an opportunity to partake in the more traditional forms of extortion and blackmail. Everyone in the Restroom Regiment had enough cash, which is why at the Mid-Town he was able to . . ." His voice trailed off.

"Take it out in trade instead of cash?" I said.

"Precisely," said Uncle Brendan.

"I never heard any of this," I said. "How come I never picked up any of this stuff?"

Uncle Brendan smiled faintly. "You really weren't around the station house that long, now were you, Jack?" He looked away from me again. "I mean, as I recall it, it didn't take long for you and your particular talents to catch the eye of City Hall." He paused again. "And I daresay this wasn't the type of graft the mayor and the rest of his Beautiful People liked to discuss over chardonnay at the Parkman House. A little too . . . old Boston, wouldn't you say?"

There was nothing there for me to respond to. I kept the conversation moving.

"Would the Inspector take a drink under extreme social pressure?" I asked.

"He had a thirst so great it would cast a shadow. Which is probably why he never had a pot to piss in, despite all those years on the Restroom Regiment."

What was that old saying? God invented whiskey so the Irish wouldn't rule the world.

"Always broke, the Inspector was. Always ducking out the back door at District Four for a wee small taste of the creature. But that all changed back in— But I'm getting ahead of myself. Does the name Wimpy Hogan ring a bell?"

After World War II, before the blacks arrived and the whites started stampeding out of the city, Wimpy Hogan was the top guy in the rackets, at least in our neck of the woods—the South End, Roxbury, and generally everything in north Dorchester.

The three Hogan brothers called all the shots—Wimpy, Aloysius, and William. They had a garage on Columbus Avenue, a bar in Uphams Corner, a funeral parlor on Tremont Street, later a TV store in Dudley Station, and a piece of just about everything else, which back then was mainly numbers and loan-sharking.

Sometime in the mid-1970s, the Hogans started vanishing off the face of the earth, one after another. The theory was that Wimpy, the brains of the family, had made a severe error in recruiting as muscle a young man from Mount Pleasant Street in Roxbury named Anthony Massimino, soon to be better known by his underworld moniker of Tony Miami.

Ancient history now, and as I glanced furtively down at my watch, Uncle Brendan frowned again.

"I know," he said, his voice a mixture of frustration and regret, "you gotta get going. Let me give you the shorthand version. The last Hogan to go was Billy, who I knew a little bit, from all my years on the beat. I run into him in their bar this one evening, and he tells me, strictly on the q.t., that he's getting shaken down by a detective. Not the usual stuff, you understand, the weekly payouts to the captain's bagman, which he could budget for. This detective, he was freelancing. And he was looking for big money. Or so Billy said."

"Was it the Inspector shaking him down?"

"Billy Hogan wouldn't tell me. I asked him, flat out, but he knew better than to spill."

"But what do you think?"

"All I can tell you is this—the Lynches had been shanty Irish on Warren Street since the days of Honey Fitz, that much I know for a fact. I used to hear him railing all the time about the niggers moving into Roxbury, not that he was the only one complaining, of course. He never moved out, though. I figured he was drinking up his paycheck, an occupational hazard as we all know. But then all of a sudden, Billy Hogan is being shaken down by some unnamed cop, and then he vanishes, like his brothers before him, and suddenly the Lynches are out in Oak Square, with two toilets no doubt. Quite a step up back in those days, maybe it still is, I wouldn't know."

"Let me get this straight," I said. "The Inspector starts shaking down Billy Hogan, Billy Hogan does a Dixie off the face of the earth, and suddenly the Inspector is lace-curtain Irish in Brighton. Is that it?"

"You always were a quick study, Jack."

"Who might know more about this?"

"Tony Miami."

"Other than Tony Miami, I mean."

"Well," he said with a sigh, "they had a bunch of kids, all the Hogans did, but as far as I know they all moved away over the years. Didn't care much for Boston anymore—imagine that. There's only one still around here that I know of. Billy's boy. He still runs the family bar in Uphams Corner. It's right before the bridge. Wimpy's Lounge."

"I thought they busted out that joint years ago."

"It just looks that way. He might talk to you, he might not. I don't know. I heard he's not too tightly wrapped, but can you blame him?" He looked at me and frowned. "Who are you working for?"

"No comment, Uncle."

"I'm just warning you, it seems like a hundred years ago, but let me tell you something else you may find interesting. When the boy, the Speaker now, got out of law school, he didn't go the usual route. Remember when the district courts used to have those Saturday morning sessions?"

Another blast from the past. The Saturday sessions were also where novice lawyers met their future clients, as the older, better-established attorneys nursed Saturday-morning hangovers down on the Cape.

"The Inspector's boy," he said, "didn't have to work Saturday sessions in the district courts like everybody else coming out of Portia and Suffolk. He hangs out his shingle, a one-man band he is, and suddenly he's got more work than he can handle from all these old-time cops who worked with his old man, the Inspector. The funny thing is, a lot of those guys had third-rate lawyers in their own families who I'm sure would have been hungry for the work. Just simple boilerplate things like closings and wills, that's all he was doing. Yet these old-timers chose to go with the Inspector's boy."

"Are you suggesting the Lynches were shaking them down?"

"I'm suggesting no such thing," he said, taking a sip of his tea. "I'm just mentioning another one of the Sorrowful Mysteries involving the Lynches. Like the way the Hogans start disappearing, and all of a sudden, the Lynches are nigger-rich, pardon my French."

"What would he have had on them?"

"Don't you mean," he said, "what would his father have on them?"

"How long can that sort of shakedown go on?"

"Long enough to build up a bankroll that you can use to get elected state rep from Brighton, apparently." He paused again. "You're not talking to any cops about any of this, are you?"

"What kind of cops?"

"Good question," he said, "because I would watch my back, especially with the feds. I wouldn't turn my back on any of 'em, especially if you've got anything on Tony Miami or that other sweetheart there, the one they call Knocko. Did you ever run into Special Agent John Finnerty?"

Chapter Five

AFTER A FEW more minutes of pleasantries and insincere promises to keep in touch, I headed back into the city. It was getting dark as I cruised my block a couple of times. Then I noticed Plain View's guy, Willie, standing on a corner, smoking a cigarette, trying to look nonchalant, but failing miserably. In my co-moon-ity, he was sticking out like the proverbial sore thumb.

I finally found a legal spot about two blocks south, and began hoofing it home. Willie didn't spot me until I was less than one hundred feet from him. As soon as he made me, he began openly staring at me, which I now realized was Willie's real game all along. He wasn't hiding, he was there to make a statement. Plain View wanted to let me know that this was serious police business. Thanks for the bulletin, Plain View.

I was no more than ten feet from my front door when suddenly an unshaven little Irish-looking guy, about sixty, wearing a scally cap, materialized behind me. He must have been waiting in a parked car or a doorway for me to return.

"Mr. Reilly," he said, and as I stopped to acknowledge him, I noticed two trim, clean-shaven younger white guys standing across the street like they owned it, which they probably figured they did, because they were feds. And yes, they both made the little guy. Tough luck, old-timer.

"Mr. Reilly," he repeated. "I'm a friend—was a friend—of Bucky Bennett, and he asked me to give you this."

He took a plain business envelope out of his pea jacket and handed it to me.

"It's a key to a locker at the bus station," he said. "The number's on the key."

"The bus station down by South Station?"

"Damned if I know," he said. "I been away myself. I thought the bus station was on St. James Ave., but everything's different now with that Big Dig." He paused. "I know your brother Marty too."

Then the purpose of his banter dawned on me. He wanted a tip, like he was a bellhop or a room-service waiter. I reached into my pocket and came up with a double sawbuck. Now that I think about it, more than likely it was Bucky's twenty that I handed him. Jinx money.

I thrust the bill at him and said, "Don't look now, but this street is lousy with cops."

He followed instructions, slowly allowing his eyes to take in the scene. "Shit," he said. "Heat everywhere, and I never even noticed. I been in too long."

"How long?"

"Since Hector was a pup," he said. "That long enough for you?"

"Just keep walking, don't look back, and maybe they'll leave you alone."

"Yeah," he said, "and maybe the tooth fairy'll be leaving me a little something under the pillow tonight too."

Then he gave me an old-fashioned tip of his scally cap, turned on his heel, and vanished once more.

I never saw him again.

I STOOD on the sidewalk, fingering the key in the envelope in my pocket and wondering what to do next.

This was not the moment to make a rash move, so I went inside to kill some time and hope that the cops outside would grow tired of doing the same in the cold. I tried to put Bucky out of my mind and think about paying jobs—Jiggs's, to be specific. I needed a better understanding of the Speaker's recent fire sale of his properties in Brighton. And I knew just the convicted-felon millionaire who could give me a crash course on real estate in Ward 22.

I called one of the biggest landlords in the city, a guy I once did some sneaky stuff for. His name was Teddy Gold and his secretary put me right through.

"What a coincidence," he said. "I was just thinking of you. Are you still a fervent believer in the Second Amendment?"

"When guns are outlawed," I said, "only outlaws will have guns."

"I know one outlaw who's in the market."

"Anything special?"

"Just something . . . light. It's for protection only."

Isn't it always? I considered my Army trunk, and then told him I'd see what I could do, and would it be possible for him to sit down with me to discuss a little business matter involving one of his neighbors, a member of the bar named Lynch? He didn't seem surprised at the subject of my inquiry. He said we could meet tomorrow afternoon, and I appreciated his promptness, although I figured it had more to do with the fact that he wanted something that has killed fewer people than Ted Kennedy's 1967 Delmont 88 Oldsmobile, as an old NRA bumper sticker used to point out.

THE PHONE rang again. I checked caller ID, and saw that it was Katy Bemis. This time I picked up. She said she was working on a follow-up, that her "sources" were telling her Bucky Bennett had crossed the two guys. That didn't seem like much of an advance on this morning's story, and I told her so.

"I'm not after you," she said, and I said, "Riiiight."

"Look," she said, "can we go off the record here?"

"I'll bet you say that to all the guys."

"Ha ha," she said, without mirth. "All I'm asking you is, if something happens, will you at least let me know? I mean, until yesterday, there hadn't been a gangland hit around here in years. This is big."

"You think?"

"Well, if you don't want to cooperate, there's nothing I can do about it. But I hope you don't think you can trust the *Globe*."

"No, I don't think I can trust the *Globe*."

"That's something, I guess. But listen, if I find out something, I'm not going to run with it until I call you. That's the way I operate."

She didn't have to tell me the way she operated. They all operate the same way. They call you twice, so they can write that you did not return "repeated" calls. Once reporters make the call, they can basically write any damn thing they please about you, because the calls prove they don't have "reckless disregard" for the truth, which is as big a joke as "absence of malice."

The Supreme Court decision they always cite is *Times v. Sullivan,* which covers public figures, a category into which I fit, alas, during the time I was working for the mayor. I learned all about libel law during my photo finish with the grand jury. My lawyer, Danny Goodis, who was also the mayor's lawyer, used to explain *Times v. Sullivan* to me every morning, after each new alleged exposé about me on page one.

I said to Katy Bemis, "Your editors are real interested in the Mob this week, is that what you're telling me?"

"Absolutely," she said.

"In that case," I said, "I've got a tip for you, and we'll see just how committed they are to rooting out organized crime."

I filled her in on the land transfer Jiggs had told me about up on Route 1. I gave her the number of the bill, and who had filed it. By the time I finished, she was already writing the headline to the story in her head.

"Mob clout at State House," she mused aloud. "Speaker's lackey greases skids for underworld."

"Good luck getting that into the paper," I said. "It's one thing to blast the likes of me out of the saddle, but now you're going after one of the Beautiful People. What do the papers care as long as he's for gay marriage?"

"That's the *Globe*," she said. "I work for the *Herald*. I can get it in. You just watch."

"Oh, I will, believe me," I said. "Now can you do me a favor?"

"What's that?" she said, warily.

"Lose this phone number."

EVENTUALLY THE cops broke off their stakeout, the feds first and then Willie. I figured the shift change was my opportunity to get down to the bus station. First I ripped open the envelope, just to make sure it contained a key, which it did, to locker 465. I put my father's Kennedy's topcoat on, slipped the Rossi into the right pocket, and then looked outside my window. No cops, not even Myrna. I had already changed my mind about Willie's presence. Now I missed him—even Knocko's dimmest plug-uglies could make Willie, and as long as he was loitering on the corner, the chances of a home invasion were slim, fat, and none.

The bus station was within walking distance, about ten blocks away. I made good time, crossing the Mass. Turnpike into Chinatown, then cutting right on Kneeland Street. I worked my way past the twenty-four-hour hipster diner and through the narrow winding streets of the old leather district, past the new South Station, before I reached the bus station across the street.

First I located the lockers—they were emptied every forty-eight hours, according to an obviously post–9/11 notice on the wall. Whatever was in the locker, I needed to get it now, just to be on the safe side. I found 465, looked both ways, established that no one was paying any particular attention to me, and then made my move. He who hesitates is lost. I took the key out of my coat pocket, slipped it into the lock, and opened the locker.

What I saw, when I looked inside, was a whole pile of something that I couldn't immediately identify, because it was covered with an ancient, grease-stained wool hunting jacket. On top of the pile was another envelope, addressed to "Mr. Reilly."

I pocketed the envelope. Then I lifted the jacket and peeked at the pile beneath it—stacks of mostly unsealed manila envelopes, overflowing with what looked like Xeroxed documents. On top of them I saw two pistols—a revolver and a semiautomatic—and I also counted three silencers, one of which had to be close to eight inches long. I looked both ways and then pushed the locker door closed just enough so as not to arouse the interest of any nosy goddamn civilians, but not enough to relock it.

I wasn't sure what my next move should be, so I sought guidance from the beyond. Still leaning up against the lockers to keep the door shut, I took out the envelope I'd just removed from the locker and tore it open. It contained another key, as well as a short note:

> *Mr. Reilly (or whoever gets this): These are my own personal effects and not what I discussed with you. If you are here then I have no further use for them, so do with them what you will. What you need will be in PO Box 3889, Government Center Station, next to Ch. 7. Enclosed please find PO box key. All the best, BB.*

You bet, Bucky. All the best indeed. If he'd organized his life of crime as carefully as he orchestrated his postmortem career, he might still be among the living. He must have dropped everything in the locker just before he called me, a little more than twenty-four hours ago.

How much would it cost to rent the locker for another day? I looked at an eye-level sign on the wall. The price was two bucks a day, in quarters, which I didn't have. I would have to take my chances that no one else would grab the locker for however long it took me to obtain some quarters. I pushed the locker door shut, with the key in it. I pulled on the handle to make sure it was secure, then sauntered over as casually as I could to the mini–Burger King across the lobby, where the first thing I saw on the cash register was a barely legible scrawled sign that said "No quarters. No even ask."

This was my lucky day.

I grabbed a Danish and handed the temporary guest worker behind the cash register a five and told him to give me back eight quarters and keep the rest of the change. He smiled and shook his head. He must have been watching me all along.

"Ees against policy," he said. "Make it a ten."

I briefly considered haggling with him—would seven bucks close the deal? But I couldn't afford to bargain. That would make me stand out from the crowd even more than my swollen face already did, when the cops might soon be showing mug shots, mine included, to this illegal alien innocent fucking bystander from Burger King. So I silently handed him a ten-dollar bill, and he gave me back eight quarters.

"*Muchas gracias,*" he said, flashing the gringo a gotcha smile.

I thought about saying "*De nada,*" but *porque*? As I walked back to the locker, I tossed the stale Danish into an overflowing trash can. I inserted the eight quarters, opened the locker door once more, and briefly pretended to look inside. Then I shut the door and removed the key. I had control of Bucky's personal effects for another twenty-four hours, plenty of time. I dropped the key into my coat pocket and made for the door.

By now it was dark, almost six o'clock, but since I was less than a mile from the post office, I decided to hoof it there before they locked it up for the evening. Another 9/11–related hassle—most post offices are no longer open all night. I got there with about five minutes to spare, quickly located "my" box, and peeked inside. Nothing, not even a catalogue or credit card solicitation.

I left the post office and walked the hundred feet or so to the nearby Starbucks. I bought one of their ever-popular four-dollar coffees, walked back outside, and fished the cell phone out of my coat pocket.

I dialed Plain View on his cell phone.

"This is your friend," I said.

"My friend," he said. "That's a good one."

"I noticed my other friend outside," I said, "the one of the colored persuasion."

"I'll tell him you were asking for him."

"I assume you were trying to send me a message."

"You, among others."

"If I were you," I said, "I might want to have a peek inside a rental locker at the bus station, number four sixty-five. Four-six-five."

"Go on," he said.

"I would say if management won't give you a key, it would definitely be worth your while to get a search warrant, because I think you would quite interested in what's inside."

"Like?"

"Like at least one 9mm. And a revolver. And silencers."

"Did you see them, personally?" he asked.

"Absolutely," I said. "They were in plain view."

MY FAINT hope was that whatever Tony Miami and Knocko were looking for would be found in the locker in all those manila envelopes. But even if what they wanted wasn't there, it would take them a while to track down that information from their police department sources.

I grabbed a cab home. Once I got inside, I had one beer, and then another. They say drinkin' doubles don't make a party, but you couldn't prove it by me. I could have made a few calls on be-half of what few nonpolitician "clients" I had on the string, but why bother? Their cases were all of the wink-and-a-nod variety. I say I'll try to find somebody, and then I don't, for which they say they'll pay me, and then they don't.

In the end it all works out even, more or less, except in my bank account.

Sitting at my kitchen table, sipping a beer, I decided to switch over to my one registered firearm, namely, my Beretta 9mm. I much prefer a revolver, because they won't jam on you. Unfortu-nately, all my revolvers were of the unregistered variety.

Even the one that I was going to give to Teddy Gold.

I got the Beretta out of my steamer trunk and drew a bead on my Kenmore refrigerator, one of the few non-SubZeros left on my gentrified block. The more I drank, the better I liked the heft of the automatic, which was good, because until this thing was resolved, my new motto was going to be from the twenty-third Psalm: my rod and my staff, they comfort me. Mostly my rod.

Feeling just medicated enough to take the edge off, I spread out all the public documents that Jiggs had included in his packet on Mr. Speaker. Two years ago, he had reported ownership of his seven condos and/or apartments, two three-deckers, four single-family homes, and a summer "cottage" in Chatham. Even with mortgages on some of them, I figured his equity had to be at least five million. With that kind of net worth, he had to have a lot of bagmen, I mean lobbyists, out there pounding the pavement, soliciting payoffs, I mean contributions.

But then something had happened. His financial collapse was recorded in last year's filing, which was already almost ten months old. In it, he reported the sale of everything he owned except his own single-family home in Oak Square and the Cape property. Why hadn't this been in the papers? Just how much cover does being pro–gay marriage buy you around here?

The phone rang.

"Mr. Black?" It was Jiggs. "Making any progress?"

"Why would he want to sell everything?"

"Isn't that what I'm paying you to find out?"

"Yeah, but I thought you might be able to point me in the right direction."

"Have I overestimated you, Mr. Black? Did I or did I not tell you about his new secretary?"

"You know his father was a cop," I said. "Is it possible this might have something to do with the old man shaking down some people who don't take too kindly to being shaken down?"

"Now I'm regaining my confidence in you," Jiggs said. "Is this other thing, the Foley's thing, blowing over, so that you can get down to business for me?"

"I sure as hell hope it's blowing over," I said, and I hoped he couldn't hear the doubt that had crept into my voice, not to mention the alcohol.

I USUALLY don't get too many calls during normal business hours, in large part because most of my paying clients are politicians. They work in public buildings where, as the old joke goes, no one looks out the windows in the morning because they want to have something to do in the afternoon. And when they're not looking out the window, they're eavesdropping on everybody else. That's why they all whisper, even when they're talking to me, in the privacy of their own home or car, after business hours. It's just a habit they've gotten into, talking softly, so no one can hear what they're saying. My office hours generally run from seven to eleven. Most of the time I'm yelling at them, "Speak up! I can't hear you."

As the evening wore on, I took a few more calls. One payroll patriot whispered to me from his home in Fitchburg. I'd driven out there a couple of days earlier to meet an off-duty cop in the parking lot of a Dunkin' Donuts off Route 2. In return for three crisp new hundred-dollar bills the cop had handed me a police report that involved my client's boss, a former mayor who happened to be the $110,000-a-year aide to a statewide politician who had once run for president. The police report detailed how this john, the ex-mayor, had been arrested for the old "attempted solicitation." In other words, he had tried to pick up a twenty-bucks-a-trick working girl.

Now my man had a follow-up request: He wanted the story planted in one of the Boston dailies, he didn't much care which one. Once it hit either paper, he figured, he would quickly succeed his boss as the politician's chief of staff, for the aforementioned 110 large a year.

"How much?" he whispered.

I told him I'd drop the dime for another thousand, on top of the grand he'd already paid me. He said no problem. What's another grand when you're about to be making 110K?

At 9:01 my phone rang again. It could be someone who had forgotten Miss Manners's admonition never to call after nine at night or before nine in the morning. Or it could be someone calling from a federal penitentiary. My money was on the latter.

"Hey," said Marty, after I accepted charges. "They're still very concerned."

"I haven't got anything."

"Yeah, they're pretty sure of that, but they think maybe you will be getting something, very soon, and they want it."

"They made that pretty clear already."

"They'll make it clearer, if they have to. But mainly what they want is, they don't want any trouble."

"I got that message firsthand today at the Chinese place there." I was referring to Fo-Lee's.

"I heard about that. I'm just here to reiterate the message."

I wondered how they were communicating with him. Probably a guard on their pad with a cell phone. He'd hand the phone to Marty, and Marty would dial them, or vice versa. I doubted my brother had volunteered for this assignment.

"Can't they call me themselves? Why do they have to use you?"

"You don't know?"

"No, Marty, I don't know."

"They want you to know how easy it is for them to get to me."

Finally I stumbled into the living room to watch a little TV, the Beretta in my right hand and a beer in my left. I watched the eleven o'clock news, and every newscast led with a live shot from the bus station. Plain View looked pallid, as if he hadn't been sleeping well lately. That made two of us.

Chapter Six

WHEN MY CELL phone rang, I was still dozing fitfully on the couch, in my clothes. The digital clock on the coffee table told me it was 9:14 A.M. I picked up the phone.

"Hi honey," Plain View said. "I'm home."

I muttered a few obscenities, and he laughed.

"No," Plain View said. "I'm home. Look out your front window."

I did, and sure enough, there he was, by himself this time, double-parked in an unmarked car.

"Come on down," he said. "And don't give me any bullshit about how you're afraid to come out and play, because what could you possibly be frightened of, given the exemplary fucking life you lead?"

"Is this a social call?" I said.

"This is fucking police business." No more kidding around now. His tone was stern. "Haul your ass down here or I'm coming up."

And after all I'd done for him yesterday. What did Slip always say? No good deed goes unpunished.

"What took so long?" Plain View said as I climbed into the front seat beside him three minutes later.

"I was shaving," I said.

He scowled and reached into his coat pocket to pull out a mug shot. It was without question a younger version of the scally-capped ex-con who had given me the key to Bucky's locker yesterday afternoon.

"He looks vaguely familiar," I told Plain View.

"The key word is 'vaguely,' I'm sure."

"And here I thought maybe you were stopping by to thank me for that nice tip I gave you yesterday."

He rolled his eyes, so I decided to press my advantage.

"It all panned out just like I told you it would, didn't it?"

"It better have, after I put my ass on the line to get that warrant. You ever try to find a judge after five o'clock—a sober judge, I mean."

"You were the lead story on every station."

"You know why they led with it," he said with a shrug. "It was the silencers. They look scarier on the tube than cocaine or cash. All these idiots still got *The Sopranos* on the brain." He paused for a moment. "That was Bucky's stash in the locker, as if you didn't know."

"So why are you busting my balls?"

He sighed deeply. "You gave me something, I'll grant you that, but it's cold as ice, and in the meantime, I get another missing-persons report that lands on my desk."

Missing person? As the old song goes, I had a funny feeling I wouldn't be feeling funny very long.

"Look at the mug shot again," he said. "Do you, or do you not know this bum?"

I took the photo in my hand again and pretended to study it some more.

"I told you, he looks familiar, but I'm guessing that if we drive down to Braintree today and walk around the South Shore Plaza, we'll see a million guys look just like him."

"This guy ever give you anything?"

Plain View was calling my bluff. Willie had been staking out my place yesterday. It had been just a shot in the dark on Plain View's part, sending Willie out, to show the flag as it were, and now he had me tied to another guy who was MIA.

"Has something happened to him?" I said, handing back the photo.

"I'll ask the questions here, okay? I want to know, who is he, and what did he give you, and don't tell me you don't know him, 'cause Willie seen you with him."

"So did a couple of feds. Did Willie tell you that too?"

"He told me," he said. "I suppose they got their reasons for keeping you under half-assed surveillance, just like I got mine. You're trying to change the subject. I'll ask the question again. What did this guy give you, and don't give me no bullshit that he didn't, because Willie seen you duke him some cash."

"I don't know who he is," I said. "I really don't. He just came up to me and handed me something."

"And . . ."

"And what?"

"What did he hand you? I mean, I know what he handed you, given the time line here, but I want to hear it from your own mouth that he gave you the key to the locker at the bus station. This isn't a deposition. I shouldn't have to be pulling teeth here."

Teeth. Get it? I got it all right.

"Let's review the sequence of events, shall we?" he said, sounding like one of my old teachers at Boston English. "An ex-con who has a drink with you turns up murdered about ten minutes later. Now another ex-con who did time with the dead ex-con and who gives you something from the first ex-con turns up missing immediately afterwards. I gotta figure, the way things are going, there's at least one more guy slated to do the Houdini."

I ignored that. I wanted to know about the old geezer.

"Okay, so I did run into this guy yesterday," I said. "If there was anything sneaky going on, do you really think I would have given him some money in front of Willie and a couple of feds? Plus, you can't tell me the cops are interested in every ex-con who goes missing overnight."

Plain View rolled down his window and spat onto the sidewalk, surely a violation of some city ordinance. Where was Myrna when I needed her?

"I see I got your attention now," he said. "But since you've asked me about him, I can tell you that this gentleman had a hearing scheduled late yesterday afternoon over in the family court. He was in contempt, most of 'em are, he owed child support or some such shit. It was short money, but one of those new lesbian judges was threatening to throw him in the can if he didn't come up with the dough. So he got a cashier's check—we confirmed that. He paid cash for it just after he met you."

"What exactly does this have to do with me?"

"Other than the bank teller, you were the last person to talk to him before he disappeared."

"Disappeared?" I said. "Maybe he went on a bender."

"Maybe," said Plain View. "But when you think about it, he's got the check in his pocket—we know that, 'cause first thing this morning we got the time stamp from the bank, which is right across Post Office Square from the courthouse. All he has to do is walk across the street and hand the check to the clerk and then he doesn't have to worry for a while about getting lugged. But he never made it across the street to the courthouse."

"So what happened to him?"

"That's what I was hoping you could tell me," he said. "But if you were to ask me, I would say that unless we catch a real break here, we have seen the last of Alan 'Suitcase' O'Malley."

"That was his name, Suitcase O'Malley? Wow."

"He was living in the same halfway house on Huntington Ave. as the late Bucky Bennett, as if you didn't know. They were also in Otisville together, along with your brother."

"If Suitcase only disappeared yesterday afternoon," I said, "why is there already a missing-persons report out on him?"

"Are you listening to me or not?" he said. "He was in contempt; he didn't show at the hearing, his ex-wife is there all in a dither, no doubt more worried about the money than the ex. So the judge, who hates all men to begin with—and that's off the record—issues a default warrant. They move a lot faster on deadbeat dads than on terrorists or illegal-alien carjackers, in case you haven't noticed. They already had his mug shot, he's such an upstanding citizen, or was. And when Willie's going over the orders of the day this morning, he recognizes the guy and puts two and two together."

"Willie?" I said, in surprise.

"Yeah," Plain View said, smiling. "Maybe Willie ain't the sharpest knife in the drawer, but there's not a lot gets by him. He works a lot harder on the job than you ever did, I'll tell you that right now. He's got a real work ethic."

Plain View glanced down at his watch—reverie over.

"I ain't got all day here," he said. "I got more dead ends to chase down on the Bennett hit in addition to this new thing here."

"Is it safe to say," I asked, "that this string of homicides and missing persons has left the police 'baffled'?"

"Yeah, we're baffled all right," Plain View said. "And what's really baffling us is why you haven't disappeared yet too."

"I'm as baffled as you are," I said.

"Okay, if that's the way you want to play it," he said, and then he extended his hand. "And if I don't see you again, I wish I could say it's been a pleasure knowing you, but I gave up lying for Lent."

BACK INSIDE my house I considered my next move. The safest thing to do would be to give Tony Miami the key to the post office box. But suppose whatever they wanted didn't turn up in the next forty-eight hours or so? Then Tony might conclude, erroneously, that I was jerking him around, and that kind of misunderstanding can start you down a road where the last exit is an unlicensed dental office in a basement in North Quincy.

And I still didn't know for sure what was in the package. Maybe some of the old Hogan records, but at this late date they hardly seemed worth at least two murders, not to mention a couple of million dollars from the Speaker. So there had to be something else involved. I didn't know what exactly and I was pretty sure Suitcase O'Malley hadn't known either.

Whatever, I couldn't stay inside the house any longer. I was getting antsy. I grabbed the Beretta and decided to visit the last outpost of the once-mighty Hogan criminal empire.

BACK IN the day when I read the *Globe* regularly—and it's been a while now—occasionally I'd come across a story about the "renaissance" of certain neighborhoods, blighted areas that are allegedly "coming back." What a crock.

I was getting that déjà vu feeling now, driving into Uphams

Corner. Just recently I'd read yet another piece—okay, the headline of a piece—about how local "community advocates" were concerned how so many rich white people were gentrifying their multicultural rainbow oasis of a neighborhood, falling all over themselves to move back into Dorchester to celebrate diversity in the rich urban mosaic of graffiti, crackhouses, lowriders, rodents, immigration lawyers, whooping cough, methadone clinics, drive-by shootings, pit bulls, rent-to-own furniture stores, diphtheria, empty Goya containers, MassHealth cards, tuberculosis, storefront preachers, leprosy, SSI crazy checks, WIC fliers, abandoned houses, and pregnant thirteen-year-olds.

The renaissance of Uphams Corner must have been taking the morning off, because I was able to find a parking space directly in front of Wimpy's Lounge. It had to be the last place in the world with a "Time Out for Dawson's Beer" sign hanging above its entrance. It was three doors down from the renovated Strand Theater, a city boondoggle and a white elephant if ever there was one, except in Uphams Corner it would have to be an elephant of color. The Strand's last big get had been Louis Farrakhan of the Nation of Islam, complete with a controversy about how women weren't allowed in, or only into the balcony, or something. That had been at least a decade ago.

Getting out of my car, I sidestepped a wino sprawled, literally, in the gutter. I tried to avoid making eye contact with a couple of junkies nodding off as they propped themselves up on the sidewalk against the barroom's walls, which last appeared to have had a fresh coat of paint sometime during the Johnson administration—Andrew Johnson.

You know what they say about the War on Poverty. It's over. Poverty won.

I opened the barroom's heavy, windowless, Molotov cocktail–proof metal-frame door, and stepped into a gin mill so dark and foreboding that it took more than a moment for my eyes to adjust to the absence of light. Finally I was able to make out a couple of uniformed black bus drivers from the nearby T car barn hunched over in a corner booth, whispering and engaging in civil disobedience against the citywide ban on smoking in public places. Slip would have been proud.

In the adjoining room, two off-duty black firefighters were playing pool. On a stool at the bar, another black guy, much older, snored softly, his head resting on the fraying foam padding that rimmed the edge of the bar. On the other side of the bar, the bartender, white, stood with his arms folded, a mixed brown-water drink in front of him on the bar.

I braced myself against the bar and noticed a puddle of water on the bar slowly advancing towards the passed-out black guy's head.

The spillage seeped ever closer to the "customer." Crunch time was near, and options were few. Either the bartender could attempt to wake the guy, or he could mop up the water with the filthy dishrag in his hand and let the bum continue his nap.

Billy Hogan Jr. made an executive decision—he semi-deftly wiped up the puddle and let the black guy keep snoozing. The crisis was over until the guy either fell off his stool or started throwing up, whichever came first. Actually, there was a third potential outcome—a liquor inspector could stumble in for an impromptu inspection and write up the bar for any number of code violations. But the likelihood of anyone from City Hall appearing in this neighborhood was less than remote. There was no money to be made shaking down anyone at Wimpy's Lounge these days.

Hogan was maybe ten years older than me, but he looked seventy—emaciated, bitter, hands shaking ever so slightly. I pegged him for the sort of drunkard who would neglect to eat for days on end. Just from his general pallor, I guessed he had maybe five years, tops, before the cirrhosis kicked in. It's a hard way to go, but Billy Hogan Jr. was buying himself a ticket, one drink at a time.

"What can I do you for?" he said to me without interest, and I introduced myself, sort of. He brought me a draft beer and I told him I was investigating the murders of his father and his uncles, although I used the weasel word "disappearances." I may have also flashed a square badge, and I'm sure I neglected to mention who I was working for, an omission he was still sober enough to pick up on.

"Who wants to know?" he asked. Always, the recurring question.

"Some concerned citizens," I said.

"What's in it for me?"

"Maybe you get to the bottom of this thing."

He laughed, and it had a brittle edge. "That'll be the day. You know my mother went to her grave not knowing for sure that her husband, my father, was dead. Do you know what kind of hoops the insurance company makes you jump through if there's no body? They got billions, and they push you to the wall for ten grand."

I just stood there, politely sipping the house beer. Old Milwaukee.

"You have to go to court to get someone declared legally dead. And my mother, she never got no, uh, whaddaya call it, what's the word?"

"Closure?"

"Yeah, closure. She never got no closure." The bus drivers yelled for a couple more beers, so Billy Hogan Jr. interrupted his soliloquy to serve them. That gave me a chance to look around the joint, and it was even grimmer, and grimier, than it had appeared at first glance. The jukebox was dark, unplugged. A familiar and unpleasant smell lingered in the air, emanating from the general vicinity of the toilets in the rear hallway. From where I stood, I could see a hand-lettered sign on one of the restroom doors, I'm guessing the ladies' room, and I'm also guessing that the sign said "Out of Order." But not out of odor.

In the late eighties and once again in the late nineties, a lot of these neighborhood dives had gone under. The only real value they had were their liquor licenses, and if he'd been paying attention, Billy Hogan Jr. probably could have sold his to one of those chi-chi boutique hotels or a waterfront bistro for at least a hundred grand. But that was before the dot-com bust. Taxi medallions were worth maybe half what they once were, ditto liquor licenses. I had a hunch it wasn't the first time Billy Hogan Jr. had missed out on a big payday.

I noticed a slightly damp *Herald* lying on the bar about five feet away from the sleeping drunk. I didn't think he'd be needing it anytime soon, so I walked over, picked it up, and brought it back to where I'd been standing.

The headline on the front page made me smile: "Speaker's Hand Seen in Mob Land Grab." The byline was Katy Bemis's. I didn't have to read the story, but I did anyway. She'd done a nice job on short notice. Now she definitely owed me one. . . .

I wondered if she'd call today to at least thank me. Probably not—in my experience, reporters would rather think of themselves as relentless gumshoes ferreting out the truth, rather than admit that in most cases they're just stenographers, taking a handout, recording the settling of old, or not so old, scores. Still, I was hoping she'd phone. Hope springs eternal, right?

I looked up and into the twisted face of Billy Hogan Jr.

So much for my little daydream.

He was back behind the bar, and from his slight swaying I deduced that sometime during his trek to the outer limits of Wimpy's

Lounge he had managed a nip or two to replenish his stock of bile. He must have had another bottle, or at least a drink, stashed somewhere over there. Once again he stood facing me across the bar, and this time he practically spat his words out at me.

"She had multiple sclerosis, my mother," he said. "They said my father was a criminal, but he dressed her every day, took care of her. All he done was run this place and keep the books for his brother. You know, Wimpy. They didn't care, they killed him anyway. I had to drop outta high school to take care of Ma. But she died two months later. Doctors said it was a broken heart."

As if they'd say anything else, at least to the grieving son.

"The Hogans ran everything around here, not that anybody remembers anymore. Everything but Southie and Savin Hill. And then it was over, just like that. As soon as there was finally some real money on the table, they killed my father and my uncles. My family missed out on the real money."

Real money—that meant drugs. I tried to imagine Wimpy and Billy Sr. and Aloysius living on into the disco seventies, still in their fedoras and suspenders but now also wearing bell bottoms, cutting lines of coke, selling to hippies and project rats and Rastafarians. I drew a total blank. But who was I to step on his fantasy? It surely beat the dismal reality that he was living, and dying.

"Billy," I said, "did a cop steal your father's ledger books?"

"How'd you know about that?" he said, suddenly even more sullen and resentful, if that was possible.

"I need to know what was in those books."

He picked up his rag and furiously mopped the bar, then looked up again. "Who'd you say you were again?"

"I might be the guy who gets you those books back."

"Yeah?" he said. "Lotta good they'd do me now. Everybody's dead or retired to Florida. Mostly dead by now. Cripes, that was over thirty years ago, and most of those cops my family had on the pad were no spring chickens even then. You must know what was in them books, if you're talking to me. Why are you so interested?"

"Just background for something else I'm working on. Who stole them?"

He stared at me, trying to figure out who I was, who I was representing. The booze was not improving his powers of concentration. He grimaced as he tried to think it through, of who might have sent me.

"You must know who grabbed 'em, or you wouldn't be down here." He reached across the sink and picked up another glass I hadn't noticed. No ice, just brown water. Maybe it was tea, but I doubted it. He took a sip and put the glass back down.

"Why don't you tell me who took them?" I said.

But he said nothing. So there was no way around it. I had to put at least some of my cards on the table.

"Was it an inspector named Lynch?"

"You know it was. That's the prick all right, Lynch. My old man always told me and Ma, if anything ever happened to him, we were just to put those books in a safe place and then tell either Wimpy or Aloysius where they were, and they'd make sure everything was taken care of."

Unfortunately for Ma and Billy Hogan Jr., the family muscle, Wimpy and Aloysius, were gone before bookkeeper Billy got clipped. So my godfather had called it. I hadn't really doubted him, but you always have to confirm the information no matter how much you trust your source. It's always unfortunate when someone gets whacked over a rumor that later turns out to have been untrue.

"Lynch comes over to the house one morning about a week after Pa disappears, he waits 'til I'm out shopping for groceries, and he shows up at the front door to get Ma alone. He says to her, I got a search warrant. The fuck he did. But what does she know? She's from County Clare, she's in a wheelchair, she's dying for chrissake. She lets him in and he goes straight to the cabinet where my father always kept the books—he knew exactly where they were—and he takes them and then he leaves."

"And let me guess—he didn't give her a receipt?"

"What do you think? Later on, when I call the cops, he just denies it. What am I gonna do? It's his word against Ma's."

Now that I had what I needed, Billy Hogan Jr. couldn't shut his yap.

"I used to watch my old man every afternoon when I came home from school. He'd be sitting at the kitchen table, writing down names and numbers. That's all they were, those ledgers. Names and numbers."

In the background, a glass crashed to the floor off the pool table. A firefighter cursed. Billy Hogan Jr. ignored the commotion.

"I heard they buried my father and my uncles at some rod-and-gun club somewhere out around Hopkinton. I even heard Tony Miami still laughs about it. He says they still need to plant one more stiff out there so's they can all play hearts together, instead of whist."

That sounded like Tony Miami all right. A real joker, more fun than a barrel of monkeys.

"I had no idea what my old man was talking about when he kept telling me the books were pure gold. But I sure do know now. He had the goods on half the cops in the city. No wonder they didn't look too hard when he disappeared. I used to go down to headquarters, on Berkeley Street there, every month or so. I'd ask 'em what they were doing to find my father and my uncles. They'd just shrug, the bastards. Playing Mickey the Dunce. They're all on the take, they were then and they are now. And then that prick

Lynch used my father's ledger books to shake down all the cops on the job that my family'd been paying off."

How do you like them apples? Life sucks, then you drink yourself to death.

"And do you know what the worst thing of all is?" he said. "Do you know who that bastard's son turned out to be?"

I knew, but I let him have the satisfaction of telling me anyway.

Chapter Seven

LOOKED BOTH ways for muggers before I got back into my Oldsmobile. I had to check the mailbox again in Government Center. Last night I'd done it myself, but that was after business hours, when no one knew that Bucky's personal effects had turned up. They might be keeping an eye out for me now. I considered calling Plain View and just handing him the mailbox key, but that wouldn't really solve my problem. The two guys would still be coming after me for double-crossing them after they'd acted in such good faith by not killing me.

Just in case someone had picked up my tail, I took a circuitous route back into the city, drifting all the way down to Gallivan Boulevard, into Jiggs's district. I passed the old Eire Pub where President Reagan had once raised a mug of Ballantine Ale draft. Not a single white face on the street. No wonder Jiggs was in an up-or-out mood. He'd be needing to annex ever larger parts of Milton to his district if he wanted to remain in office beyond a couple of more terms.

As I headed up Dorchester Avenue I got on the phone to my second-floor tenant, Bruce the waiter. I woke him up.

"We've got to stop meeting like this," he said.

"I need a favor," I said.

"This is such serendipity," he said. "You need a favor and so do I—I need a rent freeze for a year."

"I don't need the favor that bad."

"Six months?"

"It's a deal," I said. "Now here's your part of the deal. I want you to meet me . . ."

. . . somewhere within walking distance of the Government Center post office. We finally settled on Murphy's Tap, an old joint on Canal Street with a bar that ran the length of the block from Canal to Portland Street.

I'd first thought about the gin mill across from the new courthouse, on the lot where JoJo Langone's old funeral home had once stood. But then I remembered I'd seen Tony Miami hanging there, plus the day bartender worked for the Racing Commission, so I couldn't take the chance of him reporting anything back to the State House. Bruce then suggested a gay bar on Merrimac named the Boston Rifleman (I shit you not), but I nixed that on general principles.

As for my familiarity with Murphy's Tap—well, let's just say that if you have a liquor license in the city and you don't want a lot of heat, it makes good business sense to stay on the right side of the mayor, and there's one way in particular to do that. It's green and you can fold it. Of course the mayor himself can't be accepting beer-dampened wads of small bills, so there has to be a buffer, a cushion, someone to whom it's second nature to be accepting wads of somebody else's money, and who better in such a supporting role than a connected plainclothes cop out of City Hall?

"This pickup you want me to make," Bruce asked me over the cell phone as I drove through Dudley Station. "Is it dangerous?"

"I don't think so," I said. "I'm pretty sure they don't know which box it is, if they know anything at all."

"Do I want to know who 'they' are?"

"I wouldn't, if I were you."

"I'll bet I could make a pretty good guess, though, couldn't I?"

"No extra credit for guesses," I said.

He said he would need at least a half hour to get to North Station, so I decided to keep driving around. I headed into Kenmore Square and from there on into the Speaker's district. There was one address on Com. Ave. I wanted to eyeball now that I knew the Speaker had once owned two apartments—or should I say condos?—in the building.

I slowed down to check out the building, and above the front door I saw an awning. That was always the sign that an apartment building had gone condo. When they install a ceiling fan in the "master bedroom," that means it's become a "luxury condominium." On the front of the building was a large CONDOMINIUMS FOR SALE sign, listing a Back Bay telephone exchange. I wondered how many times they'd been flipped since the Speaker unloaded them in his own personal little fire sale.

I turned around in Cleveland Circle and headed back into the city.

It was around eleven thirty when I reached Canal Street, a narrow old horse path of a street across from the Boston Garden. Bruce, who had wisely eschewed his customary flamboyant South End garb for more mainstream, Gap-esque attire, stepped out of the doorway of Murphy's Tap. I pulled over in front of a fire hydrant and he climbed into my car.

Once he was inside, I handed Bruce the post office box key and told him that after he checked the PO box, he was to call me. If there was nothing in the box he could return home. If he picked up anything, he was to head back to North Station and meet me on Track 10. It was the least he could do, for nine hundred bucks, because I had been planning on jacking up his rent a hundred and fifty a month.

"One thing, sir," Bruce said to me in the car. "What if I notice I'm being followed by some knuckle-dragger in a scally cap?"

"Swoon," I said. "Faint dead away."

Bruce smiled weakly at me, but finally opened the door and got out. I drove away to park my car in an alley around the corner from the Garden–Fleet Center–TD Bank North–TD Bank-whatever. The alley gave me a clearer view, and a quicker getaway, if necessary. I unlocked the glove compartment and took out my ancient dog-eared Official Police Business placard, signed by the commissioner before last. I threw the placard on the dashboard, pocketed my legally registered Beretta, grabbed my cell phone, locked the car, and walked over to North Station.

Ten minutes later, I got the call from Bruce. Nothing. I offered him a ride back home, but he said he'd walk.

So I was out nine hundred dollars for nothing. Thanks Bucky. Thanks Marty.

Chapter Eight

BACK ON SHAWMUT Avenue it was once again an ordeal to find a parking space. Myrna must have radioed for reinforcements, and they were swaggering up and down the block in such an obnoxious manner that I decided to leave the Olds in the little lot behind Foley's and walk home from there.

Then I showered and dressed. I'd have preferred to schedule my appointment with Mr. Gold in the morning, but after working for him, I knew that his mornings were reserved for the real-estate business. He explained to me once that if you wanted to collect rent from deadbeat tenants, which his generally were, morning was the time to do it, because they (most likely) weren't drunk, and they were (probably) too hung over to take a swing at you.

If anyone understood what the Speaker had been up to with all these real-estate transactions, it would be Teddy Gold. At the time I did a piece of work for him a few years back, he'd just been indicted—bribery, perjury, obstruction of justice, mail fraud, wire fraud, racketeering; in short the usual potpourri of federal white-collar crimes.

Working for the Gold defense team, I was in charge of shit, first its procurement and then its disbursement. Mr. Gold needed one prosecution witness in particular dusted up, a certain city hack who had been wearing a wire the day Teddy Gold handed him a bag of cash in the KFC in Union Square in Allston. With the invaluable assistance of large sums of Teddy Gold's cash, I soon learned that this rat bastard was very handy with a computer, and his biggest mistake turned out to be using the one in his office at the Inspectional Services Department to download some, well, let's just say there is a reason Boston is known in certain born-again Republican circles as Sodom and Begorrah.

When Mr. Gold's attorney made the feds aware in very general terms of what we'd dug up on their star witness, they folded and settled for a suspended sentence. Mr. Gold ended up with four hundred hours of community service. He taught tennis in Roxbury—a regular Great White Father, you might say.

Before I left the house, I checked my bedroom closet one more time for my old BPD shoulder holster, and finally found it, underneath an ancient bulletproof vest I'd forgotten I even owned, although actually, I'd never owned it, I just signed it out from the department one day, and never returned it. So sue me, garnish my kiss in the mail.

I strapped the holster on for the first time in years, and was pleasantly surprised to see how snugly the Beretta fit. I wore one of my father's old tweed sport coats—he'd put on weight in his final years, and it was a size too big for me. Perfect, in other words, for concealing a bulge under my left armpit. I positioned myself in front of the full-length mirror in my bedroom and buttoned the coat. Then I turned from side to side. Couldn't see a thing, from any angle. There wasn't even the hint of a bulge.

Teddy Gold's office was up on the third floor of the first building he'd ever bought, on Brighton Avenue. The only view he had was from a fly-specked window into an alley where his tenant "activists" periodically released rats which they claimed they'd found in one or another of his ten-thousand-plus units.

Mr. Gold emerged from his inner sanctum to greet me in the lobby. He didn't look a day older than the last time I'd seen him, maybe three years ago. He had to be close to eighty now, a small, wiry guy with a year-round tan. City guys his age, for some reason, consider a winter tan a big status symbol. We shook hands and he looked at my swollen face, frowned, and said, "I won't ask who did that to you."

"I walked into a door," I said.

"A door?" he said, opening his own door, and motioning me inside his private office. Once we were both inside, he shut the door and I handed him the small paper bag I was carrying in my left hand.

"Is it hot?" he asked, peering inside.

"Not particularly," I said. "It used to belong to my brother."

"The one in prison?"

"Yeah, but he was always kind of fastidious."

"Is that why he's in prison, because he's so fastidious?"

"You of all people should know better than to ask that question," I said. "He's in prison for the same reason you're not—money. You had it, he didn't."

"Touche," said Mr. Gold, dropping the subject. He was more interested in the gun he was holding in his hand. "Tell me about this fine revolver."

"It's a Taurus .38," I said. "A Smith and Wesson knockoff. Brazilian."

"Like more and more of my tenants," he said, looking up, smiling. "Why is the grip taped?"

"No prints that way."

"No prints? I told you, I want it for self-defense."

"Of course you do."

"I can't buy legally, you know." He was looking at me now, to establish his sincerity. "I'm a convicted felon. Even if I wasn't, the papers'd kick me in the balls if I went down to police headquarters to get a license. I've fallen off all the Forbes 400 richest-bastards lists but I still got enough dough to give the straphangers a chuckle or two."

The straphangers, reading newspapers? He hadn't been on the T in awhile.

"Mr. Gold," I said, "you don't have to explain anything to me."

He put the Taurus back in the bag with the two boxes of bullets I'd thrown in. It was a shame to part with the Taurus, but what are you going to do? I watched him open the bottom drawer of his battered desk, place the bag carefully inside, and then carefully close the drawer.

"How much?" he asked.

"Don't worry about it," I said. "Consider it a token of my esteem."

"In other words," he said, "now it's my turn to do something for you."

I nodded and sat down across the desk from him. He folded his hands and smiled.

"Did I tell you yesterday on the phone, your friends from the State House are calling me again?"

"It's an election year, Mr. Gold."

"That's what they always tell me," he said. "Is it ever not an election year?"

In the odd-numbered years, it was the city pols coming around. He paid them because he needed protection from City Hall assessors and building inspectors—like the guy he'd almost gone to prison for bribing. In the even-numbered years, it was the legislators and the statewide candidates who came knocking. Mr. Gold had to pay them for protection from the mischief the legislature could stir up, on everything from lead-paint and rent-control bills to hiking the capital gains tax. When I worked for him, I'd watched him handle other developers, and contractors, and whoever else he'd done business with. If somebody had a beef with him, the first thing he always said was, "I'm sorry you feel that way."

If the person persisted, he'd always say, "I'm sorry you feel that way, but that's not American law."

And usually that was it. If they still wanted to argue the point, he'd just start over with his first standard line: "I'm sorry you feel that way."

That was it. No compromise. He figured he had more money than almost anyone he had to deal with, which meant he could outlast them, if push came to shove. But he always rolled over for the pols. He truly didn't want to fight City Hall. He'd learned his lesson when he was indicted. Smart guys usually do. They make sure it never happens again. Now the politicians were calling again.

"I always read in the paper," Teddy Gold was saying, "that these politicians are being 'urged' to run. Tell me, who is doing this urging?"

"The working families of Massachusetts," I said.

"You know I own some convenience stores," he said. "And what does a convenience store have to have to make it work?"

A lottery franchise. The lottery is controlled by the state treasurer, who this year was running for governor.

"And of course," I said, "a convicted felon can't be a lottery agent."

"How right you are," he said. "So I have to move a table for the treasurer's time at Anthony's." He smiled again. "As long as you're here, Jack, would you like to sit at my table—I won't be there, of course, and I suspect you won't be either. It'll cost you five hundred bucks."

"Let me make another guess, Mr. Gold. You've got a job for me that pays, oh, I don't know, a thousand."

"How ever did you read my mind?" he said. "You know, it's nice to have paid my debt to society, but it was a lot cheaper when I was a pariah and on probation and they couldn't shake me down. So it's a deal then—I cut you a check for a thousand dollars, and you duke him five hundred."

I nodded. The way it was working out, I had sold him the Taurus for five hundred bucks. Then we got down to my real reason for being there. I asked him about the Speaker.

"I know him, of course, and basically he's no different from the rest of them. He has his bagmen, I'm sure you know them better than I do, these third-rate Irish lawyers who will someday be judges in the district courts. They ask me, do I want to go to Speaker Lynch's time? As if I have any more choice in the matter than I do with the treasurer. So I buy a table, because that is what is expected of me, as the richest Jew in his district."

He smiled, so I smiled. Then he continued:

"So I go to Anthony's Pier 4 to see Mr. Speaker, and we look at the palatial new courthouse across the water that replaced the old one where I copped a plea—"

"And where I stonewalled before the grand jury—"

"We have so much in common, you and I," he said dryly. "Anyway, the Speaker and I, we make small talk, and until very recently I always had the impression that he and I shared the traditional view of real estate."

"Which is?"

"Never sell. Buy and hold. Make the payments and sooner or later, between inflation and appreciation and the monthly rents coming in, you're in the black. They talk about the miracle of compound interest. Real estate puts compound interest in the shithouse."

I saw him glance quickly at a framed photograph on the wall that I had never noticed before. It was new, a digital snapshot of a little boy on a beach, and then I remembered. At age seventy, he'd become a father for the first time, by a secretary in his office. Teddy Gold now had a stake in the future.

"He wasn't stupid, your friend the Speaker," Teddy Gold said, slipping into the past tense. "He was buying up the stuff that not even I would touch, and I have my own maintenance crews which I need to have out working forty hours a week. So I'm always on the lookout for even the most dilapidated properties. But our friend—until very recently he would buy absolutely anything. Lead paint, leaky roofs, broken furnaces—he'd pay off the tax liens and bring in his own crews. And it was all cash."

So it was just as I had suspected. The Speaker had been laundering his cash payoffs through the buildings—the fixer-uppers, the handyman's specials.

You can't use cash to buy buildings, of course. The deed has to be recorded at the Registry, tax stamps bought, etc. So you use the cash you've extorted to pay the contractors who fix up the buildings. The contractor loves it because he doesn't have to pay taxes on it, so he gives you the 20 percent cash discount, plus none of his subs have any incentive to drop a dime either, because they're taking cash as well, which makes them as guilty as the contractor who's paying them.

"Let's say you buy a three-family for two hundred thousand," Teddy Gold said. "You put in a hundred large in renovations, cash, for which you get maybe a hundred and fifty grand worth of work, if you're sharp. Then you raise the rent and get yourself some new tenants. If you can hang on for three or four years, you're in the black."

"And everything is totally laundered," I said.

"That's the beauty of a rising real-estate market," he said. "It's hard to prove how much money you dumped into the place, but when you sell it, everything is laundered, and even if you don't use the money to buy something else, the only tax is capital gains."

"Which is still only 20 percent," I said, and he nodded.

"As opposed to a top marginal income tax rate of 35 percent on a bribe, plus they can throw you in jail for accepting it. And what's even better is, if you roll the money from the sale over to buy more property, they call that a 1031 exchange, and you don't have to pay taxes, period."

"But now the market sucks," I said.

"That it does," he agreed. "But your friend should have been able to ride out a slump. He never overpaid, as I recall, and even in a down market people need a place to live—"

The phone on his desk rang. He picked it up and grimaced. He told his secretary to put the call through and then he cupped his hand over the receiver and whispered to me, "It's the Senate president."

I smiled. Another candidate for governor.

"Hello, Mr. President. . . . Of course I appreciate you getting back to me. . . . Oh, I understand. . . . Believe me, I know how difficult it is to keep those chairmen of yours under control."

Teddy Gold glanced over at me and rolled his eyes. Blame the chairman for whatever bill had just been filed to croak Teddy Gold, and then ride to Teddy's rescue on a white horse—for a price. It was so transparent that even a Harvard man could have figured it out.

"Mr. President, allow me to add my humble voice to the swelling chorus urging you to run," Teddy Gold was saying. "You can count on me . . . under other names, of course. . . . I agree, no need for any headlines. . . . One hundred percent . . . Put me down for a table . . . Governor."

A few seconds later, he was putting the phone down and shaking his head.

"You ever hear people say someone oozes charm? That guy just oozes." He was wound up now. "And the scam is so transparent. He gets that dolt of his from New Bedford to file a bill calling for the reinstitution of rent control—"

"Which would be very expensive for you."

"That's right, but it's not going to happen, ever, and everybody knows it's never going to happen, but I still have to pay protection money to him, me and every other big landlord in the state, so he can run for governor and get his ass kicked like every other Senate president who ever ran for anything outside the building. I'm sure if you own a cab or a drugstore or a racetrack, he's got some other chairman of his shaking you down too on a different bogus bill. And he'll lose and next year there'll be a new chairman filing bills for a new president who'll be calling me up to buy a table at Anthony's."

Then we got back to Mr. Speaker. I told him most of the sales listed in his most recent Ethics Commission filing had been to realty trusts, yet another legal dodge, in this case to conceal the names of the real owners. From my experience in the shit business, I knew that the only name that has to be listed on the incorporation papers is that of the trust, and of course the trustee, who can be anybody, and usually is.

The only drawback might be if the straw on the deed reneged and decided he really owned the property. But in most of these deals, before the property even changes hands, the real, hidden owner gets an undated letter of sale from the straw. Purchase price: one dollar.

So whenever the real owner wants to claim title, he just dates the document.

"Is it possible," I asked Teddy Gold, "that he's selling the properties to Knocko Nugent and Tony Miami?"

Teddy Gold looked surprised. "Hadn't considered that possibility, although I guess I should have." He glanced again at the photo of the little boy on the wall. "This is no place to raise a child."

What place is, these days? I stood up and thanked him for his time. He walked me to the door, put his arm around my shoulder, and said, "About the gun, Jack."

"Yes?" I said.

"I ask you again," he said. "Is it hot?"

"Compared to what?"

He smiled and handed me a voucher. "On your way out, don't forget to pick up your check."

"A check?" And then I remembered. I was going to a time for the state treasurer and receiver general, or at least I was buying a ticket to the fundraiser.

"Now that I think of it," Teddy Gold said. "I have another job for you, if you're interested. Give me back that voucher." I handed it back to him, and he took a pen out of his breast pocket, put the slip up against the wall, crossed through the thousand-dollar figure, and wrote above it "$2,000." He handed it back to me and grinned.

"Have you ever broken bread with the Senate president, Jack—I think he could be just the man we're looking for to get this great Commonwealth of ours moving again."

"For the children," I said.

Chapter Nine

I N THE CAR, my cell phone rang.

"Mr. Black?" It was Jiggs.

"Did you see that story in the paper this morning about that certain thing we discussed?" he asked, and I knew just what he was talking about—the Speaker's own one-dollar land transfer on behalf of the Mob.

"You didn't plant it, did you?" he asked.

"Me? You're kidding, right?"

"Because I don't want any freelancing until after the vote," he said. "You clear everything with me before you make a move. Got that?"

I'd thought Jiggs would be grateful to me for dropping the dime, but I'd forgotten one thing. The Speaker had to be kept alive until he finished getting through the repeal of the term limits provision in the House rules. Let Lynch take the heat from the media about "one-man rule" and "bossism." Once Lynch was speaker-for-life, his life expectancy would be about a day, or at least that was Jiggs's plan. But until the vote, Mr. Speaker had to be propped up as much as Jiggs could manage.

"That was a tough piece," he said. "It frightened some of the goo-goos from the suburbs. Now they're thinking they might take some heat if they vote for the Speaker."

"They frighten easily, don't they?" I said.

"No freelancing," he repeated. "I'm serious."

"I understand," I said. "I'm making some progress on your matter, but it may take a while longer."

"Take as long as you need," he said. "Just don't finish before the day after tomorrow. Understand?"

I understood all right. The vote was tomorrow afternoon.

AS I drove downtown toward the post office, I checked my answering machine back at the house.

The first message was from my ex-wife. Gee, I wonder what she wanted. Strike that—I wonder how much she wanted. They say you never really know a woman until you've tangled with her in court, and they're right. The next message was from Katy Bemis, and she sounded a lot friendlier than she ever had before. She wanted me to give her a call.

Driving up Tremont Street, I called her right back at the direct landline number she'd given me in the city room. When she picked up the phone I said, "Do you know who this is?"

"Yes," she said. "You're another one of those guys who won't identify himself because he thinks I might be taping the conversation."

"You better not be," I said, turning onto New Chardon Street. "This is a two-party state."

"How would you know that?" she said.

"I know plenty," I said, and it occurred to me, it had been a while since I'd done anything remotely like this kind of boy-girl bantering. It was almost flirting. "And now that I think about it, aren't you going to thank me?"

"You never struck me as the kind of guy who wanted a pat on the back," she said. "I always thought of you as more of the I-didn't-see-you-you-didn't-see-me kind of guy."

"You've 'always' been thinking of me?"

"Always since Monday," she added quickly.

"So . . ." I said, as I grabbed a ticket to park in the Government Center garage. "I'm returning your call."

"I did want to thank you, actually," she said. "And, you know, if you've ever got anything else . . ."

"You'd like another story, is that what you're telling me?" I said. "I do have one you might be interested in. I don't have the details right on me, but I can fax 'em to you."

"Faxing?" she said. "How quaint."

"I can't e-mail police reports yet," I said. "I don't have a scanner. But how'd you like a story about a former mayor who just got lugged for trying to pick up an eighteen-year-old hooker in his hometown. He's the chief of staff for a certain Vietnam veteran who lives on Beacon Hill and ran for president."

"You got that solid?"

"All wrapped up with a bow on top."

"That's a good story." She sounded like she meant it.

"It's a great story," I said. "It's a national story."

"Listen," she said, "could I, uh, meet you somewhere?"

So it was an even better story than I'd thought. She didn't trust the fax machine, and I didn't blame her. The senator surely had his own sets of eyes and ears in the newsroom, and since fax transmissions are nothing more than phone calls, they can be easily traced. So it would be in my own interest—and my client's—to hand deliver the documents.

"I can meet you somewhere later," I said. "Not Foley's though."

"I agree. How do you feel about Southie?"

"Not so good right now. How about Harry's King of Draft."

"You mean that place on Albany Street with the pool tables next to the day-labor place? Yucky."

"Okay," I said. "What about the Chinese joint there on East Berkeley?"

"You mean the place with the eel tanks?"

"Is that yucky too?" I said. "I mean, I can try to wangle us a table for the Cotillion at the Myopia Hunt Club, but how soon do you want this stuff?"

"ASAP," she said. "I'm sorry. The Chinese place is fine. What time can we meet?"

We settled on five. I told her I'd be the guy eating sweet 'n' sour eel. She said yucky, but she was kidding, I think.

I TRIED to appear nonchalant as I sauntered into the Government Center post office to see if anything had turned up in the afternoon delivery. I'd have preferred to use Bruce again, but his rates were too steep, and I was going to have to check twice a day until whatever it was arrived, if it ever did arrive. But it was another wasted trip—Box 3889 was still empty, not even a pitch from the Jimmy Fund or the Home for Little Wanderers.

I drove home, trying to imagine a line of banter to impress Katy. How many years older than her was I—couldn't be more than twelve. As soon as I got home, I was planning to Google her and then run her name through peoplefinders.com, to learn what I could about her. Just a little mild fantasizing on the Internet, that was my plan. But as soon as I opened the front door, the phone rang, and that was the end of my daydream, because it was good old Marty on the other end of the line.

"I haven't got it, okay?" I said.

"That is not the answer they are looking for," he said.

"Well, it's the only one I got."

"You don't want to have to tell them that to their faces, believe me." He sounded nervous.

"If I haven't got anything," I said, "there's nothing I can give them."

"Well, you better find something then." *Click.*

I guess I had my marching orders. I needed to be making what is generally known as a good-faith effort, as if Knocko and Tony Miami were men of good faith. I had to give it the old college try, at least for a couple of hours, until my "date" with Katy.

For some reason it feels more like I'm working if I make calls from my kitchen rather than the living room. The kitchen table seems almost like a desk. So I sat down with a legal pad, a couple of pens, and a cell phone and began calling everyone who might know anything about the friends of Bucky Bennett.

The first guy I phoned was one of the old mayor's precinct captains with whom I'd worked at City Hall. He knew plenty of guys in Charlestown, and although he wasn't exactly brimming with good cheer, he did refer me to another ex-Boston cop who, like me, had gone out on disability. This ex-cop kept telling me how he'd "really took" a heart attack, as if to distance himself from me, in case the call was being taped. He was another one who apparently hadn't gotten the memo about this being a two-party state.

Finally, after much cajoling, the ex-cop mentioned that Bucky was known to hang on occasion with a guy named Pigeon. An interesting moniker—Pigeon. I pressed him on where I might find Pigeon, but all he could cough up was the name of a bookie in Magoun Square, Somerville.

The bookie in Magoun Square referred me to a guy in a fish-processing plant on Northern Avenue on the waterfront, who told me to call Pigeon's cocaine dealer, who hung out at a bar on Fifth Street in Chelsea. It was at that this point that I began identifying myself as Captain Evans of the BPD—that is, Plain View. Whenever I'm impersonating a cop—technically, a felony, although I don't recall anyone ever being prosecuted for it—I always give the right name and the wrong rank. That way, on the off chance that the guy you're talking to someday ends up on the witness stand, your lawyer can impeach his faulty memory. If he can't remember an officer's correct rank, ladies and gentlemen of the jury, how long are the odds that he can recall the details of what he claims my client was allegedly saying to him all these months ago?

It wasn't likely to come to that, but better safe than sorry is another one of those hackneyed sayings to live by. Anyway, my pitch, or should I say Plain View's, was that I was looking for some information on Bucky Bennett's associates.

The coke dealer steered Plain View—I mean, me—to a Laborers Union business agent in Maverick Square who put me in touch with a guy who ran a bar for Tony Miami in Roslindale Square (although I figured this guy had already been, how shall I put this, debriefed). Since I was now claiming to be a cop, the guy in Roslindale Square felt compelled to tell me that, as far as he could tell, Pigeon had flown the coop, but, not for nothing, I should maybe call an old-timer named Bruno from Lowell, who might know different. So I called Bruno, who sounded like he was about eighty years old. He immediately lost interest in Pigeon and began telling me a story about how he'd once bumped into Joe Barboza, the old hit man, "back in sixty-five" when he was stalking Stevie Hughes, or maybe it was Connie Hughes. I can't remember, and I don't think Bruno could either.

About the third time Bruno punctuated his interminable tale

by saying "come to find out," I realized that the coke dealer had given me a swerve. Bruno from Lowell was softer than a sneaker full of baby shit.

"Who'd you say you was again?" Bruno asked me.

"Captain Evans, BPD," I said. "Thank you very much for your cooperation, sir."

"Who wants to know?" he said.

"Bucky Bennett," I said.

"You mean that mook that hangs over the Four Brothers on East Broadway?"

"In Somerville?"

"I ain't talking 'bout Guys 'n' Dolls, bub. Who'd you say you was again?"

"The Four Brothers?" I said, ignoring his question, which he'd probably already forgotten. "That name rings a bell."

"It would, if you was any kind of a cop, which I'm beginning to doubt you are."

"Four Brothers? Didn't the organized crime squad padlock that dive?"

"They did," he said. "But then one of the brothers got hit, and they reopened it. Come to find out, City Hall felt sorry for them, especially once the aldermen got taken care of, you follow me? Now it's the Three Brothers Cafe."

"So you saw Bucky there?" I asked, just to confirm that I could finally get off the phone with Bruno from Lowell.

"Not Bucky, you stupid flatfoot," he said. "Bucky's dead. It was on TV. I seen his pal, Pigeon. Bucky's friend. I seen him there yesterday."

Yesterday? What was yesterday to Bruno?

"Yeah, I seen him," he said. "He tells me Phil Waggenheim is after him."

Phil Waggenheim used to work as a strong-arm for In

Town—the Mafia. If he were alive today, which I was positive he wasn't, he'd be at least ninety.

"His name is Pigeon," Bruno said.

"I thought his name was Waggenheim," I said.

"Not Phil, Pigeon," he yelled. "Cripes, who'd you have to pay off to get to be a captain, Captain?"

Two hours of legwork, and I was talking to a guy who belonged in Marion Manor. He was the nearest thing I had to a lead.

"Pigeon is a friend of Bucky's?" I asked.

"Was—was a friend of Bucky's. How many times do I gotta tell you? Bucky's dead. I seen it in the *American* yesterday, front page. Pigeon's scared now too. Thinks he's next. Got the twitch back, like he always does right before they lower the boom on him. Who'd you say you was again?"

I figured that was my cue to say good-bye to Bruno. If Bucky had been hanging out in Somerville, then I was going to have to take a ride over there. It was a very long shot, but I needed something to tell Tony Miami, even if only for Marty's sake. It was the least I could do for Ma.

But before I drove to Somerville, first I had to meet Katy across from Foley's.

Chapter Ten

I GOT TO the Chinese restaurant first. I ordered a tea and sat down by myself in the corner where I could check out the eels swimming aimlessly around the tank. They had a second tank as well, teeming with fish of some sort, probably carp, but it was the eels everyone remembered. Everyone who wasn't Chinese, anyway.

About five minutes after I arrived, Katy blew in. She was wearing a pants suit, and damn, did she look good. The counterman was so impressed he forgot to address her in Mandarin to put her in her place. She waved over at me and asked if I wanted anything, and when I shook my head, she bought herself a cup of tea and then walked over. As she sat down, she put her cell phone on the table.

"I haven't been here for years," she said, looking around. "I came here for lunch the first day I went to work at the paper. The city editor took me out for lunch here. Then he came on to me."

I wasn't certain how I was supposed to react to that so I nodded noncommittally. She looked at me and frowned, and I had a feeling about her next question. There was only one thing anyone noticed on my face these days.

"I know it's impolite to bring this up, but how did you cut yourself under your chin?"

"I was shaving," I said, and she laughed.

"What were you shaving with—a bayonet?"

Busted again. This date of mine wasn't exactly getting off to an auspicious start, so I decided to shift back to business. I pushed a folded-up *Herald* across the table toward her.

"It's all in there," I said.

"It better be," she said, opening the paper and glancing at the arrest reports. "I called the senator's office two hours ago and told this week's flack that I had everything."

"You ran a bluff on them?"

"It was no bluff," she said. "You said you had everything, and you've never lied to me."

Was she giving me a compliment? Again, I wasn't quite sure how to respond. After a few seconds of contemplation, I decided to take it as a compliment. Katy trusted me. I smiled and nodded and waited for her to begin reading the reports. But she didn't pick up anything. She just looked at me with what appeared to be genuine curiosity.

"You know," she said, "I was just starting out at the paper when you were, umm, leaving City Hall. But from what I'm told, you were a regular jack of all trades."

"Hack of all trades is more like it."

"I know you were the mayor's boss in Ward 3 for a while, and I know you had an office at the State House where you took care of all the little things for the reps—"

"Tickets, mostly," I said. "Playoffs and parking. That, and girlfriends. If they couldn't get her on up there at the State House, then we could usually work something out at City Hall, if their boyfriends were high enough up in leadership or at least tight with the Speaker."

"So what happened to you?" she said. "I don't mean to rub it in, but you must know the Jack Reilly storyline. Champ to chump, penthouse to outhouse—"

"Didn't you read the clips on me before you wrote that story about Bucky the other night?" I said.

"I did," she said. "And I was wondering, how does a cop from the South End—an Irish cop—get to be the ward boss in the North End?"

"It's the same ward—"

"Yeah, but—"

"I know a lot of people in the North End."

"Like Tony Miami?"

That brought me up short once more. Did she know something? I would have to feel my way along to see if she was on to that part of the story. "Sure, I know Tony. My brother, well, you know about him. But Tony's not from the North End. He's from Roxbury. And he's never really gotten along that well with In Town. He's with . . . the other guys."

"How do you know?"

"I read it in your newspaper," I said, smiling. I briefly considered mentioning my Italian mother, but decided against it. I didn't have to explain anything to her. Katy was studying me closely, sizing me up, not as a boyfriend but as a source.

"Who do you think set up Bucky for the two guys?" she asked.

"I have no idea, but if what you're really asking me is did I set him up, the answer is absolutely not."

"That's not what I was asking, but— Oh, never mind."

At least she was taking an interest in me, although I suspected it was more along the lines of an anthropological inquiry. Dr.

Margaret Mead Bemis, among the primitives, or maybe even the primates. If she knew I'd sat down with Tony Miami at Foley's, then I'd seriously underestimated her abilities as a reporter.

"Can I ask you about what happened at City Hall?" she asked, and I shrugged. It's ancient history now, and I've explained it to everyone else, or tried to.

"I mean, I've heard all the stories," she said. "But everybody who was there at City Hall then is gone. I never talked to anybody who was inside at the time."

"Pretty simple story," I said. "We're off the record here, right?"

She nodded. I know, you're never really off the record with a reporter, but what could she do with this stuff now, it was so old.

"Basically," I said, "the feds wanted the mayor bad, but to get the ball rolling, they had to flip somebody high enough in the organization who knew where the bodies were buried. So how do you get somebody to roll? You know this part of it. You set somebody up to take a fall, and then you give him an out—the option of going before the grand jury or maybe even wearing a wire. I was the perfect candidate for a sting. I was inside, had been for years. I knew everything, they had me on tape, so they wanted to flip me. They figured I could lead them right to the mayor."

"So that's why you had Danny Goodis as your lawyer? The mayor gave you his own lawyer because he couldn't afford to have you go down."

"I was never going down, despite what was said at the time. Look, I don't know how much you want to know—"

"I want to know everything," she said. "Tell me. All I remember is, the feds wired some cop who wanted a promotion, and sent him down to Doyle's to meet you, and they got you on tape telling him what he'd have to do, money, payoffs, that kind of thing. Right?"

I listened impassively. At least she knew the difference

between Foley's and Doyle's. Doyle's is in Jamaica Plain, used to be under the old elevated Orange Line, but these days it's more of a hangout for the Beautiful People. What happened there turned out to be the key event in my life, at least so far.

"Listen to me," I said. "I never said anything on that wire that could even be construed as illegal. Like you said, this guy, this drunk, wanted a promotion. I told him I couldn't take cash, it's gotta be checks, made out to the campaign committee. It's not illegal to take a check, as long as it's not over five hundred bucks. And all I told him was we'd try—try—to do the right thing by him. I also explained to him he'd have to take the exam if he wanted a permanent promotion, that anything we gave him—if we gave it to him—would be provisional, meaning the next mayor could take it away."

From her expression, I could tell Katy wasn't interested in the minutiae of the civil service system. She was more interested in politics than cops.

"You could have brought the mayor down," she said.

"That's what everybody said. I'm not so sure myself. Maybe he wasn't as dirty as everyone made him out to be."

"Do you ever talk to him?"

"Never." Maybe after the statute of limitations runs out in another eighteen months or so, but even then, I doubt it. Not that I would ever tell her that, or anyone else. She looked directly at me and said:

"And this is what you do now? You peddle dirt?"

"'Peddle dirt'?" I said. "You ask me if I've got anything, I tell you I do, and believe me, there's plenty more where this came from, but now you're acting like you don't want to soil your hands with it. If you don't want it, there's other people who do."

I reached for the folded *Herald,* but she put her hand over mine. It felt good.

"I'm sorry," she said, using her other hand to pull the paper closer to her. She flipped it open, removed the top police report, and began reading it. After a few seconds, she looked up from it; a wide grin on her face.

"This is beautiful," she said. "He told the hooker he was going to be working in the White House? Do you know how much he makes?"

"About one ten."

She looked up. "How would you know that— Oh, wait a second. I know exactly how you'd know that. Somebody wants his job, and they knew about this, so you got the . . . what do you call it? An assignment? Or a contract?"

I ignored that. "You're going to need some kind of official confirmation from the police department out there, right? I'm pretty sure the police chief will confirm everything for you."

"How sure are you?"

"Would you like his direct line?" I said. "How about his cell phone?"

She smiled again. "You know some old guy called me this morning at the paper after reading my story about the strip joint. The guy sounded Italian, old North End, and he asked me, how come I didn't put in the story that Sal DiGrazia used to be one of Jack Reilly's precinct captains? He whispered your name, the way Southie wiseguys do with Knocko."

She was staring at me. She wanted an answer about my association with the state rep Sal DiGrazia.

"Did Sal work for you?" she said, and I thought for a moment. There was no point in lying. What did I have to be ashamed of, unless she knew Sal better than I thought she did?

"Did Sal work for you?"

"Yeah, Sal was my guy," I said. "I plead guilty. You know Ward Three, it's, like, four different worlds—North End, Chinatown,

Waterfront, South End. I'm South End, he's North End. I inherited him when I took over as ward coordinator." The mayor always insisted we call ourselves ward coordinators. Ward boss sounded so . . . machine.

"How long were you the ward boss?" Katy asked.

"Only a few months, until I . . . left. See, what happened was, the guy who was the ward boss—this was probably before your time—he was from the North End. Back then the two precincts in the North End probably had over half the voters in the ward. It's changed now, in more ways than one. Anyway, the guy who was running this ward for the mayor—my ward, Ward Three—they had him stashed in a no-show at Public Works. He went down on a mail fraud rap. He finagled a UDAG grant, forged a bunch of documents, and used the dough to put in a pool in his backyard— must have been the only private pool in the North End. But he made a fatal mistake—he didn't invite any of the neighbors over, so they dimed him out. See, he'd been bragging how he stole the money, and then he didn't cut them in on the score. Not too bright."

I watched her, and God did she look fine. Only a minimum of makeup, but she didn't need even that. Her eyes were gray-green, and they were twinkling. She put her chin on her right hand and leaned forward.

"Do you know anyone who isn't crooked?"

I was trying to think of a snappy comeback for that, but just then, her cell phone rang. She picked it up and I could hear her end of the conversation:

"Oh, Senator, thanks for getting back to me. . . ." She reached into her purse and came up with a pen and a steno pad. "He's resigned? . . . Wants to spend more time with his family. . . . Have you seen the actual police report? . . . Let me read part of it to you. . . . The common nightwalker said he asked her, and this is a quote, 'How much for a blowjob?' and when she responded thirty dollars, he showed her a badge and said, 'How about a discount? I work for the next president of the United States. . . .'"

I stood up, took out one of my business cards, and then jotted the chief's cell phone number on the back of it. By now, she was deep into the interview, and it wasn't easy to make eye contact with her. She was in another dimension with excitement, but finally she glanced over at me and told the senator to hold on. She cupped her hand over the receiver, smiled brightly, and said, "I'll call you tomorrow. Thanks."

Walking past the eel tank, I tried to look on the bright side. The good news was, I'd just made a thousand dollars. The bad news was, I should have charged two grand.

Chapter Eleven

THE THREE BROTHERS Cafe was in a nondescript two-story building about a half mile over the Charlestown line, which is Boston. East Somerville has changed, as they say, over the past ten years. There's now a heavy Brazilian presence—restaurants, travel agencies, cash wiring outfits, all of them flying the Brazilian flag out front on East Broadway.

I parked the Olds in a legal space on the south side of Broadway, the Charlestown-bound side. If something happened, I didn't want to have to drive west, past the McGrath-O'Brien Highway and up Winter Hill. That was terra incognita to me. I needed a quick way to get over the line back into God's country—the City of Boston, Ward 2.

The name on the liquor license at Somerville City Hall may have been changed to Three Brothers, but the fourth sibling survived in the neon sign above the door. In the front window was a clock advertising Holihan Ale, which had gone out of business around 1970. I was still packing the Beretta in the shoulder holster under my coat, just to be on the safe side.

But really, what trouble could I get into at dusk in East Somerville?

I opened the barroom door and stood in the entrance, trying to adjust my eyes to the darkness. Foley's, Longo's, Jiggs's joint in Central Square, Wimpy's Lounge, now the Three Brothers—I was really on the Michelin tour of world-class Boston barrooms this week, and all I had to show for it so far were some ugly bruises and a nasty gash on my chin.

Most gin mills like the Three or Four Brothers usually come equipped with one or two toothless tigers hunched over at the bar, old men in their seventies drinking up their Social Security checks on musties—Pickwick Ale and, in the old days, Narragansett. Dimeys, they used to call them when I was a kid, a long time ago.

Most nights, the old farts would be yapping about events that happened way back when. Like the night in '52 when Tip O'Neill stole his first election to Congress from Mike LoPresti, or the time in '65 when Buddy McLean got picked off by Stevie Hughes with an automatic rifle as Buddy and his guinea bodyguards strutted out of Pal Joey's, or maybe it was the Peppermint Lounge they were calling it that year. . . .

If you're sitting on the stool next to them, you're wishing the old-timers would call it a night and go home. But this evening it would have been nice to have a couple of bystanders on hand. Alas, their Social Security checks apparently hadn't arrived yet. The geriatric fixtures at the Three or Four Brothers had run out of drinking money and wouldn't be back until the eagle shit, as we used to say at Fort Bragg.

Behind the bar I saw a guy about my age who looked like he

lifted weights. He had a thick mane of slicked-back black hair and was wearing an apron. I liked that apron—it meant he was a pro. Bartender, that is. Whatever else he was a professional at, I didn't want to find out.

Sitting across from him at the bar were two younger guys, smoking cigarettes. Somerville must be another one of those places keeping the health Nazis at bay. One of them wore a scally cap and in front of him on the bar was a set of brass knuckles, in addition to the shot glass and the beer chaser—the proverbial beer and a ball. I guessed enforcer—pardon me, associate business agent—for one of the mobbed-up local unions, teamsters, most likely. The brass knuckles indicated he was on his way to a general membership meeting of the International Brotherhood.

The third guy, sitting farthest away from me, leaned forward and stared past the brass knuckles on the bar to check me out.

As he looked me over, I did the same to him, and what I saw was a large scar across his neck. These guys over here don't use knives, so the cut could only mean one thing—prison. He was in his late thirties, with a shaved head.

The thought occurred to me that discretion is indeed the better part of valor, and that I should just turn on my heel and beat feet back to my car. These were not Bucky Bennett friends, these were Bucky hunters, and I'd already used at least two or three of my own nine lives.

"Yeah?" said the bartender. If this were Foley's now would be the moment to spring for a round. But in East Somerville, a stranger offering to buy a round is considered an egregious breach of etiquette, an affront to common decency. Unless you've been okayed first by a friend of theirs, you're assumed to be a cop. Make a wrong move, and you don't get a beer, you get a beer and a beating.

I glanced back at the front door. It was close, no more than ten feet away. And I was armed. What the hell, I decided to try to shoot the moon.

"I'm looking for a guy named Pigeon," I said.

"Pigeon?" said the guy with the brass knuckles. "That's a funny name for a guy. Is he?"

"Is he what?" I said.

"A pigeon. You know, a rat."

"I wouldn't know," I said, over the guffaws of my fellow barflies. "Look, I think I got some bad information here."

"No, you didn't," said the bartender. "Not at all. Matter of fact, he's expected. Pigeon always stops by here, this time of night. Ain't that right, guys?"

I was suddenly in a bad B movie. The two closest to me shifted their weight ominously on their stools.

"Take a load off, pal," the bartender said, continuing his run of film noir patter. "You can wait here with us. What'll it be?"

"You know what?" I said. "I think I got the wrong address here. I should be in Ball Square. Have a nice day."

I turned and decided to make a run for it. Once I got onto Broadway, I would be safe. I was a mere ten feet from safety, a quick dash. And then I saw him—another huge thug had silently entered the bar behind me, and now he stood directly between me and the door, blocking my escape. He had to be six four, 260, in a scally cap and a windbreaker with the initials MCCA—Mass. Convention Center Authority. In other words, he belonged to the Speaker, or to a friend thereof. He held a rolled-up *Herald* in his left hand, and it was obvious the paper was covering something heavy, and hard. It was also clear that he wanted to hit me with whatever it was.

A voice behind me yelled, "Hey, Tommy, he's looking for Pigeon."

The hulking thug, Tommy I presume, smiled and said to me, "I think that can be arranged."

"Excuse me," I said, reaching into my coat for the Beretta while simultaneously trying to step around him. But Tommy moved in front of me. The door was still blocked. Out of the corner of my eye I saw him waving his right hand and then I realized that he was actually dangling what appeared to be a hundred-dollar bill in front of me.

"What's the rush?" Tommy said. "Didn't you hear—the first shot's on the house."

And after that you have to use your own bullets. It was an old joke. Now he moved to the right, so I shuffled to the left. He did the same. I kept my eye on the bill—it had to be some kind of trick. Behind me I could hear barstools squeaking. The others were coming after me from behind. I felt them closing in. Too bad I hadn't been wearing a better-fitting coat, because they might not have made a move if they'd known I was carrying. Or maybe it wouldn't have mattered. I drew my gun and pointed it at Tommy.

"I'm a cop!" I yelled. "Police! Freeze! You're all under arrest!"

Behind me I heard somebody mutter, "Bullshit." Then the two from the back grabbed me, pinning my right arm, and the gun, against my body. They just missed grabbing my left arm, which I was trying to keep in front of my face. From behind the tap, the bartender yelled, "Hit him one, Tommy."

Tommy raised the newspaper, as I kept flailing at him with my free left arm, trying to deflect the blow, but he was a lefty, and he hit me square on the right side of my head, just above the ear. It hurt like a bastard. I dropped the Beretta onto the floor, but the blow didn't put me under. The second one did.

"IT'S PROBABLY a concussion, Captain. He should be okay but we need to get him to the hospital for some X-rays."

That was the first thing I heard after I got a whiff of the smelling salts. I was lying on my back in something that was both sticky and gritty, and I wondered for a moment where I was. Then I remembered. This was not a dream, and I would not awaken in my own bed to the mellow sounds of the all-night jazz radio station.

"Hey, Jack, a little far from home, aren't you?" It was Plain View. I opened my eyes and looked up. I didn't feel up to saying anything as Plain View scratched his chin.

"I'll bet your head hurts like a sonuvabitch."

I looked straight up and saw him casually turn to the guy standing next to him in plainclothes.

"He's a fucking Timex, Jack is," Plain View said. "Takes a licking, keeps on ticking."

Then I noticed a guy in uniform, but no gun—an EMT. The other guy with Plain View looked about fifty-five, with a large gut hanging over his belt. Cheap suit, unpressed pants, and his shoes—who knew they still made Hush Puppies? He had to be a cop, but I didn't recognize him. A cop that old, I should have known. Everything was very confusing.

The fat cop said to the EMT, "Give us a couple of minutes with him, and then he's all yours."

I tried to prop myself up on the floor, but that just made them all step forward to push me back down. I know, they were concerned about possible concussions and broken bones and all that standard EMT 101 stuff. Then I realized that I was in Somerville. No wonder I didn't recognize the cop. But that raised another question: What was Plain View doing here, outside the city? With my head throbbing the way it was, it took a few extra seconds to put my words together, but finally I asked Plain View how he happened to be in Somerville.

"You finally noticed, huh?" He glanced over at the other cop.

"He can't be that bad off if he remembers where he is." He glanced over at the other guy again and then back at me, on the floor.

"Pardon my manners," he said. "Jack Reilly, this is Lieutenant Steve Marini, Somerville PD. Steve, Jack."

I managed a pleased-to-meetcha and then, still woozy, I inquired again if I could sit up. Marini and Plain View both shook their heads.

"What happened?" I said.

"We were hoping maybe you could tell us," said Marini.

"I was looking for somebody."

"The guy with the lead pipe who hit you upside the head?" Marini asked.

"Him, I wasn't looking for," I said, slowly, feeling the pain more now. "I was looking for another guy."

The Somerville cop nodded and said, "A guy by the name of Pignarole, by any chance."

"I don't know," I said, and Marini glanced over at Plain View.

"He might not even know his real name, but I guarantee you he was looking for the same guy we were," Plain View said, as if I wasn't even there and I certainly wasn't—all there, that is. The Somerville cop asked me to describe everyone who had been in the barroom, and I did the best I could, but nothing clicked with the Somerville cop until I mentioned the guy waving the hundred-dollar bill.

"Tommy Nickerson—Tommy Nick, they call him," Lieutenant Marini said to Plain View. "That's his MO." Marini looked down at me. "You were lucky. Usually, instead of a lead pipe, Tommy Nick's carrying one of those old longshoreman's hooks. He waves the C-note, drops it to get your attention, and when you're bending over to grab it he buries the hook in your back. So it could have been worse."

I touched a hand to my throbbing head. Somehow I didn't feel very lucky.

"I don't think I'd be able to identify him, though," I quickly put on the record.

"Of course you wouldn't," said Plain View.

"Are you sure you're not from Somerville?" said Marini with a smile. He turned to Plain View. "I think he's going native on us."

From the back of the bar I heard another voice.

"Hey, Lieutenant, I think we got something here."

Marini excused himself and headed off toward the back of the bar, leaving me alone with Plain View. I was still lying dazed on the floor, with him towering over me. Being in such a prone position made me uncomfortable, so I tried to sit up again and this time he didn't stop me.

"You're lucky to be alive," Plain View said. "We don't show up at the exact moment we do, you could be with Bucky and Suitcase and Pigeon. They were lining you up for a dental procedure."

"These guys? These guys were ham-and-eggers."

"Yeah," he said. "But they know some guys."

"What happened?" I asked Plain View.

"Do you mean why am I here, outside the city?"

I nodded, but said nothing, to conserve what little strength I had left. Now my stomach was churning.

Plain View said, "I was trying to find him for the same reason you were, namely, to ask him some questions about Bucky, et al. Unlike you, though, I have to pick up an escort from the Somerville PD before I can roust the place. So we get here just behind you and we try to open the door, but it's locked, which seems wrong, this time of night, so we knock, and that's when we hear 'em taking off."

I noticed that the front window was now broken out, and the

ancient Holihan Ale clock lay in pieces next to it. Too bad about the clock—it might have generated some decent bids on eBay. Once they took me down, they must have bolted the front door. The cops had quickly realized they couldn't batter it in, so Plain View and Marini and a few other Somerville cops had climbed in through the front window after breaking it.

"They got away?" I asked.

"Of course they got away," Plain View said. "This is Somerville. Nobody saw nothing, including you. The bad guys always get away in Somerville."

"Where's my gun?" I said.

"You had a gun and they still did this to you?"

"I've lost a step, I guess."

"More than one, I'd say, if you include your shaving accident," he said. "The way things are going, maybe you oughta think about spending less time in bars and more time in the Christian Science Reading Room." He paused. "You want I should tell Lieutenant Marini about the gun?"

"It's registered," I said. "Dammit. My Beretta."

He squatted down beside me. "I don't mean to say I told you so, but . . ."

I ignored that. What response could I make? Tell him four-on-one is Somerville fun. He'd just laugh in my battered, puffy face.

"Who owns the place?" I asked. "I mean, whose name is on the license."

"The ward alderman, Marini tells me." Plain View flashed me a big grin. "Ain't that convenient? And the manager of record is the ward alderman's wife. It's a small world over here in the All-American City."

"She wasn't tending bar here this afternoon. He can put that in the report."

The Somerville lieutenant sauntered back, gave me the quick once-over to make sure I was still breathing, and then turned his attention back to Plain View.

"There's blood on the floor back there, and gasoline," he said. "It looks like they were getting ready to torch the joint." He looked at me. "With you in it, Reilly."

HAVE YOU been in a hospital emergency room lately? If you speak English and appear to be American citizen, you are indeed a stranger in a strange land.

After the EMTs wheeled me in, the young doctor gave me a handful of Percs or some such thing, which were much appreciated. When they asked me to sign for them, I even used my real name. Then they took some X-rays of my head, and an Indian physician came over and tapped me on the knee with a hammer, after which he became the third person in an hour to tell me how lucky I was, and by the way, since they would be needing to send my X-rays somewhere, who was my primary care physician?

Thank God I'm a retired City of Boston employee. I can't imagine what it must be like to have to actually pay for health insurance these days. If I were the average Joe, without the city-paid health plan, I'd just tell them I was illegal. Charge everything to Tio Sam. Just to be on the safe side, give the gringos a false name—they can't call you on it or it's a hate crime. It's all free—for the illegals, that is. As for the rest of us—or should I say, the rest of you—well, have you checked the price of your health insurance lately?

If you're an American citizen, if you don't pay your bills in ninety days, the collection agencies start up with the dunning letters, followed by the nasty phone calls, and finally they haul your ass into small-claims court. If you don't pay, you'll end up with a lien on your house. You won't be able to renew your driver's license. Illegal aliens, of course, don't have driver's licenses. Don't need 'em either, because most cops are under orders to let 'em go. You and me, they'll handcuff us and tow our cars, but illegal aliens don't even get a warning. . . .

I popped another Percocet.

The Indian doctor said he couldn't force me but that he would recommend that I spend the night in the hospital, "for observation." I shook my head no, and the doctor didn't argue, because he had some knifed Guatemalan MS 13 gang member to sew up. Then he wrote me a prescription for two dozen Vicodins, which he warned me were "the party drug of choice in California," as if I didn't know, and as if they weren't here too. I'd have preferred Dilaudids, but any opiate in a storm.

Finally, as I put on my coat, I realized I didn't know quite where I was. I took a deep breath and walked carefully over to the reception desk. I didn't want to appear unsteady on my feet. I told the woman at the desk where my car was parked and asked if it was within walking distance. She took one look at me and told me, in broken English, that she would call a cab if I wished.

No, I said, I did not wish that, at least not immediately. I reached for my cell phone, then realized I'd left it in the glove compartment of my car. I asked the receptionist if she could direct me to a pay phone, if such things still existed. They did, and she did, and I dialed the main number at the Somerville PD. It took about three transfers, but I finally got Lieutenant Marini on the line.

"Is it safe to pick up my car?" I asked.

"It's dark," he said.

"Does that mean no?"

"There is no part of the city of Somerville that is unsafe for any member of any ethnic group, at any hour of the day or night. That's a direct quote from the mayor."

"So the answer is no, it's not safe."

"You tell me when you're leaving the hospital and I'll have a cruiser double-parked on Broadway outside Three Brothers in front of your car," he said. "I'd pick you up at the hospital myself and give you a ride, but that's against regulations."

I understood. Even though I already knew the answer, I politely asked him if they'd had any luck in their investigation.

"Did I talk to the manager of the Three Brothers?" he said. "Is that what you're asking me?"

He was obviously speaking on a recorded line. Cops record everything nowadays, even on normal business lines.

"Does the alderman really own the bar?"

"No," he said. "The alderman's a convicted felon. He can't own a liquor license."

"Gotcha. He oughta treat himself to a pardon next Christmas. I hear the governor's going to be giving out bulk discounts."

"Unfortunately," Marini said, "it was a federal rap."

I felt dizzy again, and leaned up against the wall as I watched a couple of weeping muchachas cha-cha down the hall. I assumed they were coming to visit the stab victim. One of them had a Jennifer Lopez-style ass, only saggier, and the other was about ten months pregnant. They were both crying. Where would they get their crack now?

Marini said, "So I called the 'manager,' and yes, he does bear a certain resemblance to the bartender you saw, but he swears the bar was closed this afternoon, and he's got witnesses who place him at the racetrack—"

"Which one?"

"Does it matter? He's got guys to back him up, or will have, if he needs them. He said Suffolk, but if it turns out Suffolk wasn't open, they'll get some witnesses from Wonderland, not to mention some losing tickets and a parking stub. You know these guys.

You can drive over and ID the other guys if you want to, but you know the drill."

Then he gave me his cell phone number. In the old days if you were a cop and you had something sensitive to discuss, you didn't use the police-band radio, you went to a "landline," a "secure phone." Now you have to use a cell phone for the sneaky stuff. Without a federal court order, it's a felony to listen in on cell phone transmissions. The things you learn in my line of work.

I called him back from the pay phone, after punching in about a thousand numbers on my telephone credit card. This was the type of call that could end up costing me almost as much as a night's stay at the hospital.

Marini answered on the first ring and immediately began speaking.

"I wish I could help you, I really do, but—"

"You don't have to explain anything to me."

"—but I've only got eight months left, and then I'm out."

There was nothing more he could add on that subject, so I decided to change it.

"What about Pigeon?" I said. "You think his body'll ever turn up?"

"If it does, I hope it's at least nine months from now. I mean, someday one of these guys will flip, and we'll find out where they're burying them. I just pray I'm retired to Florida by then, because I can't take the smell, never could. Gotta be six or eight missing just over here. Boston, I can't imagine."

"I'd say close to twenty," I said, and then I remembered how close I'd ended up to being number twenty-one, or maybe I would have counted as Somerville's number nine. I thanked Lieutenant Marini and asked him if he could have the patrol car on East Broadway in ten minutes.

———

WHEN THE cab dropped me off in front of Three Brothers, I walked over to the SPD car and told the uniform I was going to remove something from my glove compartment and keep it in my lap all the way to the Charlestown line, and that I was not talking about my cell phone. I told him that I had a license for this other object I was going to remove, and if he wanted to see it, I would be happy to oblige. He waved me off, which I figured he would, and it was just as well, because I had no such extra piece. As I walked over to my Olds, the cop was picking up his cell phone, and I assume he was calling the local talent to tell them not to try to take me on the way out of town.

Somerville is my second favorite place in the world. My first is everywhere else.

All the way back to the South End I was worrying about a parking space. I really do have to get myself a handicapped placard. When I worked for the mayor, I had those "untraceable" plates like Plain View's—I could park anywhere and not worry about any tickets, because the plates came back registered to no one. Quite a perk, that was. Now the best I could hope for was a placard. Everybody was getting them, it seemed. That's why it was getting harder and harder to find a regular, nonhandicapped space.

I was back on Shawmut Ave. by eight forty-five, and for once I got lucky with a parking space two doors down from my house. When I got inside the door it was just after nine, and the phone was ringing, so I had a pretty good idea who was calling.

"Are you fucking crazy?" Martin T. Reilly said to me. "That was a provocative act, going over to Somerville like that."

"I'm fine," I said. "Thanks for asking."

"You're lucky you're not dead," he said.

"You got nice friends. Did I ever tell you that?"

"What are you, a fucking retard?"

He's in prison, I'm not, but I'm a fucking retard. The only reason I'm over there in the first place is because he tells me if I don't start producing some results, he's going to get shanked. Now I've got a concussion, and he's criticizing my sleuthing techniques. Some guys I know, their brothers set 'em up with no-show state jobs, behind which comes a pension. My brother sets me up to get whacked in Somerville.

"Do you know an ape named Tommy Nick?" I said.

"Tommy Nick?" he said. "The guy with the C-note? He's the one who worked you over?"

"Tell him I owe him one," I said. "Right upside the head."

"What'd you expect, waltzing in there like you own the place. That dump is as bad as the Ace of Hearts."

"Since you're so smart," I said, "maybe you can tell me this. If they snatch me, how do they get what they want?"

"You must have a concussion from that beating Tommy Nick gave you," he said. "They don't kill you until you've told them what they need to know."

"Suppose I don't crack?"

"Suppose you don't crack? You sound like you've already cracked, asking questions like these. When they get through with you, you'll crack all right."

"You got anything else you want to say to me?"

He just hung up.

THE SOMERVILLE sawbones had told me not to mix alcohol with the pills, so I didn't. I just had a few beers, which is not alcohol in my book, it's medicine.

I sat at the kitchen table, my head throbbing worse with every beer I drank, as I oiled another, formerly forgotten throwdown I'd found while rummaging through my old Army steamer trunk. If anybody makes a cheaper gun than the Raven, I've never heard of it.

I must have had it close to ten years. I found it one winter Saturday afternoon in the Hyde Park municipal building after a riot broke out at the Ward 18 Democratic caucus.

Once our cops had cleared the hall, after busting a few heads, some of us went back in to secure the perimeter, and in one corner at the back of the hall I saw it . . . a Raven, a .25 caliber. I looked both ways to make sure no one was watching me, and then I palmed it. The little piece of shit was loaded too, as I found out in the men's room a few minutes later when I took a moment to examine my new toy. I never ran the serial numbers, just stashed it away in the bottom of the steamer trunk, knowing that someday it would come in handy, because a throwdown always does.

Now that day was here.

By ten o'clock, I was in bed, out cold, dreaming of long-ago political brawls in Ward 18 as I brandished a Raven. It was a deep, refreshing sleep.

Chapter Twelve

B Y NOW I had a pretty good idea when the first delivery of the day reached the Government Center post office. At ten thirty I could check, and if it wasn't there today, I figured that whatever it was would probably never arrive—knock on wood.

I was up by eight, but I still felt a little wobbly. So I popped my last two Percocets from Somerville and got a moderate buzz on, although to keep it going I knew I'd need to get over to the CVS over on Traveler and have the Vicodin prescription filled. But for now I felt fine, until I wandered by a mirror and got a good look at my face. My left eye was black and the whole right side of my face was swollen from the bruises. On the plus side, the cut on my chin from Knocko's knife had finally scabbed up.

I swallowed a handful of Vitamin Es and made my way gingerly to the shower. I must have spent fifteen minutes under the hot water. After I dressed, I realized I still had some time to kill, so I called Katy Bemis at the *Herald*. She didn't answer, of course, but a recording informed me that in case of an emergency, I could leave the traditional "numerical message" on her pager. I called the pager and left my cell phone number and even remembered to hit the pound sign to send.

Two minutes later she called me back.

"What'd you think?" she said.

"About what?" I said.

"Haven't you read the paper today?" she said. "I thought that's what you were calling about."

"No, I— What's in it? The senator's guy?"

"Used to be the senator's guy, you mean. He's gone. He resigned to quote pursue other business opportunities unquote."

"Didn't I hear something last night about spending more time with his family?"

"That too. Taking time to smell the roses also figured prominently in his resignation, which the senator accepted with regret."

"And mixed feelings no doubt."

"How did you know?" she said. "Hey listen, it's funny you called—I was just thinking about you. I do appreciate you giving me the tip. It's on the Real Clear Politics home page."

I had no idea what she was talking about, but she certainly seemed pleased she'd made the Web site. Maybe from now on I should charge my clients an extra five hundred if the story I plant for them makes the . . . whatever the Web site's name was.

Katy Bemis said, "I really didn't mean to bust your balls last night."

"Forget about it," I said. I've been called worse, by the U.S. attorney, among others.

"I was on deadline, and I was out on a limb there—I mean, what if you'd been stringing me along?"

"Never happen," I said.

"I think I owe you lunch," she said. "Are you busy today?"

"I think I can you fit you in," I said. "Where do you want to meet?"

"How's the Long Wharf Marriott Legal sound?"

"A tourist trap," I said. "Still don't want to be seen in polite company with me, do you?"

"I hadn't thought of it that way," she said. "But maybe it's not such a bad idea."

"Can I can order the jumbo shrimp cocktail?"

"Five shrimp for fourteen bucks—it's a steal." She laughed. "Listen, after the last two days, you can have the fisherman's platter as far as I'm concerned. It's on me—well, the paper anyway."

I hung up and suddenly I didn't feel nearly as sore. This was practically a date. I didn't need any more Class A controlled substances, I was high on life, well, at least as high as I ever get. If only Bucky Bennett hadn't decided to inject himself into my life I'd be ready to make my move. But then, if Bucky hadn't appeared on the scene, I wouldn't be having lunch with Katy Bemis. I turned on the all-news radio station and heard that today was the big day for Speaker Lynch, with the House "poised," as they put it, to repeal the term-limits rule on the Speaker.

Jiggs would be all in a dither. He would be too busy to call me today, and anyway, he was the last guy I needed to talk to right now.

Outside, it was a sunny day. The radio said it would reach fifty degrees. Warm, but still cool enough to need a coat, a coat that would hide my latest throwdown, the Raven. Hit the street without the equalizer? Quoth the Raven, Nevermore.

At least not for another few days.

I put on the shoulder holster and then decided to wear a newer, tighter-fitting jacket, which theoretically would make me look a bit less destitute when I met Katy for lunch, although the swollen black eye and the bruises Tommy Nick had left on my face didn't exactly enhance my matinee-idol profile.

Maybe if I walked to the Long Wharf I'd at least look a bit ruddier. Plus, I'd save the thirty dollars I'd otherwise have to fork over for a parking space in a waterfront garage.

The morning walk to the post office was uneventful. I trudged through what used to be the Combat Zone. The old red-light district was gone now, overwhelmed by a variety of factors, the most significant of which is the easy accessibility of downloadable porn on the Internet. Thanks for the mammaries, Pilgrim Theater and the Intermission Lounge's All Nude College Girl Revue.

In Downtown Crossing, I glanced at the headless mannequins in the display windows of what used to be Jordan's and was now Macy's, and then walked past an ATM outside a Fleet bank which used to be a BankBoston which used to be a BayBank which used to be a Provident Institute for Savings branch. Am I starting to sound like Jiggs?

I crossed onto City Hall Plaza, a Gobi Desert in summer and a polar icecap in winter, and soon I found myself standing in front of Bucky's post office box in Government Center.

I looked in and saw a postcard. I fumbled with the key but finally got the box open. The postcard directed me to the counter, where I could pick up a package that was too bulky to insert into the box. I silently took my place at the back of a long line.

There were two clerks—one an efficient young guy with light brown hair, and the other a fat fiftysomething guy with a florid face and a bad gray comb-over. The older guy looked like someone who could get in over his head with loan sharks. Let me rephrase that—he looked like a guy who had gotten in over his head with loan sharks.

I was hoping for the young guy, but it was not to be. I handed Combover the postcard and he studied it, then looked up at me with his beady eyes.

"This your box?" he asked.

"I got the key, don't I?"

He pondered that conundrum for an instant. I couldn't cite any exact statutes, but I doubted he could either, so if he decided to raise the issue, I'd have to fall back on that old saw about possession being nine-tenths of the law. To end the debate before it began, I held up the key. He frowned and studied me some more. I suspected the throbbing black-and-blue bruise on the side of my face had not escaped his attention.

"Don't I know you from somewhere?" he said.

"South Bay House of Correction?"

"No," he said, shaking his head. "Were you in the service?"

"First Cav, Iron Triangle, 1968. Kill 'em all and let God sort it out."

"You look kinda young to have been in 'Nam."

"Look, pal, I gotta get moving here. Can you get me that package?"

He gave me a dirty look and shuffled off in the general direction of the back of the room. The young clerk watched him moving, slower than cold molasses, and shook his head before he went back to his next customer. If this was the day Bucky's "marital aids" arrived, I was going to be sorely embarrassed.

Finally Combover returned, still giving me the evil eye, holding in his hand a bulky manila package, taped up all around the sides. I studied the package and saw that it was addressed to Bucky Bennett, in the same handwriting as the note in the bus station locker—namely, Bucky's. The return address was the halfway house in the South End that Bucky had lived in, with, among others, Suitcase O'Malley. Combover had been studying the label on the long walk back to the counter, and apparently nothing had escaped him.

"You ain't Bucky Bennett, are you?"

"I'm a friend of his."

"Didn't he get shot the other day?"

"Couldn't prove it by me," I said, grabbing the package. "I just got back to the world."

Once I got outside the post office, I took out my cell phone. Then I realized Combover was still staring at me through the full-length glass windows, so I moved away from the building. It was still early in the day for Slip—10:50—but I needed a favor. I called his apartment in Roslindale and he answered the phone, sleep heavy in his voice.

"Can I use your office at the Hall?" I said.

"Shit yes," he said, and he didn't say anything more, which was just the response I was looking for. You know the old saying, Friends help you move, good friends help you move bodies. I asked him to call his secretaries at City Hall and tell them that I would be there in five minutes.

"I might need to use the Council copying machine," I said. "Is that okay?"

"It's okay by me," he said. "But you better watch out for Magoo."

Owen "Magoo" Sullivan was the city councilor from South Boston. He and The Man were tight as ticks. As kids, they'd been in different street gangs, but time heals all wounds, especially if the wounded are heels and if the time is accompanied by large amounts of cash. His nickname came from the Coke-bottle glasses he'd always worn. His vision was as bad as Mr. Magoo's, hence the moniker. Magoo had been the president of the Council a few times, including, I'm almost positive, when Knocko was lining the mayor and me up for head shots, if you get my drift.

Anyway, Slip said he'd be right in, but coming from Roslindale, he was at least forty-five minutes away from City Hall, plus before he even got in the car he had to shave and dress.

I tried stuffing the package under my coat, but it was too bulky. So I just carried it in my left hand, keeping my right hand in my coat pocket—after all, nobody knew my piece was under my left armpit. I drew a few stares as I walked into City Hall, but that was to be expected. At City Hall anybody from the old regime is persona non grata until the new mayor says they're not, and I wasn't expecting a commutation any time soon.

Rather than take the elevator, which meant enduring more chilly stares, I walked up the stairs in the center of the lobby to the fifth floor. The mayor's office is on the harbor side, with great views, which is only fitting and proper since he controls 100 percent of the juice in the city. The councilors are shunted off to the less desirable inland side, facing out onto City Hall Plaza and Tremont Street.

I nodded at the Council receptionist, whom I knew from the old days, and headed straight into the labyrinth of Council offices. Then I saw him—Magoo, a little bantam rooster of a guy, tough as hell and a nasty drunk who hadn't touched a drop in twenty years. Slip's office was less than thirty feet away, but Magoo was blocking the way.

"Jack Reilly," he said, extending his hand. "How's da family?"

I smiled wanly and gripped his palm. When he finally let go, he was still blocking the hallway, and he seemed to notice my face for the first time.

"Jesus Christ," he said, "what happened to you?"

"I fell down," I said.

"Anybody I know?" He was smirking.

"I'd love to catch up on old times," I said, "but I gotta meet Slip."

"Slip?" He rolled his eyes. "It's not even noon yet. Slip won't be in for at least an hour."

"I know," I said, stepping around him, "but I've got some business to attend to."

He moved aside to let me pass. "Don't do anything I wouldn't do," Magoo shouted after me.

SLIP'S SECRETARIES had been expecting me, and they ushered me into his office. Once inside, I bolted the door and took off my coat, then removed the Raven and set it down carefully on Slip's desk, within easy reach. Then I sat down at Slip's desk, took a deep breath, and opened the envelope.

It contained two smaller packages, each in a manila envelope. In the first one I found two yellowing, dog-eared old ledger books. On one cover page was scrawled "1974" and on the other "1975," which was the year Inspector Lynch stole it. I didn't even bother to look through that one. I knew generally whose names were in there, and more important, whose weren't—my father's and Uncle Brendan's. Ancient bribes to long-dead cops—interesting stuff to pore over at some point down the road, but not terribly relevant at this moment. I quickly put Wimpy Hogan's ledger books back in their own envelope.

The second package contained two items. First there was an eight-by-fourteen-inch legal pad. The first dozen or so sheets on the pad were covered with initials and numbers. The other item was an old-fashioned savings passbook from, of all places, Cooperative Trust, the little bank in Medford that Bucky and his crew had burglarized.

I flipped through the passbook and saw that the account had most recently shown a balance of $189,982.76, with most of the deposits made in nice round numbers—$8,000, $9,000, $7,500, etc. Every deposit was under ten grand, the threshold at which any transaction must be reported to federal banking regulators. I closed the passbook and then studied the cover. The account belonged to a corporation, Fourth Suffolk, Inc. The Speaker was from Suffolk County, and all the districts in every county are numbered. What number would you suppose the Speaker's district is? I didn't know for sure, but I had a hunch, and I'd have bet a bunch.

Speaking of hunches, I opened the passbook again, and saw that the last deposit had been made two years ago on May 25. Just before Memorial Day weekend. The Memorial Day weekend when Cooperative Trust was robbed. Just as I'd suspected.

My hands were trembling as I put down the bank book. I reached for the legal pad and flipped through page after page of handwritten notes, in different pens, with dates from eight separate years, ending two years ago, in late May.

Once I began studying the writing, it didn't take me long to realize it was basically another, newer ledger, with initials next to numbers. For instance:

FLP, RMV . . . $10,000
RQK, SD . . . $5,000

Lobbyists, no doubt. And if the dates were correct, almost all the payoffs were well within both the state and the federal statute of limitations.

Bingo! I had exactly what Jiggs wanted.

A speaker—this would be my biggest takedown ever. Top o' the world, Ma, top o' the world! I had exactly what I was looking for, so I set the more recent legal pad aside for a moment, picked up the big, outer envelope, and removed the old ledger books. I laid aside the 1975 ledger, which looked relatively unused, and started reading the 1974 records. I went past the familiar names of the crooked cops of my youth and kept turning pages until I found what I was looking for—notations of money flowing in and out of the various Hogan criminal enterprises of Roxbury, the South End, and Dorchester.

Everything was painstakingly recorded—the incoming revenue from the barrooms and one-armed bandits. The figures also included the loanshark money on the street, as well as the daily number, which was known as "nigger pool" because of its popularity in the black neighborhoods. But nigger pool was a huge racket across the entire city, organized crime's biggest money maker in the days before the State Lottery Commission was created to muscle in on the underworld's money machine.

What a treasure trove it must have been for the Speaker's father to come into possession of such damning evidence, especially on all his fellow cops. They'd been on the take, and the Inspector was on the make. Suddenly, instead of getting paid off, all the crooked cops must have themselves been paying off. It must have made the Restroom Regiment racket seem like small potatoes. The Inspector had been lucky no one had capped him, because God knows cops hate to pay for anything, especially protection, which they figure they should be selling, not buying.

I finally laid the old 1974 Hogan ledger to one side on top of the unopened 1975 book and returned to what appeared to be the Speaker's own records. And these were the originals—the records of years of ever-increasing shakedowns, in the Speaker's own hand, as he had moved up through the legislative leadership.

When Bucky had realized that Knocko and Tony Miami were closing in on his little crew two years ago, he must have made copies of the ledgers and then put them back with the rest of the bank loot. Now he was dead, and I had the originals. Who knows why he'd done what he did. He was just a small-timer in way over his head, with maybe some coke or angel dust thrown in to even further distort his already-poor judgment. He was, after all, from Charlestown.

I wondered how Knocko and Tony Miami had discovered what gold they had unearthed. I doubted they'd gone through all the documents—guys like them don't have that kind of patience, or eye. Perhaps Bucky's late cohort Happy Teeth told them, under duress, after Bucky had bragged a little too loudly about what he'd come across. However it went down, it was just another lucky break for Knocko Nugent and Tony Miami. Good things happen to good people.

I heard a tap on the door and I snapped to attention, grabbing the Raven.

"Yeah?" I said. "Who is it?"

"It's me, Slip. How's it going?"

Still sitting at the desk, I yelled, "I'm sorry, Slip." I looked down at my watch and saw that I'd been in his office for almost an hour, reading and rereading the ledgers. Time passes quickly when you're studying incriminating documents.

With the gun still in my hand, I got up and walked around Slip's desk to the door. "Hold on," I said. "I'll be right there."

I walked over to the door, turned the bolt, and opened the door just an inch. Slip did a double take when he saw the gun.

"It's that good?" he said, stepping inside and then closing the door behind him, bolting it once more before the secretaries could see. Then he took a closer look at my face. "I hope it was worth the beating you took."

"Yeah," I said. "It was. It is that good. Bucky was right."

Slip smiled. "I'm not even going to ask what it is, because I don't want to have to deny anything down the road, but now that you've got the goods, what are you going to do with them?"

Good question. The only thing that mattered now was getting the story out, so that Knocko and Tony Miami realized they no longer had proprietary interest in it, and that they therefore had no reason to kill me. Of course, from a "professional" private-eye point of view, my job was to hand off the radioactive material to the guy who'd hired me to find it, namely Jiggs. But getting killed is not included as one of the services that I offer for five hundred dollars a day.

"If I was you," Slip said, "I'd be making copies of whatever I had, for self-preservation, not to mention you'll be needing some extra copies if you're planning on going into the blackmail business yourself."

"No thanks," I said, recalling Bucky Bennett lying in the gutter outside Foley's. "I've never seen a blackmailer come out on top in the end."

"If they do come out on top, then you'd never know it, now would you?"

He had a point.

I walked back around to Slip's desk and picked up the newer legal pad, the Speaker's list of payoffs received. I counted the number of pages of entries—fifteen. I closed my eyes and tried to think how many copies I would need. Slip was watching me, his eyes wide open, a big smile on his face. Something was finally happening at City Hall again. At least for a day or so, it might be almost as exhilarating as busing.

"Can I use the copy machine?" I said. "I need five minutes, tops."

He nodded.

"I'll go with you," he said. "And bring everything with you. Around here, the walls not only got ears, they got hands."

The nearest copy machine was in the Council mailroom, no more than twenty yards down the hall. As soon as Slip and I stepped out of his office, I noticed that from down at the end of the corridor, Magoo was eyeing us.

I looked at Slip and whispered, "Would he call The Man?"

"He'd damn well better," Slip said, "if he wants to keep picking up his envelope at the Ace of Hearts every Christmas."

We walked quickly, and I went straight to the machine. I didn't want to detach the sheets from the pad, which meant it would take a little longer, to turn each one over after I'd run four copies. Then I was also going to have to make copies of the pages in the Cooperative Trust bank book. Slip planted himself in the doorway so that no one else could enter the mailroom.

I was up to page four when I heard Magoo's voice in back of me, at the door.

"Ah, come on, Slip," he said petulantly, "you know the rules. The machine's for the use of the councilors only."

"He's working for me, Magoo. I just hired him. Now screw."

"This is not a friendly gesture," Councilor Sullivan said. "Remember, I'm the councilor from the town that gives you a third of your votes every two years."

"You're right, Magoo," Slip said, as I listened over the noise of the copy machine. "I apologize for not treating you with the proper deference. So let me rephrase my request. Councilor Sullivan, you fucking reprobate you, will you please get the fuck outta here?"

"This ain't right, Slip," Sullivan said. "Friends of mine got an interest in this thing here."

"Friends of yours got an interest in a bar too," Slip was saying, as I Xeroxed, "not to mention a liquor store, neither of which convicted felons are supposed to be hanging in, let alone owning, and The Man's never heard me say boo to the Licensing Board about either one, has he, not even last year after them two project rats from D Street got clipped in the car right across West Broadway from that dive of his."

"Council rules—"

"Council rules my ass," said Slip, and I heard change rattling. "Look, Magoo, you wanna dime me out to the papers, here's a fucking dime." I heard a coin hit the floor. "And if you don't use it to call the papers, stick it up your ass. Now make like a fucking tree and leave."

There was a brief pause, and then I heard Magoo's voice again. "Don't push me, Slip," he said. "I could take you."

"You and how many Marines?"

Then I could hear Magoo Sullivan muttering as he walked off. He wasn't used to being treated that way, except maybe by Knocko. As I closed the lid on page eight, Slip came up behind me and looked over my shoulder.

"Make it snappy," he said. "That was not the curtain call. That was intermission."

"I'll be out of your hair in a minute," I said. "I owe you one, Slip."

"One?" he said. "You owe me a lot more'n one."

"You want a copy of this stuff?" I said.

"Jesus, Mary, and Joseph, no," he said.

Chapter Thirteen

NOW THAT I finally had what the two guys had been looking for, I wasn't going to have much time to off-load it before Magoo Sullivan reported back to the Ace of Hearts.

But no way was I going to skip my lunch with Katy Bemis, not because I had a death wish, but because I'd decided to cut her in on this. If I gave her a set of the ledgers, that would be my insurance policy—one of them, anyway. Because the two guys would never dare snatch a reporter, would they? In Slip's inner office, I stuffed one set of the copies into an oversize envelope. That would be Katy's set. Then I put another set of copies, and the original, into a second envelope. Those I would keep with me. Then I put another set of duplicates into a third envelope, which I sealed.

I thanked Slip, said quick good-byes to his girls, and then headed across the street to the Government Center post office, where I bought twice as many stamps as I needed out of the machine. I addressed the third envelope, put the postage on it, and then dropped it in the chute for B. Bennett at PO Box 3889, Government Center 02114. Maybe Combover would intercept the missive, but probably not. If he got caught, it would cost him his pension. I doubted he'd take the chance, even if he saw the package.

Then I headed east, to the Long Wharf Marriott. Katy Bemis was waiting for me in the lobby at the Legal Sea Foods there. She was wearing leather boots, and a short denim skirt. Over her blouse she wore a tweed business jacket. Her brown hair was pulled back into a ponytail, of all things. She was dressed like a million bucks—a million bucks in a trust fund packed full of tax-free municipal bonds and governed by an ironclad, irrevocable set of codicils that prohibited any of the heirs from ever touching the principal.

There's money, and then there's . . . old money. Katy Bemis was old money. She was dressed preppy, but not I-don't-give-a-damn preppy, a fashion statement more commonly associated with the likes of, say, Michael Skakel, or any of the other third-generation now middle-aged Kennedy riffraff. Katy Bemis was dressed appropriately. She was not unbecoming, as Governor Romney used to say.

As I approached Katy at the restaurant entrance, I wasn't sure how to greet her. Everybody on TV nowadays, from D-list celebs to the president, slobbers on each other with a big wet kiss like they're great pals. But Katy Bemis and I weren't great pals. She was a reporter and I was a source. As I reached her, I extended my hand and she took it perfunctorily, as her eyes trained on something else.

"What's in the envelopes?" she said, and I liked that. Business first, even before mentioning my bruised, puffy face. She wanted to know about the envelopes—if there was something there for her.

"We'll get to that," I said, as the maitre d' guided us to our table, right on the water, prime location, especially at the height of the luncheon rush. Somebody had some pull here, and it wasn't me.

"I know Roger," she said by way of explanation.

"Roger?" I said.

"Roger Berkowitz, the owner," she said.

"Oh," I said. There was an awkward pause, then I said, "I wasn't sure you'd make it, I thought maybe you'd be covering the big vote in the House today."

"You mean on the term limits repeal?" She frowned. "That's a done deal. No suspense there. Besides, they pretty much let me do what I want."

"Does that mean you're like a columnist, only you don't have a column?"

"So you noticed too?" she said, smiling demurely as she motioned the waiter over. It doesn't take much to massage a newspaper reporter's ego. She ordered a glass of chardonnay, and I went for iced tea.

"Are you another one of those recovering Irish drunks?"

"No ma'am," I said. "I'm a practicing Irish drunk."

She grimaced, and then said, "I'm sorry, and I know it's not polite, but I've got to ask. What happened to your face?"

"I fell down."

"You fell down? It looks more like you got pushed—off the Hancock."

"You just asked me if I was a drunk."

"Oh, I get it," she said, nodding. "Did you get a bad ice cube, as they say at Foley's?"

"There you go again," I said.

"Well, I don't believe you fell down, any more than you cut yourself shaving," she said. "I think somebody worked you over—again."

I shrugged, and then she leaned across the table and tapped the left side of my coat. She had spotted the gun.

"I assume you know what you're doing," she said. "I also assume that this is probably connected to the other night at Foley's. Am I right?"

"Are we off the record?" I asked, and she hesitated.

"You're never really off the record with a reporter, are you?" I said.

"No, you're not," she said. "Did you figure that out for yourself, or did you pick that up from some wise political sage somewhere along the line?"

"It amounts to the same thing, doesn't it?" I said. "But to answer your question, it was the mayor—the old mayor—who told me that. He was right."

"So do you want to tell me about the gun?"

"In a while," I said. "First, I'm going to hold you to your promise on the shrimp."

She grinned, and that loosened things up. I went for the jumbo shrimp cocktail, and the fisherman's platter. The whole-bellied fried clams are good, but I like the scallops even more. She ordered a cup of clam chowder and a shrimp Caesar salad.

She said, "I wanted to thank you again for the tips on the two stories."

"My pleasure," I said, not mentioning that I had my reasons, because that was understood.

"Well, I shouldn't be doing this," she said, and right away, just from the way she said it, I knew she'd cleared whatever she was about to tell me with somebody. "But I wanted to tell you, our Probe Team is doing a piece on pensions—"

"And I'm in it?" I said, and then I laughed. "That's your big heads-up for me? I appreciate the thought, Katy, I really do, but that story gets done about every other year, and I'm always in it.

If it's not the newspapers, it's one of the TV stations. Usually during sweeps, May or November. They always run this same grainy video of me walking behind the mayor. I got black hair, and more of it, and I have long sideburns. Disco Jackie, my brother calls me whenever it comes on."

"Is that the brother that's in prison?"

"The same. But how did you know about him that first night at Foley's? Did some wise political sage fill you in, or did you find him when you were running a LexisNexis search on me?"

"You know about LexisNexis?"

"Ah, come on, Katy," I said. "I'm not a caveman. I know how to dig up shit on people, just like you do. I just don't have a trust fund."

"Uh-oh, the traditional Boston ethnic tension rearing its ugly head once more," she said, smiling just a bit. "But listen, tell me about these pensions. It's a city thing, isn't it? I know what they call them in Southie. White man's welfare."

I leaned across the table and looked her in the eyes.

"First thing, I'm not from Southie, okay? You been around long enough to know that. Second thing, my pension is totally legit. Tell your friends they can come after me 'til the cows come home and they won't get shit, because like I told you last night, I was never even indicted, let alone convicted. As for my disability, my mental problems, when it comes down to just two, I ain't no crazier than you."

"David Crosby?" she said.

"Either him or Stephen Stills, I can never keep it straight."

"Whatever, I understand what you're saying," she said. "I know you didn't slip on a patch of ice inside City Hall that nobody else saw."

"Listen, a slip-and-fall is nothing," I said. "I know a guy, he was on the job with me, he's on a domestic call in Hyde Park, routine shit, code brown, he's heading up the walk to the house and somebody rear-ends his cruiser, and he runs back to the car, jumps back inside, and files a claim for whiplash."

"This a guy from District E-18?"

"Who wants to know?" I said, but she wasn't deterred in the least.

"You got a name to go with that story?"

"I do, but not for the newspaper. I gotta live here too."

"So how come you're having lunch with me?"

"Because how else could I get a free meal at Legal Sea Foods." She nodded, and decided to change the subject.

"How long have you lived in the South End?"

"My whole life," I said. "Which means since before it went gay, and if that's what you're asking me, the answer is no, I'm not. Gay, I mean. What I am is divorced, I got two kids. You want to see their pictures?"

"I was just making conversation," she said. "Besides, what does being divorced mean? You must know about—"

She named a big-shot local media type who is divorced and by all reports gay.

"I wouldn't know," I said.

"Because nobody ever hired you to dig up dirt on him, right? I mean, if somebody paid you to find out something, it wouldn't take you long, would it?"

I had to smile at that one. "How long would it take you, if someone made it worth your while? Aren't we pretty much in the same racket, you and me, when you get right down to it?"

"Maybe, but in my case, I'm doing it for the public. They have a right to know."

Right to know? I was instantly disappointed in her for spouting such insipid high-school civics pap. If she believed it, she was stupid. If she didn't believe it but said it anyway, she must have thought I was stupid.

"People don't hire me to assassinate people," she said, taking a sip of her wine.

"You might get an argument on that from the senator's aide with the hooker problem. You got him fired yesterday with one phone call."

At that point the waiter brought our appetizers—lucky for her, because I don't think she had a ready retort. We were doing more eating than talking until our main courses arrived. She looked longingly at my fisherman's platter (fried, not broiled), and asked, "Can I have a scallop?"

"Go ahead," I said. "Take 'em all."

"Are you sure?"

"I can take 'em or leave 'em," I lied. "Go ahead."

There were only four or five of them to begin with, but she took me at my word. What the hell. The things you do for . . . lust. We passed on dessert, ordered coffee, and then she fixed me with those gray-green eyes.

"So if you won't talk about the gun," she said, "then tell me what's in those envelopes you're carrying."

"How about if I tell you you can have one of the envelopes, if you'll keep it under wraps until tomorrow," I said.

"Are there any other strings attached?"

"Just don't take a peek. Is that too much to ask?"

"Depends on what it is. Then I can tell you if I can restrain myself."

"If I tell you, you won't be able to restrain yourself. Nothing against you personally—it's just too good."

"What's in it for me?"

"You get it first when it's time."

"When is it time?"

"When I say it's time."

"When is it going to be time?"

"Tomorrow, I should think." After the House vote on term limits.

"And what do you get in return?" she said.

"What do you think I want in return?"

"I think you want to get in my pants."

"I thought you thought I was gay."

"I changed my mind."

I reached down under my chair and brought up the envelope in which I'd placed copies of all the pages from the legal pad, in addition to Xeroxed copies of the bank book from Cooperative Trust. In my haste to escape Councilor Sullivan, I'd used an envelope with the city seal and the return address of the Boston City Council. I handed it to her and her eyebrows arched.

"I know," I said. "It's a city envelope. Call the FinCom. Take it out of my pension check."

She held the envelope up and said, "Does this have something to do with the gun?"

"Maybe," I said, "and I wouldn't be waving that thing around like that, if I was you."

"Suppose something happens to you," she said, matter-of-factly.

"Supposing it does," I said, "that frees you right up. You can run with it—as a matter of fact, I'd advise you to do exactly that, ASAP."

"Or something might happen to me, is that what you're saying?"

I shrugged. *"Que sera, sera."*

"How will I know what it is, if you're not around?" she said.

"First of all, I'll be around, more'n likely," I said. "But if I'm not, believe me, you'll be able to figure out what's in there. If you can't put two and two together on this, you'll never get that column. And if you do have any questions, call Slip."

She instantly frowned. "Slip Crowley hates me, in case you haven't noticed. His mother worked for my grandfather on Beacon Hill as a scullery maid, or so he claims. He told me once my grandfather made his mother scrub floors on her knees in Louisburg Square because he was too cheap to buy a mop for her."

"Well?"

"Well what?"

"Well, is it true? Did your grandfather really do that to Slip's mother?"

"How do I know—this would have all been back just after World War Two, if it happened at all, which I very much doubt, by the way," she said. "All the time I was at City Hall the only nice thing he ever said to me was that I was the only quote-unquote Yankee broad he'd ever seen who didn't have a flat ass. If you consider that nice."

I suppressed a smile and decided to get back to the topic at hand.

"What I would do with this envelope, if I was you, I would put it somewhere safe, under lock and key, and then I would forget about it until you get a call from me, or until—"

"Your picture turns up on a milk carton."

"You got a way with words," I said. "So, have we got a deal?"

She stuck out her hand, which I'd already noticed wasn't as dainty as it might have been. It was tennis that had strengthened her grip, would be my guess. We shook across the table.

"Really, though," she said, "they are coming after you on the pension."

"Every knock a boost," I said. "That's what Curley always said."

"Are you another one of these Irish hacks who's always quoting James Michael Curley?"

"Half Irish," I said. "Get your facts straight."

KATY BEMIS and I parted ways outside the hotel. I didn't ask her where she was going, because that would have been prying. I hoped she was headed for her safe-deposit box, the way I was headed for mine, but I didn't know, didn't want to know, for that matter. I watched her take off on foot toward the North End. I wanted to confirm, just for myself, that Slip was right about her ass, and I did. He was. After that I kept on watching, just because I could.

Finally, I walked over to 60 State Street, the building with the big bank on the ground floor, where I've had a safe-deposit box ever since I started working at City Hall. It took about five minutes to stuff the Speaker's original documents inside, on top of my buffalo nickel collection from when I was a kid, what Marty hadn't stolen from me anyway to buy coke down at the Waltham Tavern. I tore out a couple of pages of Wimpy's ledger book—what the hell, the statute of limitations had long since expired on those crimes— and I also took one Xeroxed set of the Speaker's records with me.

Jiggs said to do nothing until after the vote, and I planned to follow instructions. My plan was not to return home until tomorrow, after I'd dumped everything in Jiggs's lap. If they tried to grab me in a hotel in the meantime, well, that's why I was packing the Raven. For the present, I figured I might as well make a few bucks on another job I'd been neglecting. So I hoofed it over to Causeway Street and walked into the Tip O'Neill federal building. That's the location of the U.S. Bankruptcy Court, an occasionally important destination if you're a lawyer, a creditor, or, like me, a titan in the excrement industry.

I had an assignment—a state rep wanted copies of the recent Chapter 11 filing of a local selectman who had been making noise about taking on my dear friend, the incumbent. The filings are public, and I have yet to see a bankruptcy case folder that didn't include at least one or two humiliating pieces of information.

The rep could have sent his aide down, but odds are, he'd have left some fingerprints somewhere along the line. But not me—if the selectman later tried to try to identify who had whacked him, the only name he'd find as having perused his bankruptcy records was one Kevin Hicks, of Malden. I had decided to borrow his name a few years back because he was born in Boston, two days after me. It was simple to get a notarized copy of his birth certificate at City Hall, and once I had the birth certificate, it didn't take long to get both a Social Security number and a driver's license.

"Here you go, Mr. Hicks," said the clerk, handing me back the license. "The copy machine's right over there, and no, we don't make change."

That was fine by Mr. Hicks. I'd gotten two rolls of quarters at the bank after visiting my safe-deposit box. They'd set off the metal detector at the front door, but the marshals let me take them in, even though they confiscated my cell phone and my Raven, which they did not like, not one little bit, for all the obvious reasons. Fortunately, I was able to calm everyone down by producing my Boston Police ID, which, now that I thought about it, did not identify me as Kevin Hicks. Someday soon I must call Secretary Napolitano to alert her to some of these continuing gaps in Homeland Security.

Anyway, the only interesting creditor I discovered was a casino in the Grand Caymans, but I made copies of everything, so that my employer could study them at his leisure. Not being from the tank town in question, I might not recognize some glaringly scandalous tidbit. For instance, perhaps the local strip joint had a staid corporate name that I wouldn't catch, but the rep would.

It was after three when I took the elevator back downstairs. The marshal handed me back my gun and cell phone.

"I'm glad you're back," he said. "That phone of yours has been going off every five minutes ever since you went upstairs."

I didn't even have time to check the numbers on the calls before it rang again.

I glanced over at the marshal, a G-13 lifer if ever I saw one. He was pushing sixty, definitely rounding third. He wasn't concerned about security, he was just plain nosey. I shot him a mild do-you-mind? look, and as he reluctantly turned back toward the metal detector I slipped the Raven into my shoulder holster. Then I put the receiver to my ear and said hello.

"Where the hell have you been?" It was Plain View.

"I'm at the Christian Science Reading Room," I said. "I took your suggestion, and you were right—Mary Baker Eddy is a wonderful solace in these troubled times."

"Cut the shit," he said, sounding both angry and excited. "Katy Bemis just got snatched off the street about an hour ago, and you were the last one to spend any time with her, and don't deny it, because I got witnesses."

My knees buckled. I took a step toward the marshals' counter to regain my balance.

"What I need to know from you," he said, "and I need it right now, is why was she grabbed, and I don't need any more of your tap dancing—do you hear me?"

"Did anyone get a look at who grabbed her?"

"Yeah, one of them was— Wait a second, didn't you hear me? I'm asking the questions here. Why were you having lunch with her?"

"Since when is it against the law to have lunch with a reporter?" As I spoke, I was thinking. Two facts seemed indisputable. Her life was now in grave peril because of me, and me alone. And the corollary was that if I told Plain View what I knew, and what I had given her, then she would certainly be killed, because at that point, the records would no longer be of any value to the two guys. They'd just be looking to cut their losses, which meant cutting her throat.

"Jack," he said, "I haven't got time for any more of your bullshit. It's bad enough you fuck with me on the Bennett murder, but nobody gives much of a shit about Bucky one way or the other, me included. A reporter getting snatched, though, that's different. You oughta see the live vans that're already out here in front of her apartment, and we only got the call an hour ago."

"Where are you?" I said.

"I'm at her apartment," he said. "Get over here, right now, or I'll send Willie 'round for you."

"What's the address?"

"The address? You know the address. You been tagging her, haven't you?"

"Who told you that?"

"The waiter. He said she was eating food off your plate. Says he very seldom sees that kind of spit-swapping going on, especially at lunch, unless the two people are playing doctor with the shades drawn. And I concur with his analysis."

"That's bullshit," I said. "I am not fucking Katy Bemis."

The marshal looked over at me, and I realized how loudly I'd been speaking, even by the usual cell-phone-in-public-places standards. On the other end, though, Plain View was pleased.

"Now we're making some progress," he said. "That's the first definitive statement you've given me all week. I don't believe it for one instant, but I finally have you on the record about something."

"Please," I said. "Where does she live?"

"Like you don't know, after all this time you been playing bury-the-brisket with her. But I'll tell you anyway. It's 451 Commercial Street, apartment three."

No wonder she'd been heading north on foot after we left the Long Wharf Marriott. Her condo was no more than three blocks from the hotel. She must have been headed home to stash the documents. And they must have watched us all through lunch. Magoo, the great statesman that he was, had probably been the one who placed the call to The Man, to let them know about the commotion at the copy machine.

By the time I left the Hall, they'd had a tail on me who had followed me to the post office, then Legal, then the bank, and probably all the way to the courthouse. At the restaurant someone had seen me pass her the envelope, they'd watched her waving it around, they'd noticed her spearing those scallops off my plate, and they'd jumped to the same conclusion the waiter and Plain View had. They'd grabbed her hoping that she had the originals, and if she didn't, then I did, and they'd hold her until I coughed them up to save . . . my girlfriend.

"I'll be right over," I said. "I'm at North Station."

"North Station?" he said, in surprise.

"The Tip O'Neill building," I hastened to explain. "Bankruptcy court."

"Oh, I get it," he said. "Some poor bastard out in the sticks who watches *Meet the Fucking Press* every Sunday morning and thinks politics is on the level is about to get slimed."

Now the selectman could keep on watching *Meet the Fucking Press* in peace, at least for another week or so.

I WALKED quickly, skirting the North End, down past the Charlestown Bridge and the MDC skating rink and Parmenter

Street, which the Brinks' robbers had traveled on their way to the garage back on that cold January evening in 1950. I kept moving, past the site of the Great Molasses Spill of 1919, which rolled down Commercial Street like lava, or so they said. The old-timers always claimed that on a hot summer day, you could still smell the molasses, bubbling up from between the cobblestones.

Today all I could smell was urine, spilled beer, and dog shit.

When I got within a block of Katy Bemis's, I couldn't miss the media circus Plain View had been talking about. The yellow tape was up around the crime scene, and the sidewalk on the harbor side was blocked off. So the TV crews were doing their live shots from the other side of Commercial Street. This was huge. North of Tijuana, reporters are seldom snatched in broad daylight, especially good-looking females from blue-blooded families in Top 10 markets.

Suddenly the breaking news out of the State House about the impending repeal of term limits for the speaker didn't seem nearly as important. The Speaker had caught a break.

Katy's apartment building was standard North End/waterfront Yuppie. Four stories, exposed brick, about a hundred years old. It had probably been built as a warehouse or maybe even a small factory. Thirty years ago, before the revival of Quincy Market, it had been, at most, a garage, or even more likely abandoned. Now it was condos, and the ones with harbor views were worth well over a half million each, even in this depressed market. I wondered how much Katy had paid for hers.

The uniform at the entrance stopped me from going inside, so I politely asked him to fetch Detective Evans. Across the street, the roped-off reporters were keeping a close eye on the situation, looking for any new scraps of information. One of them spotted me and started yelling and pointing. I looked over and recognized him as a *Herald* scribe who hung at Foley's on Thursday nights—payday. Katy'd probably told someone at the city desk where she was headed for lunch and now the *Herald*, among others, was trying to track me down. I ignored the reporter's shouts until Plain View appeared at the top of the steps and waved me into the lobby.

Once inside, I could look into what I took to be her apartment. The front door was wide open and what seemed like dozens of cops, plainclothes and uniform, were milling about, doing the same type of simple cop chores they'd performed two nights earlier outside Foley's with their customary lack of results—dusting doorknobs for fingerprints, taking photos, and cop-whispering to one another. Once again, to my jaundiced eye, the message of their pointless scurrying was clear: they had absolutely no idea who or what they were looking for.

I took two steps toward the front door of the apartment, but Plain View stopped me. He took me firmly by the arm and led me into the back hallway, where the building's mailboxes lined the walls. There were eight of them. I stood with my back to the mailboxes with Plain View in front of me. He didn't even mention my face, or how bad I looked. He was too busy working a case—a big case.

"I need to know something," he said. "Were you fucking her?"

"You already asked me that question."

"I didn't like the answer I got the first time, so now I'm asking you again."

"The answer is no, I was not fucking her."

"Because if you were, that would make you the prime suspect."

"I was at the bankruptcy court," I said. "I told you that too."

"I suppose you got witnesses."

"Witnesses? Try the marshal at the metal detector at the entrance, he's a real busybody. My phone was going off all afternoon. It was bothering him. You kept calling me, remember?"

"You could have snuck out, maybe, and then snuck back in."

"Obviously you haven't been in a federal courthouse lately," I said. "Which is good, I guess, considering the way most Boston cops end up in federal courthouses. But I'll tell you, they're like airports. Before they even let the judges into the garage now, the marshals got these poles with mirrors on them, so they can check under everybody's cars, even the judges', for bombs. They got one entrance. One."

"How do you know so much about the federal courthouse?" he said in a snide tone. "You got any other proof where you were, other than this alleged marshal?"

"Yeah, you go up to the clerk's office there, on the sixth floor, and you'll see I signed out a document—" Then I remembered Kevin Hicks. "Well, it's not my name on the log sheet, but it's me. Kevin Hicks."

"Oh, so now you're into identity fraud too." He paused. "I suppose you got the dirt you dug up on the poor bastard."

"I do indeed," I said, holding up a large brown envelope. He silently decided to take my word for it.

After a couple of final deep sighs and dirty looks, Plain View filled me in on what had happened. When she and I split up outside the hotel, Katy had apparently decided to walk back to her condo, instead of grabbing a cab back to the *Herald,* or maybe the State House. Once again, Plain View was baffled.

"Why would she decide to walk back to her condo?" he asked.

"I'm afraid I can't help you there," I said.

"I'm afraid you can, but I'm also afraid that if I try to push you, you'll just start lying again, and that's worse than not saying anything."

Then he resumed the story. As she approached the building, witnesses said later, they noticed a rusted-out old car, probably of American make, that seemed to be following her. Finally, as she walked up the steps, the car pulled up in front of a fire hydrant, and two guys jumped out, grabbed her, wrestled her into the car, and drove off.

Fortunately, witnesses had been able to give police a description of the vehicle. It was a Ford, or a Chevy, or maybe a Dodge, and it was blue-black-brown-gray, and the license number was, uh, well, they didn't have time to get that, and maybe there wasn't even a plate on it, and as for the two guys, they were somewhere between, well, nobody was quite sure of their ages, because they were both wearing ski masks.

"In other words," I said, "you've got nothing."

"The only thing we got is you," he said, "and I'm about one hundred percent certain you can at least tell us why she got snatched."

What could I say? If I talked, she was dead. It was as simple as that. The guys who had ordered her grabbed were not the types to leave behind a lot of loose ends like witnesses.

"Don't think, talk," said Plain View. "You're the only person who can help me that I have in custody."

"I'm in custody, am I?"

"Ever hear of the 'material witness' statute?"

I shook my head. "Nice try, but no, you can't hold me, Captain."

"What'd you call me?"

"Captain," I said. "Why?"

"I ain't no captain," he said, "and you know it."

"I was just checking to see if you were paying attention."

"Funny," he said. "This morning, I get a call from some maggot over in Chelsea. He wants to know, can I help him out on a forged-prescription beef he's got over there. I says, who the fuck are you, and he says I'm only the guy that helped you the other night, trying to find a guy who knew Bucky Bennett. He kept calling me captain."

"You ain't no captain," I said.

"You're telling me," he said. "So anyway, there's this guy out there, impersonating me, only giving me a promotion, and now it turns out you're using the same rank as this joker, who by the way I'm told sounds like he's a cop."

"I'm not a cop, so I guess that lets me out as a suspect, right, Captain?"

He'd had enough of my little diversion. "You gotta spill, Jackie. Now. The waiter says he saw you give her something. What'd you give her, and I ain't got much time here."

"If I tell you what I know," I said, "she's dead. This is my fault that she's in this mess, and I have to get her out."

"That's very touching," he said, "assuming for a second that I believe you. But why do I have this feeling that you're less concerned with the broad than with trying to work a score?"

"Believe me, I'm not trying to work any angles here."

"I know, I can trust you, you're not like the others." He paused for just a second. "Now, turn around, so's I can frisk you, because I got another hunch you're carrying something for which you do not have an FID. And when I get a hunch I bet a—"

I shook my head no no no, but he began advancing on me. If he found the Raven on me, he could arrest me, and I'd be locked up until I talked, and if I talked . . .

Suddenly there was a commotion outside Katy's front door. The FBI had arrived. A couple of the TV camera crews, who had previously been kept at bay by several uniforms out on Commercial Street, had breached the perimeter along with the G-men and were now inside the front hallway, in the lobby, not ten yards away from Plain View and me.

"Look what the cat dragged in," whispered Plain View, instantly forgetting about the frisk as we both watched the melodramatic entrance of FBI Special Agent John Finnerty—Agent Orange.

PLAIN VIEW walked quickly to the front door, while I lingered behind and watched the fed preen for the cameras that he had dragged in behind him in his wake.

"We got no comment here, fellas," Finnerty said to the TV crews, after he turned around to face them in the doorway. "All I can tell you is, at two seventeen this afternoon, the Boston Police Department received a nine-one-one report of an abduction in progress here at 451 Commercial Street. The victim's name is being held pending notification of her relatives—"

One of the reporters yelled, "Is it Katy Bemis?"

Finnerty replied, "You said that, not me. I cannot comment, but as you know, by federal statute the FBI has jurisdiction in all kidnapping cases, and that's all I can tell you for the moment. Now if you'll excuse me—"

On TV you see the G-men at crime scenes with navy blue all-weather jackets with FBI stitched in huge yellow letters across the back. Not for Finnerty the longshoreman's look. He was dressed like a Mob guy—and not even an Irish one at that. Except for the coarse red hair, he looked Mafia, New York LCN. In his early fifties, about six two, he had that early John Gotti look, hair combed straight back, a huge pinky ring, and a double-breasted Armani suit. He was not dressed for a stakeout.

After ordering the camera crews back outside and across the street, Finnerty theatrically slammed the front door to Katy's building, then turned and pointed a finger at Plain View.

"You, Evans," he said. "What kind of cluster fuck are you running here?"

Plain View glanced over at me and said nothing. Then Finnerty quickly shifted his baleful stare over toward me, aiming his right index finger straight at me.

"You, Reilly, I put your brother in prison and I can do the same to you."

Something snapped, and it was my turn to take one step forward. "You point your finger at me again," I told him, "and I'll personally shove it up your crooked fed ass."

Finnerty managed a flat smile.

"You're plenty tough all right," he said. "I can tell just from looking at your face what a working over you gave those hoods in Somerville last night."

I took a step toward him, but Plain View quickly got between us and I took a couple of deep breaths, trying to calm myself down. I don't usually fly off the handle, especially around cops, not to mention when I'm carrying an unregistered handgun of unknown provenance.

"Easy, Finnerty," Plain View said. "Back off. Jack's okay. He just had lunch with her. His alibi checks out."

"Bullshit," Finnerty said. "He's dirty, always has been. I can smell him from over here. Did you brace him for a piece? I guarantee you it's unregistered. He's a fucking wiseguy like his brother, and wiseguys are always trying to set up a quick score. Is he carrying?"

"I frisked him already," Plain View said. "He's clean."

Score one for me. I always say, I'd rather be lucky than good. Finnerty snorted and stalked into Katy's apartment, with all cop eyes trained on him. Police are quite sensitive about jurisdictional prerogatives—it's the big-fish-in-a-small-pond syndrome—and over the years they've gone to great lengths to formalize procedures to minimize any potential hard feelings. Finnerty with his bluster was observing none of the traditional protocols.

"Can I go, Mike?" I said to Plain View, loud enough for Finnerty to hear me.

Plain View nodded, then winked. "Don't lose the cell phone again."

"Hey Reilly," yelled Finnerty from inside the apartment. "I may need to talk to you. Where are you going to be?"

"I'm in the book," I shouted back. "Evans can always reach me."

"Yeah?" he yelled. "Well, I can always reach you too. Keep that in mind."

It wasn't so much Finnerty I was worried about reaching me, it was the guys he was working for, and I don't mean the taxpayers. I glanced over quickly at Plain View and he slowly shook his head. The bad news was, Finnerty was in the picture. The good news was, the "captain" and I appeared to be bonding.

IN LIFE, I have learned, when one finds oneself behind the eight ball and in dire need of assistance, it often behooves one to seek out a Life Member of the National Rifle Association. Which was why, as soon as I got down the stairs and back out onto the sidewalk on Commercial Street, I took off at a brisk trot for City Hall. The camera crews briefly gave chase, but soon peeled off. They had orders not to leave the stakeout outside Katy Bemis's apartment, and anyway, except for the *Herald* guys, no one knew exactly what my connection to the case was.

I wanted to get to Slip because I needed both a driver and someone to back me up. Someone armed. It was now late afternoon, and Slip was always in City Hall at that time of day. He never missed Channel 56's lineup of ancient sitcoms.

I entered City Hall from Dock Square, the back door. Then I took the Council elevator up to the fifth floor and ducked into Slip's office unannounced. His two secretaries—the "girls"—had already left for the day. As soon as Slip saw me he rose from his desk chair and zapped off *Green Acres*. After telling me to sit down in one of the chairs across from his desk, he sat back down behind his desk and lit up a Kool. I mentioned Katy's name and he said he'd already heard the news on the radio. He told me how sorry he was.

"Is it who I think it was who did it?" he said.

I nodded.

"Anything I can do to help out?" he said, and he meant it.

"As a matter of fact," I said, "would you be up for riding shotgun for me tonight?"

"Only on one condition."

"Which is?"

"That I get to shoot somebody."

I had to smile. "Let's both keep our fingers crossed that such an opportunity presents itself."

"Or doesn't, is what you're thinking," Slip said. "But I mean it."

"I know you do. That's why I'm here."

"You know, a lot of the liberal assholes around this building put the knock on ole Slip for packing heat," he said, and I knew where this rant was headed. "But someday—someday there's going to be a nut in the gallery at one of our meetings, and that's the day these Munsters'll be glad Slip Crowley is armed and dangerous."

We had to get going, but I needed a few minutes to cool off, and there are worse ways to calm down than by listening to one of Slip's timeworn stump speeches. After quickly filling him in on the details of the snatch, I settled back in my chair and let him carry the conversational ball.

"Don't get me wrong—I feel bad about what happened to that broad," he said. "But you know, she looks down her nose at people like us. Her kind always has. She goes to a wooden church."

Slip was drifting into one of his oldest monologues, one that he'd begun at Foley's Monday night, but had never gotten around to finishing. Where exactly he could now deliver this peroration to electoral advantage I had no idea. Even in the nursing homes of Southie and West Roxbury his anti-Yankee rhetoric would seem curiously antique, an archaic relic of a bygone era.

"Curley was right about them people," he said. "The bastards drink Dubonnet and they wear straw boaters and they still have cuffs on their pants. I see 'em walking down Beacon Hill to the Somerset Club for lunch. They all ride the train in from Wenham and then they walk from North Station to one of them office buildings on Tremont Street. They're all 'investment counselors,' that's what they call themselves on those directory boards in the lobby. Throckmorton Crowninshield the Third, or should I say, da Turd. And under that it says, 'Investment Counselor.' Or 'Trustee.'"

On and on he went. They all strutted across Slip's stage, those Irish wraiths of yore that had fought the good fight against those cheap chinless blue-blooded Unitarian-Universalist Watch and Ward Society bastards. James Michael Curley, of course, and Martin Lomasney and Honey Fitz, not to mention the ones now lost in the mists of time. John J. Kerrigan, John F. Kerrigan, Pea Jacket Kennedy, Jimmy Craven, Kitty Craven, and Jim "I'll Take a Buck" Coffey . . .

Finally Slip paused for a breath and I was able to ask him a question.

"Are you ready," I said, "to hit the road?"

JUST THEN my cell phone rang. Slip leaned over to extract his .38 Police Special from the bottom desk drawer while I picked up the phone and said hello.

"Finnerty, FBI," he said. "I've got a deal for you."

My bullshit detector went off, big time.

"I think I can get her back, but first I need what you've got—you do have it, don't you?"

"Tell me, what exactly am I supposed to have?"

Slip stared at me, and when I silently mouthed the words "Agent Orange," Slip's upper lip curled in silent distaste.

I asked him again, "What exactly is it that I'm supposed to have?"

"Some things that belong to them, not copies, but the originals." He was cute all right—too cute by half. If he were on the level, he wouldn't be trying to give me the swerve with these vague answers. An honest cop doesn't have to worry about being wiretapped.

"I'm trying to set up a meeting with them," Finnerty said.

Oh great—just what I needed, another sit-down with these guys. Another beating, or worse.

Finnerty asked, "You do want to meet with them, don't you?"

"Not really."

"Well, you may have to speak to them if you want the girl back," he said. "They want to make sure you haven't made any more copies."

Any more copies? There was only one way Finnerty could have known that she was carrying a set of copies—if the people who had snatched her told him.

"If I may ask," I said, "what's in this for you?"

"I'm just trying to get the girl back alive."

I said, "So you're not at all interested in why they want this certain thing back that I may or may not have?"

"First things first," he said. "That's a lesson I learned early on at Quantico."

I was born at night, but not last night. He was trying to

sound as straight as Inspector Lew Erskine used to every Sunday night at eight on ABC. When I was a kid and my father was on the job, the Boston police commissioner was a former FBI agent. He was perfect for the job, everyone agreed, because the FBI was like Caesar's wife—above reproach. That was a long time ago.

Finnerty said, "You're going to have to play ball with me on this one, whether you like me or not. The BPD is hopeless. You of all people should understand that." He paused. I think he was considering whether to mention his plans for the department when he became commissioner, but then he thought better of it. "State Police—a great outfit. If you need a speed trap."

As I listened, I watched Slip strap his shoulder holster on. Then he dropped his .38 into the holster and put his suit coat on over it. He walked over to the window, stared out over City Hall Plaza, and lit a smoke. He was ready to roll, and so was I. But Finnerty was still trying to close his deal.

"Well, what's it going to be?" he said. "Time's a-wasting."

"I want you to deliver a message to them from me," I said. "If they want something from me, I am going to have to hear from Katy Bemis. No Katy, no you-know-what. You got that, Finnerty?"

He said nothing. He was obviously not familiar with being talked back to.

"A word to the wise, jerk-off," he finally said. "You're not shaking down shacked-up state reps anymore. You're playing with the big boys now."

"They're tough all right," I said. "That's why they snatched a broad, because they're so big and brave."

"Don't be an asshole, Reilly. It should tell you something that they didn't just snatch a broad, they snatched a newspaper broad. What does that tell you?"

"That they've got the FBI in their pocket?"

"You're a funny fella for a guy who commits one count of wire fraud the third of every month when he has his phony city disability check direct-deposited into his checking account."

Phony? Prove it, pal. Prove it beyond a reasonable doubt. Like I told Katy Bemis, I never claimed a physical disability. What I am is mental, and if I tell a psychiatrist that I have dreams about turning my service revolver on myself and others, who can disprove it—beyond a reasonable doubt?

"What you don't seem to want to understand," he said, "is that these people you're crossing have some very important people, capitalize V-I-P, in their corner, and it'd be better if you learned to go along with them, more profitable probably, and certainly safer. Where are you right now, by the way?"

I ignored that question and asked him one instead.

"Whose tab are *you* on right now, Finnerty? The taxpayers' or Knocko's?"

"I just want the girl back, and I'm doing my best to get that through that thick harp skull of yours."

Good cop, bad cop, all in one. It saved The Man some money; he only had to pay off one guy in the Boston FBI office, although I suspected Finnerty liked to spread his master's cash around, grease a few guys here and there. I wondered idly if Finnerty had a Mob expense account to bribe other cops with, in addition to his federal cheat sheet. It would be money well spent, because both Finnerty and Knocko wanted something on everybody, and what better dirt than cash payoffs to cops from the Ace of Hearts? Once a cop takes their cash, they own him.

And the irony was, Finnerty probably didn't even think of Knocko as his boss. The way he most likely saw it, they were comrades-in-arms, fulfilling their noble mission of taking down In Town—the Italians. Assisted, of course, by their faithful Italian companion, Tony Miami.

Sometimes, when I was working for the mayor, we would put third and occasionally even fourth candidates into primaries to drain votes from the renegade councilor or rep we were trying to knock off. If we wanted to kill someone named O'Neill, for instance, we'd find another guy named O'Neil, or O'Neal, or maybe both. Straws, we called them.

The mayor always used to say that the best straw was somebody who didn't even know he was a straw. Agent Orange was a straw cop—he could no longer even tell the difference between bent and straight. Denial is the clinical term for such a condition.

"I'm going to tell you one more time, Finnerty," I said. "I want to talk to Katy Bemis, or the two guys don't get back the Speaker's ledger books. You got that, the Speaker's ledger books, the originals. You understand?"

"I understand."

"Repeat it back to me what I got in my possession."

"I can't right now."

"So you're in the office is what that means. You're on Uncle Sam's dime in Pemberton Square shaking down a citizen, namely me, to protect a pair of serial-killing gangsters I'll bet you got in your precious secret files as Top Echelon Criminal Informants with their own little numbers and codes and files and everything. And you're doing it all under color of your official duties, isn't that the phrase they always put in the indictment of a crooked cop?"

Finnerty said nothing. What could he say?

"You got some nerve, looking down your nose at me," I said. "You're the crooked cop here, not me. Do you hear me, fuckface?"

"Loud and clear."

Chapter Fourteen

I GOT OUT of City Hall lying on the backseat of Slip's car, covered with a blanket. Before we left, I'd given Slip a shopping list for the evening, and he'd rounded everything up in ten minutes flat without even venturing off the fifth floor.

He had borrowed a billy club from one of the new mayor's police detail. He had also come up with a small tape recorder, which he told me he'd purchased a few years back when he was claiming the *Globe* reporters were misquoting him. The batteries still worked. At the first stoplight, I threw off the blanket and sat up as Slip studied me in the rearview mirror.

"Where to, Chief?" he said.

I told him the State House and he just nodded and asked me if I wanted him to come in with me. I said no, because if people knew he was with me it would make him a target too. He said he understood, and I told him I'd call him on his cell phone when I was through with my business.

"Do I have I time to wet my whistle?" he said.

"I think you owe it to yourself."

He dropped me off under the dome, and I walked quickly inside, taking the stairs straight up to the third floor. The last thing I'd checked before leaving City Hall was the live coverage of the legislature on the Internet. The solons were still "deliberating," as they called it. Mainly, it was a handful of shabbily attired dissident reps from obscure outlying districts screaming "Outrageous!" over and over again, accusing the Speaker of delaying his inevitable abolition of term limits until late in the evening, too late for the TV newscasts, as if there would be any local stories tonight on TV besides Katy Bemis's kidnapping.

But the prolonged harangues, as futile as they were, did serve one purpose. They would keep the Speaker in the building for as long as it took. He had to get the term limits rule repealed, because as long as the rule was on the books, he was a lame duck, and at the State House, lame duck is everyone's favorite dish.

Meanwhile, the lobbyists had already booked Anthony's Pier 4 for a "time" tomorrow evening, to salute Mr. Speaker on his marvelous victory and fill his already overflowing campaign war chest with another two hundred grand or so. It was but a mere token of their esteem for his ability to do whatever they paid him to do, no matter how unsavory the request, at least as long as the price was right, and he could keep his fingerprints off the worst of it, more or less.

By the time I reached the third floor of the State House, it was way past five o'clock quitting time. The only ones left in the building were the reps, their staffs, the lobbyists, and a handful of reporters. At the top of the stairs, I nodded to a heavy-lidded plainclothes state cop providing alleged security for the governor, who was long gone for the evening, probably in a very public place, so as to establish his alibi for the inevitable federal grand jury that would be empaneled in the wake of this latest democracy in action, State House style.

As for me, I turned right and walked the sixty feet or so to the Speaker's office. Opening the door to his office, the first things I noticed were the iced tubs of imported champagne. Once the time for debate had expired, the leadership was going to let the good times roll.

Already lurking thirstily around the buckets were a few reps whom I half recognized as vice chairmen of rinky-dink committees, guys on the make for seven-year terms on the Industrial Accidents Board, at the end of which their nicknames would be "Lump Sum" or "Seventy-Two," as in the percentage of your salary that you collect, tax-free, if you go out on a full disability pension. I should know, right? One of the solons was wearing a sky blue polyester suit. He must have been from Fall River.

Another sport was attired in matching white shoes and belt, a look that went out of fashion everywhere but North Adams sometime around 1981. The two fashion-plate reps were amusing one another by telling lame jokes to a couple of sweaty, equally fourth-string lobbyists who were guffawing with great enthusiasm.

"That's a good one, Mr. Chairman," I heard one of the lobbyists say. Then I noticed them glancing over to check me out. My swollen club-fighter's face kept their attention for an extra few seconds, but they quickly lost interest once they realized that I wasn't in their club, which meant that I must be a square, whom they could neither shake down nor suck up to.

The secretary looked up at me from her desk, equally unimpressed. But after eyeing me for a moment, she recognized me and just as swiftly put two and two together. She was good—she was, after all, Tony Miami's sister, which meant that if there were any flies on her, they were paying rent. Unlike the reps, she instantly understood that my unannounced appearance this evening could not bode well for her boss, or possibly even for her brother.

"I need to see him, Ms. Massimino," I told her. "Tell him you've got Mr. Ledger Books out here."

"But that's not your—"

"Just tell him it's Mr. Books, L. Books. Tell him I need to see him alone, now."

She stood up, nodding, silent, taken aback.

It was not a diplomatic way to handle something as delicate as this. I was attempting to threaten the politician who was on the verge of becoming the most powerful man in state government. Forget the governor—he could be replaced by the voters every four years. A governor needs well over a million votes to win his race. The Speaker, any speaker, running in a tiny House district, seldom got more than 7,500. All he needed to govern were 81 votes—50 percent plus one of the 160-member body, a motley collection of mama's boys, housewives, problem drinkers, problem gamblers, problem eaters, problem diddlers, goo-goos, and union pawns, all of them accustomed to being knuckled. When the Speaker said, "Jump!" they responded, practically in unison, "How high?"

I usually try to be polite to everybody I run into—some of the most soothing words in the English language, whether you mean them or not, are "We don't want any trouble." Tony Miami had used those very words on me just yesterday afternoon. But Katy Bemis was running out of time, if she'd hadn't already, and Tony Miami's sister was not helping as she just stood motionless at her desk, still staring at me.

"Stalling is not an option here, Ms. Massimino," I said. "Go tell him I have to speak to him, immediately. I haven't got all night, and neither does your boss."

The reps and lobbyists had now turned away from the

champagne buckets and were watching me intently, their inane chatter at a standstill. One of them would eventually realize who was barging into the Speaker's office. Jiggs, wielding the gavel at the podium, would know within five minutes. He would not be pleased. He didn't want any trouble either, not right now anyway. But for once he would have to keep his mouth shut. The Massimino woman was still eyeing me warily and then I realized what she was thinking.

"The Speaker wouldn't want you to call the cops. Neither would your brother. Trust me on that."

She gave me another dour look, then turned and walked to the Speaker's door. She knocked perfunctorily and then walked straight in. A few seconds later she reappeared at the door, shooing a couple of the Speaker's underbosses ahead of her. One of them I didn't know personally, but the other one I recognized as Sal DiGrazia, my old precinct captain from the North End.

As they left the inner sanctum, both of them glared at me. This was my night to get the dagger eyes. These two were irate that anyone should dare intrude on their quality time with the Speaker, especially on this night of nights.

Sal looked beyond me toward the foursome of reps and lobbyists lurking about the iced tub of champagne.

"Hey, what are youse doing here?" he said to them with a smile. Youse—I'd forgotten that Sal DiGrazia thought "youse" was the plural of "you." Now he was the number-three guy in the House. So much for the theory of evolution. He turned to me, finally acknowledging my presence.

"Jack," he said, trying on a weak smile and extending a limp hand, "how come I never see you down Hanover Street no more?"

"'Cause there's a new mayor and he's got a new guy collecting from your constituents."

Not that I was a bagman. I can't say that often enough. Cops make lousy bagmen. The mayor used to say he hated it when a cop handed him three hundred dollars from somebody, because he never knew if the cop had stolen two hundred or seven hundred. I only made the pickups if nobody else was around that day.

Sal used to sit on the edge of his seat when I regaled him and my other precinct captains with stories like that, because I was his boss. Now I wasn't, and I bored him. He had a swagger about him that I'd never noticed before, maybe because when I knew him he was just an underling, and like most bosses, I never paid enough attention to my minions. No wonder Jiggs was as restless as a fart in a mitten. This was the guy just beneath him on the leadership's depth chart. Sal was just stupid enough to be very dangerous.

"Come on by sometime, Jack," he said. "After your face gets better. We'll talk about the old days."

"Maybe you can get us some comped lap-dance tickets to the Golden Melon too," I said, and his lip curled slightly, but he said nothing.

Sal and the other rep who was with him knew they were expected to leave, and as they reached the hallway door without saying anything, their lackeys likewise took the hint and followed them out into the marble hall, muttering darkly as they cast doleful eyes back toward the buckets of bubbly. They hated to leave all those chilled, imported magnums unattended, because the building was teeming with thieves and tosspots. The legislature was in session.

The Massimino woman watched them leave but didn't move. She was blocking the entrance to the Speaker's inner sanctum with her body and keeping both hands behind her back on the doorknob. Once they had all disappeared from the office, she silently stood aside, motioning me inside the Speaker's office with her head. She watched me enter and then closed the door behind me.

Whatever happened next was going to be one-on-one. His word against mine, if it ever came to that.

The Speaker rose from his leather-upholstered swivel chair and came around his ornate mahogany desk to glad-hand me. Like Sal, he tried to smile, but he couldn't quite pull it off either. I was the snake at the garden party tonight, the turd in the punch bowl.

I couldn't recall ever seeing the Speaker in person before, although I suppose I must have met him more than once back when I used to arrange the mayor's annual breakfast for the Boston legislative delegation at the Parkman House. Lynch was maybe five years older than me, but I was already one of the mayor's top fixers when he was first elected to the House. In person, he seemed leaner and taller than he appeared on TV. He had thick steel-gray hair, combed straight back, working-class style, and he was wearing a two-thousand-dollar Continental-cut suit from somewhere in the Back Bay.

To sum it up, he looked like a mid-market weekend TV anchor with his eye on the six and eleven at a bigger station in a bigger town. There'd been talk once of him running for Congress, but ultimately he'd decided that even if he won—always an uncertain bet at best for a legislative leader—he couldn't absorb either the pay cut or the power cut.

"Jack, my friend," he said without tripping over the word "friend," "long time no see."

He stopped again. We were still standing, facing one another. The logical next topic of conversation would have been something along the lines of: you probably don't remember me but . . . That, however, would have been awkward, considering the way our roles were now reversed, power-wise.

"How's the family?" he said, as if we were old buddies.

"Marty's still doing a bit at Devens—he took a fall for some guys. Not that he had much choice, if you know what I mean."

The Speaker nodded vacantly. It was information he didn't need and couldn't use. He silently motioned me over toward the couch and leather-lined chairs in the corner by the crackling fire. The walls were all wood-paneled. Except for having no direct view out onto the Common, the Speaker had a far better office than the governor. We sat facing each other in comfortable armchairs in front of the fire, our legs crossed.

"What can I do for you, Jack?" he said quietly.

"You can call the people who've been blackmailing you and tell them they'd better let Katy Bemis go or the jig is up." Bad choice of words—jig. A Freudian slip no doubt, and although it undoubtedly reminded the Speaker of his faithless floor leader, his face betrayed nothing.

"I'm sure I don't know what you mean, Jack. Terrible thing about that reporter—I heard the news on the radio—but what does it have to do with me, or you for that matter?"

I just stared at him. He shifted uncomfortably in his chair and recrossed his legs. I still said nothing. Finally he said, "Are you in some sort of trouble as well?"

"Yes, I am. But not as much as you, because I don't have nearly as much to lose, Hal."

"Don't call me Hal."

"Sorry, Mr. Speaker," I said. "What I'm telling you is, your problem right now is not term limits. It's making sure Katy Bemis stays alive, because if she doesn't come back in one piece, then you're going down too. Do I make myself clear?"

His brow furrowed. He was feigning confusion. If he truly hadn't understood, he'd have been bolting for the door, crying out for the sleepy Statie down the hall outside the governor's office. As it was, he was trying to process how to deal with a problem he should have anticipated long ago, but apparently never had. For once the delivery of a low-digit license plate or an assistant clerk's job in the Boston Municipal Court would not suffice.

"Jack, if there was anything I could do to help bring that poor woman home to her family and friends, apparently including yourself, well, you know I've got a family of my own. There's Erin and Eamon and Shannon and Gaelan and Brendan—"

"Save that Vaseline for *The Pilot*," I said, pulling some ancient papers out of my breast pocket. "Here's the deal. Recognize this stuff?" I tossed the papers at him. "Those are a couple of sheets from the ledger books your father stole from Wimpy and Billy Hogan. The real McCoy, you'll notice. The Man doesn't have the originals, never did, despite what he may have told you. I've got 'em now. You sold all your real estate for nothing, Hal, I mean Mr. Speaker."

He glanced down at the sheets I'd ripped from the book, and his jaw dropped, slowly. He breathed through his mouth. "Peaked" is the word my mother would have used to describe his complexion.

"And to answer your next question," I said, "I've got your records too, including the Cooperative Trust savings account passbook. In a safe place, a very safe place. That was real clever, just writing down the lobbyists' initials. No one could ever possibly crack that code."

He looked at me and his eyes blinked uncontrollably.

"Who?" he stammered. "Who—"

"Who knows, is that what you're asking? Right now that's not your concern. I'm calling the shots here now, and this is what you're going to do—"

"You can't prove anything."

"Maybe not," I said, but I knew I had him. When they start telling you that you can't prove it, plea bargaining has begun, even if the perp doesn't quite realize it yet. "I don't have subpoena power, if that's what you mean. But the feds do, and so does the AG."

I let that sink in, just long enough, but not a moment longer. There was no need to bully him. I needed his cooperation, at least for the moment.

"I counted the names of at least twenty-five lobbyists on your little legal pad there," I said. "Most of them work for publicly traded corporations or state-regulated utilities, and I believe the SEC frowns on using corporate funds to bribe public officials. And here's one other issue for you to consider. I've been out of the loop up here for a while now, Mr. Speaker, so you would probably know better than me. Do lobbyists stand up?"

"If I do what you want," he said, "you'll give me back everything—is that the deal?"

"I haven't thought that far ahead," I lied. "But if anything happens to Katy Bemis, you're going to prison, guaranteed. It's your choice, until it's not your choice."

"What do you want?"

"I want her released, unharmed. You make sure that happens tonight, and then we'll talk about what happens next."

"Let's talk about it now."

"Not until Katy Bemis is released."

"Doesn't your wife have a job down in Canton at the courthouse?"

"My ex-wife, and don't even think about it." He had done his homework. He was obviously either in touch with the two guys, or he knew every single job on the Trial Court payroll, or both.

"It wasn't meant as a threat," he said evenly.

"Whatever you meant, she's off the table. My kids too. That is nonnegotiable. I'm calling the shots now. Your only job is to get Katy Bemis back. You got that, Hal?"

He stared at me, and I stared back. Neither of us said a word, and finally I stood up. I handed him one of my business cards, with my cell phone number handwritten on the back.

"You will get her back tonight, won't you, Hal?"

"What if I can't?"

"You can, and you will," I said. "Your word is your bond, and you're giving me your word."

"I am?"

"Yes, you are, Hal," I said. "And after she's released . . . we'll talk again."

"How do I know I can trust you?"

"Because I'm giving you my word," I said, "and my word is my bond."

I CALLED Slip and he picked me up under the dome. This time I got in the front seat. I was pretty sure no one had had time to put a tail on me, but one way or the other, I wasn't going to make the thirty-minute ride down to Slip's house in Roslindale under a blanket in the backseat. It wasn't like it was easy to miss the Slip-mobile. On one side of the back bumper was a campaign bumper sticker with only one word: SLIP. On the other side was another bumper sticker that said LIBERALS: AN AMERICAN CANCER.

Somewhere, Slip had picked up another gun, which he handed to me. It was a fully loaded Bulldog, a great piece. When I was on the job, whenever we would fire our personal Bulldogs on the police practice range on Deer Island, everyone would always ask each other, "Did you hear the Bulldog bark?"

Slip had barely turned onto Bowdoin Street when my cell phone rang. I was hoping it wasn't Jiggs, and it wasn't.

"Here she is, hero." It was a strange, filtered voice, an underling's.

"Jack?" It was Katy. They hadn't done anything to her—yet. It hadn't taken the Speaker long. He certainly had their cell phone numbers.

"Katy?" I said. "Are you in Southie?"

"Watch it, hero," said the voice. "We're listening too."

"Are you okay?"

"I'm all right, Jack. They haven't hurt me."

"You're going to be all right, I swear." Meaningless words, like a bishop's homily. "I just have something they want, and when I get it back to them, they'll let you go."

I waited to hear her voice again, but all I heard was the other, male voice.

"Now you're on message, hero. Try to stay there." I heard a click. "You can talk to her again later. Now, do you have that something with you that doesn't belong to you?"

"Talk to the Speaker about it," I said.

"That's not part of the deal." Whatever happened to "hero"? "You know better than to use a middleman."

"You talk to him and get back to me. And when you call back, I want to talk to her again."

"You want a lot for a guy who's holding no cards."

"I got one ace up my sleeve, and it's the only one that counts. I get her back, or you don't get it. Your choice. Now call me back when you make up your mind." It was my turn to hang up. Slip continued driving south silently through the South End and into Roxbury, letting me think. Finally, as we neared Dudley Station, I made my decision. We would bring the war back home. We would go to Southie.

"It's your call, Chief," Slip said. No backtalk, no unsolicited advice—I appreciated that. He knew how to take orders, something everyone used to learn back in the time when universal military service really was universal, before Vietnam really got hot, and draft-dodging became all the rage, and not just in the suburbs either.

Of course, besides the Army, Slip and I shared another, even more formative experience. We'd both started out as drivers for politicians, me for the mayor, and Slip for a one-term Democratic governor way back in the sixties, when Massachusetts still had two-year terms. One thing driving for a pol teaches you, or reinforces if you were in the military, is that there is a reason why you're told over and over again in basic training that an enlisted man shall not speak to a superior officer unless spoken to.

The pol you're driving has his job to do, which is shaking hands and making speeches and putting the arm on guys with dough. Your job is getting him there, not chewing the fat with him or critiquing his last speech. The pol doesn't need to be trading quips with you, any more than a bird colonel needs to be batting the breeze with a buck private.

Sometimes you have to take orders, and the only way to learn that is by taking the goddamn orders. Thirty-six months in the Army can do wonders for a young guy's character. Look what it did for me and Slip.

"You know," Slip said, "that Plain View ain't such a bad guy."

"No, he's not," I said. Talking up Plain View was Slip's way of gently suggesting that maybe we should take a pass and leave this matter in the hands of the cops.

"Here's my problem, Slip," I said. "If I tell Plain View everything I know, including the dirt on the Speaker, that means the blackmailing is over, and then they have no reason to keep Katy alive; in fact, they have every reason to kill her."

"I understand," he said, "but tell me again why that's your problem?"

"Because I gave her the stuff that got her snatched."

"But she's one-a them know-it-all broads, Jack, and I understand you and her been getting along, and I don't mean to kick her when she's down. But I know her from the Hall, and believe me, she always makes it clear she wants to be treated like she's one of the boys. Well, now she is one of us—she's hit the fuckin' jackpot. The only difference is, she volunteered for it. You and me, we didn't. This ain't a fuckin' lark for guys like us, this is the hand we were dealt. For her it's a game, and she always figured if push came to shove, she could hop on her polo pony and trot back to Dover Fucking Sherborn or Manchester by the Fucking Sea or whatever la-de-da suburb she's from. The way I look at it, she should have known who she was dealing with."

"She was dealing with me, Slip," I said.

"Look, all I'm saying is—it's just I get tired of all these fucking victims. You're supposed to treat them like they're equals, until they get between a rock and a hard place, at which point they start screaming about how unfair life is, and it's all the fault of guys like us. Why do we always have to answer the bell for somebody who don't even like us?"

He said no more. He had spoken his piece. He just wanted to get it on the record. What could I say? I had screwed up by giving her the copies, and now it was my duty—a word I seldom use—to make it right. Slip had screwed up by volunteering to back me up, and now it was his duty not to break his word. We were in it together, a couple of fuckups, up to our eyeballs in . . . duty.

"We're crossing the frontier," Slip said as we drove over the new Fort Point Channel bridge into South Boston, the largest Irish stronghold left in the city, although not nearly as monolithic as it had once been. But even now, with blacks and Hispanics in the projects and Yuppies up and down East Broadway and with tiny condos in converted three-deckers in City Point going for upward of four hundred grand, at least until the recent real-estate collapse, it was still a rough-and-tumble little spit of land, harbor view or no harbor view.

Slip said, "Where to now, Boss?"

What he meant was, which of Knocko's haunts were we going to hit, because Katy had to be over here, somewhere. This was The Man's turf. As for Tony Miami, Southie was mostly where he hung now too, but like Slip, he was really a man without a country, or at least a neighborhood. Tony Miami and Slip were both white guys from Roxbury—DPs, as they used to call them after World War II, displaced persons. Slip had moved to Roslindale, and Tony Miami now spent most of his time over here, although he had several apartments scattered across the South Shore, plus a "club" over on Southampton Street as his forward base in Roxbury.

Knocko owned Southie, which meant he had all the eyes and ears in "the Town" looking out for his interests. Slip and I were up against it, in more ways than one. We had the element of surprise, but not much else. We would get just one shot, and then we'd have to scurry back across the bridge to civilization, and if that sounds like I look down my nose at Southie, so be it.

The question we had to consider now was, which of their outposts would we strike: the liquor store on Old Colony Avenue, the gym on Dorchester Street, or the barroom in the Lower End, the Ace of Hearts, which was out of the question—way too many plug-uglies.

"I'm thinking gym," I said.

"Good call," Slip said, nodding. "Fewer hostiles, and I hear bad stories about that place."

"What kind of stories?" I said.

"I don't even want to repeat 'em," he said, making the sign of the cross. "You know I pull a lot of votes outta here."

In Wards 6 and 7, as Magoo Sullivan had reminded him earlier in the day, they don't count Slip's votes, they weigh 'em. Which was one reason why he was so antsy—he couldn't be seen throwing his weight around over here on behalf of an outsider, which is what I was, and forever would be, even from ten blocks away. Slip had been over here practically every night for thirty years, and although they always voted for him, the Southie natives still widely regarded him as a refugee from St. Patrick's in Roxbury.

He drove down West Broadway to Dorchester Street, then turned right. The darkened gym lay just ahead, on the other side of the street.

"You just drop me off right here," I said. "Give me ten minutes and then pull up in front and I'll jump in. If it looks like there's trouble, you know that alley just on the other side of Fitzie's package store?"

He surely did. He brightened and pulled over. He liked the new plan—the alley was dark, and with any luck, no one would spot him or the Slipmobile. I got out of the car and he drove off, probably to buy a pack of smokes at the variety store on D Street across from the projects. As long as he was over here, he might as well plant the flag. I wondered if they had a jukebox that played "Far Away Places."

As for me, I walked quickly across Dorchester Street, gripping the Bulldog. This was definitely a job that called for a throwdown. With my left hand I grasped the well-worn BPD regulation billy club that Slip had borrowed for the evening.

Fortunately, this was not your usual Southie gym, with the flat-chested female MBAs working out after a thirteen-hour day at one of the formerly flush mutual fund companies that had been struggling since the collapse of Lehman Brothers and all that followed. This gym was an open front for organized crime, and everyone knew it, even the blow-in drifters from New York who the Southie natives claimed were ruining their quaint fucking neighborhood, except of course for when they were overpaying for the shitbox three-deckers in the Lower End, thereby allowing one dysfunctional family of natives after another to finally flee the ravaged gin mills and the ruined schools, thirty years after busing. Better late than never, I suppose. I pounded on the front door of the club.

"Closed," someone inside yelled back.

"Police," I said sternly. "Open up."

An eye-level slit opened in the door. "Let's see the badge."

I flashed my old BPD badge, and then I heard the bolt move, even as the voice said, "You're making a mistake. Somebody's gonna hear about this."

I took out the Bulldog, and as soon as the door opened, I stepped inside and stuck it in the face of the sweatsuit-clad goon who had opened the door. He was about twenty-five, with bad acne scars, and from his build, it appeared he was a serious abuser of steroids, which also meant he was very likely clinically insane. I instantly made an executive decision: If this thug made a move for the Bulldog, he was getting it in the face, with as many shots as I could squeeze off. No way could I survive, let alone prevail, in hand-to-hand combat with such an ape. For now, though, he was awed by the equalizer. He backed away.

"Who the fuck do you think you are?" he said.

"I'm the guy with the gun," I said. "Anybody else here?"

"Just me," he said. "We're closed for business."

Regular business maybe. But for monkey business, I'd bet this place stayed open 24/7.

I looked down the corridor, and saw light coming from one room, way down near the end of the hall. Figuring that for the office, I marched him down the hall, past the men's and women's locker rooms and a couple of closed doors that led to what I presumed were tiny exercise rooms. As we turned left into the office I noticed another door beyond the office, at the very end of the hallway. The sign on that door said EMPLOYEES ONLY. Once we were inside the office, the ape, his back still turned to me, started talking again over his shoulder.

"You're making a big mistake," he said. "This is The Man's place."

"Keep your hands up and don't move," I said, pushing him farther away from the door, poking him in the back with the billy club that I held in my left hand. In my right hand, I kept the Bulldog trained directly at the back of his head.

"I got one question for you," I said. "Where's the broad?"

"I, uh, I don't know nothing about no broads." He was lying, and none too convincingly either, double negatives notwithstanding. Knocko and Tony Miami just couldn't bear to employ anyone whose IQ reached even room temperature. It was understandable enough, given the nature of the periodic hostile takeovers in organized crime, some of which the two guys themselves had been involved in over the years. But sooner or later, in any field of endeavor, there is always a price to be paid for surrounding oneself with morons.

I noticed his arms starting to droop, which was unacceptable. "I said hands up, shit-for-brains."

He got his hands back up.

"I don't have much time," I said, "so you'd better tell me where she is."

"She, she—she's with The Man."

"With Knocko?" Now this was a surprise, and not of the pleasant variety.

"So where are they?"

"I don't know. The Man left with her, afterwards. I thought he was taking her home."

"Home?" I said. "Who do you think I'm looking for, ass-hole?"

"I, I don't know," he said, over his shoulder, craning his head around. "I mean, I thought maybe you was her father."

"Whose father?"

"The girl's. The kid that The Man picked up and . . . you know."

"How old is this girl?"

"About fourteen—he don't go for 'em if they're much older than that." He stopped, realizing he'd gone too far. "But don't tell him I said that."

Then he added, pathetically, "Please."

I rammed the gun right up against the back of his neck. "I'm looking for the girl reporter you guys grabbed this afternoon. Where is she?"

"Her?" He almost sagged with relief now that he knew I was inquiring about a mere kidnapping. "She ain't here, I swear. I don't know who's got her or where she is. All I know about her is what I seen on TV tonight. Only ones in this place now are you and me."

I thought about the girl who had been here today—no more than fourteen years old, the thug had said.

"So The Man likes jailbait, does he?" I knew I was veering off the track, but this must have been what Slip had heard rumblings about. "Let me guess, he doesn't know they're underage. They show him their library cards."

"You think I ask them kinda questions?" he said, his voice quivering. "I just work here."

"Yeah, I bet you handle a few chores on the side too, like maybe dragging a body or two down the stairs at the Ace of

Hearts after hours. I think I seen you around." Did I really say "I seen"? Hang with these guys for even a few minutes and your brain cells start to shrivel up and die. He began to turn his head around again but I shoved the Bulldog up against his neck.

"Don't even think about trying to get another look at my face." The bruises on my swollen face would be a certain giveaway, although maybe he'd already noticed them at the front door. But probably not. He didn't strike me as someone with an eye for the telling, novelistic detail.

I snarled, "How many floors in this dump?"

"Three, but I swear the girl—the reporter—ain't here."

"Where is she then?"

"I told you, I don't know, all I know is, they said—" Once again, he'd gone too far, and by the time he thought better of it, it was too late. I asked him again what "they" had said about the girl.

"Nothing," he lied. "They don't tell me nothing."

"You don't say?" I said. "Well, let me tell you something, I got a good mind to torch this dump, and The Man is gonna be plenty pissed when he comes back here and he realizes you were the sentry when his little underage trick pad went up in smoke."

His hands were still high, but now they were shaking. "I thought you was a cop."

"You got five seconds to tell me what you know about the reporter," I said, poking him in the ribs again with the billy club, "or I shoot you. What'll it be, moron?" I began the countdown. "Five—"

He used up maybe, oh, four-tenths of a second. "I keep tellin' you, I don't know where they took her. All I heard was The Man telling Tony over the phone that two of the guys had her, and they had to bang in sick at the garage to keep an eye on her."

That would be the Under-Common garage, the cash cow of

the Stadium Authority, where Jiggs had said all the hoods were being larded onto the payroll, to get some reportable income to show their parole officers. The Speaker was going to have even more explaining to do, to somebody, I wasn't quite sure yet just who.

"That's all I know," the thug said, again trying to glance back around at me. "I swear."

I shifted the gun from his neck to the small of his back, his spine specifically. One wrong move, and he was a paraplegic, if he didn't bleed to death before the ambulance arrived.

"Now I want a little tour of the place," I said. "Maybe I might want to join the club, become a member."

"I told you, nobody's here."

As if I'd take his word on anything. As my father used to say, Trust everybody, but cut the cards. I wasn't following him up or down any stairs—that would be tempting fate. But as long as I was here, I might as well take a quick look around the first floor.

Specifically, I was wondering about the room at the end of the hall, the one with the sign that said EMPLOYEES ONLY. In most clubs, that would be the janitor's closet. But this was Knocko's place, so at the very least, he might have a few revolvers and the odd 9mm stashed along with the mops and the cleaning supplies. Maybe I could replenish the dwindling supply of firearms in my old Army steamer trunk.

"You're an employee," I said. "Let's visit 'Employees Only.'"

"It's locked," he said. "The key's in the drawer over there."

"Then go get it," I said, "but don't make any sudden moves."

He made no sudden moves, just turned slowly around and then practically tiptoed over to the desk. He averted his eyes from my face, a wise move, as he opened the drawer slowly and extracted a ring of keys. There was apparently no gun in the drawer, not even a knife. Unlike the Boy Scouts, they were not prepared. The two guys had gotten complacent over the years. In Town was down if not out. And there was nobody coming up behind the two guys—blame busing, white flight, and the birth dearth. They'd gone soft. They were out of shape. Maybe not Knocko and Tony Miami themselves, but their underlings.

Key in hand, the punk walked the twenty feet or so toward the back of the building with me following behind at a safe distance. He asked my permission before he opened the "Employees Only" door. He then announced to me that he would now turn on the overhead light, if I wanted him to. I wanted him to, and so he did, again in slow motion. Once it was on I could see that one wall had a door that opened into another shabbily appointed free-weight room. Paint was peeling off the walls, and a trash can in the corner was overflowing. Except for the door, the entire far wall was dominated by a window which I immediately realized was a two-way mirror.

In the free-weight room, you would look at the wall and see a mirror. You'd never know someone could be looking at you on the other side. I'd never seen a two-way mirror outside of a police station before, but knowing the kinds of contacts Knocko had, I was willing to bet he probably used the same glass guys as the BPD—and that he got a better deal on his work because, of course, he would be paying cash.

Besides the two-way mirror, the free-weight room had one other distinguishing characteristic. There were more mattresses than free weights, and they were scattered haphazardly all over the floor.

"What does Knocko use the two-way mirror for?" I asked.

"What do you think?" he said, a little too belligerently for my liking.

From where I stood, through the window I could see all of the small room, and I noticed a banner on the back wall that said SOUTHIE RULES! Then I spotted a tiny state-of-the-art camera hanging from the ceiling inside the free-weight room. Mattresses, a camera, underage girls . . . I suddenly realized I was standing near a soundstage of sorts, the Southie Rules! XXX-rated grind-house. The Man, it appeared, liked to retain a record of his con-quests. He was a regular Rob Lowe of the underworld, running his own personal jailbait version of *Girls Gone Wild* in Southie.

"Let me guess," I said, "this weight room is not open to the general public?"

"You're dead now," the ape said calmly. "You might as well shoot both of us, if he finds out we was here in the dog room."

"The what?" I said. "What did you call it?"

"Nothing," he said.

"You called it the dog room." I shoved the gun farther into his back. "So he has this room where he does the jailbait, and he videotapes it under this banner that says Southie Rules exclama-tion point, and he calls it the dog room and sometimes when he's in the mood, I bet he sits in here, by himself of course, and watches other guys rape the little girls."

"You better forget I ever mentioned it to you, or we're both dead."

"What's that mean, 'the dog room'?"

He shook his head again. "I keep telling you, I don't ask no-body nothing."

I glanced around the viewing room again, and this time I noticed a metal cabinet, about four feet high, and on top of it, some DVDs haphazardly stacked. Katy Bemis wasn't here, I was pretty sure of that now, but I still had a minute or two before Slip would pull up. If I could just grab some of those DVDs. . . .

"Man, you are in such deep shit," the ape said. "We're both dead, do you understand that?"

I looked again at the cabinet and this time saw, on top of the DVDs, masks—ski masks. Probably an extra little kink on some of the tapes, the masks might make a nice souvenir back home on Shawmut Ave., along with some DVDs, of course.

"Get a bag, ape."

"You're going to need a body bag," he said.

"If you push me I'll drop you right here," I said. "I don't give a shit, if that's how you want to play it. Then I'll have all night to go through these tapes. Your call, sailor."

He muttered an obscenity or two under his breath, but finally grunted something about a bag in the other corner. He pointed, and I could see it. It was a brown paper shopping bag, from Flanagan's Supermarket. I told him to fill it with as many DVDs as he could, which he did, in his own lumbering way. As he loaded the bag, I got a good grasp on my billy stick. When the bag was about two-thirds full, I ordered him to put a couple of the ski masks on top. After he did that, I told him, "Turn back around again—I don't want you facing me. And then take off your clothes."

"What are you going to do?"

"I'm going to shoot you if you don't stop asking questions," I said. "Make it snappy."

He made it snappy. Once he was naked, his hairy backside still turned to me, I got a good solid grip on the billy club and I sapped him, as Slip would say. Hit him right on the side of the head, as hard as I could. He went down, not out exactly, but he was moaning, in great pain, semiconscious at best.

Once he was down, I leaned over and struck him once more on the side of the head. He stopped moaning. Then I grabbed a few of the remaining DVDs, ran out into the hall, and threw them toward the front of the building. I quickly went back into the mirror room, gathering up his clothes. Then I dashed back out into the hallway and scattered his clothes just as I had the tapes.

If he did come to anytime soon, the first article of clothing he'd need to find was his sweatpants, so I draped them over my arm. Then, after taking one of The Man's ski masks from the bag and putting it on over my face, I turned out the light in the office, took the Bulldog out of my coat, and fired it twice at the window/mirror that faced out onto the dog room. The double-thick glass exploded, and I was certain it would take some industrial-strength vacuum cleaners, not to mention thousands of dollars' worth of custom-made, special-order replacement glass, to get the dog room back into working order. Most likely, its days as a statutory rape romper room were over.

I took off for the front door, shutting off all the lights behind me as best I could. If it was dark inside, that would slow down the police, because cops learn early on that unless a place is on fire, you don't go barging into a darkened building where shots have just been fired. The last thing I did before exiting was turn off the light in the front lobby, so as to minimize the chances of any civilians getting a good look at me; not that I was greatly concerned, now that I was wearing a ski mask. For once, some witnesses in South Boston would be able to tell the cops that the perp was wearing a ski mask, and they wouldn't be lying.

I bolted down the stairs and into the street, with no pedestrians on the sidewalk to see me. Once I got onto the sidewalk, I balled up the ape's sweatpants and hurled them as best I could under a parked car.

Then I turned back toward the "gym," took out the Bulldog, and fired two more bullets, this pair going straight through the club's front door. Almost immediately, lights began going on in all the upper-floor apartments above the storefronts along Dorchester

Street. I scanned the street and saw the Slipmobile. Slip had heard the shots too and was making a U-turn.

I took off at a sprint and made the two blocks to the alley in what seemed like about fifteen seconds flat. Slip's car was idling, and I jumped in the car, tossed the bag of DVDs into the backseat, and told him to hightail it south for Dorchester.

Chapter Fifteen

THE BEST THING about Dorchester is there's a million ways in and out. No way the cops could cover every street, not that there was a chance in hell that they gave a rat's ass about a few shots being fired on Dorchester Street, at least as long as no one called 911 to report any casualties. We would hop onto the Expressway at Gallivan Boulevard and drive south until we could be reasonably certain we weren't being followed. Then we could head home to Slip's apartment in Roslindale, an easily defensible third-floor walkup just outside the square on Washington Street.

There was only one problem. We still hadn't found Katy.

Slip said nothing as he drove down Morrissey Boulevard, nearing the *Globe.* I took the Bulldog out of my coat, removed the two unused rounds, and began dissembling the old revolver as Slip glanced over.

"I knew I heard the Bulldog bark," he said.

"You did," I said, "and now I'm going to have to put it to sleep."

"Damn shame," he said. "It's one fine piece."

"Was," I said, tossing the barrel out as we passed by the *Globe*. I kept throwing out pieces every five hundred yards or so until there was nothing left. Then I tossed out the two remaining bullets, and a quarter mile later, the four spent cartridges. It's much more difficult to do a ballistics test or trace a gun's lineage if you only have a couple of pieces of it. Plus, juries tend to frown on parties who heave loaded weapons onto the sidewalk because, well, you know how the little tykes of all ages, from eight to eighty, love to play with a new toy they've just found.

"That gun didn't belong to me," Slip said.

"I'll replace it," I said.

"Do I even want to know what just happened?" he said.

"I don't think so," I said.

"But the broad wasn't there?"

"No, she wasn't."

"So it was just a routine little shoot-out then," he said, touching his cigarette lighter to a Kool. "Mother o' God, it sounded like D-Day back there."

Yeah, I thought. D as in dog room.

"You're sure I don't need to know anything more?" he said.

"I'm sure, Slip. And I'll say no more."

"You're damn right you won't," Slip said.

AND I didn't. I just sat there silently in the shotgun seat, staring out the window, pondering my next move as Slip drove at a steady sixty-five, a safe ten miles per hour above the speed limit. At the Braintree split he took Route 3 south toward the Cape for a couple of exits before getting off in Weymouth at Route 18. It was outside the city, but he knew the turf. A lot of his old friends and neighbors from Dudley Street in Roxbury, who had long since moved out of the city, were now old enough to be ending up at the South Shore Hospital.

At times like this, Slip wouldn't say shit if he had a mouthful. And that was just as well, because I had a lot to consider as I gazed out at what had once been farmland, as recently as the midsixties. Now, in place of the dairy farms and the drive-in theaters, we drove by palm readers and tattoo parlors and "multi-service centers" in buildings taken over from now-defunct regional discount store chains like Zayre's, Ames, Bradlees, Caldor. . . .

We passed a new high school under construction that was going to include a day-care center for all the teen moms. The city was coming to the suburbs. Slip drove past a Catholic church where the old Cardinal had posted not one, but two pederast priests. We passed a drug store with a large sign out front that said "We no longer stock OxyContin." We drove by branch banks with ATMs that were now all bilingual—Press 2 for English. We saw gas stations where you had to converse with the attendants through bulletproof glass, and liquor stores where the bulk of the sales were now in nip bottles.

"This whole stretch reminds me of Mattapan in sixty-six, sixty-seven," Slip finally said. "Just waiting to tip. I'll bet you there's more pit bulls and rottweilers registered down here than goldens, or would be, if illegal alien drug dealers ever registered their dogs, which of course they don't, any more than they register their cars."

Finally, we started seeing signs for businesses that had "Brockton" in their names, so I told Slip to turn back around. As to what I should do next, I was stumped. We got back on Route 3 heading north and had just reached the Southeast Expressway when my cell phone rang. It was Plain View, calling from headquarters.

"Got anything for me?" he asked.

"Not yet, but you'll be the first to know."

"Why am I not reassured?" he said. "But I got some dirt, don't ask me why I'm passing it on to you. Agent Orange is shaking every tree over here, trying to figure out where you might be holed up."

"That's what I call good police work."

"Yeah," he said dryly. "Another thing—the boyos already tossed your apartment. I drove by there just to see if anything was shaking, and sure enough, the front door was wide open."

"Where was Willie?"

"I told you," he said, "Willie was just there to make a statement that one time. I can't have a man over there all the time." He paused. "Anyway, when I saw the door open, I went in. I hope you don't mind. I didn't have a search warrant."

"That's okay. You didn't find anything, did you?"

"Nothing I could use, if that's what you mean. Just some old newspapers and an old London bobby's hat on the floor."

"Shit," I said. "That hat belonged to my grandfather."

"I didn't know your grandfather was English."

"I'll explain it to you some other time."

"I guess the question is," Plain View said, "was there anything for them to find?"

"Not unless they were looking for my discharge papers from the Army, or the phone numbers of my brother's last three parole officers. There's not much else there. Did you at least shut the door behind you?"

"Ten-four, good buddy," he said. "Don't you want to ask me anything about Katy Bemis?"

"I just talked to her," I said, neglecting to add that it was more than an hour ago now. "They still have her, but she's okay, for now."

"I thought you didn't have anything for me." Suddenly there

was a frosty edge to his voice. "I've been straight with you, why are you holding out on me?"

"If I was holding out on you, would I have told you I'd talked to her?"

"Maybe not," he conceded. Then he thought a little longer. "I know I sound like a broken record, but it might help if I had an idea exactly why they're so interested in Katy Bemis and you. You could tell me what it is they want, for instance."

"I could," I said, letting it hang. "If only I knew myself."

"Oh, please," he said.

Neither of us spoke for a few seconds. I thought maybe he'd hung up on me. But then a thought suddenly occurred to me.

"Are you still there?" He was. "Let me ask you something, Evans, what're the odds we could ever tie Knocko or Tony Miami directly into any of this?"

"I wouldn't hold my breath if I was you," he said.

"So who's the highest up we—you—could bring down in this?" Other than the Speaker, of course, but that notch would be carved on my belt later. I wanted to know who Plain View thought he could take out now, with a little luck and the right plan. The more notorious the crew Plain View believed he could round up, the more likely he'd be to cooperate with me. I asked him again who he thought he might be able to make a case against. I had a pretty fair idea what his answer would be.

"Agent Orange maybe, if we got lucky," he said. "Jesus Christ, is that guy bent. He's not even hiding it down here at headquarters. It's all Knocko said this and Tony Miami told him that. We're supposed to be very impressed."

"If you gave him a lead, would he bite?"

"Oh God, yes. That's one thing about a cop who goes south on the job. He gets lazy. Let's just say Finnerty doesn't have a whole lot of sources down here, or anywhere else, would be my guess. Other than his two dear friends, that is."

"So he'd bite?"

"He'd bite all right," Plain View said. "So what do you want me to tell him, first off, and secondly, what's in it for me?"

AFTER I got off the phone with Plain View, I told Slip we were going back to the South End, to my place. Slip didn't care. The night was young and there weren't a lot of his voters to alienate in the South End anyway. To make my plan work, Plain View had to put the story over, but that didn't appear to be Mission: Impossible.

Finnerty was head over heels in love with the Mob. Most likely it had started with simple access, the occasional tip on an impending armored-car robbery like the one Bucky Bennett had gotten nailed on, or my brother's truckload of hijacked cigarettes, or the whispered address of a warehouse full of weed in Southie whose owners had neglected to pay off The Man for "protection." Plus, Knocko no doubt furnished him with a steady supply of inside underworld gossip to spice up those field reports every G-man has to file for the deskbound pencil-pushers in Washington to get their cop rocks off on.

But soon after Finnerty "recruited" his Top Echelon Criminal Informants all those years ago now, cash had begun changing hands. After all those years of "protecting" every non-Mafia hood in the city, including drug dealers, Knocko was rolling in dough, and Finnerty was a cop, which is to say broke, at least if he were honest. Maybe in the beginning Finnerty rationalized it by telling himself that no matter what the Jesuits teach you at BC High, the ends do indeed justify the means, and the end was taking down the Italians on Prince Street. As he pocketed the cash in the envelope that Knocko handed him in an unmarked car at Castle Island, perhaps Agent Orange told himself he was merely bonding with his Top Echelon Informants, accepting a "loan."

Talk about baiting the hook. You can bet Knocko and Tony Miami knew exactly what they were getting—an insurance policy, their ace in the hole if they ever got in a serious jam. Anybody can trade up a cop, except maybe a state senator.

"So let me get this straight," Slip said as we stopped at a traffic light near the Cabot T garage in Southie. "You want me to go into your place before you do and hide in the closet downstairs."

"Affirmative. Then Finnerty will break in and wait for me to return, because Plain View told him I had everything with me, and that I was heading back to my place."

"Why would he believe Plain View?"

"Because he's so fucking crooked he's gotten stupid—and careless."

"Okaaaay," Slip said, doubtfully. "So why doesn't he just take you out on the street?"

"Can't risk the possibility of witnesses. He'd rather do me inside."

Slip frowned. "What if he decides to hide in the same closet as me?"

"He won't. You'll be too far back from the front door, and he won't dare turn on the lights, so he'll just hide right inside the door."

"You hope."

"I hope," I said. "That's right. I hope."

Slip did not seem impressed with my spur-of-the-moment plan. "So then, if everything goes the way you hope it does—"

He again emphasized the word "hope." Seldom is heard a discouraging word from Slip to his friends, but now he was making up for lost time. The bell was ringing, and Slip was shaking his head, *No mas.* He didn't want to come out of his corner.

"Here's what I still don't get, Jackie. How come he doesn't just cap you right then and there once you're inside, then grab the stuff and screw?"

"Because he's a cop," I said. "Corrupt, yes, but a cop nonetheless. He'll want to find out what I know."

"Know about what?"

"It doesn't matter what I know. He just has to find out whatever it is I do know. He can't help himself. To a guy like Agent Orange, information is power. He uses it to impress his superiors. He gets the inside dope. It's like spreading gossip at a cocktail party. The desk jockeys are impressed he's got so many quote-unquote underworld informants, so they tell him the inside stuff they get from the other feds, the honest ones, to impress him back. And he turns around and tells Knocko what the honest guys in the office are up to."

"And both sides are paying him?" Slip said, putting it into his own terms. "Are you telling me he's a double-fucking-dipper?"

"That's exactly what he is—I thought you knew," I said. "Information is the coin of his realm. He gives them information, they give him—"

"Money." Slip had the blinders on now. He hated the bum. The prick was collecting two paychecks, and Slip was only getting one. Agent Orange was a double-dipper. He had to go.

"He's taking payoffs from the wiseguys," Slip said.

"No doubt about that. It explains how he can afford to fly first class to Florida, unlike you, and it's also why he wants me to spill to him before he clips me. That way he earns his money from The Man, by bringing him some new information. Plus it's no fun for him if I don't know he whacked me."

"I don't get that, Jack."

"Neither do I," I said, as the Slipmobile glided up East Berkeley Street past Foley's. "If it was Tony Miami, or Knocko, they'd just drop me. They only want the money, or whatever it is that can get them more money. Finnerty's on some kind of cop power trip. He's gotta show me who's boss before he kills me. And that's where you come in, Slip."

"That's when I clip him?"

"I'd rather you didn't, Slip. I mean, get the drop on him, and that way, we can use him to get Katy back."

"I hope you don't take offense at this question, Jack, but what makes you think she's still alive?"

"I—I just have to hope for the best, I guess." That was the best answer I could come up with. "I mean, you heard me talking to her, what, about an hour ago, and I told 'em they'd get nothing unless I talk to her again."

"But what happens if Plain View sells Finnerty on this setup and then Finnerty calls Southie and tells 'em he can take you and get the stuff back?" The doubts were creeping back into Slip's mind. "At that point do they even have a reason anymore for not whacking her?"

Slip was making more sense than I wanted to admit.

"Suppose I do get the drop on him," Slip said. "How does that get Katy Bemis back in one piece?"

"I'll offer Agent Orange as a trade, him for Katy, straight up. We'll have him call Southie and tell them to bring her over, because that's the only way I'll let him go." Now that I was outlining the plan again, it didn't sound nearly as much like a slam dunk as when I'd described it to Plain View.

"At least," I said, "that's what I hope happens."

"You hope?" said Slip. "I'll tell you, if I ever got in a hole like the one you're digging for Finnerty, I would not be calling the Ace of Hearts expecting the cavalry to come riding to my rescue. If

I'm Finnerty, and you get the drop on me, what I do is, I dummy up and sit tight. Any calls I make are to my lawyer."

Slip had obviously been doing some calculating of his own while I'd been talking to Plain View. He kept talking.

"Let's just say everything goes according to plan and we collar Finnerty. You call nine-one-one and say you caught a burglar and he's FBI. If he shuts up he may be through as an agent, but he probably walks on any criminal charges, which means he keeps his pension, because whoever heard of a district attorney indicting a fed on a bullshit housebreak? After the heat dies down, The Man most likely finds something else for him somewhere else, plus the eagle still shits for him once a month. Not a bad life, all in all. You following me here, Jackie?"

I was following him all right.

"But," Slip said, "if he calls The Man and tells 'em he screwed up, well, we both know how those kinds of problems get straightened out. Not with a pension, that's for sure."

But what options did I have? There was no other way to play the hand.

"Another thing," Slip said. "Suppose Finnerty doesn't know how he's supposed to play it, and he clips you as soon as you open the door. What then?"

"Then you clip him," I said, and Slip laughed.

"But then what about my gun?" he said. "I've got my .38, and it's registered."

I didn't quite understand what he was driving at, so I said nothing.

"If you shoot somebody," he finally said, "the gun becomes evidence, right? That means it goes into the cops' evidence room. You used to be on the job. You know what happens when evidence goes into the evidence room. Nothing ever comes back out of the evidence room. It's a sad fucking state of affairs, cops stealing. My cops. They endorse me every two years, so I can't say nothing. But . . ."

Now I got it. Slip loved his .38, he loved it so much he didn't want to have to use it, because if he did, it would be gone forever.

"How about my Raven?" I said. "I'll trade you."

He muttered something under his breath that I couldn't quite make out, but as soon as we reached Shawmut Ave., he pulled over, put the Slipmobile into park, and we exchanged guns.

"If this Raven is such a good gun," he said, "why didn't you use it at The Man's gym?"

"Because I wanted to make a statement," I said, "and I prefer the Bulldog's bark."

"This is a real piece of shit," he said, looking down at the Raven in his palm. "This is a fag's gun."

"What can I tell you?" I said. "I'm hoping you don't have to use it, but if you do, you'll be firing at practically point-blank range."

He studied it some more, a tiny piece in his oversized paw. He grimaced and gritted his teeth.

"This is a peashooter," he said.

"You want the .38 back?" I asked.

"Oh God, no," he said.

"Suppose you do have to shoot him," I said. "How do you explain the Raven?"

"I found it in your place," he said, as he pulled up in front of my house. "You got broken into tonight, right? Who the fuck knows what some jailbird reprobate junkie left there? I grabbed it in the melee."

"You've been thinking about your story, haven't you?"

"All the way back from Brockton," he said. Then he climbed stiffly out of the car and I slid over into the driver's seat. He handed me his little tape recorder.

"One last thing," I said. "Suppose something happens and I have to use your .38."

"Don't you dare," he said.

I watched him walk into my building and then I drove around the block. I parked on a one-way side street about two blocks south of my house. I took the bag of DVDs and the envelope with the copies of the Speaker's ledgers and locked everything in the trunk. I pocketed the gun and the tape recorder, and then I walked back to Shawmut Ave., keeping as close as possible to the buildings, in case Finnerty was already prowling the neighborhood.

About three doors down from my house, across the street, was the O'Shaughnessys' house, as it was still called, even though they'd long since cashed out to Westwood, selling out to a rich gay couple who spent the winters in Key West.

Between the O'Shaughnessy house and the next one over, on the south side, there was a narrow opening between the buildings, a corridor that led to the two backyards. That little alley was where I set up shop.

If Finnerty came in from the north side, of course, I wouldn't be able to see him, but that was the Foley's side, which meant potential witnesses. I figured his approach would be from the southern, Roxbury side. Unlike Foley's patrons, gays and illegals would be much less likely to recognize him.

The one possible complication was if Finnerty decided to bring a couple of Knocko's hirelings with him, but I figured if ever there was a job to work solo, it was this one. Finnerty was crooked, but I doubted he wanted to whack somebody in front of witnesses, especially hoods.

The problem with witnesses is that sooner or later somebody gets arrested and tries to cut a deal. So if you're involved in a capital crime with somebody, odds are eventually you'll have to kill him, or vice versa. This is why so many guys get whacked right after they make bail—once they start thinking about doing another stretch, a lot of them begin considering whether 'tis better to drop a dime than suffer the slings and arrows of another eighty-nine-month sentence, of which they must serve 85 percent.

The way someone like The Man looks at it is, better safe than sorry. Hit the guy in the head, drop him where he stands. Who needs the fucking jeopardy? Even my brother Marty has figured this out. Whenever he gets lugged, he just sits there, in jail, where they can't get to him, or at least not as easily as they could if he were out on the street. When he's sentenced, the judge calls all those months "time served." On the outside, Marty may be a half-assed hood, but once he's back inside, the wiseguys at the Ace of Hearts were right—he does do time like a million bucks.

I stood in the alley, occasionally peeking one way and then the other, shivering a bit in the damp March darkness. I made sure the tape recorder was working, and then I checked out Slip's .38. Double a-okay.

Then I saw him shuffling up the street, weaving a bit, as if he were drunk. Nice touch, Finnerty. He was probably the smartest guy Knocko and Tony Miami had ever had on the payroll. It requires a certain minimum level of intelligence, or at least cunning, to set people up and basically frame them, even losers like my brother.

When he reached my building, Finnerty fiddled and diddled with some keys and then let himself in the front door. I'd told Slip to leave the inner door unlocked; I figured Finnerty was already aware that Knocko's boys had burgled my place earlier this evening, and as far as he was concerned, it would be just like the piss-poor BPD to fail to properly secure the crime scene. Whatever, I had to get the supercilious fed inside, and I had my doubts whether he could solve a serious lock, which mine is.

I waited about five minutes, to give him time to settle in and to assure myself that he didn't have anybody backing him up. Finally I crossed the street and walked up the steps to my front door.

Then I hit the Record button on Slip's little tape recorder.

Inside the foyer, I looked down at the pile of unclaimed catalogues and prospectuses that had piled up for me and my tenants since the last time I'd cleaned up the place. I leaned over and picked up a sealed envelope, which would serve as my stage prop— the secret documents that Knocko wanted back.

Envelope in hand, I fumbled noisily with the key at the door, mostly because I didn't want to surprise Finnerty. As I opened the door and stepped inside, I held my breath so I could hear him in case he decided to act like a real Mob guy and just cap me, no questions asked. If he tried that, well, at least I'd hear him coming and have a second or so to react. Two steps inside the door, I saw a figure step from the shadows and I heard his voice.

"Freeze, motherfucker."

He was still FBI, all right, right down to the bogus macho lines. Thank goodness. I didn't hear him identify himself though. He was speaking loudly enough even for Slip's cheap little transistor tape recorder. It's amazing what you can do these days with digital audio enhancement, especially if money is no object, and for the feds it wouldn't be, if I could just stay alive long enough to deliver the recording to them.

"Drop it," he said, "and get your hands up."

"Yes, sir," I said, letting go of the envelope. I put my hands up as the package thudded to the floor. Finnerty leaned over to pick it up. He didn't even notice that it was sealed, or that the return address belonged to a mutual fund company on Franklin Street. He just chuckled with pride at the magnitude of his own accomplishment.

"Thought you could put one over on us, huh?" he said, not specifying who "us" were. "I oughta plug you right here and now."

On a scale of 1 to 10 in the admissible evidence department, that checked in at about a 12.

I squinted in the dark. "Don't shoot, mister." That was pouring it on thick, that "mister." "Who . . . are . . . you?"

"I'm the last guy you'll ever see if you don't tell me everything you know, punk."

THE LAST guy I'll ever see? Finnerty really knew how to put someone at ease, so he'd open up and spill the beans. Slip interpreted it just the way I did and decided to make his move. I watched his shadow as he stepped out of the closet behind us, gun in hand, and said evenly:

"Now you freeze, Finnerty, or I blow your brains out."

I immediately hit the deck as Finnerty wheeled around and Slip squeezed off two shots from the Raven. I heard the crack of the shots, and Finnerty was suddenly hurled backward across the room. His gun seemed to fly out of his hand as he landed in a heap, all crumpled up, right beside me. He moaned.

"I got him, Jack," Slip yelled. "I got him! Is he dead?"

"Jesus Christ, I don't know," I said, rising to my knees and staring down at Finnerty's prone form. "He's bleeding like a stuck pig. I think you shot him in the ass, as he was turning around."

"Shit," he said, "your popgun fucked up my aim. It's too light."

"I don't know," I said. "He looks pretty bad off to me."

Finnerty was groaning, louder now. I turned on the light overhead and noticed that the puddle of blood under him seemed to be widening before my eyes. I glanced over at the wall and saw a bullet hole. Slip was one-for-two—not bad for firing in the dark.

I picked Finnerty's gun up off the floor.

"Hey Slip," I said, "check this out. It's a revolver, .44 caliber, Ruger Blackhawk. Is that regulation?"

"In a pig's arse it is," Slip said. "The dirty double-dippin' reprobate bastard was going to waste you with a throwdown."

I looked down at Finnerty, pointed his own piece at him, and smiled. Agent Orange was suddenly living two of the oldest cop cliches: Payback is a bitch, and don't do the crime if you can't do the time.

This shooting complicated matters. I bent over Agent Orange and asked him if he could hear me. He let out a louder groan, which I took to be an affirmative response. He slowly turned himself over onto his stomach and dragged himself along the floor toward a chair, leaving a trail of smeared blood behind him. Finally he propped himself up against my favorite easy chair. His head bobbed and his breathing was labored.

Slip stared down at him, his hands on his hips, the Raven tucked inside his belt. He smiled; this was a victory for everyone flying coach over all the shitheads up in first class.

"Lucky for you I shot you with a girl gun," Slip told him. "If I was using my own piece, I'd have upgraded you, asshole. To dead."

Then my little gun had indeed served its purpose. Slip turned around to whisper in my ear.

"I think he's going into shock. There's no time to waste."

I nodded, took the tape recorder out of my coat pocket, and knelt down beside Finnerty as though I was administering last rites, which maybe I was. I didn't see too many more West Palm winter weekends in his future.

"I am John F. X. Reilly and I am in my first-floor apartment at 125 Shawmut Avenue, Ward Three, City of Boston, at nine twenty on the evening of March 2 with FBI agent John Finnerty and Boston City Councilor Slip Crowley and we all agree—assent—to this audio taping. Do you assent, Councilor Crowley?"

Of course he did.

"Do you assent, Special Agent Finnerty?"

"Fuck you," he said hoarsely. "Call nine-one-one. Get me an ambulance. Get me Bob Mueller on the phone. Louie Freeh. Somebody. I can't believe you let that idiot shoot me."

Slip took a belligerent step toward him. "Who are you calling an idiot, sucker?"

I stepped in front of Slip and theatrically turned off the tape recorder. "Finnerty," I said, recalling one of my favorite old B-movie lines, "we can do this the easy way, or we can do this the hard way."

"What's the hard way?"

"You bleed to death."

"You wouldn't dare. I'm an FBI agent."

"An FBI agent who didn't identify himself as such and who was pulling a black-bag job. An FBI agent who was using what I presume to be an unregistered, probably stolen, handgun in the commission of a felony. Finnerty, I'm not calling anybody until we get everything on tape."

Slip chuckled. He lit a cigarette, then bent over Finnerty and blew smoke directly into his face.

"Some fuckin' sleuth you are," Slip said. "The only things you ever investigated were the sales in Filene's Basement."

Slip took another deep drag and then exhaled still more secondhand smoke into Finnerty's face. The fed groaned.

"I am John F. X. Reilly," I repeated, "and I am with FBI agent John Finnerty and we agree—assent—to this taping. Do you assent, Mr. Finnerty?"

"You'll never get away with this. I'll see both you assholes behind bars."

"Do you assent to the taping, Mr. Finnerty?"

"Hell yes. I'm shot."

"Agent Finnerty, what was your purpose in illegally breaking and entering into the home of Mr. Reilly this evening and threatening to murder him in cold blood?"

"I wanted to get back the shit you stole from the Speaker."

"Are you referring to certain documents burgled from Cooperative Trust Savings Bank in Medford, Massachusetts, which were given to me by the late Bucky Bennett, copies of which were used by James J. 'Knocko' Nugent and Anthony Massimino, aka Tony Miami, to extort money from House Speaker Harold Lynch?"

"Yes, yes, yes," he croaked. "Enough with the *Adam-12* shit. Call nine-one-one."

"Were you sent here by Nugent and Massimino to burgle the apartment and retrieve the Cooperative Trust documents and murder me?"

He let out a long, low moan. I lowered the tape recorder even closer to his mouth, and Finnerty wheezed.

"They don't operate that way, you know that." His voice had gone from a croak to a rasp. "Things just . . . get done. I figured . . ." His voice trailed off. Either he was thinking, or he'd expired. Then he moaned again.

"I just figured it out," he said, "that homicide dick set me up. I got set up by two Boston cops and then this hack"—he waved weakly at Slip, his voice fading—"shoots me."

"Who are you calling a hack, sucker?" Slip demanded.

I asked him, "How much do they pay you for your, uh, services?"

"They're my informants," he said, a little too quickly, as if he'd rehearsed this answer. "You have to establish a bond of trust with your criminal informants, especially if they're Top Echelon. Little things. Gifts at Christmas, favors here and there."

He was going to murder me so his underworld paymasters could keep blackmailing the most powerful man in state government. That was his idea of a favor. I had more than enough tape now. Maybe it would be admissible at trial, maybe not. But it was the end of his career in the FBI, not to mention his bid for police commissioner.

"Finnerty," I said. "Where have they got Katy Bemis?"

He managed to look up at me with sad eyes. "I have no idea," he said softly.

"Well then I have no idea whether I'm going to call nine-one-one."

"Jesus Christ, you can't let me die like this," he said. "You're a cop."

"An ex-cop. A crooked ex-cop, remember?"

"Please—" he said, looking directly at me. His mouth was open, but no words came, and I realized why he wasn't speaking. He was trying to remember my name. He had been seconds away from killing me and now he couldn't remember my name. "Please, man, all I have is a phone number to call."

"Then give it to me, scumbag." He recited it, and I called Slip over and whispered in his ear to keep an eye on him. Then I noticed my grandfather's bobby hat, still on the floor, about two feet from the widening pool of Finnerty's blood. I picked up it, took it into the kitchen, and gently placed it on top of the refrigerator.

I began dialing Plain View on my cell phone, but quickly thought better of it. I cut the connection and looked at the number Finnerty had given me. It had one of those unfamiliar cell phone area codes. Since I've been off the job, I know the cops have new technology for tracking cell phone calls, satellites, and everything else, but the bad guys would be using disposable phones. One call, two at the most, and then they ditched it. Remember those old cop-movie scenes when the serial killer calls the starlet and the detective, Robert Taylor, tells the woman to keep Richard Basehart talking until they can trace the call? Then they cut away to stock footage of a busy switchboard with all female operators. There would be none of that tonight. Do they even have switchboards anymore?

All I knew was that if Knocko's guys detected the slightest hint of a setup, they would kill Katy. No doubt those were their exact instructions. I had to get her back tonight, and the only way to do that was to lure Knocko's gunsels out of Southie, with her in tow.

I counted to sixty, very slowly, after which I walked back out into the living room, cell phone still in hand.

Slip was still standing over Finnerty, smoking another Kool, brandishing the Raven. Finnerty looked about the same—not so hot.

"Did you call nine-one-one?" Finnerty asked, his voice still weaker.

I shook my head and bent over to offer him the cell phone.

"Not until you call the boys—on your cell phone. Tell them you couldn't close the deal. Tell them they don't get the Speaker's ledgers back until I get Katy. And we aren't crossing the bridge either. They have to bring her here. Do you understand?"

"They won't bite," he said. "You might as well let me bleed to death."

I shrugged. "That's your call." Slip and I both stared down at him. I concentrated on his pinky ring and idly wondered how much it would fetch at Uncle Ned's Money to Loan on Washington Street. Then Finnerty made up his mind. He began reaching into his coat pocket, muttering, "Cell phone," as if I were still afraid of him pulling a weapon. He retrieved the phone and then handed it to me.

"Dial the number for me," he said, spitting out the words with as much energy as he could still muster. "The one I gave you."

I did, and handed it to him on the first ring. They picked up immediately.

"Kevin?" he said. "Yeah, it's me . . . I couldn't finish it. . . . Doesn't matter . . . he wants the broad back in return for that shit he's got. . . . It's take it or leave it. . . . The cop set me up . . . tell me about it . . . I'll handle him myself later. . . . There's nothing wrong with my voice, whaddaya talking about? . . . I'm fine . . . I got the drop on 'em, it's, like, a stand-off. . . . I'm telling you, The Man would want you to have them bring her over here. . . . Believe me, all the two guys care about is getting their stuff back. . . ."

He looked up to me, to show he was a team player. The problem was, he was on the wrong team. Still, I gave him a thumbs-up and a nod. I'd trust him about as far as I could throw him, and apparently the other side felt the same way, which was why he was having difficulty convincing them to walk into a trap.

"Look," he said, clearing his throat, sounding terrible, "believe me, he's gonna be plenty pissed if you shit the bed on this deal . . . okay, okay, it's Reilly's place, Shawmut Ave. . . ."

He couldn't remember the number. He looked up at me and I silently mouthed it for him.

"One-two-five Shawmut Avenue," he repeated. "Kevin . . . tell 'em no funny business . . . you know what I'm saying . . . make it quick . . . bye."

He looked up at me and then handed me the phone. His eyes were starting to glaze over, his jaw was going slack, and it couldn't have happened to a nicer fellow. I grabbed the phone, told Slip to keep an eye on him, just in case, and then I walked back into the kitchen. I sat down at the kitchen table and called Plain View. He picked up on the first ring.

"Slip Crowley just shot Finnerty," I said.

"Aw, shit," he said with a deep sigh. "Is he dead?"

"No, but he should be. He was trying to kill me."

"Save it for the uniforms. Speaking of which, I assume you've called nine-one-one."

"Actually—" I stopped myself just in time, before I admitted I hadn't. He'd go ballistic on me if he knew there was no ambulance on the way for a "man down." Even a crooked man.

"Tell me you've called nine-one-one," he said. "I'm going to check, but tell me you've called."

"I thought I'd let you make the call."

He considered my offer for a moment or two, then said no.

"You make the call," he said. "Then call me back, on my cell."

He was right. If I called 911, it was just a case of shit happens—a corrupt cop finally getting his comeuppance. If Plain View had to make the call, his ass was in a sling, because it would mean that he was taking some responsibility for what had gone down. If Finnerty survived, he could accuse Plain View of setting him up, although at that point, what credibility would he have?

I made the call to 911 and gave them my address, and then I phoned Plain View back on his cell phone and told him the ambulance was on its way.

"Thank you," he said. "This will make it a lot easier on both of us."

"Up to a point," I said, and then I told him the part of the plan I hadn't mentioned to him earlier in the evening, about the next group of visitors that I was expecting.

"They're on their way over now?" he said. "You're shitting me, right?"

"What else was I supposed to do?"

"I really wish you hadn't played it this way," he said, "but I'll be right over."

ONCE THEY arrived, the EMTs quickly realized that Finnerty was down almost a quart of blood. As they lifted him onto a stretcher, the rubber soles of their shoes squeaked in the puddles of Finnerty's blood on my living room floor. They kept asking me and Slip what had happened, and we told them we had found him lying there, shot, when we arrived home. They didn't believe us, but it's not a crime to lie to an EMT, and they had more pressing duties anyway—like trying to get him to the emergency room before he expired from shock and loss of blood.

As the gurney reached the door, with his last bit of strength Finnerty propped himself up on the stretcher and pointed at Slip and me.

"Arrest these men," he said. "They shot a federal agent."

The EMTs looked at us in confusion.

"He's obviously hallucinating," I explained to them. "Poor bastard—he's just lucky we got here in time." I looked at Slip. "Right, Councilor?"

"Damn straight," Slip said to me, glancing over at Finnerty, who had collapsed back onto the stretcher. "Don't worry, Agent, we'll find the reprobates who done this to you while you were burglarizing the place."

Then Plain View arrived and began assuming command, more or less. The first thing he did, once the ambulance was gone, was get the police cruisers off the street and into the alleys, far enough back that they couldn't be seen from a car being driven slowly down Shawmut Ave. We didn't have much time, but for once the cops moved fast. My building was quickly surrounded by SWAT snipers. They have a lot more toys now then when I was on the job. If they'd had more time, the cops would have brought out their tank, an armored personnel carrier or two, and maybe even the bomb defusers. Your federal law-enforcement grants at work.

Inside, in my living room, Plain View and I stood in opposite corners, two of the few places in the room where the rug wasn't soaked through with Finnerty's blood. I knew he'd have plenty of questions that I didn't want to answer, so I tried to take the offensive.

I said, "They gotta come, right?"

He gave me a funny look. "They don't gotta do anything."

"Yeah, but they have to get Finnerty out of this jam."

Another puzzled look from Plain View. "They do? Why?"

"Because," I said, thinking aloud as I went along, "because . . . he might crack."

"Why would he crack?" he said. "They don't know he's shot, do they? I mean, he didn't tell them on the phone that he was shot, did he?"

"I don't think so."

"You don't think so? You mean you don't remember?" He was rapidly gaining the upper hand on me and would soon be the one asking the questions. It was my house, but he was the cop, so he was in charge, at least until the deputy superintendent or whoever arrived. The building's front door would be left open, so that Knocko's men could get in. Once they were inside, there would be no getting back out.

I looked out the window and was relieved to see that the street appeared deserted again. Now Plain View was explaining how we would handle Finnerty's absence once we got them inside. No one, he said aloud, should try to imitate Finnerty's voice. As he said this, he was staring at Slip.

"You must think I'm stupid," Slip said, patting my gun, which he'd stuck into his belt. Plain View couldn't help but notice.

"Is that the gun you shot him with?" Evans asked.

"Who wants to know?" Slip replied.

"Is it your gun, Councilor?" Plain View asked, and Slip glanced over at me.

"It's mine," I said, making an instantaneous decision to tell the truth, because I realized now that Plain View would be insulted if we tried to peddle him the lame story about the gun being abandoned by Knocko's burglars.

"And no, it's not registered," I added. "It's a throwdown I've had for years, from back when I was on the job."

"You never learn, do you?" he said, and I knew I was about to get a lecture. But then his radio crackled, as someone out front alerted him to the fact that our guests had arrived, in an old Chevy van they were double-parking directly in front of my building.

That told me they weren't planning a lengthy visit.

Plain View nodded at one of the uniforms by the door. He turned off the lights. Now we watched from the front window as they got out of the van. There were two of them, plus Katy, who was pushed out of the van by a guy wearing a scally cap and a windbreaker with a Mass. Convention Center Authority seal on it. The guy had to be at least six four—it was my pal from Somerville, Tommy Nick. What goes around comes around.

He shoved Katy ahead in front of him, his gloved left arm tight around her neck and what looked like a 9mm in his right hand. I wondered if it could be my Beretta, the one he took off me last night in East Somerville. I didn't see any C-notes, though. Tonight Katy was his shield, and if he went down, she was going with him. Her face was death-mask pale, and she was obviously terrified, but at least she was still breathing. She was wearing the same skirt she'd worn to Legal Sea Foods for her lunch with me all those hours ago.

Tommy Nick kept pushing her across the sidewalk, toward the front steps and the door. Behind him, the second guy had his right hand in the waist pocket of a nylon Bruins jacket. He was wearing a ski mask.

I drew Slip's .38 out of my coat, which was a clear no-no for a civilian, but it was too late for Plain View to pull rank. He just drew his own automatic and stepped back into the darkness as Katy and the boyos reached the front of the building. As he shoved her up the steps, Tommy Nick whispered something in her ear and she raised her leg and pushed the door open with her foot.

Tommy Nick pushed Katy inside the foyer, his gloved hand still around her neck. The second guy, the one in the Bruins jacket, tagged along about ten feet behind them, his hand still jammed into his pocket to deliver the unmistakable message. Bruin looked over his shoulder, scanning the street behind him, before he turned back around and joined Tommy Nick and Katy in the lobby.

Tommy Nick now spotted the open door to the apartment.

"Ah shit, Carmine," he said. "I don't like this one bit."

He paused a moment, then hissed: "Finnerty? You there? What happened to the lights?"

From inside the door I watched their shadows playing off the hallway walls. I couldn't believe they had walked into such an obvious setup.

They inched closer to the threshold, and now I could see them more clearly through the door. They were wearing sweat-pants, as I knew they would be. For the Mob, every day is casual Friday.

"Finnerty," Tommy Nick said. "Either you answer or we walk right back out this door."

I looked over at Plain View. He shook his head—he didn't want any response. But I disregarded his silent instructions.

"Aaaarrrrrgh," I said, gurgling.

"Finnerty, motherfucker," Tommy Nick said doubtfully. "What the fuck is up?"

"Shot," I coughed out. There was no response, which meant they weren't buying. I hadn't expected them to.

"We been set up," Carmine said, drawing the gun from his jacket.

"Let's screw," Tommy Nick said to him. "Cover the street."

Then, in a louder voice, he said, "Whoever's in there, don't try nothing, or she gets it first."

Carmine then muttered something I couldn't quite catch, but I gathered he wasn't happy. Carmine disappeared from my line of sight and then I heard the door onto the front steps open, and that was apparently when he spotted the cops because the next thing I heard was, "Police! Freeze!" followed by one shot from a pistol and then the *pop-pop-pop-pop* of multiple gunshots from rifles, shotguns, and sidearms. Carmine would not be coming down for breakfast.

Inside, I could see Tommy Nick listening, trying to figure out his next move. He was grimacing, and he tightened his grip around Katy's neck. Then he made his decision.

He turned her around and pushed her toward the front door.

"Don't shoot," he yelled to the cops outside. "I'm coming out and I've got the bitch in front of me."

I made my move then. It was my turn to step out of the shadows and into the doorway, where I had a clear bead on Tommy Nick's back. I said nothing, just took aim with Slip's .38 as he pushed Katy nearer the door. I kept the gun aimed right at his back as he approached the door.

"I've got the broad in front of me," Tommy Nick yelled to the cops outside, oblivious to my presence behind him. "Don't shoot."

The outer door was about half open to the street. They were halfway out the door. I was now standing just inside the door of my apartment and I knew it was time to step up.

"Drop it or I shoot," I yelled, and Tommy Nick turned around, instinctively, as I knew he would, into the now half-open door. To do so, he had to turn Katy around with him, to keep her in front of him, as his shield. That was his final mistake, just as I had hoped it would be, because it gave the cop snipers outside on the street a clear shot at his back. As soon as his back was exposed, I instantly heard the crack of shots from at least two police sniper rifles outside. First his left hand dropped from Katy's throat, and she ran to me, past me, into my apartment. Tommy Nick lurched one step forward toward me, dropping his gun and staggering backward two steps, into the doorway. A sharpshooter's rifle popped again and this time the back of his head exploded, blowing the scally cap off his head.

More shots rang out from the street, automatic-weapons fire this time, now that Katy was no longer in the line of fire. It sounded like the Fourth of July and Chinese New Year's rolled into one on Shawmut Ave. His eyes wide open in shock, his jaw agape, Tommy Nick took one final baby step toward me before pitching forward, facefirst, onto the lobby tile. He was dead before he hit the floor.

I stepped back into my apartment and dropped Slip's .38 back into my coat pocket. Plain View rushed out into the lobby, as the cops on the street rushed forward, surrounding the two bodies. My only regret was that I had no time to rifle Tommy Nick's pockets for the hundred-dollar bill. He wouldn't be needing it anymore.

Chapter Sixteen

IT TOOK KATY a while to calm down. The detectives asked her some perfunctory questions—did she know where she'd been held? Had she seen anyone else? Did they ever say who they were working for? The answers were no, no, and no. After a few minutes the cops went back to assessing the carnage outside. Ambulances were parked wherever the cruisers weren't, catty-cornered on the street, in the alleys, even up on the sidewalk. Blue and red lights played off the windows of the houses.

It didn't take long to get the two bodies into the meat wagon. The entire block was sealed off with yellow tape as a crime scene, which meant the TV crews would have to park on Washington Street and hoof it up. When no one was looking, Slip quietly reached into my coat pocket and retrieved his .38. Then he walked outside and started talking to the reporters. This was going to be a big night for the Re-elect Councilor Crowley Committee, Delbert Raymond "Slip" Crowley, Chairman.

I stayed inside the house with Katy. At first I thought about sitting her down on the couch in the living room, but the carpet was soaked through with Finnerty's blood, so we adjourned to the kitchen. No cops, just us.

"Is this your house?" she said in a faraway, trancelike tone.

"I live here my whole life, except for the Army and a few years in Canton," I said, babbling. "Canton, I lived with my wife. Now my ex-wife, I mean. I was married to her at the time. My ex-wife."

"Does it always look like this?" she said.

"If you mean does somebody get shot here every night, the answer is no."

She managed a flat smile but said nothing.

"The reason it looks like this," I said, "is that some of the same guys who grabbed you tossed it tonight, earlier."

"Did they find what they were looking for?" she asked calmly. "And what exactly were they looking for?"

I pretended not to hear and handed her my cell phone.

"Anyone you need to call?" I said. She brushed the hair out of her eyes, wiped a lone tear from her left eye, and nodded.

"My parents," she said, "and the paper. They're in Florida, my parents I mean."

No boyfriend, though. I filed that information away for future reference. That first night in Foley's, I'd noticed that she wasn't wearing a ring on her left hand, but these days you never can tell.

"I'll leave you alone," I said.

"No," she said, "please stay. It's your house."

Well, if you insist. She continued looking at me as she dialed. Her parents picked up quickly. I wondered if they had even known, until the call, what had happened to their daughter this afternoon. It didn't take her long to reassure her folks. She said "Don't worry" a lot, almost as often as she said "I don't know."

Sometimes when she would say "I don't know" she'd stare

across the table at me. A couple of times she also said "They didn't touch me."

She finally hung up, and turned her full attention to me. Her tears were gone now, but she still dabbed at her eyes with a crumpled tissue.

"We haven't got much time," she said. "I have to get back to the paper, but first I want you to tell me why this happened to me."

"They didn't tell you?"

"Those two? They're messenger boys. Were. What was in that envelope that made it worth their lives, and mine too, almost?"

"It was a copy of some stuff, in case something happened to me. I told you that."

She shook her head. "It was more than that. It had to be. You used me as a decoy, didn't you?"

"I didn't mean to. I had no idea." That much was true.

"Why'd you give me this stuff? You don't know me."

What could I say? That I was like Bucky Bennett, fresh out of friends? Guys like me, it's hard to round up a posse, even under the best of circumstances.

"Why didn't you give these documents or whatever they are to Slip? Isn't he your friend?"

I had to keep Slip out of this. Shooting a crooked FBI agent was one thing—that would win him votes in the fall. But holding out on Knocko and Tony Miami was not a smart move on any level. I knew what Katy thought of Slip, which was what a lot of people thought of him who didn't know him except from TV, or the newspapers.

But they were wrong about him. Slip was not a stupid guy. He'd made a career out of pissing off a lot of people with a lot of clout, and at the age of sixty-seven he was still walking around.

For a guy like Slip, Slip had survived a very long time. Which was why when I asked him at City Hall if he wanted a set of the papers, he turned me down flat.

"I could have been killed, you know," she said.

"I know. What can I say? I apologize, but I understand that doesn't begin to make up for what you went through, on account of me, and my stupidity." I shook my head. "I don't blame you for being angry at me. I wouldn't blame you if you never spoke to me again."

"Do you think I'm angry at you?" she asked evenly.

"Do I think you're angry at me?" I needed time to frame an acceptable response. "Well, I guess I would be, if I were you."

"I'm not exactly mad," she said. "I mean, I'm numb, I think I will be for a while, I don't know how long. I really did think about dying, but . . ." She paused. "But sometimes things—I don't know quite how to put it, but sometimes things . . . work out for the best. You know what I mean?"

She looked down and a single tear ran from her eye down her cheek and then dropped onto the kitchen table. She sighed deeply and raised her head to look me in the eye.

"When I get back to the paper, I have to show 'em what a tough girl I am, and that part of it I think I can handle. But they're going to want to know why I was kidnapped, and why these two got shot tonight, at your house of all places, and I need something to write in my story. . . ."

"You have to write for tomorrow's paper?" I asked.

She nodded. "I think you owe me something, Jack, for this whole ordeal. I think you owe me the whole story."

And if I didn't come through now, it was over between us before it ever started, assuming it ever would have started in the first place. She didn't leave me much choice.

"Off the record?" I said.

"What do you mean, off the record? It's all over now, isn't it?"

"Not hardly," I said.

ONCE I had her word she wouldn't spill everything, at least for a few hours, I gave her the *Reader's Digest* condensed version. I didn't bother with the ancient Wimpy Hogan stuff, just concentrated on the Speaker's ledger books, only I didn't tell her his name. Those were my orders from Jiggs, or at least that's the way I decided to interpret them. She was not pleased that I wouldn't give up the name. First she played the guilt card, and when that didn't work, she started in with the interrogation.

"Is it the governor?" she said.

"I'm not playing that game," I said.

"Is it the Senate president?" she said.

"I told you, I'm not playing that game," I said.

"Your game almost got me killed," she said. "I think you at least owe it to me to tell me who's being shaken down."

"If you wait 'til tomorrow, it's a bigger story."

"If I wait 'til tomorrow, the *Globe* may get it."

"Not from me."

"I've heard that one before," she said.

She was right, of course. Still, if I couldn't get the Speaker on tape, he'd just deny everything and try to ride it out. Could he get away with it? Probably not, but more outrageous miscarriages of justice have occurred in Massachusetts. Chappaquiddick comes to mind.

"I'll give you everything tomorrow," I said, "including the ledgers."

"Are you the only one with the ledgers?"

"Yes, I am."

"But for how long?"

"It'll all be over tomorrow, one way or another."

"I need to know his name," she said. "Is it the Speaker?"

"If I tell you his name," I said, ignoring the question, "you'd want to put it in the paper, and you'd have to call him, and that would tip him off."

"But you've got to tell the cops." She was whispering now, on the off chance that some of the police milling about in the living room could hear her. "If you tell the cops, they'll tell the *Globe*."

"I promise you you'll get the story first."

"Once you tell somebody else, it's out of your control."

"Which is why I'm not telling anyone."

"Can I call him a 'prominent politician'?"

"No," I said. "That's too close to home. Call him a 'prominent member of the community.'"

"That's too vague."

It went on like that for a while, Katy bargaining with me about what she could put in the paper that would give her a scoop without screwing up my plans. Jiggs would have blown a gasket if he'd known I was conducting freelance negotiations over the disposal of what he would no doubt consider his intellectual property.

Finally, as Katy kept looking at her watch, we got down to negotiating the exact wording of how she was to describe the prominent politician. I hung tough for "a prominent member of the community," and just as we seemed to have reached an impasse, Plain View strolled back into the kitchen.

"Okay," he said to me. "No more bullshit from you—pardon my French, Miss Bemis." Nice touch, that "Miss."

His hands were on his waist as he stood over me. "Why'd Knocko and Tony Miami grab her—and those names're off the record, Miss Bemis."

"Too late," she said. "It's on the record unless you say it's off the record—"

"I know, I know," he said. "It's only off the record if you say it's off the record before you say it. I haven't got time to argue with you, Miss Bemis. You know who grabbed you anyway, or who ordered it. So I'm going to concentrate on your boyfriend here."

She didn't object to the characterization. Under different circumstances I might have been heartened.

"I got two bodies out there," Plain View said, "and an FBI agent in critical condition—"

"Correction," I said, "you got a burglar in critical condition. Make that a home invader."

"Yeah, that's your story. Yours and Slip's."

"And what exactly is Finnerty's version of how he came to be in my living room?" I said. "You can listen to the tape. And you know damn well that throwdown of his is unregistered, and how much you want to bet that ballistics can maybe trace it back to some major felony, maybe even a hit or two?"

"Don't try to change the subject," he said. "If I don't have a coherent story, the reporters out there are going to crucify me, and if they crucify me, guess who I'm gonna take it out on?"

He looked over at Katy Bemis. She just sat there, her legs crossed, staring vacantly ahead. He was talking about reporters as if she weren't there, and in a way, she wasn't. She was over her initial shock, I could tell that much. In her head, she was composing the story she'd be writing when she got back to the paper in a few minutes.

"Jack," Plain View finally said, "did you tell her what I did for—" He stopped as he thought better of informing her of the circumstances of Finnerty's arrival on the scene. "I'm not saying anything more because I don't know if I can trust either of you."

"You can trust me," she finally said, still not looking at him. "We're off the record now."

"I'll bet," he said. "By the way, did you happen to look to see what was in that package Loverboy here handed you?"

"Loverboy?" she said, finally absorbing one of his needles. "But to answer your question, no, I don't recall being given anything by Mr. Reilly."

"That's a very amusing story, Miss Bemis, especially considering the circumstances," he said. "You and Jack share that same dry sense of humor, I can see that now."

Then he turned back to me.

"At the risk of repeating myself here," he said, "I need to know everything that's gone down since Bucky got whacked outside Foley's. And let me say something else to you, Jack. You know as well as anyone, or should, how many more wiseguys they have in the bullpen over there, and you also know that tonight is not the end of this if they think you have something of theirs that is still worth something on the open market."

Katy said, "Isn't that his problem?"

"You stay out of this, Miss Bemis," he snapped without even glancing over at her. "This is between him and me."

"You disappoint me," I said to him. "You know better than to disrespect a member of the press, especially a female. The mayor's going to have you up on charges of insufficient political correctness if you don't apologize."

"I got some problems with both of you," Plain View said, turning back to her once more. "I know you had a tough time of it, and by the way if you need any victim counseling here tonight, it's only a phone call away. Just say the word." He paused. "But right now, I don't hear nobody thanking me for putting my ass on the line, which is what I did. My problem now, Miss Bemis, is I got to sweat what happens if I pick up your paper tomorrow and it's on the front page what this whole thing is all about, and I haven't told the brass, mainly because I don't know myself. If that happens I'm gonna have to spend all day tomorrow apologizing to the commissioner, and to City Hall, and the *Globe,* and the TV stations, and God only knows who else, and after I get through saying how sorry I am, I probably get busted back to pounding a beat out of that trailer at the corner of Blue Hill and Morton."

Then he turned to me.

"I'm speaking to you now, Jack," Plain View said. "What you ought to think about is that if I'm gone from headquarters then there won't be nobody down there in the future covering your ass like I did for you here tonight, because all anybody on the job's gonna remember about you is how you hung me out to dry, and I'm sorry for making a speech, but if you two don't like me, well, the feeling is getting to be pretty fucking much mutual."

Neither Katy nor I said anything for a moment. Finally she stood up and fixed Plain View with a perfect debutante's smile.

She said, "I'm the one who should apologize to you. I'm sorry, Detective. You're right, Jack did tell me about how you were the one who got Finnerty here, and I understand that's why I'm free now, and unharmed. I do appreciate that. You saved my life, I know that. Thank you. I mean it."

His face brightened instantly.

"You're welcome," he said. "And I mean that too. But please, if you really want to thank me for what I done, then shut up about it, okay?" He seemed to unwind a bit, and he even managed a wry smile. "Incidentally, if you watch the eleven o'clock news tonight, you'll find out it was Slip who saved your life. He's outside telling every reporter in the city about how he masterminded the whole deal."

We all chuckled, but it tailed off into an awkward silence, which Katy finally decided to break.

"Detective Evans," she said, "there is going to be nothing in the paper tomorrow that you don't know right now, you have my promise on that, and nothing that will get your ass in a sling. You have my word. I owe you big time, and I know that."

Plain View smiled, not at me but at her. He thanked her, although not profusely, because a cop never knows when a reporter will turn on him, and vice versa. Then he looked back to me.

"You want some advice, Jack? Wait, don't answer that, because I know you don't, but I'm gonna give you some anyway. We're all three of us damn lucky we pulled this off tonight, but you better watch your back from now on, because those guys don't forget, and it's you they're going to blame."

"Oh, don't you worry about me," I said, hoping that my new cache of DVDs would prove to be as good as I hoped they would be, which also reminded me that I had better retrieve them from Slip's car. I live too close to the Cathedral projects to leave potential life-insurance policies lying around in the trunk of anything less than an Abrams tank.

Plain View said to Katy, "I'll be needing your formal statement in the morning. Do you need a ride anywhere?"

She looked over at me and I shook my head. "I'll get her home."

"I'll bet you will," he said.

OUTSIDE, THE reporters wanted to talk to Katy, but she called the *Herald* and they told her to get in ASAP, knock out a first-person account, feed what she could into the main story, and pose for a few pictures, after which she was expected to do as many live shots with the TV stations at eleven as she felt up to.

My plan was to drive her to the *Herald* in Slip's car, which I still had the keys to. I was sure Slip wouldn't mind, because he was continuing to give interview after interview, and for the first time in years no one was calling him a racist, or a homophobe, or a troglodyte. For this one brief shining moment he could bask in the media spotlight as a hero. In the meantime, I'd be driving around in the Slipmobile, since my own car was parked on the block, part of the crime scene and therefore stationary until further notice.

Plain View asked me when I'd be back and I lied and told him about an hour. He yawned, looked at his watch, and told me to return by midnight.

Then he extended his paw to Katy.

"I'm glad you're back in one piece," he said, shaking her hand.

"That makes two of us, Detective," she said.

IT WAS only about a two-minute drive to the *Herald,* so Katy didn't say much, not that I expected her to. When I pulled up in front of the newspaper, before she opened the door she turned to face me, thanked me once more, and finally offered me her hand. I was getting the same treatment as Plain View.

"Will we be having lunch again anytime soon?" I asked, and then she leaned over and gave me a kiss—a peck, they used to call it—on the cheek. She said she'd see me tomorrow and then stepped out of the car and strode toward the front door.

She was almost there when I remembered something and yelled for her to come back. She turned back around quizzically and walked back over to the car.

"We got a deal," I said. "Right?"

She looked confused.

"What I mean is," I said, "whose ledger books did you have copies of?"

"A prominent politician's."

"No, no, no," I said. "That wasn't the deal."

"Okay," she said, "a prominent member of the community."

"You swear?"

"Cross my heart and hope to . . . well, you know." She blew me a comic-book kiss and I waved good night.

Chapter Seventeen

A S SOON AS Katy disappeared from sight on the up escalator, I took out my cell phone and dialed Jiggs's home phone number in Dorchester.

Of course Jiggs didn't pick up, but I left my number and thirty seconds later my cell phone rang. He mentioned a bar in Jamaica Plain and a half hour later he was sitting beside me in the front seat of Slip's car on Green Street outside a neighborhood gin mill.

As we sat in the darkened car, watching lesbian couples stagger out of the bar arm in arm, I filled him in on what had happened. I kept on talking, waiting for him to get excited about my discovery of the incriminating ledger books, and my ultimatum to Mr. Speaker, not to mention the Speaker's impending political demise.

Jiggs just listened, nodding occasionally but saying next to nothing. He was already plotting his next move. With the Speaker on his way out, there would be a war now for the gavel. It would be a treacherous time, and the higher up you were on the totem pole, the more precarious your perch. One wrong move and your career was over, because you can't really stick around in the House after you lose a fight for speaker. It's winner take all. Nobody pays off to a loser.

For the moment, however, Jiggs had the edge. Unlike everybody else who would be running for speaker, he knew what was about to happen to the present occupant of the office. He could start rounding up votes immediately. The early bird gets the worm.

I got to the end of my story and Jiggs still hadn't said anything, so I asked him a question.

"So what do you do next?"

"That's my concern, isn't it, Mr. Black?"

In other words, butt out. But I was too wired to let it go, so I made a foolish decision. I decided to give him my advice.

"I think your best play," I said, "would be to resign as majority leader."

He snorted at that. "Stick to peeping through keyholes, Mr. Black. I'll handle the strategic planning around here."

"Why not just send the Speaker a letter of resignation?" I persisted. "I'm not saying you have a press conference, because later on that'll look like you were piling on. You just say that due to irreconcilable differences with the Speaker, you can no longer serve as his floor leader."

"Irreconcilable differences?" he said. "What am I, married to him?"

"That's just it, Jiggs, you need a divorce decree ASAP. One you can show to the media. Tomorrow he's all done. He's going to resign."

"Why? He ain't even got a target letter yet."

"I told you already, I'm giving Katy the ledgers."

"I did hear you say that just now," he said, "and I remain in utter disbelief. You offered her something of value, something she did not even ask for, because she had no idea they existed, if your account is to be believed. Since when did you of all people start thinking with your dick, Mr. Black? And when did you start freelancing, for that matter? This is a new Mr. Black I'm seeing here tonight, and I must tell you I am not at all impressed. Information is power, and you have now forfeited my power, my advantage."

"She earned it, wouldn't you say?"

"Earned it?" he said. "What happened to her today is bigger than going to jail for a couple of days to protect a source. You just made her career, on my dime I might add."

"Giving her the ledgers tomorrow is the best way," I said. "They snatched her to get the stuff back and Finnerty's on tape explaining who ordered the ledger books seized. It's all wrapped up with a big bow on top."

"Tell me again how you fit with this woman."

"I'm a . . ." He had me there.

"Are you her boyfriend?"

"No, I'm not."

"Not yet, you mean. And you're not going to be either, stop kidding yourself about that. She's not one of us, and if this doesn't get her over to the *Globe,* nothing will. And as much as I don't see you and her together now, once she's over there on Morrissey Boulevard, surrounded by her chinless la-de-da kinsmen with the bow ties who have trust funds and clip coupons on their tax-free munis . . ." He allowed himself a slight chuckle. "Are you by any chance in the throes of a midlife crisis, Mr. Black?"

"Please," I said, a bit defensively. "No fucking way."

"Whatever you want to call it then," he said, "promising to give her The Man's records tomorrow is forcing my hand, and it does not please me that I find myself in this predicament because of a guy who's on my payroll."

I thought I'd done the job he'd hired me to do, but Jiggs was pissed. If I were one of his state reps, tomorrow morning he'd have had the State House door-openers dragging everything out of my office down to the subbasement of the State House next to the prehistoric furnaces. I'd be evicted along with everything except my watercooler. That would be gone, period. A rep knows he's really on double secret probation when they confiscate his Belmont Springs watercooler.

"I got a question for you," Jiggs said. "You're hot to trot to give her those ledger books, but what if Lynch has been giving me some of the dough? Then I'm in a bind."

I pondered that for a moment, trying to think like Jiggs. It was easy.

"First of all," I finally said, trying to answer the question as if I were in a class, which in a way I was, "the money is always kicked upstairs, not down. I mean, if that was you that was speaker, would you be cutting your floor leader in? Of course not. Why would you give him any cash? That would just be show-ing him how much he could be grabbing for himself if he some-how disposed of you. Plus, by cutting up your ill-gotten gains with him you're just creating a potential corroborating witness against yourself, that is if the lobbyist who gave you the dough ever flips."

Jiggs nodded and smiled. "I was just checking, to make sure you could still at least somewhat get around on the old fastball."

"Nothing on the level," I said, quoting a snippet of Jiggs's old observation. "Now, what do you want me to do?"

"Tell me again how you were thinking of handling this, with the Speaker, I mean."

I told him, and he listened quietly.

"Okay," he finally said. "Do it. My only concern is the reporter. She doesn't know about me, does she? Tell me the truth."

"She doesn't know who I'm working for," I said.

"Let's keep it that way, Romeo." He stared straight ahead at yet another party of loud butch-looking women stumbling out onto the street. Things had certainly changed since the days of Inspector Lynch at the Mid-Town lesbian bar (at least on Tuesday nights). The love that dared not speak its name was now keeping the entire neighborhood from getting a good night's sleep.

"You're in good shape," I told Jiggs. "You got all the cards, Mr. Speaker."

"Nobody's got all the cards, Mr. Black. Not you, not me, not now, not ever. Have you forgotten everything the mayor taught you? And never call me Mr. Speaker until I am."

Slapped down again. It's no fun, being a wage slave. Then I remembered something. Tonight had been the night of the big vote on repealing the eight-year term limit on the speaker. I asked Jiggs if it had gone through.

"Like shit through a goose," he said calmly. "Roll call was 123–22, something like that."

"So even a few Republicans went along?"

"They did if they knew what was good for them." He rubbed his eyes. He was very tired, but like me, he was still too wired from the day's events to start winding down quite yet. "The Man is so far gone he can't grasp the long-term ramifications of doing away with term limits."

Jiggs was a real student of the game, just like the old mayor. He was giving me another lecture now.

"If you're the speaker," he said, "what you have to do is preserve the illusion of upward mobility. You have to create vacancies—handing out judgeships or clerkships, encouraging your chairmen to run for higher office—"

It's usually called up-or-out.

"—but whatever you do, you gotta sell the rank and file on

the myth that they can move up, because if they ever realize that they can't, and that the game is rigged, then they start plotting against you."

Like you did, Jiggs, I was tempted to say.

"What Lynch doesn't understand," Jiggs said, "is that some of these guys have been docile only because they've figured that with term limits, if they hung in there long enough something would eventually fall to them. Pretty soon now, they're going to realize that's bullshit, if they haven't already."

"You just happened to realize it first," I said.

"You are correct, sir," he said, allowing himself a tiny smile. "I just happened to realize it first."

"When does the insurrrection start?" I asked.

"When do you expect to meet with the Speaker?" he said.

I DROVE back to the South End, and although BPD cruisers were still double-parked all over the area, the blue lights had been turned off, the yellow tape was down, and the street was open to such traffic as could get by. I parked the Slipmobile down the block, took out the copied ledgers and the DVDs from Southie out of the trunk, and walked casually to my own car, which luckily for me was parked just far enough from the house so that no cop eyes could follow my movements.

I quickly unlocked my trunk, carefully placed the ledgers and the bag of DVDs inside, and covered them with one of my late father's fraying, oil-encrusted blankets. Then I strolled back into the house, after showing some identification to a uniform who looked like he was about fifteen. He resembled an old city councilor I used to run errands for when I was a kid, and I asked him if he was related.

"Yes sir, Mr. Reilly," he said. "That's my grandfather."

His grandfather? As my Uncle Brendan had said, it's unsettling enough when you get old enough to start meeting authority figures and you realize they're the children of people you hung with on the corner thirty years ago. When you're a kid, one of the sure signs that someone is an old fart is when he tells you, "I knew your father." And now I was running into . . . grandchildren.

Back inside my apartment I saw Slip snoring in my easy chair, his arms folded, a couple of empty beer cans beside him on the coffee table. Plain View was talking to a couple of plainclothesmen when he saw me.

"Where the hell have you been?" he said.

"I needed to take a walk, get a breath of fresh air."

"That was some stroll. Where'd you go, Worcester?"

Then he introduced me to a couple of the younger cops he'd been talking to. Fortunately, I didn't know any of their grandfathers, although they said they'd heard of me. To which I responded, as I always do, don't believe everything you hear. Then they drifted away, and I inquired about Slip.

"Is he drunk?" I asked Slip.

"I don't think so," Evans said. "He did about eighty-five live shots, and then he got into your beer stash, said he owed it to himself. I think he's just tired, mostly. How old is he now, anyway?"

"Sixty-seven," I said. Twenty years younger than my father would have been, that's how I remember.

"Jesus," said Plain View. "What do you think you'll be doing when you're sixty-seven?"

"Whatever I'm doing," I said, "I hope I'm doing it in Florida someplace."

"Sixty-seven years old," Plain View said, "and he's chewing me out because I made him hand over his .38, so we could send it to ballistics as evidence. He claims he feels naked without it."

"I believe him," I said.

"So do I," Plain View said. "He says to me, 'Why do you have to take my gun? I shot the bastard with Jackie's.'"

"That's true too," I said. "You know, he is the chairman of the Public Safety Committee, for whatever it's worth, which we both know is nothing. But the man did perform a public service this evening, did he not?"

Plain View looked at me warily.

"I think you owe him a favor," I said.

"Oh, now I get it," he said. "You want him outta here and you're asking could your old pal Plain View handle the job? And the answer is, yeah, I think we could find a car to accommodate the councilor."

I told him Slip would also really appreciate it if one of the uniforms could drive the Slipmobile back to Roslindale. Plain View nodded at one of them, and after I handed the cop Slip's keys, he left. I woke Slip up—Plain View was right, he was mostly tired, it seemed. The thought of continuing his nap during the twenty-minute ride home to Roslindale trumped any objections to accepting a favor, so we got him quickly out the door.

Once Slip was gone, Plain View asked me, "Are you staying here tonight?"

"Where else would I be staying?"

"Touchy, ain't we?" he said.

"Of course I'm staying here. Why shouldn't I?"

"No particular reason," he said, "except it's kind of a mess, what with being tossed tonight, not to mention all this blood in the living room and all. Plus, suppose you was to cut yourself shaving again? I'd hate to see that happen, after all this, you know what I mean? So that's why I'm leaving two uniforms and a car in front of the building."

"My tax dollars at work," I said.

He stifled a yawn. "I'll be needing your full statement tomorrow, and I do mean full, so why don't you call me in the morning? After ten."

"Ten-four," I said. "Go ocean-frank in peace."

I was starting to fade, but then I remembered something. I asked him if he had IDs yet on Tommy Nick and Carmine.

"Yeah," he said. "And let me tell you, the district attorney is a very unhappy man this evening—morning."

"Why? You did him a favor here tonight. Two fewer dirtbags he has to worry about."

"He don't quite see it that way is the way I'm hearing it," Plain View said with a weary smile, idly scratching the stubble on his chin. "See, these guys were cashiers at the Under-Common garage—"

"Which is owned and operated by the Stadium Authority," I interjected.

"Bingo. And since these two got hired about six months ago, revenues had fallen off so steeply that a sting had been undertaken, complete with surveillance cameras—"

"And our boys are on videotape, robbing the till?"

"It's even better than that," Plain View said. "The grand jury handed up sealed indictments just yesterday. Thomas Nickerson and Carmine Mottola—these are, were, their names, if you care— they were going to be arrested when they showed up at the garage for work tomorrow—today now. To say the district attorney is rip- shit would be an understatement. You ruined a photo op he'd been setting up for six months."

I shrugged. Win some, lose some.

"By the way," he said, "Mottola was wearing exactly the same outfit as one of the guys who whacked your friend Bucky—ski mask, Bruins jacket."

"You don't say."

"I do say," he said. "They were very busy in their final hours in this vale of tears."

"Do you suppose they found the time to make a good Act of Contrition?" I said. And then I told him how I was now certain that Tommy Nick was indeed the fellow whose acquaintance I had made over in East Somerville a little more than twenty-four hours earlier.

"No shit?" he said. "I'll have to call Marini over in Somerville in the morning. Funny how last night you said you couldn't pick him out of a lineup, but now you're able to make a positive ID."

I nodded. "Another thing I noticed—Tommy Nick's Beretta looked an awful lot like mine."

"You don't say."

"I do say."

"We'll check the serial numbers," he said. "And then it goes into the evidence room. We'll make sure you get a receipt for it." He smiled, then paused before continuing.

"I heard something else you might be interested in," he said. "Word is, Mottola is Tony Miami's cousin."

"Now that's not good news, is it?" I said. "For me, I mean."

But how much of this was my fault, really? The scenario seemed obvious: Tony Miami and Knocko, with their impeccable law-enforcement sources, got a tip about their minions' impending arrests. One way or another, they had to be hit. Knocko and Tony Miami don't like to leave a lot of loose ends dangling, especially if the loose ends might start thinking about the three magic words: Witness Protection Program.

So the two guys most likely decided to have the cops eliminate the most-likely-to-flip members of the organization, but only after they finished one or two final pieces of business. Cousin or no cousin, when you gotta go, you gotta go. If they succeeded in retrieving the ledger books, fine. Then they'd have been whacked. If they failed, well, let the cops handle the contract. I mentioned my theory to Plain View.

"Am I being paranoid?" I asked.

"Actually," he said, "I was thinking along those same general lines myself. By the way, you weren't in Southie earlier this evening, were you?"

"No," I lied, "why do you ask?"

"Just another senseless street crime," he replied deadpan. "Somebody shot out the windows in Knocko's gym, inside and out, and then we find one of his apes crawling around inside naked with a concussion, or close to it, with DVDs scattered all over the hallway on the floor."

"Strange," I said. "Any suspects?"

"Knocko's boy says it was a gentleman of the colored persuasion."

"In Southie?" I said. "What is this world coming to? You know, in the old days, you never would have gotten an ID like that, because in the old days, everybody in Southie wore a ski mask, just like Carmine Mottola. Or so the witnesses always said."

He shot me a sideways glance. "Funny thing, one of the people across the street, who heard the shots and looked out her window—she did say she saw a guy in a ski mask running away."

"Now that's more like it—I'll bet she knows all the words to 'Southie Is My Hometown' too." I was trying to keep it light, but Plain View was talking more to himself than to me.

"We always heard a lot about that quote-unquote gym, but we never had probable cause to go inside." He shook his head. "From what we've been told about what goes on in there, I'd like to have gotten a look at some of those DVDs, but even with all the shoot-ing, I would've needed a search warrant, just to be on the safe side. But by the time I find a judge, probably not until tomorrow morning, get the warrant, and get back there—"

"No videos," I said. Sometimes it pays to work private. Prob-able cause never stops me from making my appointed rounds.

"Don't you want to ask me," he said, "what we think they're doing over there in that gym?"

"I'll bite," I said. "What do you think they're doing over there in that gym?"

"Sorry, can't tell you. Police business." He grinned, the simple bastard.

"But we did get one break," he continued, "on the gun the reputed Negro used."

"Should I ask what the break was?" I said. "Or is that police business too?"

"About thirty minutes after we get the call," he said, ignoring my question, "a *Globe* pressman is having a smoke outside the building—you can't smoke inside there no more, of course, just like you can't smoke anywhere else, unless you're Slip Crowley. And under the streetlight there on Morrissey Boulevard, he sees a couple of pieces of a gun in the gutter, and sure enough, they're practically warm."

"Well, there you go," I said. "That may be just the break you've been looking for."

"Yeah," Plain View said, as he began tiptoeing gingerly through the coagulating blood in the living room, toward the front door, with me just behind him. "Unless of course we can't find the rest of the gun, or even if we do it turns out the serial numbers are filed off, and then even after we put it in the acid and the numbers come back up, it turns out the piece was stolen off an old dairy farm in Westford in 1986."

"Well, you can't win 'em all," I said as we reached the front door, where he introduced me to the cop on the door. We shook hands all around, and then I went back inside and locked and bolted the door and went to bed.

Within moments I was in a deep sleep, and in my unquiet dreams, the Speaker was in cuffs, hands behind his back, being led away by the bloody corpses of Tommy Nick and Tony Miami's cousin.

Chapter Eighteen

I WOKE UP around six and turned on the radio. On the AM band, Slip was regaling an older talk radio audience—his voters, in other words—with tall tales of his Dirty Harry–like adventures. I looked out the front window and saw that the police car was still there. Good, because I needed to retrieve the DVDs before Plain View pulled the detail, probably at the end of the overnight shift.

As I dressed I glanced around my apartment, and in the dim light of sunrise I saw for the first time just how thoroughly Knocko's henchmen had trashed the place. It would take days to get it totally back in shape. They had even gone through my medicine cabinet. Thank God they hadn't bothered my bottle of saw palmetto prostate support pills. That was where I stashed my Vicodins.

I popped two and wondered what the deductible was on my homeowner's insurance. I had no idea where I even kept the policy, or whether it was paid up. I surely hoped so.

But first things first. I walked to the front door and told the same young cop I'd met five hours earlier that I had to make a run to my car. He shrugged and I ambled down the sidewalk in the forty-degree March dawn.

When I got back to the house with the bag of DVDs, with the ski masks on top, I asked the cop on duty if he wanted some coffee and he said that would hit the spot. I went inside to make some and while it was brewing I went onto the Internet to check out the newspapers.

Both papers had sketchy accounts, the *Herald*'s less so, for obvious reasons. Katy's paper again called me a "rogue ex-cop" and the *Globe* described me as "a one-time reputed City Hall bagman." I wish I could collect royalties on that phrase every time they use it. The *Globe* was less concerned about the two dead hoods—they were, after all, white—than about the shooting of an FBI agent by Slip. It's never too early to start dusting up a conservative candidate, no matter how justified his actions or how minor the office he seeks. My favorite paragraph from the *Globe* story was:

> *Asked to comment early this morning at his home in Roslindale, Crowley shouted an obscenity and hung up on a reporter.*

Good for you, Slip.

In both papers, the FBI declined all comment on the mysterious circumstances of Finnerty's shooting, not exactly a resounding show of support. By tomorrow, I guessed, Finnerty would be demoted to "embattled," which is newspaper code for "on the way out, soon to be indicted." For a while there a few years back, I used to be "embattled" every morning in the papers too. In the end I got lucky, something that I just didn't see in the cards for Finnerty. They had way too much on him.

In the *Herald* I first read the main story, in which Katy shared a byline with the police reporter. And yes, she did keep her end of the bargain—she had been grabbed, she said, because of a false rumor that she had "apparently" received documents belonging to "a prominent member of the community." False rumor—nice touch, and she'd thought that one up all by herself. That would give the Speaker at least a glimmer of hope that he was still in the clear.

As for her own first-person exclusive, she began it this way: "In this business, you never know what a day will bring."

I had a pretty good idea what today would bring her— another scoop, involving the guy who was getting top billing in the only other major local story in either paper this morning, the repeal of term limits for the House leadership late last night.

The Speaker was quoted in both papers as saying he was "deeply gratified" by the "overwhelming" vote. The taxpayers could not be reached for comment.

I took the coffee out to the kid cop, and he thanked me and said he was sorry, but Plain View was pulling the detail at the end of the shift. If it was okay by me, he said, he'd just knock on the door before he left and leave the coffee mug right outside the front door. It was okay by me.

I waited until he left just before eight, and then I pulled the front-window shades back down and went into my bedroom, where I had a DVD player hooked up to my second TV. I dumped the Knocko DVDs onto the bed. I counted eight of them, all marked with hand-scrawled double-entendre porn-film titles— *No Fly Zone, Cuckoo for Cocoa Cocks, the Sopornos, Weapons of Ass Destruction,* etc. But none of these were commercial-grade XXX porn. This was amateur night in Ward 7, and it was also child pornography.

As I fast-forwarded through them, one after another, my

palms grew damp, as I began considering just how many years I could be looking at, merely for having these DVDs in my possession. You know the old saying: fifteen'll get you twenty. I'm no expert in these matters—Traci Lords always looked legal enough to me in all of her now-proscribed features. But only one of these Southie females appeared to be even close to non-jailbait. And if that kid had spent as much of her allowance on braces as she had on tattoos she might have been presentable enough to appear in some "mainstream" porn like, say, *Bright Lights, Big Titties* or *Don't Talk With Your Mouth Full.*

These DVDs were all undeniably from Knocko's personal stash. He was the star, The Man in every way. At least I assumed Knocko was the guy, because in the first four tapes the Johnny Wadd of Southie was wearing one of those ski masks. All the shots appeared to be from a handheld camera. It was what they call "gonzo." The overhead camera must have been a new twist, or kink, that they hadn't gotten around to mastering yet. Or maybe I'd just grabbed the golden oldies, the ones they had just transferred to DVD.

In every one of them, the girls, usually between twelve and fourteen, would either beg for mercy or appear completely zonked out on whatever drugs Knocko had plied them with. The stoned girls were the lucky ones, considering Knocko's preference for the back door, a predilection he most likely picked up during a youthful stretch at Alcatraz for bank robbery. The girls who weren't high were quickly weeping, begging for mercy, and, in a couple of cases, bleeding. It was sick stuff, but to what use could I put it? The perp was wearing a mask, and somehow I suspected that these girls from the projects would be unwilling or unable to recall anything of consequence for a grand jury.

On the fifth tape—titled *Organ Grinders*—I hit pay dirt.

Knocko had apparently misplaced his mask, because you could see his face, in full frame, in all its glory. It was him, no doubt about it. You could see the girl clearly too, and she couldn't have been much more than twelve. He took her right under the SOUTHIE RULES! banner as she begged, unsuccessfully, for him not to . . . well, you know. I pressed ahead with the last three, and there he was, sans mask, on two more. The girls didn't look any older either. On the last one, entitled *Journey to Uranus*, he was doing a whimpering black girl doggy-style. She appeared to be about thirteen, utterly wasted, and the cameraman, who had remained totally silent in all of the other tape-rapes, zoomed in tight on Knocko's face.

Then I could hear the disembodied yet familiar voice of the cameraman say, "Christmas comes early this year for Seamus Nugent."

Seamus—that's Gaelic for James. They're raping little kids and celebrating their priceless Hibernian heritage at the same time. A little inside joke, I suppose. Sometimes I'm glad I'm only half Irish.

Anyway, when the cameraman mentions his Gaelicized name, Knocko looks up, his hands still on the black girl's hips as he thrusts deeper into her. Looking totally demented, he stares into the camera, smiles, and says, "Christmas is for cops and kids."

I hit the remote control to rewind back to hear the cameraman's voice once again.

"Christmas comes early this year for Seamus Nugent." It was just who I thought it was. It was Tony Miami.

I pressed the Eject button, took the DVD, and scrawled "Seamus's Christmas" in pencil under *Journey to Uranus*. Then I put it and the other two with Knocko's face in the original Flanagan's bag, after which I placed the other five in a larger plastic Target bag. Christmas is for cops and kids—I'd never heard that one before. In the kitchen, my phone was ringing. I tiptoed out through the stickiness of the drying blood and waited for the answering machine to pick up. It was Plain View, and he sounded like he was back to his usual exasperated self.

"I know you're there," he said. "I'm just warning you, don't even think about not coming in this morning. I need that statement. You got my numbers."

When the phone don't ring, Plain View, you'll know it's me.

I sat down at the kitchen table and picked up the phone. I needed to reach out to Tony Miami and The Man, but not directly. So I called a number in South Boston and that party gave me another number and two or three calls later I was dialing another South Boston exchange in the Mary Ellen McCormack projects. I also had the name of the gorilla I'd slugged last night, or should I say I had his moniker—Sully. What else would it be, except Fitzie, or maybe Murf? Tony Miami's guys, I'm sure, were named Chickie and Buddy and Rico.

The phone rang three times before an old lady with a raspy cigarette voice picked it up. I asked for Sully and she replied, in a heavy Southie accent, "Who shall I say is calling?"

"A colored gentleman," I said.

"Joey," she yelled, "it's some nigger for you."

Beautiful. I waited a moment and then heard a sleepy voice.

"Yeah? Who's this?"

"You know who this is. It's the colored gentleman from last night."

"Listen, you got some nerve calling here. The Man is looking for you all over town."

"Oh yeah?" I said. "Well, I guess that means you're going to have to tell him about those things of his that I took off you last night."

"You tell him."

"No," I said, "I'm leaving that to you, because if I don't hear back that he knows what I have, then I am going to have to start telling certain parties that you gave the videotapes to me, and how do you think that's going to go over with The Man?"

"You wouldn't dare."

"Try me, pal."

"You don't even know who I am."

"How'd I get your phone number then?"

Another long pause. "Well, it's all lies anyway. If he asks me—if—and I ain't even saying who 'he' is, if he does ask me, this guy whose name I'm not saying, I'll tell him it's all bullshit."

"Okay," I said, "if that's the way you want to play it, it's no skin off my ass. Just make sure your life insurance is paid up, so Ma can still afford her two packs of Marlboro Lights every day."

I gave him time to think. It took more than a few seconds for the rusted gears in his brain to mesh together. Finally, he said, "How do I know you are who you say you are?"

"I'm through talking with you," I said. "All you need to know is that I have the DVD of Knocko boning a little black girl, and he says, quote, Christmas is for cops and kids, unquote. And the cameraman is Tony Miami, and he calls The Man Seamus. The title on it is *Journey to Uranus*. You got all that?"

"Tell me again why I'm supposed to tell him you've got this DVD."

"Because if you don't, he'll kill you."

"Maybe he kills me anyway."

"That's definitely a possibility," I agreed. "Let's call it sixty-forty you're gonna get whacked in the next couple of days one way or the other. But if he thinks you took it and then willingly gave it to me, then your chances of getting two in the bonnet rise to approximately one hundred percent, because then he'll think you're going to use the DVD to blackmail him."

"Why would he think that?"

"Because why else would you take it?"

"But I didn't take it, you did."

"Good-bye." I hung up on him. How can you have a conversation with a dead man?

I took the bag of the masked-Knocko DVDs and spread an old towel on top of them, to discourage any unnecessary peeking by any concerned goddamn citizens.

No way could I keep them in my apartment, not with the feds trying to figure out how to manage the unfolding public relations disaster of Agent Orange. Thank God the steamer trunk was empty. If they can't pin anything else on you, the G-men will always settle for a gun rap. But the DVDs would be infinitely worse. Laying a kiddie-porn rap on the guy whose apartment Finnerty had burgled would go a long way toward making the heat die down. I hated to throw away something that might be of value to somebody someday. Waste not, want not. But what choice did I have? I took the bag with me out into the foyer and walked up the stairs to the second floor. Bruce the waiter answered the door.

"Landlord," he said at the door, standing behind the bolt lock in a bathrobe. "That was some party you had downstairs last night. Should I be offended that I wasn't invited?"

"Be thankful for small favors," I said.

"Did it have anything to do with my visit to the post office?"

"Do us both a favor and forget about the post office," I said. "This is a lot easier, this next thing I want you to do."

"Does it involve that shopping bag in your hand?" he said.

I STILL had to smuggle the other damning DVDs out of my apartment before the local feds again started acting like bulls in the nearest china shop in the neighborhood, namely mine.

I ransacked the closet and way in the back I found a particularly oversized tweed topcoat, a couple of sizes bigger than my late father's from Kennedy's. I figured it was Marty's, purchased hot out of the back room of the Ace of Hearts back during his Quaalude days. He ballooned up to three hundred pounds for a while before he took the collar for sticking up a diamond sales-man. It had not been a happy time in Marty's life, even by Marty standards, but finally some good was coming of it—the coat's bulk made it easy to stash the DVDs on my person. With a shop-ping bag under my arm inside the coat, I called a cab and took it to 60 State Street, where I had my safe-deposit box.

This time the young Asian teller remembered my name. I waited until she shut the vault door behind me, and then I made the switch—retrieving the original copies of the Speaker's ledgers, and replacing them with the DVDs.

I was packing my last throwdown in a waist holster on my belt. My main concern today was G-men in wingtips, because the Southie guys were surely under orders to lay low for a few days. But suppose someone didn't get the message, or was too coked up to follow orders. So I was carrying.

After I left the bank, I walked across the street to a Copy Cop, made more Xeroxes of all the ledgers, and split them up into two big manila envelopes. On one I wrote Katy Bemis's name, slipped my spare safe-deposit box key inside, and then sealed it. The copies I'd given her the day before had no doubt been taken off her when she was snatched, and she needed a fresh set for today's stories. Once I had them I hoofed it over to the Parker House and grabbed another cab. I told the cabbie to take me to the *Herald*, and on the way, I called Katy's cell phone. She picked up immediately.

"Are you at the paper yet?" I said.

"Yeah, I just did a live shot with MSNBC from the city room. Evans called here, looking for you."

"Plain View?" I said. "If he calls again, tell him you haven't heard from me either."

"Look," she said, "you told me last night—"

"Go downstairs in three minutes. There'll be an envelope at the front desk for you."

"Is it—"

"It is. There's also a key to a safe-deposit box at the Bank-America branch at sixty State Street, which you should put in a very secure place."

"Uh-oh," she said. "Haven't I heard this one before?"

"I'll fill you in later," I said. "What you're interested in today are the sheets—"

"Is this another copy of what you gave me yesterday?"

"It is. Listen to me because I'm going to be out of pocket for a while—"

"So what else is new?"

"Please, Katy, just listen. The initials belong to lobbyists, and they're next to numbers and their clients, and it's all in the Speaker's handwriting. It's the Speaker that all this stuff belongs to."

"I knew it!" she said in exasperation.

"There's only one thing I ask—don't start calling the lobbyists until I go see the Speaker—"

"Yeah," she said. "But—"

"Yeah but nothing," I said. "That's the deal. Take it or leave it."

She took it. Two minutes later, with the cab double-parked outside the front of the paper, I ran the envelope inside and handed it to the security guard. I got back into the cab and had the driver wait until I saw her appear at the front desk and take the envelope. She looked outside, and I waved, and she smiled and waved back.

Five minutes later, I was back inside my house, where I split up the contents of Bucky's estate. I stashed the older stuff from the Hogan brothers in the hall closet, and put the Speaker's more recent incriminating documents into a shopping bag. I considered calling Plain View, then decided against it. He'd be pissed, that's for sure, but he'd get over it.

Chapter Nineteen

I CALLED THE Speaker's office and arranged to meet him at three in his office at the State House. Hey, I'd given him my word, and my word is my bond. Tony Miami's sister made it clear by her tone on the phone that she had absolutely no use for me, but maybe she was just in mourning for young Carmine. Then I grabbed another taxi, which took me to the McCormack Building at the top of Beacon Hill. I was headed for the twenty-first floor, the attorney general's office. In the lobby I was met by a couple of Staties now nearing retirement. I used to knock around with them when I worked for the mayor, before I got jammed up.

Now they were the top cops in the attorney general's political corruption unit. I had called ahead, and after we went upstairs I showed them Mr. Speaker's ledgers. They were quite impressed. They'd read Katy's story in the paper, and like everyone else they'd been trying to figure out the identity of the prominent individual in the community. Now they understood that this could be the biggest pinch of their careers, if they could sell it to their boss, the attorney general. They brought me into his office for a rather uncomfortable face-to-face meeting.

Attorneys general never have much appetite for going after political corruption. Professional courtesy, there but for the grace of God and all that. It's okay to hunt down and humiliate a nobody—a tree warden in Spencer, say, who spends seven dollars in town funds to buy a dozen crullers from his brother-in-law's doughnut shop. It's a lot dicier to take on somebody who might be able to fight back, especially when it comes time to approve your budget for the next fiscal year. That's why most elected prosecutors are quite skilled at leaving no stone unturned, except the one the rich guy or the connected pol is hiding under.

But a prosecutor always needs a notch or two on his belt for the next campaign, and if you can ever bring down a guy like the Speaker, it permanently inoculates you against the charge of being one of the Beacon Hill boys. The AG himself, an ambitious sort from Middlesex County, knew enough about my background to instantly develop a profound skepticism about my motives, which he expressed in no uncertain terms.

But I didn't take the grilling personally. They were all just trying to anticipate the grounds for the inevitable post-conviction appeals, when the lawyers for the Speaker, who would by then be the ex-Speaker, would describe the ledgers as the fruit of the poisoned tree, etc. I answered their questions truthfully, as much as I possibly could, and after an hour of so of the third-degree, the AG personally signed off on the sting.

By twelve fifteen, my Statie friends, now joined by a couple of intense-looking young prosecutors, walked down Beacon Hill from the McCormack Building to the McCormack Courthouse—both of them named after a former U.S. House Speaker from South Boston named John McCormack, whose brother was the original Knocko, a 350-pound bookie who owned a block-long bar in Andrew Square. His real name was Seamus too, although as far as I knew, no one had ever referred to the first Knocko as "Seamus." Assimilation was the big thing back in those days.

As always, locating an honest or at least semisober state judge took longer than anything else. Eventually the Staties found a distinguished jurist who could be counted upon to dummy up. He was nearing retirement and he was bitter. I've never met a judge yet who wasn't. With a big grin he signed a court order authorizing me to wear a wire to my afternoon meeting with the Speaker.

By two fifteen, I was quittin' the grinnin' and droppin' the linen. They were putting a wire on me.

THIS TIME the Speaker's secretary, Miss Massimino, didn't give me the third degree. She may have wanted to, but her instructions were otherwise. Still, she managed to be even more unpleasant in person than she had been on the phone earlier. I hadn't really expected to see her this afternoon, considering that her beloved cousin Carmine had died so . . . unexpectedly.

As I entered the Speaker's outer office, I was carrying Bucky's manila envelope, stuffed with copies of the legal pad ledgers, as conspicuously as possible. She regarded it warily, as if it were some kind of hair-trigger bomb. It was.

She ushered me into the Speaker's office and again the fire was roaring. I wondered how much the firewood was costing the taxpayers, but whatever the price, it was certainly worth it, at least as far as the Speaker was concerned. As much as the wood paneling, the fire made him seem somehow more . . . substantial.

More deserving of a larger bribe.

As I walked into the inner chamber, the Speaker rose from his desk and strode purposefully over to me to shake my hand. He nodded at Tony Miami's sister, and she departed without a word, closing the door silently behind her. He again turned up the radio too loud, although the Staties had assured me that wouldn't be a problem for their new high-tech recorders. Once we were both seated on either side of the fire, he clasped his hands together prayerfully and leaned forward toward me.

"Thank God they got Katy Bemis back. What a terrible, terrible ordeal." He shook his head. "I know what kind of people these are, believe me. And I think you do too."

Was he talking about my brother, or his secretary? I didn't need to respond, though, because he had his list of talking points, and he wanted to hit each one.

"You know I did call them last night," he said, and I just stared at him, not speaking unless spoken to, just as the prosecutors had instructed me. If nothing I said could reasonably be construed as entrapment, the grounds for appeal would be significantly narrowed, if not eliminated.

"You do believe me, don't you?" he asked. "I mean, that I made calls to . . . them. For the girl."

"Did you talk to Knocko?"

"Oh, heavens no." He lowered his voice to a whisper. "Please, don't even mention that name here."

"Okay," I said. "Let's get to it. I want you to resign as speaker. You don't really have a choice, do you? Not with what I've got on you. But I'm reasonable. You quit, and I'll forget about these ledgers."

"I don't believe you, Jack," he said. "I wish I could, but I just can't picture you as the kind of guy who 'forgets' about something like this."

He pursed his lips as if he were considering my ultimatum.

"What do you really want from me?" he asked. "Name your price."

"My price is your scalp. You're through."

He shook his head without saying a word. Then he looked directly at me.

"No," he said again. "I'm not resigning as speaker. It's out of the question. I've spent twenty years struggling to get to this office, and I'm not leaving, especially not after last night's courageous vote of confidence from the members."

Courageous? Hal Lynch had become the proverbial legend in his own mind.

"It is perhaps the greatest honor of my life," he said, "and my only regret is that my sainted mother—"

"Save that bullshit for the *Globe*," I said. "I haven't got all day. You have two alternatives here. You can resign 'voluntarily,' or I can leave right now and walk down to the JFK building and give this package to the feds."

As I raised the envelope an inch or two, the Speaker smiled.

"Jack, you know as well as I do, the same people who have a certain entree, shall we say, in this office, also have a presence at the local FBI office. Speaking of which, I strongly suspect there was more to the shooting of Special Agent Finnerty at your apartment than was reported in the papers this morning."

The Speaker looked at me, but he'd said nothing that I needed to respond to. So he took a deep breath and decided to try to create the illusion of confiding in me. "I have seen Agent Finnerty in the company of our mutual friends, if you know who I mean."

I knew who he meant.

"Why was Finnerty inside your house?" he persisted. "A B and E? A tail gone bad?"

I shook my head. "This may be your office, but we're on my dime, not yours. So your answer to my eminently reasonable offer to allow you to resign is no? You won't quit?"

"Why should I? So Jiggs can become speaker? I might as well hand the job over to Slip Crowley. Jiggs has no vision."

"But you do? You have vision? I read those entries in your ledger. You got some vision all right—you shook down one of the big insurance companies for fifty grand in cash not to kill the demutualization bill."

"Demutualization, Jack? I'm impressed, I really am. From your tenure up here for the mayor, I always thought you were just a—"

"A reputed bagman?"

"Your words, Jack. Not mine." He stood up and walked over to throw another log on the fire. "Surely we can come to some sort of understanding."

"How many people can you let blackmail you—are you going to put a fourth mortgage on your house, Mr. Speaker?" They'd told me not to call him Hal. Show him some respect, the AG's people had said; refer to him the way everyone else does. That will put him more at ease.

"Knocko and Tony Miami have drained you already, Mr. Speaker, judging by how much of your property you've had to sell. Now you're going to let me get my tentacles into you too?"

"How much?" he said. "In the end, that's always the only question, isn't it? How much is this going to cost me?"

"It's going to cost you your job. I want you to resign."

He sat back down, neatly folded his hands on his lap, and slowly shook his head.

"When did this good-government epiphany of yours occur, Jack—on the road to Foley's rather than Damascus, I'm sure." He tapped the arms of his leather-bound chair with his fingers. "I hate to be such a cynic, Jack, but if you do happen to be working for someone else, perhaps you would allow me to bid against them."

I ignored that too. My job was to get him on tape, admitting to felonies, the more the merrier.

"Why did you write everything down? Why put yourself in this position?"

"Do you think I knew the bank would be robbed? The records were in a safe-deposit box. I wasn't the only one who was taken advantage of, as I'm sure you're aware."

"But by writing it down, you're acknowledging that you've extorted money." This was the money shot I was going for. "Why do it?"

"My father kept Wimpy's ledgers all those years, didn't he? I'm sure you looked through them as well. My father used those records to extract money from crooked cops. That's how he tried to pay my tuition through college and law school. It wasn't easy raising a family on a cop's salary in those days, as you no doubt recall. There was no Quinn bill, no phony disability pensions, no Big Dig overtime, not nearly as much overtime period. Details weren't nearly the racket they've since become—and that's off the record."

Off the record? Did he really think it mattered what he said about political issues now? Talk about being in denial.

"You may think of those dusty old books as Wimpy's records," he said. "I think of them as my old man's. So I kept them around for sentimental reasons, I guess you could say. And me, I was just following in my father's footsteps. He had his ledgers, and I had mine."

After last night's vote, he must have thought he was bulletproof. Why else would he be admitting everything? Unless . . . nah, he didn't have the stones to try to pull anything on me.

"Another thing," he said. "You need to have some kind of record of past transactions, so the next time your clients need something, you can be sure you're not selling yourself short. You need to keep accurate records. Any good businessman can tell you that."

"So that's what you are, a businessman?" I said. "And the people you shake down are your 'clients.' And I guess you have so many 'clients' it's hard to remember off the top of your head just how much you've shaken 'em down for before?"

He smiled. "You know, Jack, I knew you before you were a virgin."

I said, "When you resign, you get your books back."

He stood up and walked back to his desk. "I told you, I'm not resigning." He opened the top drawer and took out a 9mm automatic with a silencer.

"Are you crazy?" I said. "You're pointing a gun at me, in your own office, in the State House." This was for the State Police detectives monitoring and recording the conversation around the corner in the governor's Council chambers. "Suppose I've made copies and left them with someone."

"Possible but not likely." He shook his head as he slowly walked back over to where I was sitting in front of the fire. He was standing over me now, about three feet away, with the gun pointing down at my head.

"Your girlfriend said in the paper this morning she didn't have them. You always played your cards pretty close to the vest—that's why the mayor liked you. I don't think you've changed that much. Who are you working for, by the way?"

"Mr. Speaker, if you want these books, you're going to have to shoot me."

He chuckled. "Please. You're even less credible posing as a martyr than you are as a citizen shocked by corruption on Beacon Hill. Now please just hand the ledgers to me, and we'll watch them burn together in my fireplace."

"I'm telling you again, you'll have to take them from me."

"Only if you insist," he said, "but what do you think the silencer is for?"

"And your secretary?"

"Angela Massimino? She didn't see me, and I didn't see her, and most assuredly neither of us saw you, if it comes to that. And sometime late this evening, if worse comes to worst, a couple of stout, strapping lads from Ward Six who do the occasional odd job for our mutual friend will roll you up in a rug and you'll go somewhere to spend eternity, probably very close to the man who put me through college and law school, Wimpy Hogan." He kept the gun pointed at me. "Now hand those books over."

Maybe I should have been worried, but I still wasn't.

"Put down the gun," I said, just on the off chance that the Staties hadn't been paying attention. "Just because you've run your office as a racketeering enterprise, that's no reason to compound the crime by killing me."

His eyebrows suddenly arched and he frowned. "'A racketeering enterprise'?" He paused and shook his head. I'd heard the phrase bandied about so often in the AG's office over the last couple of hours that I had just blurted it out. I must be slipping, and the Speaker had simultaneously come to the same conclusion about himself.

"I must be losing it," he said, shaking his head. "You're wearing a wire, aren't you, you bastard?"

That was when I dove at him. Don't ask me why, because the Staties were crashing through his office door at the same moment. My shoulder hit him right below the knee and he crumpled. He didn't weigh that much to begin with and he obviously didn't have a personal trainer. I was on top of him immediately.

I grabbed his right hand but he wouldn't let go of the gun. As we wrestled for it, he managed to squeeze off a round that shattered the glass in the door to his office. By now the Staties were all over us, and one jackbooted uniformed trooper stepped on the Speaker's right hand, hard, until the gun dropped harmlessly onto the imported Persian rug he had planned to wrap my corpse in.

I rolled off Mr. Speaker and sat up on that very tasteful carpet, panting and trying to catch my breath as the State Police cuffed him and read him his Miranda rights.

"I got nothing to say," he told them, and then he looked over at me. There was anger in his eyes.

"I thought we had a deal," he said.

"We were working on it, Hal. Then you tried to shoot me."

"Shit," he said. "The mayor always used to tell me, 'Never trust a cop.'"

And I thought I was the only one who remembered that line.

"Fuck a duck," he said, as the Staties looked on silently, taking it all in. This was a man who until a few minutes ago had controlled their budgets, including whether or not they got a pay raise next year, and/or a new unmarked car. Now he was just another perp, a perp who'd called their beloved paid details a racket. What goes around comes around.

"Never trust a cop," he repeated. "It wasn't just the mayor who told me that. It was my old man."

And Inspector Lynch should have known, right?

"I thought we had a deal," he repeated.

"We did," I said, "but you lied, Hal."

"No, you lied. And don't call me—" He caught himself.

"We both lied, Hal."

Now the Staties were pushing him out the door. I stood there in his chambers watching him leave for the last time, in handcuffs. In my time I'd seen more than a few legislative leaders in the dock in a courtroom, but never one in cuffs, at the State

House. Getting lugged in your own office was an indignity usually reserved for county sheriffs appointed by Pee Wee Dukakis.

"Just tell me one thing, Reilly," he yelled over his shoulder. "Who are you working for?"

His secretary stared through the open door at me. If looks could kill, they'd still be scraping my remains off those ancient wood panels. I waited until the posse was out in the hall before I finished dusting myself off. As the Staties' tech guys watched, I removed my sport coat and shirt, and they then disengaged me from the wires. Her arms crossed, Angela Massimino took it all in silently. Then I put my shirt and jacket back on, and nodded at the techs and the two forensic guys who'd been left behind. I walked out of the Speaker's chambers into the outer office where Angela Massimino still stood, arms crossed, staring at me with baleful eyes.

I said, "Tell Tony I said hello."

She glared back at me. "You'll be seeing him before I do."

I asked her if she minded if I used her phone, and she just turned her back with a snort and walked out into the hall. I picked up the phone and dialed Plain View's cell phone.

"Hi honey," I said. "Don't pay the ransom—I've escaped."

AFTER A while Plain View stopped yelling at me. I had said nothing in my own defense, because I had none. I'd hung him out to dry after he did me a big favor. I asked him if he wanted me to come down to headquarters and give him a statement.

"Why bother?" he said. "I've already got your statement. The attorney general's flack just e-mailed it over. It's a press release."

"I'll bet I could get your name in the next one."

"Don't even think about it," he said, suddenly lowering his voice. "Do you know how tight Lynch is—was—with the mayor?

He was the mayor's go-to guy at the State House. Had been for years. All that ass-kissing, all those no-show jobs for everyone in Brighton—everything gone in the blink of an eye."

"Tell the mayor not to sweat it," I said. "I'm sure the new speaker will be for sale too, at a reasonable price, no doubt."

"Yeah, easy enough for you to say. I mean, it's one thing to give the DA the finger. The mayor's a different story. Where are you?"

"In the Speaker's office," I said. "Where else would I be?"

I glanced around the office. Above Angela Massimino's desk was a framed, autographed photo of Mr. Speaker standing stiffly with Bill Clinton. He'd been a Hillary Clinton delegate in Denver in 2008.

"They call you a 'cooperating witness' in the press release," Plain View said. "Is that anything like a snitch?"

Then he slammed down the phone. I owed Plain View one or two, at least, no doubt about it. I wondered if he could possibly make good use of some DVDs.

The prosecutors told me to stay close by, but they had all my numbers and didn't need me immediately, so I decided to take a stroll. I bounced down the front entrance of the State House, down the flight of stairs that hardly anyone ever uses except TV stations when they're shooting promos of their new anchors supposedly rushing down them after confronting some political miscreant. The late-afternoon sun was out, and it had to be close to fifty degrees. I crossed Beacon Street onto the Common, found myself a park bench, pulled out my cell phone, and checked my messages.

Katy Bemis had called four times, leaving all her numbers. In her most recent one, she sounded quite as agitated as Plain View. I called her back, and her tone was almost as cold as the Speaker's.

"We just got a press release from the AG," she said. "I thought you said I was getting a scoop."

"You are," I said. "Nobody else has that list of lobbyists who were paying him off."

"You sure about that?"

"Sure as I can be," I said. "I told them, no leaks. The deal was, you get it alone."

"Do I get an interview too?"

"You mean with me?"

"Who do you think I mean?"

"Well, I'm talking to you now, aren't I? I haven't talked to anyone else, don't plan to either, if you tell me not to."

"I'm telling you not to."

She was focused all right.

"Another thing, Katy," I said. "About that key I left with you."

"Yeah?" She was guarded now in her response, not quite sure what I was going to ask her to do.

"I've got the key," she said. "I'm looking at it right now."

"If anything happens to me—"

"Getting a bit melodramatic, aren't we?"

"Isn't that what you said yesterday too, at Legal?"

"Point well taken," she said. "So if anything happens to you—"

"Your signature's not on file at the bank, so you can't get in by yourself, but just go to some cop you can trust—"

"Evans?"

"Possibly. Yeah, probably. But take somebody with you, for sure."

"The stuff you left in there, what is it?"

"This is not a secure line," I said, thinking of the feds' cell-phone wiretapping capabilities. "I'll tell you when I see you."

"It's that good?" she said.

"Actually, it's that bad. It's worse than this lobbying stuff, much worse. We'll talk about it later."

"What about my exclusive?"

"Ask away," I said, and she did. I gave her whatever I thought she could make best use of. She asked me if I felt I was "redeeming" myself, but that was one place I wouldn't go. Finally she told me she had enough and I told her maybe I'd see her later at Foley's. She didn't say yes, but she didn't say no either. Sitting on my park bench, I watched the early commuters scurrying across the Common in the direction of the Park Street station. Was it too early to have a cocktail? An old Yankee named Rodman Weld once said: "A gentleman never drinks before three or east of Park Street."

It was definitely after three and I was practically on Park Street. I looked across Tremont Street at the blinking neon beer sign in the package store that catered to the Common's large population of winos. My cell phone rang again. I fished it out of my coat and said hello.

"You didn't tell me you were getting wired, Mr. Black," Jiggs said immediately. "You lied to me."

"Funny," I said, "that's just what The Man said to me."

"He ain't The Man no more."

"I forgot," I said. "You The Man now, Jiggs."

"I don't care for wires," The Man said.

"So I've noticed."

"I haven't got much time right now," he said, and I could hear excited voices in the background. The Man was dead, long live The Man. The TV cameras were probably setting up in Jiggs's outer office. He would soon deliver some hideously insincere statement that would leave everyone who watched it on TV cringing in disbelief that such a loathsome human being could ever rise to any position of power and trust, even in the Massachusetts legislature.

"I need to talk to you later tonight," he said. "I'll call you in a couple of hours. But right now I need to know, are we both straight on our stories?"

"You mean, I didn't see you and you didn't see me?"

"What else would I mean?" he said. "Now, let's go over a couple of points. If someone asks you under what circumstances did you receive this package of documents, what's your answer?"

"This guy who sent them to me, Bucky Bennett, he was a friend of my brother's in the can, and Bucky said he was going to send the ledgers to me for safekeeping. Shortly thereafter he expired, after which I received the package. As any concerned citizen would do, I immediately sought the counsel of the attorney general."

"And I had no idea what was going on, none whatsoever."

"You?" I said. "How could you possibly know anything? I didn't see you and you—"

"And the broad still knows nothing about me, right?"

"She knows nothing."

As long as no one knew that Jiggs had hired me to whack the Speaker, he could lie to everybody with impunity. He could credibly claim he had nothing to do with the hit. That was his story and he'd be sticking to it. I figured the conversation was over, but he wanted to get a few things off his chest, and he surely couldn't speak to anyone else at the State House about what had just gone down.

"Do you see now why I couldn't quit the way you wanted me to? He was going nowhere without a shove."

"You were right. You called it. I been away too long, I guess."

But he wasn't listening to me. He was talking to himself.

"If I'd quit," he said, "he'd have already appointed that moron from Northampton as floor leader, and now I'd be the dissident coming after both the Speaker and his non-backstabbing Mr. Smith-goes-to-Beacon-Hill hick acolyte in their moment of need."

"Their moment of need?" I said. "Are the rank and file really that stupid? The Speaker is blackmailing lobbyists, the Mob is blackmailing him, he tries to shoot me and he's the victim?"

"This place has changed," he said. "When I started out, it was like reform school. Then they cut the House down from 240 to 160 members, the goo-goos started getting elected, and all of a sudden it was like the Perkins School."

For the blind.

"And now it's worse—it's the Fernald School."

For the retarded.

"By the way," he said, "just for my own edification, what kind of witness are you going to make against the man formerly known as The Man? I'd love to cross-examine you—'Mr. Reilly, as a sworn law officer of the city of Boston, did you ever collect or cause to be collected certain cash contributions?'"

That very subject had been broached a few hours earlier on the twenty-first floor of the McCormack Building.

"More'n likely they won't even need me," I told Jiggs. "They figure they'll flip all the lobbyists in his ledger book. Their guess is there may not even be a trial."

"There's nothing yet anywhere on the Internet about the ledgers—who's getting that piece of the story?"

"I thought we discussed that last night."

"So that's one part of the plan that didn't change?" he said. "Tomorrow morning we'll read all about the Speaker's little racket in the *Herald*?"

I heard a voice in the background, then Jiggs again.

"Tell 'em I'll be right out," he yelled, then whispered to me, "I'm ready for my close-up, Mr. DeMille. Can you leak it to your girlfriend that I was getting ready to resign?"

"How about we say it was over a matter of principle?"

He laughed at that one and so did I.

"Just make sure she spells it right," he said. "That's princi-p-l-e, not p-a-l."

"Jiggs," I said, "I believe you may be just the type of reformer that a weary, disillusioned public will seek out to restore their faith in the integrity of the Massachusetts General Court."

"I am not gladdened, but saddened for my beloved institution, the people's body," he said, giving me the dress rehearsal of the crocodile-tear-stained statement he was about to deliver to the press. "I was shocked, shocked to learn of the allegations against my dear friend and colleague, a man who like so many of us rose from a humble station in life, yet who to the very end always had a moment, not to mention a sawbuck, to share with any of his constituents, indeed, with anyone he met on the street who might be temporarily down on his or her luck. This is a calamity for so many people, and I would caution everyone out there who is following this tragedy, for indeed it is a tragedy, both for the individual and for this proud institution—I would implore all of you to remember that in our system of justice, a man—a person—is presumed innocent until proven guilty."

"You're reading this, aren't you?"

"Do you think I got 'tragedy' in there enough?"

"How many commitments do you have?" I asked.

"Enough," he said. "More than enough."

"Written pledge cards, like the old days?"

"What do you think?" he said with a chuckle.

Then I asked him when he was going to formally announce his candidacy for speaker.

"Tomorrow morning, I should think," he said. "They'll ask me about it tonight, but I'll just give 'em a little of the old soft-shoe. Tonight Speaker Lynch should get his fifteen minutes, wouldn't you agree?"

"Absolutely," I said. "Hey Jiggs, will you remember your friends?"

"My friends?" he said. "You mean the little people?"

There must be something about that wood paneling that changes these guys. He said he'd call me later, but I wasn't going to hold my breath.

Chapter Twenty

A S THE SHADOWS lengthened across the Common and the temperature began dropping, I sat on my park bench. The lights started flickering on in the big apartment building, Tremont on the Common. I answered a squeal there once—a local hedge fund manager had mistaken his gal-pal for a Duraflame log and tried to fling her into the fireplace. . . .

I glanced over at that flickering beer sign on Tremont Street. For four days it had been balls to the wall, and now it was over. Everybody else was still tying up their own loose ends—Jiggs, Katy, Plain View—but I had nothing more to do. Even Slip would soon be leaving City Hall to begin his nightly tour of the funeral homes, trolling for votes among grieving survivors at wakes across the city.

About twenty feet down the path that ran to Charles Street, I noticed a bum of indeterminate age in an overcoat leaning up against a tree. He was watching me, staring, and then I realized that this was his bench that I was occupying. Dinner is served early at the Pine Street Inn, and he'd returned home for a nap, and here I was, an interloper, a squatter. If it were summer and the ground was warm, maybe he wouldn't have cared so much, but it was still winter and I had usurped his bed.

I stood up and stretched, and gave the bum a nod to let him know I was relinquishing the bench. Then I started walking home.

As I passed Foley's, I looked in, but I knew that if I stopped in for one or two, I wouldn't leave until one or two. I'd close the place, and suppose Jiggs called. Aw hell, who was I kidding? I wasn't worried about about Jiggs's call or last call. I wanted to talk to Katy, and she'd be tied up for several more hours phoning frightened, corrupt lobbyists and their lawyers. When she came by later—if she came by—I had to be sober. So for once, I kept walking past Foley's. Inside my house, I didn't even bother to check the phone messages. Anybody I wanted to talk to had my cell phone number.

I decided to complete some of my own unfinished business. I retrieved the Wimpy Hogan ledgers from the hall closet, put them into a shopping bag, then walked down the street and started up my Oldsmobile.

Uphams Corner, here I come.

ON THE radio, the all-news station was carrying Jiggs's press conference live—he was humbly acknowledging that he was be-ing "urged" by certain unnamed parties to step forward and as-sume a heavy new burden of public service, although he hastened to add how vitally important it was to remember that in our sys-tem of justice a man—a person—is presumed blah-blah-blah.

Even on the static-filled AM band, you could practically hear him talking out of the side of his mouth.

I thought about the Speaker, spending his first night behind bars. When would these pols ever learn? They always set their sights so pathetically low—all they ever looked for was the quick score, a lunch bag full of cash, just enough for a down payment on a summer house in Mashpee, or a condo in Stuart—not Boca Raton or even Naples, but Stuart. That was their idea of living large, selling out to lobbyists and pinky-ring union bosses and assorted other front-runners who would gladly sell you an apple for an orchard any day of the week.

Now I was parking the Olds in a space right outside Wimpy's Lounge. Once again the urban renaissance was taking the night off in Dorchester. I grabbed Wimpy's ledgers, or most of them anyway, and walked quickly into the bar.

Billy Hogan Jr. was wiping at that same spot, and the same black guy was sleeping at the same place on the same stool. He looked up—Hogan, not the black guy.

"You're back," he said, without interest.

"I have something for you," I said. I took out the 1974 ledger and handed it to him, then reached back into the envelope to get the one from 1975, the one I hadn't had time to read the previous day at City Hall. As I pulled out the later book, a sealed envelope dropped out of it onto the grimy floor, facedown. I bent over to pick it up and saw that it was of much more recent vintage than either of the Hogan ledgers. It had been stashed at the very back of the legal pad, which was why I hadn't noticed it until now. I turned it over, saw my name scrawled on it. Underneath my name was written, TO BE OPENED ONLY IN EVENT OF DEATH.

Bucky's, I presumed.

As I pocketed the letter, Billy Jr. didn't notice—he was too busy poring over the handwritten notations and figures marked down by his father and his uncles, running his fingers along the faded, yellowing pages his father had no doubt touched. Somehow, I supposed, he was hoping to make a psychic connection. I wished him well, but it was a private moment. I turned and walked back to my car.

I felt the envelope in my pocket. I had a feeling I was about to receive a message of my own from that bourn from which no traveler doth return.

I TORE open the envelope and pulled out two sheets roughly torn from a yellow legal pad. It was indeed a final letter from Bucky. He was getting a lot more accomplished dead than he had ever been able to pull off while he was alive. By the overhead light in my car, I read what amounted to his last will and testament:

I, Robert "Bucky" Bennett, do hereby wish to tell my side of the story of the Cooperative Trust bank burglary and the subsequent events. I have just called a private detective and former Boston police officer John F. X. Reilly, and will soon meet with him to discuss this matter. I am planning to send him these documents that will prove the truth of what I am about to write, or some of it anyway.

Mr. Reilly, although we have yet to meet, I am trusting you on your brother Martin's word to do the right thing with the material you will be receiving. If I am dead, you will have a clear idea from what I am about to tell you who was behind my murder.

Let me start at the beginning, which for these purposes is when I was released from the federal penitentiary in Otisville, NY, almost three years ago.

I am the first cousin of Daniel Patrick Mahoney, the state rep from Dorchester who is better known as Jiggs. I have just called him and told him what I am planning to do. I also told him that if anything happens to me . . .

It went on from there. I read it once in the car, reread it, then stepped back inside Wimpy's Lounge and read it a third time. Then I sat alone in a booth for a while, just thinking. Billy Jr. was so absorbed in his own reading and recollections that not only did he forget to thank me, he also neglected to even send over a round.

Finally I put down Bucky's letter and considered my options.

First, I could blackmail Jiggs. I had him by the short-and-curlies, no doubt about that. I could turn him upside down and shake him, just like Knocko and Tony Miami had done with Hal Lynch.

Or I could do the right thing, as Bucky called it. I could destroy Jiggs.

I left Wimpy's Lounge, got back in my car, and started making phone calls as I drove north. Jiggs seemed surprised to hear from me so soon. But I told him it was "urgent" and he warily agreed to meet me in his office at the State House at nine. This was that rarest of occurrences—a Friday night when at least some lights would be burning brightly on Beacon Hill. My second phone call was to Katy at the newspaper, to tell her that she might have another story tonight.

It was about eight thirty when I pulled up in front of the *Herald*. Katy ran outside, took Bucky's letter back into the building to make copies of it, keeping the original for herself just as I'd instructed her. She brought a copy back out to me. This time she kissed me on the cheek, primly, but with a little more oomph, I thought, than last night, although it's possible I may have been imagining that.

Ten minutes later, I was inside the deserted State House, turning the corner toward Jiggs's third-floor office. At night, when the State House is empty, you can hear the sound of your own footsteps echoing off the marble tiles down the darkened corridors.

Already a *Herald* cameraman was lurking around the corner from Jiggs's office, waiting to grab the gotcha photograph of Jiggs for tomorrow's front page.

As a tabloid, the *Herald* relies on street sales, and other than scantily clad females and Super Bowl victories, few events move papers off the newsstands faster than a front page featuring a grainy, overexposed shot of either a perp or a pol, or better yet a perp-pol, preferably while unsuccessfully trying to shield his face.

The photographer introduced himself and said Katy had told him I was on my way up. He was a squirrelly-looking guy with scraggly black hair, a beard, and booze on his breath. He spoke in a rasp and showed me the hand mirror that he was using to keep track of all the comings and goings from the majority leader's office around the corner. He could see them, but they couldn't see him. I complimented him on his ingenuity and continued on to Jiggs's door.

I tapped lightly on the door and Jiggs opened it. The scowl on his face told me there would be no bantering this evening.

"This had better be good, Mr. Black," he said.

"Oh, it is," I said. I was early. It was just before nine, and Jiggs had the lights turned off. Otherwise, the more desperate backbenchers would still be pounding on his door, pestering the future speaker for committee chairmanships and such, wanting to get his "word" in a building where a man's word was his bond, except when it wasn't, because somebody else had offered something better, usually money. It didn't matter that under the new one-man rule imposed by the soon-to-be-former Speaker Lynch, committee chairmen no longer had any real clout. All these greedy saps cared about was that a chairman got gold-embossed stationery, one or two additional aides, and, most importantly, an extra $7,500 a year. That's why all the ham-and-eggers were making the ultimate sacrifice—getting drunk at the State House on a Friday night, rather than back "in the district," where they could pound them down somewhere on the arm and not have to worry about getting pinched by the local cops for OUI.

"I'm figuring out the new committee assignments," Jiggs said as I followed him back into his office. "So let's make this quick."

"Fine by me," I said to his back. "Did you know Bucky Bennett?"

"Bucky?" He sat down at his desk. "Bucky Bennett? The dead guy? Why do you ask?"

"He says he knows you."

"Says? I thought Bucky Bennett was dead. The present tense would not seem appropriate."

"Oh, but it is," I said, sitting down in a high-backed chair across the desk from him. "Bucky left what you might call a last will and testament."

Jiggs smiled and turned slightly away from me. "Did you hear what he said, Tony? You were right."

I turned my head and I saw him. It was Tony Miami, standing in the shadows behind me, in an unlit corner of the room, both hands in the pockets of his tweed sports coat. It looked Brooks Brothers, but no one would ever mistake Tony Miami for a Dartmouth man. So Jiggs, who hadn't even wanted me to use my real name when I called him, had now invited Tony Miami into his State House office. Jiggs had obviously put two and two together.

Tony Miami was all smiles as he stepped forward.

"Hello again, Jack," he said, offering me his hand. "Or should I say Mr. Black?"

"Hello, Tony," I said, standing up to grasp his hand. "Let me guess—you're working for Jiggs here tonight?"

"Strictly on a contingency basis," he said. "Think of me as a consultant."

Tony pulled up a chair of his own and sat down next to me,

across the desk from Jiggs. He asked me what else Bucky had said. There was no question now who was calling the shots.

I tried to ignore Tony Miami as much as possible as I addressed Jiggs directly. I said, "Bucky said you were his cousin. Is that true?"

Jiggs folded his hands and nodded.

"Bucky said you were the inside guy on the Cooperative Trust job," I said to Jiggs. "He said you never told him every gangster in the city had a safe-deposit box there, or he never would have done the job. He was pissed at you, Jiggs. He thought you set him up, because you wanted something specific taken from that bank."

"The rantings of a deceased career criminal," Jiggs said softly. "Utterly inadmissible in a court of law. Won't even make it past discovery."

"You just keep telling yourself that, Jiggs," I said. "Now, may I continue?"

"That's what we're all here for."

"Bucky said you gave him the number of one box that he had to get. You told him he had to clear that box out and bring everything in it to you. He said that was all you wanted as your finder's fee."

Jiggs stared straight ahead, poker-faced.

"I'd forgotten how you used to be chairman of banks and banking—you had it right after Lynch, am I right?" Jiggs lowered his eyes, which I took as confirmation. "So I'm guessing there must have come a day when it was time for the traditional quid pro quo. Maybe you had to sign off on, say, Cooperative's acquisition of some little nickel-and-dime savings-and-loan in Somerville. Maybe it was something else. The cops can put together the exact details easily enough. Whatever you did for Cooperative, there was a payoff for fast-tracking it, or more likely for not stopping it. The payoff was, Cooperative Trust would make you

a director, only they had to wait until you'd moved up in leadership, out of the banks and banking chairmanship, so it wouldn't
look quite so quid pro quo, am I right?"

He looked up at me again, but said nothing.

"It wasn't much of a score, becoming a director, but then, it
wasn't much of a bank. All they could give you was a small sti-
pend for every directors' meeting you attended, the occasional
winter trip to Florida, and maybe a few stock options here and
there—not a big payday but no deal too small, right, Jiggs?"

He shrugged.

"Once you were on the board, there were certain things you
had access to, and being a man of innate curiosity, not to mention
having a lot of time on your hands, being a state rep and all,
somehow you stumbled across a list of people—or should I say
entities—that had rented safe-deposit boxes there. That was when
you realized that Hal Lynch had a box there. You put two and two
together on that Fourth Suffolk Corporation bullshit right away,
didn't you, because even then you were already lining him up for
a head shot."

"Life in the fast lane," Jiggs said calmly. Tony Miami, legs
crossed, sitting beside me, listened impassively.

"Once you had the list of everyone who rented boxes," I said,
"you went over it with a fine-tooth comb, which is when, I'm assuming, you figured out that it was also a drop for people like
our friend Tony here."

Tony Miami said: "I told you he was no slouch, Jiggs."

Jiggs interrupted: "Bucky said all this in his letter?"

"More or less."

"What else did he say?"

"He said you were the one who approached him and suggested the burglary on Memorial Day weekend. You gave him a
list of boxes that seemed promising—without telling him, of

course, who most of them belonged to. But you only cared about one box, didn't you, Jiggs? Bucky said you gave him the Speaker's box number, without telling him whose box it was, of course. And you told him to put the Speaker's stuff in a separate bag."

I paused in case Jiggs wanted to fill in a blank or two. He didn't.

"I have to ask you one thing, though," I said to Jiggs. "Was it the Fourth Suffolk Corporation that tipped you to the fact that Lynch was using Cooperative Trust as a drop?"

"Please," Jiggs said, still staring straight ahead, making eye contact with neither me nor Tony Miami. "His big mouth is what put me on to him. Lynch was—is—a boozer. In vino, veritas. He bragged. Loose lips sink ships, at least they sank his. It's the curse of the Irish."

"So it wasn't a fishing expedition—you knew what was in his box?"

Jiggs frowned. "I am reminded of the perennial question, 'Who wants to know?' What are the ground rules of this conversation? I'll say nothing until I know what your intentions are."

Suddenly Tony Miami interrupted.

"He's got all the cards now," said Tony Miami, frowning. "You don't need to be pissing him or anybody else off." He slowly shook his head. "At this point, Jiggs, you gotta throw yourself on the mercy of the court, am I right, Jack?"

I glanced over at Tony Miami and permitted myself a slight smile but said nothing. I returned my stare to Jiggs and remained silent. I was interested in what their next move would be.

"How do we know he ain't wearing a wire again?" Jiggs said, his grammar failing, a sure sign of stress.

Tony Miami looked over at me. "You ain't wearing no wire for this, are you, Jack?"

I shook my head.

"See, Jiggs," he said, "I knew that already, because it'd be real bad for his business, wearing a wire against a customer. This here is different than with Lynch. He's working for you, or was. It ain't attorney-client privilege exactly, but it's close enough. And I know he wouldn't want to do nothing to hurt me." He glanced over at me and flashed me a brief, wan smile. " 'Cause we're pals, right, Jack?"

Tony Miami knew when to hold 'em and knew when to fold 'em. He wasn't worried about me, because he knew I knew he could get to my brother Marty.

Jiggs took a deep breath and glared back at Tony Miami. "I didn't ask you to come here to agree with him. I know he's got me by the balls."

"He does," said Tony Miami, "and I don't know what you can do about that."

I took note of the fact that he said "you," not "we." If he could have, of course, Tony Miami would have gladly straightened out this matter for Jiggs. Because once you straighten something out, you own whoever it was who needed that certain something straightened out. When the time comes, and it always does, the straightener-outer can tell the people he straightened something out for to straighten something or someone out for him. The people who had something straightened out really don't have much choice, do they, and the more embarrassing the problem they had to have straightened out, the less choice they have. In the end, everybody gets straightened out.

Jiggs continued staring at Tony Miami. "Your job here is to get him in line."

"How exactly do you propose that I do that?" Tony Miami said. "Do I tell him you'll pay him to keep his mouth shut? Do you really think he's gonna get in line behind me and the other guy? I told you, he ain't stupid." He scratched his chin. "Plus, Jiggs, can't you figure the play here? He's already dropped a dime to his girl-friend at the paper. Ain't that right, Jack?"

I said nothing, but Jiggs shifted his stare to me.

"What are you trying to do to me?" Jiggs asked.

"I told Bucky I would handle things for him," I lied.

"You told me you'd handle things for me too, and I paid you."

"You did, Jiggs, but you lied to me."

Tony Miami just sat there. He didn't want any trouble. He never let his mouth write a check that his ass couldn't cash.

"Let's go back to what happened here," I said. "You had to have gotten the number on the boxes and the names that went with them from someone high up in the bank, and that's another witness who'll testify against you at trial. Unless you think maybe a banker'll stand up any more than, say, a lobbyist."

Tony Miami nodded thoughtfully. Here was a man who had spent much time grappling with the eternal question of who would and who wouldn't stand up. He and Knocko had long since formulated a corporate policy concerning rats, real or imagined. The policy was: Dead men don't squeal.

I continued, addressing Jiggs: "So Bucky gives you what you wanted. Only he told you that all he had found in the Speaker's box were Xeroxes. You didn't believe him, but it didn't seem like the kind of complaint you could call nine-one-one about. Mean-time, all the Mob guys are very determined to find out who ripped them off, and pretty soon our friend here is on to Bucky's gang."

Jiggs was now sitting hunched over his desk, silent, which didn't matter much, because the guy I was speaking to now was Tony Miami.

"So you, Tony, you and the other guy snatch a couple of Bucky's crew off the street. Material witnesses, you might say. And since no one can take the Fifth Amendment when your grand jury is in session, pretty soon you not only have your own loot back but also your very own set of the Speaker's records, because Bucky did hand them over to you, just to get you off his back. And even if they were just Xeroxes, they were more than enough to begin to shake down the Speaker with."

"No comment," Tony Miami said.

I said, "What I'd like to know is, how'd you find out that Jiggs was the inside guy? I'm guessing that Bucky, being fond of a cocktail himself, told this to one of the other guys in his crew, and you discovered this information during a dental procedure. That's my assumption, anyway."

"Assumptions are the mother of fuckups," Tony Miami said evenly. "I'm sure I don't know what you're talking about. But this is a marvelous yarn you're spinning, Jack. Don't stop now. You're on a roll."

"Thank you," I said. "To get back to my assumption, Tony, I'm assuming now you and the other guy had Bucky whacked when you realized that despite what he had told you, there was in fact a set of originals, and he had them. And as if that wasn't reason enough to cap him, the Speaker told you that Bucky was trying to extract an additional pound of flesh from him. And that's not allowed, because you consider—considered—Lynch your own personal mark. So you took care of Bucky. It hasn't worked out quite the way you planned, but shit happens, right? And the only two guys who can tie you to the Bennett hit are lying faceup on slabs down at the Southern Mortuary."

Now Tony Miami grinned broadly and stood up.

"I hate to have to run," he said, "but you just reminded me, I gotta get to a wake. I'm already late, but I think they'll wait for me."

That explained the sport coat.

"My cousin passed away unexpectedly the other night, maybe you heard about it, Jack. Carmine was a dear boy. He'll be missed."

"My deepest condolences," I said.

"By the way," Tony Miami said, buttoning his jacket. "How's that reporter friend of yours doing?"

"Oh, she's fine now."

"That was an awful thing, wasn't it?" he said. "I can't tell you how pleased I am that everything has worked out for the best."

So much for cousin Carmine and the dear boy's wake.

"And that FBI agent that Slip Crowley shot," he continued. "What was his name—Finnegan?"

"Finnerty," I said.

"Finnerty," he repeated. "Imagine that, a bent FBI agent." He shook his head. "Unbelievable. Is there anything lower than a crooked cop, Jack?"

"They're lower than whale shit," I said.

"You can't really trust anyone these days, can you, Jack? You know what I mean?"

"I know what you mean, Tony."

"I thought you did. Give my best to Marty too, when you see him."

"I will," I said. "And how's your sister, Angela?"

"Well, this whole thing with the Speaker came as kind of a shock to her, as you can well imagine. I mean, she thought the Speaker walked on water."

"Who didn't?" I said.

"But she's a tough kid, as you know, and she thinks whoever the new speaker is—" He glanced over at Jiggs, still slumped in his chair. "—and you know who we're pulling for, she figures, he'll decide to keep her on, running the office."

"I'll bet she's right about that, Tony."

Then he turned toward Jiggs. "Jiggs, good luck, let me know how it all turns out."

The kiss of death. Tony had run the numbers in his head and

they didn't add up. There was no way to save Jiggs, so he and Knocko were taking their money off the table and walking away. Tony looked over at me again.

"Jack, may I have a few words with you?" he said. "Alone."

There was no reaction from Jiggs, sitting dazed at his desk. He was beyond reaching. So I just nodded and walked with Tony Miami into the outer office, closing Jiggs's door behind us, on the off chance that he might try to eavesdrop. I turned on the overhead lights. If it attracted a rep or two, so much the better. It's not healthy to spend a lot of time alone in the dark with Tony Miami. When I flipped the switch and the room flooded with light, he frowned slightly. Tony Miami preferred to do business in the shadows.

"I gotta ask you about something else," he said. "Maybe you heard, there was a stickup last night at one of our places, the gym on Dorchester Street there."

"News to me," I said.

"Yeah, it didn't make the news," he said, "what with all the other shit hitting the fan all at once there. But The Man is very concerned about it—they took some, well, you might call it senti-mental stuff."

"Really?" I said. "Like what?"

"Just . . . sentimental," he said. "I was just wondering if you'd heard anything about it. All we know for sure is that whoever robbed us had some bruises on his face, like he'd been worked over fairly recently."

"Really?" I said, resisting the urge to reach up with my hand and feel the bruises on my face. "Well, I wish I could help you, but I haven't heard a word."

"Okay," he said, his eyes narrowing. "Lemme know if you hear anything, will you?"

"I certainly will," I said. "I mean, I've never been there myself, but I've always heard a lot about that gym. This stickup guy, he didn't get into the dog room, did he?"

Tony Miami tilted his head just a bit, as if he wasn't quite sure he'd heard what he thought he'd heard me say.

"You know the room I'm talking about," I said. "It's got this big banner on the wall. 'Southie rules exclamation point.' Or so I'm told."

"Who told you this?"

"I don't recall—it's just something I picked up somewhere," I said, and then we heard a rapping on the door. I ignored it at first, but whoever it was was persistent enough to keep knocking. Greed for a $7,500 chairmanship can do that to a rep.

"Mr. Speaker," the supplicant said. "It's me, Buck, from the second division. Please, let me in. I need to talk to you."

"We're closed for business," I said. "Screw."

"But Mr. Speaker—"

"Get outta here, Buck," I growled, "or you'll end up in the basement."

The solon fled, walking slowly at first and then breaking into a trot, as we could hear from the echoes of Buck's shoe heels hitting the marble tiles. Tony Miami wasn't happy, but he managed a weak smile.

"You handled that good, Jack. Can you handle this other thing good? The Man gets a call today from that nitwit of ours who was in the club when it got knocked over last night. Now The Man is very concerned, and when he gets concerned, sometimes he loses his temper. You know what I mean?"

"Stress can kill," I said.

"So what should I tell him, to relieve his stress, I mean?"

"You can tell Seamus—that's what his friends call him, isn't it?"

"You've made your point, Jack. Now I gotta know what I should tell . . ." He paused.

"What should you tell Seamus?" I said. "You tell Seamus he's got no problem with me if I got no problem with him. But if I should disappear . . ."

"So you give the DVDs to somebody else?"

"Let's just say, as long as I'm walking around, every day will be like Christmas."

"Christmas? I don't follow you, Jack."

"You know what I always say, Tony. Christmas is for cops and kids."

It took him a second, but finally he nodded. "Oh, okay, so you grabbed that one. I got you now."

"I never knew The Man liked brown sugar."

"No need to get graphic," he said, shaking his head. "I know what you got over our heads."

"You know what they say about DVDs, don't you, Tony? It's kind of like a bullet. Don't worry about the one with your name on it, worry about the one that's addressed to whom it may concern."

I was pushing it now, but I couldn't help myself.

"Nice camera work too," I said. "Somebody's pretty handy with a videocam there."

"I hear you," he said. "Loud and clear."

I had to make sure he did, just in case he and The Man weren't as tight as they were supposed to be. For my own safety, Tony Miami had to understand that it would be a grave error if he decided to make me disappear thinking that only Seamus would go down on a kiddie-porn rap, after which everything would belong to him. Tony Miami needed to understand that he was in the same jam with Knocko.

Tony Miami said, "So you're telling The Man he has nothing to worry about?"

"That's what I'm telling The Man, and anyone else who might be concerned about their exposure, shall we say. As long as I'm okay, The Man is okay. And as long as all the people around me are okay, then all the people around The Man are okay too, if you know what I mean, Tony."

Tony Miami knew what I meant.

"Hitting me in the head, that would be *stunatu*. You know what I mean, Tony?"

He began to say something, then thought better of it. I'd pushed it beyond what I should have. But he just nodded and shook my hand.

"Don't be a stranger," he said. "We got a few irons in the fire, you know."

Not to mention hands, feet, and maybe another bodily appendage or two. I'd have to keep an eye on both of them from now on, but as long as I had the DVDs, they couldn't take a chance on whacking me. It was a Mutual Assured Destruction thing.

Tony Miami turned and walked out into the hall. I closed the door behind him and turned the bolt in the lock. I knew who was waiting for him at the end of the hall, and I didn't want him fleeing back inside. Plus, I needed to finish my chat with Jiggs. I lightly rapped on his office door and when there was no response I opened it and walked back inside.

Jiggs stared up at me with glazed eyes.

"I thought you were working for me," he said.

"That was then, this is now."

"You fucked me," he said.

"No, you fucked me," I said. "You knew everything I turned up before you even hired me."

"What do you care, as long as you get paid?"

"I don't like being played for a chump."

"But that's what you've always been. You were a chump for the mayor."

"So maybe I don't like being the chump anymore. You ever consider that? Why didn't you hire somebody who didn't mind playing the fool?"

"Because Bucky was already going to see you, and because I wasn't sure anybody else could piece it together to take the Speaker down."

Outside his office, from the hallway we suddenly heard at least two voices yelling, exchanging curses, and then the sound of footsteps pounding down the marble hall. Then I heard other, unfamiliar voices. A TV camera crew must have arrived and joined the *Herald* photographer's stakeout. Jiggs stood up and cocked an ear toward the door.

"I forgot to tell you," I said. "There's been a *Herald* photographer in the hall for the last hour with orders to shoot anybody who walked out of your office."

An hour ago, Jiggs would have come across the table at me with his meaty fists, but now he was a beaten man and he knew it. He sagged back down into his chair and said nothing as the pounding recommenced on his door. This time it was the TV crew, demanding an explanation of Tony Miami's appearance in his office.

"You fucked yourself, Jiggs," I said, above the din. "Hiring me to find out what you already knew, that was too cute by half."

He closed his eyes and shook his head. "All you were supposed to do was find out about the Mob shaking down the Speaker and then leak it, like you do everything else."

"But you told me not to," I said.

"Since when do you follow orders?" he said.

"So your plan," I said, "was to let the Speaker ram through the term limits repeal, which he did. And then, while the papers and the goo-goos were still all hot and bothered about it, I was supposed to leak the story about the Mob owning him, and you would step in, riding to the rescue of Reform on a white horse? Was that your plan?"

"Something like that," he said, and then his cell phone rang. He picked it up.

"How did you get this number? . . . Oh, I know how you got this number." He glared across the desk at me. "Your boyfriend gave it to you, didn't he?"

He kept scowling at me as he spoke.

"If you run that I'll sue your ass so fast I'll own that rag you work for. . . . If you want any comment you can call my lawyer, Danny Goodis. . . . Of course he was my cousin, everyone knows that . . . that's a goddamn lie . . . no quote-unquote gangster has ever set foot in this office, I don't care what your photographer says. . . . I have nothing more to say to you."

He slammed the phone down. "Guess who that was," he said, before lapsing again into silence.

"I don't get it," he finally said. "I didn't kill Bucky. I didn't kidnap that cunt who just called who's gonna croak me. I actually paid you, paid you well. And yet I'm going down and Tony Miami walks away from the whole thing washing his hands like he's Pontius fucking Pilate. What's the difference between him and me?"

"The difference is, Tony had his cousin killed before the kid could rat him out, and you didn't."

"Go take a flying fuck at the moon," he said, finally rising out of his chair and shaking a halfhearted fist at me. "Get outta here. I'm gonna ride this thing out. And if I do go down, well, maybe you don't come out of this smelling like a rose either."

I smiled and rose from my chair. "If you mean the thirty-five hundred dollars, it's already on a deposit slip, time-stamped with your name on it. You can't trade me up, Jiggs. You were my customer, you asked me to do something, and I did it. And do you know why? Because my motto is, The customer is always right."

"This customer wants his money back."

"I just changed my motto," I said. "My new motto is, The customer is almost always right."

"You fucked me," Jiggs repeated. "You fucked me good."

Jiggs—another victim.

Chapter Twenty-one

AFTER I GOT back to my house, I took a good long shower. I try to do that whenever I return from the State House.

I was supposed to meet Katy Bemis at Foley's after deadline, and I had a feeling Slip would be stopping by as well.

Just as I stepped out of the shower, I got a call from a state senator who was planning to run for a down-ballot statewide office against the mayor of a suburban city. The senator wanted to leak a story involving the mayor's misuse of his official city car, which was often parked overnight at the apartment house where his new young blond secretary lived. The senator was wondering if perhaps I might take some cash off his hands. I told him I'd love to bump into him on the Common tomorrow, as long as he was carrying at least twenty Benjamins in a business envelope. My price had just gone up, doubled in fact. Twenty Benjamins had a nice ring to it.

"Benjamins?" he said.

"As in Franklin," I said. "My favorite presidents are Jackson and Grant."

"I get it," he said. "Twenty Benjamins equals . . ."

"Forty Grants," I said, "or a hundred Jacksons."

The way my new client explained it, it sounded like it would work best as a TV story, and I had just the Jimmy Olsen for the job—a local TV "investigative" reporter with a trench coat and a moustache who was worried about the possibility of being laid off. But I wanted the senator's cash up front, because I don't do hits on the arm. That's for jealous boyfriends and serial killers, and I am neither. What I am is a professional—a professional shit merchant. I buy and I sell.

After the senator hung up, I went into my bedroom closet and pulled out a box the feds let me take with me when I left City Hall. It took about ten minutes of rummaging, but I finally found what I was looking for. I wasn't going to call Katy again, but if she did show up, I wanted to have a little surprise for her.

By ten thirty, I was unwinding in the Berkeley Room with Slip, who had just arrived after leaving his fifth and final wake of the evening, at O'Brien's in Dorchester. Bing Crosby was crooning "Far Away Places" on the jukebox.

Katy Bemis arrived about twenty minutes later. There was a cheer as she walked through the door—she was in the big time now. With everyone hugging her and shaking her hand and trying to buy her a drink, it took her about five minutes to break free of the crowd and make her way back to our table. She gave both Slip and me antiseptic kisses on the cheek. When Gerry Foley arrived with a round, everyone in the bar gave her another big round of applause which you couldn't call a standing ovation only because everyone in the place was already standing.

Within two minutes, the three of us all had at least five more drinks in front of us.

"Here's to that crooked fed, Agent Orange," Slip said, raising another glass of brown water. "Thanks for all the free booze, Finnerty."

Then he rose stiffly and wandered away to feed the jukebox and talk to a couple of pinky-ring guys from the firefighters' union. That gave me a chance to talk to Katy alone. She was trying to keep her game face on, but I could tell she was fading fast. She needed about three good nights' sleep in a row, followed by two weeks in Florida, or anywhere else but here. In the meantime, I wanted to keep up my end of the conversation.

"How'd the picture of Tony Miami come out?" I asked her, and she was suddenly smiling again. It must have been a pretty good shot.

"It looks like something out of the *Chicago American*, circa 1927," she said. "The only thing I regret is that he wasn't wearing a fedora."

"Look on the bright side," I said. "How often do you get a surveillance shot of Tony Miami at the State House . . . in a Brooks Brothers blazer?"

"Is he going to be pissed at you?" she said.

"He'll get over it," I said. "He's just a longtime friend of Jiggs, after all, or so his lawyer will say. They'll e-mail the statement to all media outlets tomorrow, after which both the lawyer and Tony Miami will be unavailable for comment for about a month, until the heat dies down."

"You sure he won't blame you?" she asked.

I shook my head. "Why should he? I didn't know he was going to be there with Jiggs. Tony stepped on his own dick. He knows the difference between a setup and a screwup. Besides, I think he's going to be giving me a good leaving-alone for a very long time."

"Does your confidence, shall we say, have anything to do with that key you gave me?"

I smiled. Despite her racial handicap, this girl was quick.

"I'll tell you more about the key later," I said. "Just don't lose it."

She was too exhausted to continue the interrogation, so she settled for picking up a fresh glass of Foley's domestic Chablis. She took a long sip and then leaned in close to me. I liked that a lot.

"You didn't give Bucky's letter to anyone else, did you?" she said. "Tell me you didn't give it to the *Globe*."

"I didn't give it to the *Globe*."

"You'd better not have," she said. "At least not if you're after what I think you're after."

Oh be still my heart. I counted, one-one thousand, two-one thousand, three-one thousand . . .

She leaned back again and said, "Not a bad couple of days' work for you, taking out the top two guys in the House."

"One of whom was a paying customer," I said, "and they don't grow on trees. You didn't do too badly yourself."

She looked a little embarrassed. We were at that awkward moment, linked to each other in that inextricable way in which both people understand exactly what will almost certainly happen next, only it hasn't happened yet, and you're not quite sure when or how it will happen.

The tension was palpable. Where was Slip when we needed him? I had to make some conversation fast, so I asked her how Finnerty was doing at the hospital.

"The official word is he's still in critical condition, but they're just saying that because they want to keep him on ice while they try to flip him. 'They' being agents from Washington. These feds they brought in wouldn't tell the local G-men if their coats were on fire. For obvious reasons."

"Flipping Finnerty won't be that difficult," I said. "He's got a wife, a bunch of kids, and the girlfriend from the steno pool with red hair."

"Even the wife has red hair, is what I hear," she said. "And they'd all have to agree to go into the program, because if he starts singing—"

"My money would still be on Knocko and Tony surviving," I said. "Finnerty may be able to tell them a few things, hijackings, low-level drug dealers, Boston cops getting protection money, nickel-and-dime stuff. But the offshore accounts, all the missing hoods and girlfriends—no way did the two guys cut Finnerty in on any of the heavy shit."

We sat there in silence for a moment, studying our drinks. I asked her who she thought the next speaker would be. She considered that for a moment.

"Maybe Norton, that dope from Northampton. He's the whip, next in line."

I smiled and shook my head. "He may be next in line, but I wouldn't bet the farm on him. You know what they say, when the boys from the suburbs go home, the boys from Boston go to work."

She looked at me, puzzled. "Sal DiGrazia?"

"Sal's the man," I said. "You can take that to the bank. He'll be working the phones the minute the paper hits the street, if he isn't already."

Suddenly her face lit up. "And he worked for you!"

I nodded and reached into the left breast pocket of my sport coat, then pulled out a Xeroxed copy of an ancient police report. She scanned it quickly in the dim light, reading how a twenty-one-year-old white male, Salvatore DiGrazia of Salem Street, had been arrested for operating a parking lot without a license. On Celtics game nights, back at the end of the Larry Bird era, when the Celts still owned the city, Sal had been charging fans twenty bucks a car to park in the old Boston Redevelopment Authority lot across from City Hall. Even better, the cop who'd collared him had been black, and Sal had called him a "dirty fucking nigger." And it was all right there in the Boston PD report, a public record.

"Where'd you get this?" Katy asked me.

"I was the Ward Three coordinator, remember? He was one of my precinct captains. One of my duties was to keep tabs on everyone in the organization. The mayor hated surprises."

"And now Sal gets one," she said.

"Sometimes," I said, "it pays to know people who only know crooked people."

She let that one go. "Is it enough to knock him out?"

I shook my head. "He'll just say he was misquoted, it was a misunderstanding, he's 'grown.' This is a good solid hit, but not a head shot. I just brought it along as a tease. Let Sal get settled in first, and then hit him with it. And that'll give me time . . ."

She smiled, but her eyes were glazing over. She was played out, drifting off.

"There is something else on him, isn't there?" she said weakly.

"Maybe," I said, "but I can't remember exactly what. If you give me a few days, though—"

"You're not holding out on me, are you?" She was trying to hang in, but her chin was drooping onto her chest. "I'm sorry Jack, I'm just so—"

Just then Slip thudded back into his seat. Just as well. There was sweat on his brow—the brown water was starting to catch up with him. He looked serenely at Katy, who recovered quickly enough to fold up Sal's police report and drop it into her purse. Slip asked her if we were off the record here. Stifling a yawn, she told him we were all friends and he asked again, are we or are we not off the record here? Reluctantly, she agreed. We were off the record here.

"This is going to be my breakthrough year," he said. "With the spades, I mean."

Katy and I looked at each other, and then back to Slip.

"Shooting Finnerty," he said, nodding. "A fucking cop. I shot a cop. Ain't no liberal or spade running at large that's ever plugged a cop, let alone a fed, much less gotten away with it." He took a deep breath and leaned back in his chair. "I wasn't sure at first how it would play, but mark my words—this is the year Slip Crowley carries Grove Hall."

Slip looked down at the three 7&7s that remained in front of him on the table. The ice had melted, but since when is that a problem for a two-fisted G-man-shooting city councilor at large from Dudley Street? Slip grabbed the closest one and drained it in one gulp and then stared sadly down at the last two full drinks. He hated to leave them behind, when people in India were starving for a shot of blended Canadian whiskey. But he pushed them away.

"Can't take any chances with an OUI anymore," he said. "This world is full of young pricks in prowl cars who don't care how much old Slip has done for their greedy goddamn union over the years." He looked down at us. "I don't suppose you two lovebirds would care to join me in Chinatown for a little sweet 'n' sour, chased with a jar or two of cold tea."

"Thanks for the invite," I said, "but don't let us stop you. I think you owe it to yourself."

I told Katy I'd be right back and then I stood up to walk him out to the Slipmobile. It was parked next to my Olds in the lot behind Foley's. It was a clear night, a full moon, about twenty-five degrees. I watched Slip climb in the front seat, a little stiffly, showing his age. Slip turned on the ignition, then rolled down the window. I stuck my hand in and shook his. I told him, thanks pal.

"No, thank you, pal," he said. "You gave me the opportunity to shoot a crooked fed—that's what I call a friend." Outside now, away from Katy, he lit up a Kool. "Just remember one thing, Jack. If anyone asks, I didn't see you—"

"And you didn't see me."